SF MCK

Once Upon A Spring Morn

DENNIS L. McKIERNAN

Once Upon A
Spring Morn

A ROC BOOK

ROC

Published by New American Library, a division of
Penguin Group (USA) Inc., 375 Hudson Street,
New York, New York 10014, USA
Penguin Group (Canada), 90 Eglinton Avenue East, Suite 700, Toronto,
Ontario M4P 2Y3, Canada (a division of Pearson Penguin Canada Inc.)
Penguin Books Ltd, 80 Strand, London WC2R 0RL, England
Penguin Ireland, 25 St. Stephen's Green, Dublin 2,
Ireland (a division of Penguin Books Ltd.)
Penguin Group (Australia), 250 Camberwell Road, Camberwell, Victoria 3124,
Australia (a division of Pearson Australia Group Pty. Ltd.)
Penguin Books India Pvt. Ltd., 11 Community Centre, Panchsheel Park,
New Delhi - 110 017, India
Penguin Group (NZ), cnr Airborne and Rosedale Roads, Albany,
Auckland 1310, New Zealand (a division of Pearson New Zealand Ltd.)
Penguin Books (South Africa) (Pty.) Ltd., 24 Sturdee Avenue,
Rosebank, Johannesburg 2196, South Africa

Penguin Books Ltd., Registered Offices:
80 Strand, London WC2R 0RL, England

First published by Roc, an imprint of New American Library,
a division of Penguin Group (USA) Inc.

First Printing, October 2006
10 9 8 7 6 5 4 3 2 1

REGISTERED TRADEMARK—MARCA REGISTRADA

LIBRARY OF CONGRESS CATALOGING-IN-PUBLICATION DATA:

McKiernan, Dennis L., 1932–
Once upon a spring morn / Dennis L. McKiernan.
    p. cm.
ISBN 0-451-46112-6
1. Knights and knighthood—Fiction. 2. Quests (Expeditions)—Fiction. I. Title.
PS3563.C36O527 2006
813'.54—dc22
                                    2006011818

Set in Trump Mediaeval
Designed by Leonard Telesca

Printed in the United States of America

PUBLISHER'S NOTE

This is a work of fiction. Names, characters, places, and incidents either are the product of the
author's imagination or are used fictitiously, and any resemblance to actual persons, living or dead,
business establishments, events, or locales is entirely coincidental.

The publisher does not have any control over and does not assume any responsibility for author
or third-party Web sites or their content.

Once again to all lovers,
As well as to lovers of fairy tales . . . .
And to all who seek wonder.

Acknowledgments

My dear Martha Lee, my heart, once more I am most grateful for your enduring support, careful reading, patience, and love. I know I have said this many times before, but it most surely bears repeating, *ma chérie.*

And again I thank the members of the Tanque Wordies Writers' Group—Diane, Frances, John—for your encouragement throughout the writing of this Faery tale.

And thank you, Christine J. McDowell, for your help with the French language.

And thanks to my firstborn son, Daniel Kian McKiernan, for his knowledge of ancient Greek.

(I would add, though, that any errors in usage of either French or Greek are entirely mine. Of course, the errors in English are mine as well.)

Contents

Foreword

If you have read the forewords of the first three tales of my Faery series—*Once Upon a Winter's Night* and *Once Upon a Summer Day* and *Once Upon an Autumn Eve*—you will know my thesis is that once upon a time many (if not most) fairy tales were epics of love and seduction and copious sex and bloody fights and knights and witches and Dragons and Ogres and Giants and other fantastic beings all scattered throughout the scope of the tale as the hero or heroine struggled on.

Bardic sagas were these, but as the minstrels and troubadours and sonneteers and tale spinners and bards and other such dwindled, and common folk took up the task of entertaining one another with these well-loved epics, I believe bits were omitted—fell by the wayside—and the stories grew shorter, or fragmented into several stories, or changed to fit the current culture or religion or whatever other agendas the tale tellers might have had.

And so, if I'm right, the grand and sweeping tales bards used to keep their royal audiences enthralled for hours on end became less and less as the tales were spread from mouth to mouth.

As the years went on, the stories continued to dwindle, until they became what the collectors of those tales—Andrew Lang, the Grimm brothers, and others—finally recorded and produced for others to read . . . or so it is I contend:

pale reflections of what they once were—
mere fragments—
holding a small portion of the essence—
and so on.

But guess what: they still hold audiences rapt.
They still charm.
They still are much admired by many, and certainly I am among those.

Even so, I would really like to hear some of these stories such as I have imagined them once to have been: long, gripping, romantic, perilous epics of love and hatred and loss and redemption and revenge and forgiveness and life and death and other such grand themes.

But told as a fairy tale.
Especially a favorite fairy tale.
Expanded to include all the above.
With *Once Upon a Spring Morn* this time I take two favorites of mine—woven together and mixed with what I think might have been—to tell the tale as I would have it be: an epic, a saga, a story of length.

As with my other stories, since it is a romance in addition to being an adventure, once more you will find French words sprinkled throughout, for French is well suited to tales of love.

By the bye, the best-known versions of the two central stories are but a few pages long. Once again, I thought that much too brief, and, as is apparent, I did lengthen them a bit. But then again, I claim that I am telling the "real" story, and who is to say I am not?

I hope it holds you enthralled.

Dennis L. McKiernan
Tucson, Arizona, 2006

We are in Faery, my love . . . .
Strange are the ways herein.

1

Springwood

Unlike today, once upon a time Faery wasn't difficult to reach. All one had to do was walk through the boundary—a wall of twilight—between here and there. That particular twilight wall is rather difficult to find these days, yet now and again someone stumbles across and—lo!—enters that wondrous place of marvel and adventure and magic and peril, of mythical and mystical creatures, of uncommon beings . . . along with ordinary folk—if anyone who lives in Faery can be said to be ordinary. Too, items of magic are found therein—grimoires, amulets, swords, rings, cloaks, helms, and the like, most of them quite rare. Even the lands within are numinous, for Faery itself is composed of many mystical realms, rather like an enormous but strange jigsaw puzzle, the individual domains all separated from one another by great tenebrous walls of twilight that rise up high into the Faery sky well beyond seeing. And like a mystifying riddle, some of the realms touch upon many others, while some touch upon but few. The twilight walls can be quite tricky to negotiate, for a small error in where one crosses might take a person to a domain perhaps altogether different from where one might have intended to go. Hence, care must be taken when stepping through these dusky margins; else one might end up somewhere hazardous, even deadly, though one could just as easily find oneself in quite splendid surroundings. Many who dwell in Faery ofttimes stay put rather than chance these shadowlight walls, while others—adventurers, explorers, or the driven—cross from domain to domain. Some travel well-known paths; others fare along unfamiliar routes to cross between realms. There is this as well: directions in Faery do not seem to be constant; there may be no true east, south, west, and north, though occasionally those compass points are spoken of by newcomers therein; yet when going from one realm to another, bearings seem to shift. Instead it may be more accurate to say that east, south, west, and north respectively align with sunup, sunwise, sundown, and starwise . . . though at times they are also known as dawnwise, sunwise, duskwise, and starwise. Whether or not this jigsaw puzzle makes an overall coherent picture is questionable, for each of the pieces, each of the domains, seems quite unique; after all, 'tis Faery, an endless place, with uncounted realms all separated from one another by strange walls of shadowlight, and with Faery itself separated from the common world by looming twilight as well.

Among the many remarkable domains within this mystical place are the Forests of the Seasons. One of these four woodlands is a place of eternal springtime, where everlasting meltwater trickles across the 'scape, where some trees are abudwhile others are new-leafed, where early blossoms are abloom though some flowers yet sleep, where birds call for mates and beetles crawl through decaying leaves, and mushrooms push up through soft loam, and where other such signs of a world coming awake manifest themselves in the gentle, cool breezes and delicate rains.

On one side of this mystical, springlike realm lies the mortal world, or at least one path through the twilight leads there. On the other side, though, and beyond another great wall of half-light there stands a land of eternal winter, where snow ever lies on the ground, and ice clads the sleeping trees and covers the still meres or encroaches in thin sheets upon the edges of swift-running streams, and the stars at night glimmer in crystalline skies when blizzards do not blow.

Beyond that chill realm and through yet another shadowlight border there is a domain where autumn lies upon the land; here it is that crops afield remain ever for the reaping, and vines are overburdened with their largesse, and trees bear an abundance ripe for the plucking, and the ground holds rootstock and tubers for the taking. Yet no matter how often a harvest is gathered, when one isn't looking the bounty somehow replaces itself.

Farther still and past that magical realm and separated from it by a great wall of twilight is another equally enigmatic province, a domain graced by eternal summer; it is a region of forests and fields, of vales and clearings, of streams and rivers and other such 'scapes, where soft summer breezes flow across the weald, though occasionally towering thunderstorms fill the afternoon skies and rain sweeps o'er all.

How such places can be—endless spring, winter, autumn, and summer—is quite mysterious; nevertheless it is so, for these four provinces are the Springwood and Winterwood and Autumnwood and Summerwood, a mere quartet of the many magical domains in the twilit world of Faery.

And as to these four regions, a prince or a princess rules each—Céleste, Borel, Liaze, and Alain—siblings all: the sisters Céleste and Liaze respectively reign o'er the Spring- and the Au-tumnwood; likewise, their brothers, Borel and Alain rule the Winter- and the Summerwood.

They love one another, these siblings, and seldom do tribula-tions come their way. Oh, there was of recent that trouble with Liaze and the travail on an obsidian mountain, but she had persevered in spite of the perils. Too, ere, then, there was that strangeness with Borel and his dagger-filled dreams, yet he had managed to successfully deal with that hazardous episode. And earlier still, there was the mysterious disappearance of Lord Valeray and Lady Saissa, and the dreadful two curses leveled upon Prince Alain, but Camille had come along to resolve those trials.

But after Liaze's recent harrowing ordeal, it appeared trouble was at last held at bay, though the Fates would have it that there yet loomed a portent of darker days to come. But at that time joy lay upon the land, for, in the Summerwood, Camille and Alain were wedded, and Borel and Michelle had started back from their journey to Roulan Vale, where they had visited with Chelle's sire and dam and had received their blessings; soon Borel and his truelove would reach the Winterwood, and a king would be notified and the banns would be posted and preparations for another wedding would get under way. And Liaze, with Luc at her side, was on a leisurely journey back to the Autumnwood, though she had not yet arrived; but when she and Luc reached the manse, yet another wedding would take place.

And so, at that time all was well in these Forests of the Seasons, or so it seemed.

But then . . .

. . . Once upon a spring morn . . .

Leather-clad Céleste, a bow across her lap, a quiver of green-fletched arrows at her hip, a silver horn at her side, rested in a fork among the huge branches of a great oak tree, its everlasting new leaves rustling in the cool morning breeze sighing across the Springwood. Céleste called this massive tree her Companion of Quietness, for here she came whenever she felt a nagging unease, one that seemed to dwell for days in her heart. In times such as these, Céleste would ride to this old friend and climb up within its arms and let it whisper to her of the richness of the soil and the luxury of the snowmelt and the warmth of the sun, and her unrest would abate somewhat if not disappear entirely. But on this day, though the oak gently murmured of the awakening of spring, Céleste yet felt a foreboding, for Liaze had set out nearly six moons past in the hope of finding her truelove, and still no falcons had flown from the Autumnwood bearing news of her return. And so, lost in her concern, Céleste fretted over her auburn-haired sister, and prayed to Mithras that she was well.

Even as she brooded, the Springwood princess became aware of a distant baying and the cry of a far-off horn. Céleste frowned, for she had not sanctioned a hunt that day, and yet it seemed one came this way.

Nearer and nearer bayed the dogs, and nearer and nearer cried the horn. Céleste stood and stepped outward on one of the huge, horizontal branches of the oak, the great limb easily bearing her, and she turned toward the oncoming hunt.

Louder and louder sounded the pursuit, and now Céleste could hear the hammering of hooves. Tethered below, her horse snorted and pawed at the soft ground, as if asking the princess to join in the chase.

Of a sudden, a terrified stag burst through the underbrush and fled past the great oak. A moment later, yelping dogs raced by, and not far behind, riders galloped after, the one in the lead— *What's this? A crow upon his shoulder?*—sounding the horn.

Céleste raised her own trump as they came on, and she blew a call. In the fore the man bearing the bird glanced 'round and then up as Céleste continued to bell the clarion. Ruthlessly halting back on the reins, the horse screaming in pain, the man wrenched the steed to a halt at the perimeter of the oak. The other riders—some dozen in all—momentarily passed him, and then cruelly hauled their own horses to a stop. They turned and rode back to mill about this man.

In the distance the bay of the hounds diminished.

The man looked up at the leather-clad, slender princess, with her pale blond hair and green eyes . . . and he grinned. "Well, now, what have we here?"

Céleste stared down at this brown-haired, unshaven, crow-bearing man, dressed in a red tabard emblazoned with the sigil of a black bird in flight. On his shoulder the bird shifted about and with glittering eyes looked up at her as well, as did the rest of the band, arrayed in red tabards, all.

"Who gave you permission to hunt in my demesne?" demanded Céleste.

The calls of the pack hounding the stag grew faint.

The crow turned its head, and it seemed to whisper in the leader's ear. The man frowned, and then looked up and said, "And just who might you be?"

"*Céleste, Princesse de la Forêt de Printemps.*"

The crow ruffled its feathers and turned to the man and emitted a croak as if to say, "See, I told you she was the one."

The man sneered and said, "Well, then, 'Princess of the Forest of Spring'—"

But Céleste interrupted him and again demanded, "I ask, who gave you permission to hunt in my demesne?"

"Bah! We need no permission to take that which we seek," sneered the man. "Come down from there, Princess, for, whether you like it or no, we have been sent to take you to someone who"—he grinned again—"wishes to see you." Then he barked a laugh and said, "By being out here alone, as she said you often are, you have saved us a bit of trouble."

"Brigand," spat Céleste, and she nocked an arrow.

The man sniggered, joined by all in his band. "Ah, indeed we are brigands, Princess, and sent to fetch you. So put away your little arrow and come down; else we'll have to use our own—yet dead or alive, it matters not to our mistress, for she would see you either way."

He signaled to one of his henchmen, and that man rode forward and reached for his bow.

"Call off your lapdog," said Céleste to the man with the crow. "Else you will be the first to die."

The brigand leader sighed, and then gestured a command to the man in the fore, and that henchman nocked an arrow. As he raised his weapon—*Thock!*—a crossbow quarrel took him in the ear, and he fell from his horse, dead as he hit the ground.

"*Yahhh!*" came a cry, and out from the surrounding trees an armored man in a blue surcoat charged on a black steed; even as he galloped forward, he swung a shield up and onto his left arm, and drew a glittering sword. Laying about to left and right with his gleaming blade, the rider crashed in among the brigands.

"Well, second to die," Céleste muttered, and she let fly her own shaft, and the leader fell slain. As the man tumbled from his horse, the crow took to wing and cried out, *"Revenge! Revenge!"* as it circled up and about, but Céleste paid it little heed, as she winged arrows into the mêlée below, aiming for those nearest the rider in blue, especially those behind. Man after man she felled, as the deadly blade of the swordsman reaped brigands.

Of the thirteen outlaws, only two managed to survive, and they fled into the forest—one with an arrow in his side, the other now missing a hand. Most of the brigands' horses galloped away with the two, though some of the mounts fled elsewhere, the reek of slaughter more than they could bear.

In the preternatural silence that followed, far away the sounds of the hounds vanished, and somewhere a crow calling for revenge flew beyond hearing.

The man in blue wheeled his horse about and looked up at Céleste. "Are you well, demoiselle?"

"Indeed, *Sieur*," replied Céleste, somewhat breathlessly, her heart yet pounding. "And you?"

"I have taken a cut across the leg, but otherwise—"

"Oh, Sieur," cried Céleste, "let me tend that." She shouldered her bow and began scrambling down from the oak.

The rider glanced about and then hung his shield from a saddle hook and dismounted and stepped to the base of the tree. He set his sword aside and removed his helmet; a shock of raven-dark hair tumbled out. And as Céleste came down the last of the trunk he reached up and featherlight swung her to the ground. She turned 'round in his embrace and looked up into his dark grey eyes. He held her closely and returned the gaze. "Oh, my," he breathed, "you are so beautiful."

2

Roél

With her heart pounding, "Sieur, we must tend to your leg wound," said Céleste, dropping her gaze, knowing a blush filled her features, for in addition to having dark hair and grey eyes and a handsome face, he was tall and strong and most certainly brave . . . and dangerous in battle, and perhaps otherwise, too . . . the kind of man she had dreamed of meeting one day, and here she was in his arms.

" 'Tis but a scratch," said the man, a rakish grin filling his features as he reluctantly released his embrace.

"Sit with your back to my Companion of Quietness," said Céleste, gesturing at the trunk of the oak.

The man raised an eyebrow at her name for the tree; nevertheless he eased himself down and leaned against its bole.

"Have you a name, Sieur?" asked Céleste, as she knelt to examine the wound.

"Roél," replied the man. "Son of Sieur Émile and Lady Simone, brother of Sieurs Laurent and Blaise and of Demoiselle Avélaine."

"You are a chevalier?" asked Céleste as she peeled back the edges of the slash through his leg leathers.

"Oui," said Roël, breathing in the scent of her hair.

"Oh, my, that is a rather nasty cut," said Céleste, examining the wound. She stepped to her horse, and unlike Roël's black, her grey was white-eyed, agitated by the faint smell of spilled blood, mixed with the urine of released bladders and the feces of loosened bowels of the slain men. "Shhh . . . shhh . . . ," hushed the princess, running her hand along the steed's neck, calming it. She opened a saddlebag and took out a cloth-wrapped bundle and a small waterskin and returned to the knight.

"Are you hungry?" she asked, and undid the cloth, revealing cheese and bread and an apple. The food she handed to him, but she kept the cloth. As blood welled from the cut, she ripped the fabric in two and laid one half on the grass. She folded the other and set it aside as well. Then she poured water on the wound to wash the blood away, and quickly took up the folded cloth and pressed it against the cut, and bound it there with the first piece.

"There, that ought to hold until I can get you to the manse," she said.

Yet kneeling, she looked at him, and, dagger in hand, he offered her a slice of apple. "First, demoiselle, let us finish this cheese and bread and fruit, for you never know when we might get to eat again. And, oh, might you have a bottle of wine in those saddlebags of yours?"

Céleste burst out laughing. Why, she did not know, though it might have been the incongruity of a wounded man on a field of battle calmly eating an apple and speaking of wine. He smiled in return, a gleam in his eye, and added, "Besides, my sire always told me to never pass up the chance of a picnic with a lovely demoiselle, for you never know what might happen."

Again Céleste felt a flush rising to her cheeks. *"Non, Sieur,"* she said, "I have no wine; water must do."

He sighed. "Ah, me, mere water. Still, I can drink in your beauty."

Again Céleste laughed, and she took the apple slice and sat beside him, her back to the tree as well.

"And have you a name?" asked Roél.

"Céleste," replied the princess.

"How perfect, for does it not mean heavenly?" said Roél, handing her another slice of apple along with a cut of cheese. Then he tore off two hunks of bread and handed her one of those as well.

"Did you not hear me call out my name to those brigands?" asked Céleste.

"Non. I heard you call, but I was yet at some distance away."

"What brought you?"

"The horns. I heard them and rode this way, and I arrived just as"—Roél gestured toward the slain men—"one of those bandits moved forward at the behest of another. It looked as if they were going to slay you outright, so I cocked and loaded my crossbow, and"—Roél shrugged—"the rest is history."

"Well, Sieur Roél, I am glad that you did."

They sat in silence for a while, watching Roél's black horse placidly crop grass nearby in spite of the smell of death. But at last Roél said, "Were they your enemies?"

Céleste shrugged. "They said they had been sent to fetch me to some mistress of theirs. Dead or alive, it mattered not to her . . . or to them."

Roél frowned. "Then they would have slain you?"

"It seems so."

"Too bad their mistress was not among them."

Céleste took a drink of water and passed the skin to Roél, who drained it and set it aside.

He started to reach for the cheese, but of a sudden—"*Hsst!*"

Céleste stopped chewing and listened. A horn cried in the distance. Roél leapt to his feet and slipped it on. He took up his sword and stepped to the black. "Mount up, my lady, and make ready to ride; mayhap more brigands return. If it comes to battle, flee. I will hold them off." Sword in hand, he mounted.

Céleste untethered her grey, and swung up into the saddle. She unlimbered her bow and set an arrow to string.

Now they could hear the hammer of oncoming hooves, as of a number of riders.

"Is your manse well fortified?" asked Roél, riding to Céleste's side.

"Indeed," said Céleste.

"Which way?" asked Roél.

Céleste pointed. "Yon."

"Then we'll have to circle 'round, for the riders are 'tween here and there."

An approaching horn cry split the air.

"Let us away!" said Roél, but at this last clarion call Céleste laughed gaily. She put away her arrow and raised her own horn to her lips and repeated the call.

Roél frowned. "What . . . ?"

" 'Tis my own men," said Céleste.

"Your own men?"

"From the manor," replied Céleste. "Riding to the rescue, I ween."

Again she sounded the horn, and it was answered, and in that moment a warband galloped into the open. And they swirled around the pair and came to a stop, some with swords, others with bows, and these held aim on Roél.

"Princess," called one of the men, "are you well?"

"Oui, Anton," replied Céleste, springing down from her

horse. Then she called out to the men, "Put away your weapons, for all brigands are dead save two, and they have fled away." She gestured toward the slaughter at hand and then toward Roél. "This is the knight who saved me."

Anton sheathed his sword and turned to the others. "You heard the princess."

As the warband followed suit, Roél, sword yet in hand, dismounted and removed his helm and faced Céleste. "You are a princess?"

Céleste smiled. "Oui."

A look of wonder filled Roél's face, and for a moment he stood stunned. But then he swept both helm and sword wide in a deep bow and said, "My lady."

Céleste smiled and canted her head in acknowledgment, but then gasped. "Oh, Roél, you are bleeding again." She turned to one of the men. "Gilles, did you bring your bandages and herbs and simples?"

"As always, Princess," said Gilles, even as he dismounted. He unslung his saddlebags and stepped to Roél. "Sieur, if you will take a seat by the oak, I will tend to your wound."

"Gilles," said Roél as he moved toward the tree, "have you a spare clean cloth?" Of a sudden Roél paled, and perspiration broke out on his forehead. His helmet slipped from his fingers and fell to the ground, but Roél didn't seem to notice. And then he stumbled and went down on one knee, but caught himself against the trunk of the oak. Céleste gasped and rushed forward and took the sword from him and set it aside and helped him ease down. With a sigh Roél said, "I need to wipe the blood of the outlaws from *Coeur d'Acier*."

"Coeur d'Acier?" said Gilles as he whipped open a saddlebag.

"My sword," said Roél, his voice weakening, sweat now running down his face.

"Ah, oui, Sieur, a clean cloth I do have," replied Gilles, rummaging in the bag. He murmured to Céleste, "Keep him talking."

Céleste, her heart pounding in fear for Roél, said, "Did I hear correctly, my knight? Your sword is named Heart of Steel?"

"Oui," said Roél, reaching for the silvery blade, but his hand fell lax, the effort too much.

Tears brimmed in Céleste's eyes, and though she felt as if she were babbling, she said, "Oh, Roél, neither iron nor steel is permitted in Faery except in special circumstance."

His voice still weaker, "So Geron told me," said Roél, "even as he gave me Coeur d'Acier." He closed his eyes and fell silent while Gilles pulled loose the bandage.

As the healer began cutting away the leathers about the wound, "Roél," said Céleste, "please don't leave me. Tell me more."

Roél murmured, "But Geron also said this blade would not twist the aethyr—whatever that might be—for the steel is bound by powerful runes and flashed with silver. Hence, he said I could bear it into Faery, for it would aid me in my quest."

With dread clutching her very soul, Céleste could hardly get words to leave her mouth. Still she managed—"You have a quest?"

"Oui," Roél whispered. "My sister, Avélaine, has been taken by the Lord of the Changelings, and I would rescue her and my brothers as well."

"There is a story here for the telling," said Céleste, her cheeks wet with tears. She again looked at Gilles, but with a small, cloth-tipped swab he was now fully occupied probing the wound.

Wincing slightly, his voice faintly strengthening, Roél whispered, "And tell the tale I will." And then his head fell forward onto his chest.

"Oh, Roél," cried Céleste. She turned to the healer. "Gilles, is he—?"

"Not yet, my lady, but I fear for him," said Gilles. He held up the swab; the cloth tip was covered with dark grume. "The wound itself is quite minor, you see, but a poisoned blade made the cut."

3

Awakenings

Please, Roél . . . I . . . you must not . . .
. . . Will he . . . ?

. . . Gilles . . .

. . . My lady, he's . . . We can only . . . .

. . . travois . . . we need a . . .

. . . Easy . . .

. . . Mithras, please, I beg of you . . . .

. . . Here . . . in here . . . .

. . . Careful, now . . . more water . . . .

Silvery dawn light filtered in through sheer curtains when Roél awakened, fragments of urgent conversation yet clinging to his mind. He was in a bed in a room somewhere, and someone held his left hand.

Céleste.

She sat in a chair at his side, though, leaning forward, her head and shoulders resting upon his cover, she slept, her fingers lightly touching his.

16

"Ah, my lovely," whispered Roél, and he freed his hand and stroked her silky hair; then he, too, slept once more.

When next he awakened, Gilles stood beside the bed, and dusklight filled the chamber. Of Céleste there was no sign.

"Drink?" asked Gilles.

Roél nodded.

Gilles poured a half glass of water from a pitcher, and then propped Roél up and held the vessel to his lips.

"It was a close thing, Sieur Roél," said Gilles as Roél sipped. "Twice I thought we had lost you, but twice you rallied. 'Tis good you were fit; else you would not be among the living."

"It was such a small cut," said Roél.

"Oui," said Gilles, "but such a deadly poison.—More water?"

"Please."

Gilles again half filled the glass and aided Roél to drink.

"Another?"

"Non." Roél sighed and looked about. "The princess?"

"Ah. We finally had to drag her away," said Gilles, setting the glass down. "She would not leave your side."

"How long?"

Gilles eased Roél back down and frowned. "How long? How long was she at your—? No, wait. I see. Three days. This is the third day since the skirmish."

Roél nodded and closed his eyes.

"I need to change your dressing," said Gilles, and he drew back the covers and pulled Roél's nightshirt up to the chevalier's thigh, revealing the bandage above the left knee. "This might sting a bit," said the healer.

Roél slept in spite of Gilles' ministrations.

Stars showed through the window when next Roél opened his eyes. He took a deep breath and turned, and there was Céleste, again at his side, this time awake, her face lit by a single candle burning close by.

He smiled, and she took his hand and breathed, "Roél."

"Princess, in nought but a nightshirt I am not fit to be presented to you," said Roél. "Too, I need a bath and a shave, and—"

"Pishposh," said Céleste, shaking her head. "That can come later. What you need now are food and drink."

Roél grinned. "Bread and cheese and an apple, I suppose, but, this time, perhaps wine?"

Céleste laughed and released his hand and reached up beside the bed and tugged a bell cord. Then she plumped two pillows against the headboard, and Roél hitched himself to a sitting position. A moment later a servant appeared. "Broth, Gérard, and croutons. —And tea. Honey as well, to sweeten it with. And hie."

As the man rushed away, Roél said, "What, no wine, no beef, no bread, no gravy?"

"Nothing so heavy this eve, Roél," said Céleste. "Gilles' orders, you see."

"Ah, my lady, what does a healer know of such things?"

"Well," said Céleste, "this healer saved your life." Of a sudden, tears brimmed in Céleste's eyes. "We thought you lost, Roél, but Gilles—" Céleste took a deep shuddering breath and let it out, and wiped away wetness from her cheeks.

"Do not weep, my lovely," said Roél, reaching out a hand, and even as she took it, he realized he had spoken aloud. "Oh, my lady, I didn't mean to call you my—Or, rather, I did mean it, but I-I—I mean, I—"

Roél stuttered to a halt as Céleste broke into laughter. "Ah, Roél, would you have me call you 'my handsome'?"

Roél grinned. "I shall have to think on that, Princess."

"Well, as you are thinking, is there ought else you need besides food and drink?"

"Is there a privy at hand?"

Céleste smiled. "Oui, as well as a chamber pot under the bed."

"I'd rather the privy."

"I'll show you the way," said Céleste.

"Oh, no, Princess. Have a servant—"

"Folderol," exclaimed Céleste, interrupting Roél's protest. "I am perfectly capable of aiding you."

Roél sighed and nodded and swung his feet over the side of the bed.

"Take care," Céleste cautioned. "Gilles said for you to beware the first time standing."

Roél took a deep breath and said, "Oh, my, but I believe Gilles was right."

"I'll fetch the chamber pot," said Céleste.

"Non, Princess. I would rather not embarrass myself." Bracing against the bed, Roél stood, swaying a bit.

Céleste took his arm.

" 'Ware, Princess, should I topple, step back as to not be crushed."

Céleste, from her five foot three, looked up at Roél's slender six one. "I believe I am made of sterner matter, Sieur."

"Ha! Though you climb trees, you appear quite fragile to me," said Roél as Céleste led him across the room and toward a door. "—And now that I think of it, just how did you get up that tree, my lady?"

"Perhaps, given my so-called *fragile* state, I had the Fairies fly me up," said Céleste as she opened the door. In the chamber beyond was a bronze tub for bathing, a mirrored stand with a basin and a ewer, soaps, towels, cloths, and a small fireplace. Past the tub stood another door, this one leading to a chamber-pot throne.

"My lady," said Roél, "as much as I love your company, I believe I can essay this on my own."

"As you will, 'my handsome,' " said Céleste, smiling as she withdrew, closing the doors after. Even so, she stood by in case he called for aid, for he yet seemed unsteady.

With a knock on the hall door, Gérard and two lads came bearing trays: Gérard with a tea set and a pot of honey, along with utensils and napkins; one of the lads with a tureen of beef broth with a ladle and bowl, and a second bowl filled with croutons; the other lad with a bed tray. "My lady," said the man, after all had been placed on a sideboard, "Cook says, should you want any, she has some tasty éclairs, or honeyed biscuits for the tea, along with scones and clotted cream and some wonderful blackberry preserves."

Céleste smiled. "Oh, Gérard, tell her it sounds most tasty, but Sieur Roél needs only that which you brought."

"What sounds most tasty?" asked Roél, emerging from the bathing chamber.

"Something perhaps you can have on the morrow," said Céleste, "should Gilles agree."

"A joint of beef for my famished stomach?" asked Roél, slowly making his way to the bed, his steps now steady.

Céleste laughed. "Mayhap that, too."

"My lady, would you have me serve?" asked Gérard.

"Non, Gérard, I will do the honors."

"That will be all, then, my lady?" he asked.

"Oui, Gérard, and thank you."

The trio started out the door, and Gérard, last, said, "Oh, and Mam'selle Henriette says she'll be just outside if you need her."

Céleste sighed and shook her head.

Roél clambered onto the bed, and as Céleste pulled up the covers and spanned the bed tray across his lap, he said, "You do not seem pleased that Mam'selle Henriette stands at the door."

"She thinks to guard my virtue," said Céleste.

"Ah, a chaperone?"

"Oui," said Céleste, now ladling broth into a bowl, "though I have not needed one for some while."

Roél raised an eyebrow at this, though the princess's back was to him.

The bowl now filled, she sat it on his bed tray, along with the croutons and a napkin and spoon, and then stepped back to the sideboard and began pouring tea. Roél smiled and said, "Although I am sorely wounded and abed—" Céleste glanced at him, and Roél pressed the back of his right hand to his forehead and feigned terrible weakness and emitted a prolonged sigh—

Céleste broke out in giggles and said, "You make me laugh, Roél, and I love that in a man."

Roél beamed, but continued: "—we should have one, Princess—a chaperone, I mean—for I would not sully your reputation."

As if to herself Céleste smiled and faintly shook her head, then laughed again. "Henriette was scandalized when I had you installed in this bedchamber."

Roél looked about. "What is special about this room?"

"It adjoins mine," said Céleste, nodding at a door on the far wall as she dropped a dollop of honey in each cup of tea and stirred, "and is meant for my husband."

Chapfallen, Roél now truly sighed and glumly said, "Then you are married, Princess?"

"Non. I should have said it is for my husband-to-be."

"You are engaged, then," said Roél.

Céleste placed a cup of tea on the bed tray and then stepped to the sideboard for her own. She turned and took a slow sip, her green eyes fixed on him. She set the cup back in the saucer and said, "Non, I'm not engaged. Nor am I currently involved."

"*Magnifique!*" exclaimed Roél, a great smile lighting his face, but then he flushed. "Er, that is, not that I have, um, aspirations, oh, my, I meant . . ." Roél's words dribbled away, and he studiously peered into his broth.

Céleste's mouth twitched in a brief grin, and then she took a deep breath and asked, "And you, Roél, have you someone waiting for you?"

Roél looked up at the princess, a tentative smile on his face. "Non."

Céleste's own features broke into a glorious smile. "Bon!" Her green eyes looked into his grey, his grey into her green, and, as if the aethyr itself tingled in anticipation, there came between them an unspoken understanding: he would woo her.

Yet grinning and ignoring the spoon, Roél took up the broth and downed it in one long gulp. He held the bowl out to Céleste and said, "More, please." As she replenished the vessel, he popped croutons into his mouth and happily crunched away.

4

Quest

For his second bowl of broth, Roél used a spoon, but he had taken only a taste or two when he frowned and set it aside.

"What is it, my handsome?" asked Céleste, a faint smile warring with concern on her face. "Why the grim look?"

"Oh, Princess, I just realized, the moment I am fit enough, I will have to leave you."

"Leave me?"

"Oui. My quest. I must find Avélaine and Laurent and Blaise. — Rescue them, I think."

Céleste sighed, now recalling what he had said—*When was that? Just three days past? It seems much longer.* "Tell me of this mission, Roél."

Roél took a deep breath and slowly released it, and he gazed out the window as if seeking an answer somewhere in the glitter of distant stars beyond. Then he turned to Céleste and said, "I am the youngest son of Sir Émile and Lady Simone. I have two brothers and a sister. Laurent is the eldest, Blaise follows him, our sister, Avélaine, comes next in birth order, and, of course, I am last. And ever since I can remember, Avélaine and I have been as dear to one another as a brother and sister can be."

Roél paused, his gaze lost in memory. Finally he shrugged and said, "Regardless, nearly seven years past, Avélaine was given to long restless rides, for she was sore beset by our parents. They had arranged a marriage for her to someone she did not wish to wed, and she had wanted to flee ere that day, but she knew it was her duty to follow our parents' pact with the parents of the groom. And so instead of running away, she rode off from the manor to escape the words of our *père* and *mère* and to struggle with her feelings. Always I accompanied her, for I thought she might need, not only the mostly silent companionship of someone who sympathized with her, but also someone to protect her from brigands, should any be lurking about." Roél faintly smiled. "Not that there were ever any on our estate, but you see, I was a squire at the time—no longer a boy but not yet a man—and in training to become a knight, for I would follow in the steps of Laurent and Blaise, both of whom had won their spurs apast. And so, I went along as her guardian, though I did not tell her that.

"We rode to the outskirts of my sire's estate, where deep in the forest there lie the ruins of an ancient temple. Perhaps once it had been mighty, but these days it is nought but a tumble of rock, a place our vassals shunned; even the woodcutters didn't go near. Nevertheless, Avélaine and I were out there, and at that time neither of us knew just who or what might have been worshipped therein. . . ."

Roél slashed and thrust at the air with his rapier to deal with an imaginary foe. Only half-watching, Avélaine sat on a block of stone. "Oh, Roél, why did they have to choose Maslin? It's not that he isn't a fine fellow, but for me he has no, um, no spark."

Roél paused in his duel with the air and cocked an eyebrow at his raven-haired sister. "No spark?"

"He does not move me," said Avélaine.

"Move you?"

A look of exasperation filled Avélaine's blue eyes. "He does not stir my heart."

"Ah, I see," said Roél, returning to his battle with the invisible foe.

Avélaine sat in glum thought, gazing at, but not seeing, their two horses placidly cropping grass nearby. Finally, she heaved a great sigh and said, "Oh, I wish I were anywhere but in this time and place."

"Take care, sister of mine," said Roél as he continued to slash at the air, "for you know not what magic these old ruins might hold."

"Oh, would that they did," said Avélaine, "for then I would be gone from here." She hopped down from the stone block and turned to look at the tumble, nought but a vine-covered wrack with thistles growing among the remains. As if seeing them for the first time, Avélaine strolled around the remnants, circling widdershins in the light of the early-spring midmorning sun.

Roél paused and watched her walk away; then he resumed his cut and thrust at the air. He had just dispatched the unseen foeman when as from a distance he heard Avélaine faintly call, "Roél."

He turned to see her standing there, now nearly all the way 'round the ruins. Pale, she was, almost ghostly, and she reached a hand out toward Roél as if pleading. Just behind and to the left stood a tall, black-haired, black-eyed man in an ebon cloak limned in scarlet. Over his left arm something draped, as of wispy dark cloth featherlight. A sneer of triumph filled his dark aquiline features as he gazed at Avélaine.

Roél shouted and raised his sword and rushed forward, but in that instant the man embraced Avélaine and whirled 'round and 'round and 'round and vanished, taking Avélaine with him, and when Roél came to the place where they had been, he found nought but empty air.

* * *

"What do you mean she's gone?" demanded Laurent.

"She and the man both vanished," said Roël.

"Did you not engage him in battle?" asked Blaise.

"Even as I went for him, he spun like a dervish and disappeared and took Avélaine with him," said Roël, on the verge of tears. "I searched and searched, but they were truly gone."

"Well, if I'd been there," said Laurent, "I would have—"

"Oh, leave the boy alone," cried Lady Simone, again bursting into tears, even as she stepped to Roël and embraced him.

But Roël would have none of that, and he disengaged his mother's arms and defiantly faced Laurent. "You would have done no better than I."

"Pah! You little—"

"Laurent!" snapped Sir Émile. "Enough! We are here to deal with the problem and not to dole out blame."

"But what can we possibly do?" cried Simone, wiping her eyes with her kerchief and then using it to blow her nose.

Émile knitted his brow, pondering, and then said, "I do not know, my lady. Mayhap Avélaine is lost forever, for it is clear that a powerful being has abducted her, most likely the Elf King, for 'tis said he captures mortals by stealing their shadows from them. No doubt he has taken her to Faery."

"Faery!" exclaimed Simone. "Oh, what a horrible place!"

Once more she broke into tears, and Émile embraced her.

Roël took a deep breath and said, "Sire, we can consult with Geron the Sage. Perhaps he will know what to do and where to go."

Émile nodded. "Ah, you have hit upon it, my boy. One of us must seek him out."

"I will go, Father," said Roël.

"Pah! You?" sneered Laurent. "You are nought but a child, a mere squire. I will go instead."

"No," said Blaise. "I will go."

"I am the eldest," said Laurent. "Hence it is mine to do."

"I will not accept this blame," said Roél. "I am the one to find him."

Émile called for quiet and said, "Laurent is right. He is the eldest, so he is the one to go."

The next morning, arrayed in his fine armor and armed with the best of weaponry, Laurent mounted up on his caparisoned steed and said, "No matter what Sage Geron tells me, whether he has any aid or not, still will I seek Avélaine. It might be a lengthy quest, yet surely will I find her."

Roél paused in his telling and took a long sip of tea. Céleste remained silent and waited for him to continue. Roél then set his cup down and said, "With tearful au revoirs, we watched Laurent ride away, my brother the knight quite magnificent on that great horse of his." Roél sighed and said, "But then three years passed, and we heard nothing of Laurent or Avélaine.

"By that time I had won my own spurs in the lists and in one-on-one combat as well as in the mêlées. Then war came, and over the next months both Blaise and I acquitted ourselves with honor on the fields of Valens.

"But when we returned home, Blaise set out to find Laurent and Avélaine, and he rode for Sage Geron's cottage to seek advice. I would have gone with him, but my sire was in ill health, and there were yet foemen wandering the land. So, to guard my sire and dam, I stayed behind at the manor.

"Another three years passed, and there came no word of Blaise, Laurent, or Avélaine. My sire had recovered his health, and now I would go to find my missing kindred. Mother objected tearfully, for she would not lose all her get in a futile search. My sire, too, was reluctant to let me go, yet in the end he acceded, for I was a true knight, and he could not, would not, gainsay me, his third and last son, in this honorable quest.

"As did my brothers before me, I set out to seek the advice of

Sage Geron, and a moon or so later I arrived at his cote, there nigh the edge of the mortal world, the cottage but a fortnight from the twilight walls of Faery. He invited me in and made tea, and we sat at his table and spoke. . . ."

"I'll tell you what I told your brothers," said Geron. "Contrary to popular myth, 'twas no Elf King who took your sister, but the Lord of the Changelings himself. Ah, he resembles the Elf King, yet is another altogether. He stole Avélaine's shadow, cut it free from her, he did; hence he captured a key bit of her essence and has her in his thrall."

Geron nodded.

"Then my sire was right about someone stealing a shadow," said Roél, "but was wrong about who did it."

Geron nodded.

"Then that was what he had draped over his arm? Her shadow?"

Geron nodded again.

Roél sighed. "I thought it but a wisp of dark cloth."

The sage shook his head. "Nay, lad, 'twas her shadow, stolen away. The Lord of the Changelings at times seeks out a fair demoiselle to capture, and he does so in this manner."

"Speak to me of this Changeling Lord."

Geron replenished his cup of tea and offered some to Roél, who with a gesture declined. The sage took a long sip and set the cup aside and leaned back in his chair. "Though they are rather Elflike, these beings are not true Elves, but a race set apart, a race called Changelings."

"Changelings," said Roél. "I've heard of them: babes exchanged at birth for another child."

"Oh, non, non"—Geron shook his head—"that's but part of the truth. You see, Changelings are not only babes, but adults, too. And there is this, my boy: they are called Changelings for they can alter their shapes."

"Shift into something they are not?"

"Non, shift into *someone* they are not, but always whoever they become, at heart they are still a Changeling."

"Say on, Sage."

Geron took another sip of tea. "Just as the Firbolg and the Sidhe, or better yet the Seelie and the Unseelie, there are two factions of Changelings, in appearance difficult to tell apart. Yet though they might be different from one another, they are closely akin. Regardless as to whether it is one race or two, both factions take humans for their own, for now and again they need the strength of mortal blood to restore the vitality of their kind."

"Mortal blood? You mean they mate with humans?"

"Oui. Only in this way can they remain a vigorous folk."

"Tell me of these two factions."

"One is ruled over by a queen, and she is proud and terrible."

"Terrible? Evil, wicked, you mean?"

"Non, non. Terrible in her power, in her abilities, and she does not gladly suffer the follies of humankind. E'en so, it is she who lures men unto her bed. She does not steal shadows to do so, but uses her charms instead."

Roél nodded. "I understand. What of the other faction?"

"Ah, they are ruled by the Changeling Lord, and he is also terrible, not only in his power, but in his wickedness as well. It is he who steals shadows of those he would bed."

"He would lie with my sister?"

Geron sighed and nodded.

Roél jumped up and began pacing. "My sister will never mate with that evil being."

"My boy, she has no shadow, and thus little will of her own."

Roél stopped pacing and turned to Geron. "Why did he choose her?"

"First, she was near the temple ruins, where she made a wish, one overheard by the Changeling Lord. And second, she suited his needs, for he requires someone virginal, someone who has not lain with a man nor an Elf nor any other male."

Roél threw himself into his chair. "Then he has already defiled her?"

"Perhaps, perhaps not, for lore says not only must she be a virgin; it further declares he cannot force her, for unless she enters his embrace without resistance, the seed will not take. Yet e'en if she resists, in time she will come to his bed, her will sapped, her defiance at last gone."

"How much time?"

"That, I do not know."

"Then perhaps I am already too late."

Geron shrugged. "Mayhap."

Roél slammed a fist onto the table, Geron's teacup and saucer rattling in response. "Nevertheless," gritted Roél, "I will free her."

They sat in silence for a moment, and then Roél said, "What of the children of these matings?"

Geron straightened his cup in its saucer. "The Queen of the Changelings, she woos her humans and they go willingly to her bed. And the children born of their matings are blessed."

"And the Lord of the Changelings?"

Geron shook his head. "He does not woo, but instead steals shadows, takes something of the soul; hence children of these matings lack full souls of their own."

Roél groaned, "And when these babes are swapped for human children . . . ?"

"Both factions exchange their newborn offspring for humankind newborns, and they raise the human children to live among them. In the queen's realm, some become bards and poets and thespians and artisans beyond compare, and others become warriors and they protect the queen's borders. Some, a few, return to the mortal lands and become folk of renown. For those who stay in the Changeling realm, eventually they take mates, and thus the populace is strengthened for a while. But for some reason I do not understand, at last the vigor wanes, and more humans are required to restore the vitality of the Changelings, and so both the Queen of the Changelings and the Changeling Lord must bring in new blood."

"I see," said Roél. "And what of the babes who are raised by the minions of the Changeling Lord?"

"Ah, those," said Geron. "Even though they are human, hence have the souls they were born with, most are raised to become frightful warriors or other dreadful beings, and those who return to the mortal land live in infamy."

Roél sighed and then said, "And what of the Changelings who are raised by humans?"

"If it is a blessed child from the queen's realm, then only good things come to those whose lives they touch, but if a nighsoulless child from the lord's realm, then dreadful things befall not only those in that foster household, but all who come in contact with the Changeling."

"Then, if my sister has mated with the Changeling Lord, the chances of her child turning out good are . . . ?"

"Lad, you do not want to believe her children will be evil, yet I say unto you they will be."

Again Roél slammed a fist to the table. He sat in brooding silence for a while, but at last he said, "And you are certain that it was in fact the Changeling Lord and not the Elf King who stole my sister away?"

"Yes, Roél, I am certain. Let me tell you what he looked like: he was tall, and had black hair and black eyes and his features somewhat resembled those of a hawk."

"How dressed?" asked Roél.

"Dark clothing, an ebon cloak limned in scarlet."

"Limned, or instead lined?"

"Limned only," said Geron.

Roél sighed. "You have described him exactly as I remember."

Geron nodded. "It is as I say: 'twas the Lord of the Changelings himself."

"How know you this?" asked Roél.

"I myself saw him long past when we sages banded together to destroy that temple of his, the place where he captured your sister."

"Those ruins were once a temple to the Lord of the Changelings?"

"Oui," said Geron, nodding. "A most wicked being, he was and is."

"Then that is why people avoid those ruins?" asked Roél.

Again Geron nodded, but then shook his head in rue. "Other than a handful of sages such as me, I suspect no others yet live who know it once was used thus and still holds remnants of power. Hence the ruins are now avoided out of tradition rather than from sure knowledge. It's unfortunate you didn't know better than to loiter about such a place. Unfortunate as well your sister made a wish there."

"Mistake or no, what's done is done," said Roél, though regret tinged his words. "What is important now is to retrieve my sister. —My brothers as well."

The sage took a deep breath. "As to your brothers, Roél, I would not hold out hope that they are yet alive, for when I told them what they must do, they would not wait."

"Wait for what?" asked Roél.

Geron got up from the table and stepped to a chest. He opened it and took from it a sword in a scabbard and turned to Roél and said, "They would not wait for this."

"And that is . . . ?"

"Coeur d'Acier," said Geron.

"Heart of Steel?"

"Oui," said Geron. "It is a special weapon, years in the making, for there are powerful runes bound in the blade and covered with silver flashing. It was not finished when your brothers rode through."

"Were not their own weapons adequate?" asked Roél. "They were forged from good steel as well."

"Ah, but you see, the Changeling Lord lives in Faery, where steel is forbidden except under special circumstance. After all, one must not affront the Fairies and Elves and other such beings therein; else the transgressor might find himself forever cursed."

"Did my brothers take their steel within?"

"I do not know," said Geron. "I advised them to trade their arms and armor for counterparts of good bronze."

"Trade?"

"Oui. You see, from here, the city of Rulon is on the way to Faery, and for a fee the merchants of Rulon will trade bronze accoutrements for those of steel; travellers can then retrieve their own when they come back from Faery . . . assuming they come back within a year. Rulon is just one of several cities of such welcomed trade. After all, good steel is harder to come by than good bronze, and so the merchants gain rather handsomely in the exchange with those who are fool enough to venture into Faery."

Roél took a deep breath and slowly shook his head, for his brothers had been gone well beyond the required year. Finally he said, "Tell me what I must do."

Geron nodded, and he handed Roél Coeur d'Acier. "Bear this blade into Faery with you."

"Is it not made of steel?"

"Oui, it is; yet recall, I said it was steel bound with runes of power and flashed with silver. This blade will not twist the aethyr; hence it is safe to take into that mystical realm."

Roél frowned in puzzlement, but then shrugged in acceptance and said, "What else must I do?"

"But for Coeur d'Acier, rid yourself of all iron and steel—as I say, you can trade for arms and armor of bronze. Shoe your horse in bronze as well, and change out the tack—all fittings must be of bronze instead of iron."

Roél nodded and said, "And then what? How do I find Faery?"

Geron laughed. "Ah, lad, somewhat straight on beyond the city of Rulon you will come to a wall of twilight looming up into the sky. The wall is there whether or no it is day or night, for it is one of the many bounds of Faery. Simply ride through, and you will find yourself in that wondrous but oft perilous place."

Roél nodded and asked, "And once I am in Faery . . . ?"

"Then seek the port city of Mizon. Therein lies a well-known map which, among other things, purports to show a path to the Changeling realm. It is the only certain way I know of to find that domain."

"I have one other question, Geron."

"Ask away."

Roél lifted Coeur d'Acier. "Why do you give me such a valuable blade as this and ask nought in return?"

"Let us just say, my lad, I was driven by the Fates to do so." The sage spoke no more of his part in Roél's quest, though he talked freely of other things.

Roél rode away from Geron's cottage, and days later he came to the city of Rulon, and there, but for Coeur d'Acier, he exchanged his arms and armor for those of bronze. He had the tack of his horse fitted with bronze, and the shoes replaced with ones of bronze, including the nails therein. As the merchant put away the old gear, Roél recognized Laurent's steel dagger, and Blaise's steel helm, but none of their remaining gear did he see.

A day later he espied the great wall of twilight, and just beyond the burnt ruins of what had once been a magnificent manor, he rode through the bound and entered what appeared to be a woodland where spring seemed burgeoning, though the remains of winter lay upon the world he had just left.

Roél drained his cup of tea and said to Céleste, "And so, Princess, that is my quest, and the tale of how I came to be in Faery."

Céleste stood and took up Roél's cup and stepped to the sideboard to replenish it. "Oh, Roél, I am so sorry. Your sister stolen, your brothers missing."

Abed, Roél nodded bleakly. "Yet all are in Faery, or so I think."

"This Lord of the Changelings, he took her shadow," said Céleste.

Roél nodded. "Oui. As I said, it was draped over his arm when last I saw Avélaine."

Céleste set Roél's refreshed cup of honey-sweetened tea on the bed tray and said, "Ah, Roél, it is good that you came the way you did, for to find your sister you seek a treasured map in the port city of Mizon."

Roél looked at Céleste, an unspoken question in his eyes.

Céleste smiled and said, "I know the way to Mizon."

5

Amour

"You do? You know the way to the port city?" asked Roél.

"Oui," said Céleste, smiling. "I can guide you there."

"Oh, Princess, there are Changelings involved in my quest, the Lord of the Changelings, in fact, and I would not have you in jeopardy."

"And I would not have you go alone," said Céleste.

Before Roél could again protest, Gilles strode in. "Ah, you are awake, Roél. You, too, Princess." Then he smiled and glanced at Céleste and added, "Unlike Henriette at the door. Your chaperone, I gather?"

"Oui."

A wide grin lit up Gilles' face. "Sound asleep she is, Princess, an ideal chaperone."

Yet caught up in her determination to guide Roél to Mizon, Céleste graced her features with only a small smile at Gilles' bon mot.

Gilles stepped to the bedside. "And speaking of sleep, Sieur Roél, you need to be doing that right now."

"More sleep? After three days of such?"

"Oui," said Gilles. He held the back of his hand to Roél's forehead a moment and then nodded in satisfaction. "I told you before, it was a very virulent poison, and I would have you rest well this night." He glanced at Céleste. "—You, too, Princess." He then measured the chevalier's pulse. As he released Roél's wrist, he eyed the bowl of broth and asked, "Have you eaten yet?"

"This is my second," said Roél.

"Finish it now, for I have a sleep-medick to give you."

Roél looked at Céleste and shrugged, and took up the broth and drank it down.

Gilles crumbled three dried petals into Roél's cup, and poured in fresh tea. He stirred it a moment and set it before the knight. Gilles then turned to the princess and took her cup and did the same. When he returned it to her, Gilles glanced back and forth between the two and said, "The longer it stands, the worse it tastes."

Roél sighed and raised his cup to Céleste in salute, a salute she returned, and they drank it down, each making a moue in response to the flavor. "Gilles," said Céleste, "you could have at least sweetened it with honey."

Gilles grinned and said, "Ah, but, my lady, where would be the pleasure in that?"

Céleste laughed, and Gilles said, "And now, Princess, our patient needs his rest, as do you. There will be goodly time on the morrow and in the days after for you two to speak of whatever you will."

Céleste sighed and stood. "Good eve, Sieur Knight. Rest well."

"My lady, on the morrow, then," replied Roél.

Céleste made her way to the door leading to her own quarters, and as she opened it she said, "Oh, Gilles. Waken Henriette and tell her that she can now retire, for I am safe in my own bed." Smiling, Céleste closed the door behind.

Gilles pulled the bell cord, and Gérard and two lads appeared, and they carried away the tea set and the tureen and bowls and the bed tray and utensils. Gilles took up the candle and said, "I bid you good night as well, Sieur Roél." And so saying, he left.

Lying abed, Roél peered out the window, the glitter of stars now diminished by the light of the just-risen moon. Céleste filled his thoughts—her beautiful face, her slender form, her gentle but determined way—and he knew it would be a while ere he would fall asleep . . . and the next he knew—

—there came a knock on the door.

Roél opened his eyes to see daylight streaming in through the window. Again came the knock, and Gilles entered. "Breakfast is awaiting, Roél, and you are expected."

Roél sat up.

"How do you feel?" asked Gilles.

"Quite good, though starved, Gilles."

"No dizziness?"

"Non, though I haven't taken to my feet yet."

"Then I suggest you do so and be on your way."

"But I have no clothes, and I need a bath and a shave," said Roél.

Gilles grinned, and he stepped to a tall chifforobe and flung it open and gestured within. On one side hung clothes, and beneath the garments sat shoes. "Seamstresses have been at work ever since I said you would live. Cobblers, too." Gilles pulled open drawers on the other side. "Undergarments and socks and the like are in here."

Roél eased out of bed and cautiously stood. No dizziness assaulted him. "Will they fit?"

Gilles laughed. "Oh, yes. You see, they measured you two days past, while you still had not awakened. I must say, the ladies, they found you quite, um, how shall I say? Ah, yes, utterly pleasing. Indeed, quite the man."

Redness crept into Roél's face.

Gilles smiled and said, "Now, about that shave and a bath, as long as we keep your wound out of the water . . ."

He tugged on the bell cord, and moments later Gérard and a string of lads came bustling in, steaming pails in hand.

After finishing his third helping of eggs and rashers and well-buttered toast slathered with blackberry preserves, along with slices of apple and cheese and several cups of hot tea, Roél sighed in satisfaction and leaned back in his chair.

"Ah, Roél, I love to see a man eat. In that, you are much like my brothers," said Céleste.

"We are all pigs, eh?" said Roél, grinning.

Céleste laughed. "Non. Instead, you all have healthy appetites."

"I was famished, Princess, three days with nought but thin broth and bread crumbs. 'Tis not the best way to a man's heart."

Roél was dressed in a dark grey cotton shirt, grey to match his eyes. His black breeks were cinched by a silver-buckled black belt, and he was shod in black boots. Bathed and clean-shaven, his shoulder-length raven-dark hair yet a bit damp, he cut quite a handsome figure, and Céleste often found she was staring.

As for herself, Céleste wore a long-sleeved, pale green gown, and up and across a narrow inset white bodice panel, green laces zigzagged from waist to low neckline. Striking, she was, and her face and form took Roél's breath away, and his gaze oft met hers.

They sat across from one another at a small table in a secluded, walled garden. Crocuses bloomed among moss-covered stones through which water trickled into a clear pool. A small willow tree leaned over the mere, its dangling branches astir in the springlike zephyr that had managed to climb o'er the vine-covered wall. Somewhere nearby a finch called for a mate, and was answered by the flutter of wings. And in the pale glancing light of the midmorning sun, Roél and Céleste looked upon one another, their two hearts beating as one.

"Princess, I—"

"Roél, I—"

They both spoke at once, and—

"After you—"

"After you—"

They did it again.

Roél made a motion as if buttoning his lip and pointed at Céleste, and she burst out laughing, as did he. And finally, palm up, he gestured to her, inviting her to speak.

"I don't know what I was going to say," said Céleste, and again they both broke into laughter.

"Let's go for a walk," said Roél. "You can show me this estate of yours."

"Oh, Roél, are you certain you can? You might reopen your wound."

"Five stitches," said Roél as he stood and stepped 'round the table. "That's all it took for Gilles to sew me up, rather much like darning a sock. As I said, it was but a scratch, and surely I can take a stroll. After all, it was no short journey from my bed to this table."

"But what of the poison?" asked Céleste, looking up at him.

"Ah, Gilles' vile potions seem to have entirely rid me of that. Come, let us stroll awhile."

Roél stepped behind Céleste's chair and pulled it back and handed her up. And then she was in his arms, and he leaned down and gently kissed her.

"Oh, Princess, I didn't mean—or rather I did, but—"

She kissed him again, and passion flared, and hearts hammered, and Céleste felt a glorious fire sweeping throughout her body.

Ignoring the fact that he felt himself coming erect, Roél pulled her tight against him and kissed her deeply, and he wanted nothing more than to take her then and there.

And Céleste wanted nothing more than to be taken then and there.

"Ahem," sounded a polite cough.

They broke apart and turned to see an older man standing at hand.

"Yes, Louis?" asked Céleste, somewhat breathlessly, her heart yet racing madly.

"Shall I clear the table, madam?" asked Louis, discreetly staring off at something beyond the garden wall.

Roél only half paid attention to what Céleste was saying as she took him on a wide-ranging tour. And for her part, Céleste seemed greatly distracted as she pointed out trivialities and failed to mention key points concerning the grounds and the splendid château.

Céleste directed Roél's attention to the striations in the marble floor of the grand welcoming foyer, but said nought of the great circular seal centered within the stone depicting a cherry tree in full blossom. Nor did she say ought of the skylight above, the leaded glass depicting the very same thing.

Broad staircases swept up and around each side of the hall and to the floor above, and on the third floor beyond, balconies looked down from the embracing rooms, but Céleste managed to speak of only the knurls on the balusters.

They visited an extensive library with hundreds of books and scrolls and tomes, and Céleste pointed out her favorite chair.

She took him to a game room, where portraits of her père and mère and brothers and sister looked out from gilt frames. The room was furnished with tables and chairs, and ready for play were taroc cards and échiquiers for dames and échecs; Céleste showed Roél her favorite pièce, a red hierophant with a bent miter.

In the music room laden with viols and flutes and harpsichords and drums and other such, Céleste gestured at a small violin, the one she played as a child.

Outside she walked him through the gardens, and talked of plying a trowel. She showed him the stables, and there Roél found his black placidly munching on oats. The horse seemed more interested in his next mouthful than in his knight.

They strolled past gazebos and fountains and sundials and other such objects of the manor. Although Roél now and then paid close attention, he spent most of his time admiring Céleste.

Roél was introduced to gardeners and stablemen, to servants and seamstresses, to the smith and farrier, to laundresses and hunters, to the keeper of the mews where messenger falcons were housed, and to many of the other staff of the considerable manor. But the only name that remained in his mind was *Céleste, Céleste, Céleste.* Try as he would to remember the names of the people he met, they went glimmering away in the sunbeams of this most glorious day.

And though Céleste knew she was babbling but could not seem to stop, and though Roél tried to attend but failed, they basked in one another's company, as if nothing else in the world mattered but the presence of the other.

And neither could forget the burning passion of their kiss, the desire set aflame, the wanting of one another. It was as an unquenchable fire.

That evening they had dinner in an intimate chamber, one with a table just for two. What they ate, neither could say, for they were completely entranced with one another. Later, dressed against the chill of the spring night, they sat in a gazebo and watched the moon rise.

Finally, they returned to the manor, and in the hallway they espied Henriette lurking in the shadows, waiting for Céleste's safe return. Roél escorted Céleste to her chamber door and with a rather chaste kiss he bade her good night. Roél then stepped into his own room, and reliving Céleste's every move, every gesture, every smile, he made ready for bed. He crawled under his covers and spent a long while staring at the silver moonlit world beyond his windows.

And then the door between his chamber and Céleste's opened, and dressed in nought but a filmy negligee, the princess came padding in, moonlight revealing, then shadows concealing, as she passed in and out of the silvery beams.

"My lady?" said Roél, starting up, but she gestured for him to remain abed.

"Sieur, I was not satisfied by that peck at my door," said Céleste, crawling in beside him. She curled into his embrace, and he kissed her gently and then fiercely and she hungrily responded in kind. His manhood was hard and pressing against her, and she could feel the beat of his pulse. Céleste paused a moment to pull her negligee up and off and cast it to the floor. And as he doffed his nightshirt, the garment falling aside neglected, she whisked the covers away. And she lay back and looked at him now above her.

"Beloved," he whispered, and momentarily paused, gazing into her sweet face in the diffuse radiance of moonglow. And he softly kissed her, and she him, and then he slipped inside her. She moaned in pleasure, as did he, and they slowly began making love.

Some moments later and outside the door, Henriette leaned forward in her chair and covered her ears against the sounds coming from within, and she muttered to herself over and over, "I'm not hearing this. I'm not, I'm not, I'm not, I'm not, I'm not. . . ."

6

Declarations

Covered in perspiration in the aftermath of making love for the third time, Céleste and Roél lay abed in moonlight streaming through the window, Roél on his back, Céleste on her side and propped on one elbow and gazing at him. "My lady," whispered Roél as with one finger she traced the line of his jaw, "you are insatiable."

"As are you, Sieur Knight," she replied.

"If she is yet at the door," said Roél, "what must your chaperone think?"

"That we are well in love," said Céleste, smiling. Though neither knew it, Henriette, her face flushed, her own heart racing, had long since fled to her quarters.

"I do love you, Princess," said Roél, now hitching about to look at her, "and have done so since I lifted you down from your oak tree."

"Do you recall what you said?" asked Céleste. Roél nodded. "I said, 'Oh, my, you are so beautiful.'" Céleste smiled. "That was the moment I gave you my heart."

Roél reached over and pulled her to him and engaged in a long, lingering kiss.

Céleste then retrieved and spread the covers over them both, and she went to sleep cradled in his arms. Roél stayed awake scant moments longer, gazing at this remarkable woman and wondering why she had chosen him. But even as he marveled, he fell asleep as well.

The next morn after breakfast, Gilles met the lovers and insisted Roél accompany him for a change of bandage and a dose of a needed medick.

"Another tasty concoction?" asked Roél.

"Oh, even better than those I have given you ere now," said Gilles, rubbing his hands together and cackling.

Roél looked at Céleste, and she said, "Take your medicine, Sieur Knight. Me, I have business to attend to with Captain Anton."

After Gilles' ministrations and another odious drink, at Roél's request the healer led the knight to the armory, and there Roél found his leathers waiting—cleaned and ready to wear. Several of the bronze plates—plates damaged during the mêlée with the outlaws—had been replaced on his armored jacket, and the cut on his leggings had been repaired as well.

"I'm feeling a bit out of practice, Gilles. Would it be acceptable for me to exercise at swords?"

Gilles frowned. "No swift moves, Roél. No great effort expended."

Roél spent much of the morning slow-stepping through his sword drill; he did so under the eyes of Gilles and two of the stableboys, who spent much of the time clapping and *oohing* and *ahhing* over Roél's silver-flashed sword.

Just ere the noontide, a page came looking for Roél. "Sieur," the lad said, "my lady the princess requests your company on a ride through the woodland. She waits in the stable."

Roél's black and Céleste's grey were saddled and ready when Roél arrived.

*   *   *

Anton and a number of men stood by; a frown of worry stood stark upon the captain's face. "My lady," he said, "I suggest we fare with you."

Céleste smiled and shook her head. "Roél alone is ward enough, armed and armored as he is. Besides, I have my bow and a full quiver of arrows, and surely that will be enough to deter anyone who thinks otherwise."

"But there might be more brigands abroad," said Anton.

"In which case I shall sound my horn," said Céleste.

"As you will, my lady," said Anton.

And with that, Roél and Céleste set forth from the stable. The moment they were out of sight, Anton and his men saddled their horses and followed at a discreet distance.

"They are trailing us, you know," said Roél.

Céleste sighed and nodded. "Anton has ever been overprotective. Usually I have to steal away to find solitude."

"You are a treasure not to be lost," said Roél.

Céleste laughed, and onward they rode.

They passed by the great oak, and all signs of battle were gone. Two furlongs or so beyond, they came upon a mass grave; Anton and his men had dragged the brigands this far to be well away from Céleste's Companion of Quietness; here they had unceremoniously buried them. Without comment, Céleste and Roél rode on.

Letting the horses walk for the most part, the two spent much of the time speaking of their childhoods and their dreams for children of their own. But all was predicated on Roél surviving the search for Avélaine and Laurent and Blaise.

Now and again they would dismount and lead the horses, though once in a while they raced at breakneck speed across an open dell.

And always behind, but well within a swift gallop, trailed Anton and his warband.

And the lovers rode among groves of wild cherry, their pink blossoms bursting in glory, and a storm of petals swirled about them in a roil of air.

"When will the cherries ripen?" asked Roél.

"For these trees, never," said Céleste. "And although they lose their petals in the turning breeze, when no one is looking they replenish themselves and begin anew."

"Anew?"

"Oui. These particular trees are ever petaled, for this is the *Forêt de Printemps*, my love, where spring is never ending."

"You mean the season is somehow arrested?"

Céleste nodded. "Endless, undying, perpetual."

"How strange," said Roél, looking about, wonder in his eyes. "Why then isn't the ground 'neath them piled neck-high in petals?"

Céleste laughed. "No one knows, my love; it is but another mystery of the Springwood."

"Magic, I would say," said Roél. "—Is all of the forest like this? Ever caught in the season?"

"Oui, it is."

"Oh, my," said Roél. "How marvelous. A woodland ever wakening. 'Tis a unique wonder."

Céleste smiled and said, "Let me tell you of the Winterwood, the Autumnwood, and the Summerwood."

As she spoke of these other domains and their own miraculous attributes, they passed among white-flowering dogwoods and across fields of purple crocuses, and places where mushrooms pushed up through layers of decaying leaves. They forded rushing streams and galloped by new-budding trees, and o'er fields of grasses turning green as they rode among spring everlasting.

Céleste and Roél stopped for a picnic lunch along the banks

of a stream running swiftly with snowmelt. And above the burble, Roél frowned and cocked an ear.

"What is it, my love?" asked Céleste.

"I hear a rustling."

Céleste laughed. "Ah, it is but the wee folk."

"Wee folk? Fairies you mean? Or Elves?"

"Oh, non. Fairies are quite like you and me, though perhaps a bit smaller in stature. Not Elves either, for they match us in size as well. Non, my love, the wee folk are tiny." Céleste held a hand some six or so inches above the ground. "Some smaller, some larger, some winged, others not. Perhaps you would call some of them Sprites and others Pixies, though those are but two kinds of wee folk."

Roél looked about, and now and again he caught a glimpse of furtive movement in the undergrowth. "Are we trespassing in their demesne? Is that why they gather 'round?"

A tiny giggle sounded and more rustling, and something or someone at the edge of Roél's peripheral vision dashed from behind a rock to behind a tree.

Céleste laughed. "Non, Roél. They gather because I am their nominal liege lord, and they come to pay their respects."

"You are their liege?"

"Oui. The whole of the Springwood is my demesne."

"The entire wood?"

"Oui."

Roél slowly shook his head. "Why, then, Princess, would you choose someone as me—the poor third son of a common knight, and not the prince or the king you deserve?"

Céleste took Roél's hand. "You are no common knight, Roél, but are the man I have dreamed of."

"You have nightmares, eh?"

Céleste broke into laughter.

It was late in the day when they returned to the manor, Anton and his men yet trailing, and even as the two handed their horses over to the stable master and his boys, Gérard came and discreetly waited.

As Céleste spoke to the hostler, Gérard stepped to Roél and said, "My lord, it is—"

"Oh, Gérard, I am no lord."

"Nevertheless, my lord," said Gérard, stubbornly, "it is time to make ready for dinner this eve. Your bath awaits, and I will dress you."

"Dress me, Gérard?"

"Oui, my lord," said the tall, gaunt, bald-headed man. "I am assigned as your valet de chambre." Gérard's smile lit up his face, for he was truly happy at his change of station.

Dinner was held in a large dining hall, Céleste at the head of the lengthy cherrywood table, Roél at the foot. Others were ranged along the sides, among whom were Vidal, tall and spare and with silver hair, steward of Springwood Manor; Anton, a stocky redhead, captain of the Springwood warband; Theon, brown-haired and wiry and of average height, captain of the houseguard; Gilles, the healer, dark of hair and eye; and brown-haired Henriette, petite and sharp-eyed, chaperone to the princess. Three other ladies were present, but Roél could not place their names.

And all were dressed in finery, the women in satiny gowns of topaz, of emerald, of sienna, and of azure, the men in shades of russet and grey and auburn and deep blue. Céleste wore topaz and white, with matching ribbons loosely entwined in her hair. Roél wore indigo—trews, hose, his shirt with puffed sleeves inset with pale lavender diamonds. Even his silver-buckled shoes were dark blue.

Marielle, a blonde sitting to Roél's right cooed, "Oh, Sieur Knight, do tell us of your rescue of our beloved princess."

Roél smiled and said, "Mayhap you have that backwards, my lady, for I think it was she who rescued me."

At Marielle's puzzled frown, Roél said, "You see, I rashly charged in among the brigands and found myself within a seething mêlée, and it was Princess Céleste who made certain that none came at me from arear. Had she not done so, I likely would not be here tonight."

"But surely, Sieur," said Marielle, "you slew nearly all."

"Oh, non, mademoiselle, 'twas the princess who took many down. In fact I imagine she slew more than did I."

Marielle made a moue, and Anton said, "Of the thirteen slain, seven were by sword, six by arrow."

"Thirteen?" asked Roél. "But two escaped."

"No, Sieur Roél. Of the pair who fled, we later found both dead in the woods, one with a missing hand, the other with an arrow in his side. Both bled to death."

"Ah, I see," said Roél. "What else did you discover?"

"We searched them thoroughly and, other than their arms and armor and steeds, we found gear for living off the land and a few coppers and some silvers, and little else. Their weapons and such we added to our armory; their steeds and tack are in our stables."

Roél frowned. "Were there no papers? The princess tells me that someone sent those brigands to fetch her—dead or alive, it mattered not. It seems to me that they might have had perhaps a written description, or at least a map."

"Non," replied Anton. "No papers, no map, no orders. I would be surprised if any of them could read, base outlaws that they were. All we have are the words of the brigand leader that their mistress sent them."

"Are there any notions as to just who this mistress might be?" asked Roél.

Anton looked at Princess Céleste, and she said, "There are three sisters, three witches, foe of my family entire. Perhaps it is one of them."

"Three witches?" asked Roél.

"Oui, though once there were four: Hradian, Rhensibé, Iniqui, and Nefasí. But my brother Borel slew Rhensibé—or rather did his Wolves—and now there are only three."

"Given the brigand's words," said silver-haired Vidal, "surely this points toward one of that nefarious trio."

Céleste nodded. "Oui, Vidal, I think you are right, for the bird did cry out for revenge."

"Bird?" asked Amélie, a rather staid woman with chestnut hair, Vidal's wife. "There was a bird?"

"The leader had a crow or a raven on his shoulder," said Céleste, "and when I slew that brigand, the bird took to flight and kept crying out for revenge."

Henriette gasped, "Mithras protect us all," and she and Marielle both made warding signs.

"Perhaps it was the crow that guided the brigands here," said Darci, a ginger-haired tall girl to Theon's left.

"An ensorcelled bird?" Theon asked.

Darci nodded. "Bewitched by one of the sisters."

"Oh," said Henriette, fluttering her hands about, "please let us talk of something other than bewitchments and death."

A silence fell on the gathering, and finally Gilles said, "I hear you are on a quest, Sieur Roél."

"Oui. My sister and two brothers are missing, and I go to find them."

"Missing?" said Marielle. "Oh, how thrilling. Where are you bound?"

"Wherever they are bound is where I am bound," said Roél.

Marielle frowned. "I don't understand."

Gilles smiled and said, "'Tis a play on words, Marielle. Bound and bound—one means confined or imprisoned; the other means where one is headed. Ah, and there are also the meanings 'to leap' and 'to set a limit,' but they do not apply to Roél's words. Only 'confined' and 'going' are relevant: he is bound where they are bound."

"Oh, I see," said Darci, giggling, but Marielle still looked on blankly.

Roél took pity. "When Gilles will let me, I am heading south, for that's the direction a sage named Geron told me to go, once I entered Faery, that is."

"South?" asked Marielle.

Roél looked about and took a bearing and then pointed.

"Ah, sunwise," said Marielle.

Now it was Roél who looked puzzled. "Sunwise?"

"Directions are uncertain in Faery," said Gilles. "So we name them sunup, sunwise, sundown, and starwise. Sunup and sundown are self-explanatory as to where they lie; sunwise is in general the direction of the sun at the noontide; starwise is the opposite."

"The Springwood border you head toward," said Vidal, "is very tricky—it leads to many different domains. If you cross just a few feet off course, you'll end up somewhere altogether different from where you intend, and many of those realms are quite perilous to life and limb."

"That's why we intend to escort you, Roél," said Céleste.

"Else you'll not likely reach the port city of Mizon."

Roél shook his head. "Princess, as I said, I cannot ask you to share my peril, for there are Changelings involved."

"Changelings!" shrieked Henriette, her spoon clattering to her plate. "Oh, Mithras!" Again she made a warding sign, as did Marielle and Darci.

"The princess and I have conferred," said Anton, glancing at Vidal, who nodded. "We intend to take the warband and accompany you."

Roél held up a hand of negation. "I repeat, I would not have the princess in peril."

"Did you not say that I had saved your life, Roél?" asked Céleste.

All the guests looked at Roél.

"You did, my lady, for you have great skill with the bow."

Rather like spectators at a badminton match, the guests turned toward Céleste.

"And if I were a man with that skill, would you object to my guiding you?" she asked.

Following the shuttlecock, they looked at Roél. . . .

"Princess, you are not a man."

. . . and back to Céleste.

"I am well aware that I am not a man, Roél, just as most surely are you. Even so, that does not answer my question; hence I ask it again: if I were a man with that skill, would you object to my guiding you?"

The guests waited for Roél's reply.

"Nay, my lady, a man with your skill would be welcomed."

"You object only because of my gender?"

"I object because I would not see you in dire straits and because you are my beloved."

A muttering went 'round the table, the women sighing, the men looking at one another somewhat startled, though they nodded in agreement with Roél's words, especially Captains Anton and Theon.

"Just as I would not see you in peril either, Roél," said Céleste. "You need my skill; thus I will go, for you are my very heart."

Marielle squealed and clapped her hands, and Darci pressed a palm to her own breast and said, "Oh, my." Henriette glanced about with a smug smile, and Amélie looked across at Vidal, pleasure in her eyes. Vidal grinned, for he had long wished the princess would find love, while both Anton and Theon looked at one another and then at Roél and grinned. Gilles laughed aloud and stood, goblet in hand. He raised the drink first to Céleste and then to Roél and said, "To the madness of love!"

Madness! shouted Anton and Theon together, standing as

well and hoisting their goblets and then downing their wine in one gulp.

Gaiety filled the room, and even dignified Vidal and staid Amélie joined in the many following salutes. Céleste laughed and Roël smiled, but in the back of his mind, he knew though Céleste would ride with him, into peril they would go.

7

Idyll

"You do not play échecs, my love?"

"Non, Princess. I have often thought I would find the time to learn, but I never did."

"Then I will teach you, Roél, for it is a splendid pastime."

"Then let us have at it, Céleste."

They quickly finished their breakfast, and then hurried to the game room. "Choose the color of your doom, Roél," said Céleste, gesturing at several tables, the échiquiers arrayed with men.

"Well, if it's my doom, I suppose black is as good a color as any."

The princess smiled. "Ah, then, let us sit here. I will play ebon, you the ivory."

"Ah, I see, then: you are my doom, eh?"

"Ever, my love. Ever."

After they had taken seats, Céleste said, "These are the names of the pièces: here arrayed in a row along the front are the spearmen, eight altogether; here in the back row, these two on the outside are the towers; next to those are the chevaliers, sometimes known as cavaliers; followed by the hierophants; and then the *roi* and *reine*—the king and queen—though the queen is also known as the *dame*. And this is the way each moves, and how they capture opposing pièces. . . ."

"Argh!" exclaimed Roél, "six defeats in a row. I will never master this game."

"Master échecs in six tries?" Céleste laughed. "I have spent many a candlemark at it, and still I am but a novice."

Roél frowned. "But all other games I have essayed have come easily to me. This one, though, the possibilities are endless."

"Ah, but you lasted much longer, my love," said Céleste.

"Only because you coached me, Princess."

Céleste grinned. "As was I coached by my brother Borel. He's much better than I."

"That is hard to believe, Céleste," said Roél, setting the pièces up for another game.

"Borel defeated the Fairy King at échecs," said Céleste. "No one had ever done that before. Yet, heed, Borel is not the best of us."

"Not the best? Then who?"

"Camille, Alain's beloved. She defeated Borel handily."

"Remind me to never play against her," said Roél, grinning and moving his roi's spearman forward two.

That evening, in the soft light of paper lanterns, they sat in the gazebo out on the front lawn, Céleste with a violin, Roél with a lute. Also under the roof were Marielle with a flute and Laurette, a fair-haired, petite demoiselle, playing a small harp. Gathered about on the lawn were members of the staff of the manor, those who were free of duty, all sitting and sipping wine at this impromptu concert. And they oft applauded over a well-executed, difficult riff, and over the sweet voice of Céleste as she sang ballades, as well as the baritone of Roél as he sang humorous ditties, mostly of knights bettered by wily maidens.

When it came Roél's turn again to sing of knightly exploits, he set his wineglass aside and announced, "The Crafty Maid."

Some in the audience laughed, while others looked on puzzled.

Roél struck a chord on his lute, and then began a merry tune, accompanied by Marielle and her flute, who seemed the only one other than Roél who knew the air:

Come listen awhile and I'll sing you a song
Of three merry chevaliers riding along.
They met a fair maid and one to her did say,
"I fear this cold morning will do you some wrong."

"Oh no, kind sir," said the maid, "you are mistaken
To think this cold morn some harm will do me.
There's one thing I crave, and it lies twixt your legs,
If you'll just give me that, then warm I will be."

"Since you crave it, my dear, it is yours," said he,
"If you'll just come with me to yonder green tree.
Then since you do crave it, my dear you shall have it,
These two chevaliers my witness will be."

The chevalier lighted beneath the green tree,
And straightaway she mounted, laughing in glee.
"You knew not my meaning, you wrong understood,"
And galloping away she right swiftly did flee.

"Oh, . . . chevaliers, stop laughing and take me up,
That we might ride after her down the long lane.
If we overtake her, I'll warrant I'll make her
Return unto me my horse back again."

But soon as this fair maiden she saw them acoming,
She instantly took her dagger in hand.
Crying, "Doubt not my skill, it's him I would kill;
I'd have you fall back or he's a dead man."

Said one, "Oh . . . why do we spend time galloping, talking?
Why do we spend time speaking in vain?
He'll give you a silver; it's all you deserve;
And then you can give him his horse back again."

"Oh no, kind sir, you are vastly mistaken.
If it is his loss well then, it is my gain,
And you did witness that he gave it to me."
And away she went galloping over the plain.

And so my fine gentlemen be wary of maidens,
For clever they are, and crafty they be.
If one offers something too good to be true,
Then surely too good to be true it does be.

Oh, surely too good to be true it . . . does . . . be!

With a final twang of the lute strings, Roél broke out in
laughter, as did the gathering, Céleste applauding and laughing
as well. Roél leaned over and whispered loud enough for her to
hear, "Present company excepted."

Céleste feigned a look of innocence. "Your meaning, Sieur?"

"You, my lady, are most certainly too good to be true," whispered Roél.

"Ah, my love," said Céleste, "we shall see about that anon."
And then she broke out in laughter again.

For another sevenday or so, Roél and Céleste for the most
part idled the time away, waiting for Gilles to remove the

stitches from Roél's wound, for then he would be fit for strenuous duty, hence could resume his quest. However, when he set out again, Céleste and the Springwood warband would accompany him . . . "But only to the port city of Mizon," or so Roél insisted, for he would not put anyone other than himself in peril, especially not Céleste. The princess, though, had made up her mind that she would stay with him to the end, saying, "Whither thou goest, go I."

And during this time Anton and the warband made ready for the journey—selecting horses, food stock, waterskins, cooking gear, weapons, armor, and the like. They chose the brigands' horses as pack animals, and allocated riding horses from the Springwood stables for themselves, Roche, the hostler, aiding them in their choices.

To Céleste's delight, in échecs Roél improved significantly. And in dames, he was the better player of the two.

And they often made love—at times gently, at other times wildly—and Henriette gave up entirely at being chaperone, stirred as she was by the sounds coming from their quarters, usually at night, though not always. And one morning ere dawn they slipped out early to elude Anton and the warband, and the princess and her knight rode to a high, sheer-sided rock pinnacle jutting up from the forest like a great cylinder, its rugged sides looming upward in the glimmer of the oncoming dawn.

"We call this the Sentinel," said Céleste. "From the top you can see for leagues."

"You've been to the top? The sides are sheer."

"Oui. My father taught me to climb, both with aids and without. The Sentinel I free-climb."

"Then let us scale it and take in the view," said Roél, dismounting.

"What of your leg, my love?"

Roél made a gesture of negation, but Céleste said, "I would not have you open the wound."

Roél grinned and said, "Gilles stitched tighter than a drum, *ma chérie*; besides, I will be careful."

Leaving their horses cropping grass below, they free-climbed the rough stone, to come to the flat top covered in mosslike phlox, with tiny white blossoms with a faint blush of pink just then opening to greet the new day.

"Sit, Princess, for I have something to ask of you."

Céleste cocked her head and gazed at him. "Something to ask?"

"Oui," said Roél, and he handed her down, and then he sat knee to knee before her.

He took both of her hands in his and said, "My lady, you are a princess whereas I am but a common knight. Even so, I am deeply in love with you, and never in my wildest dreams did I ever think I would feel as I do. Céleste, I cannot imagine life without you beside me. I know I am completely out of bounds here, but I love you, ma chérie, and I will love you forever. There will never be anyone else for me." Roél braced himself as if for a blow. "What I ask is, will you have me for a husband?"

Céleste squeezed Roél's hands, and through her tears of joy she replied with a simple "Oui."

A burst of air escaped Roél's lips and he said in amazement, "You will marry me?"

"Oui, my love, oh, oui," said Céleste, and she leaned forward even as she pulled him to her and sealed her answer with a kiss.

And there in the silver light of dawn washing across the spring morning sky, amid tiny white flowers with a faint blush of pink, Roél shouted for joy.

They announced their betrothal upon their return, and that eve a grand party was held, with a banquet and music and singing and dancing and festive toasts proffered and accepted. Never, it seemed, had the manor been so full of bliss, and that evening more than one happy couple found pleasure in one another's arms.

On the ninth day after Roél first awakened from his bout with poison, Gilles removed the stitches from the cut. "Well, Sieur Roél, I declare you fit for questing. Yet heed, my lad, try not to get struck again by an envenomed blade."

Roél laughed and said, "I shall do my best, Gilles."

Standing at hand, Céleste said, "On the morrow, then, Gilles?"

"Your meaning, my lady?"

"To start for Port Mizon," said Céleste.

Gilles sighed, for he, too, did not wish to see Céleste going on a quest where Changelings were involved. But then he nodded and said, "Oui, Princess, Roél is well, and the sooner started, the sooner done."

"Bon!" she said.

That night, Céleste and Roél made tender love, the princess saying, "We will be on the trail, my darling, with no privacy. There are few towns between here and the border, and few between there and Mizon. It would not be fair for us to make love while the men of the warband leave their own wives and lovers behind."

"Oui, I understand, ma chérie. But if we stop at an inn, where privacy is once again ours to have, then be certain I shall ravish you."

Céleste laughed and said, "I question as to who will be the ravisher and who the ravishee."

The next morning, just after dawn, the warband saddled horses and laded pack animals and donned armor and arms, all readying for the trek ahead. Many in the band were excited, for not oft did a venture come their way, while the veterans of skirmishes and other such went grimly about their tasks.

Roél, too, slipped into his brass-plated leather jacket and strapped on his long-knife and buckled on Coeur d'Acier. He checked his crossbow and bolts, making certain the newly oiled mechanism was fit and the quarrels well sharp. Gérard hovered nearby, tears brimming, for he was not a member of the warband, nor had he any training with weapons, yet he swore to Roél that a valet de chambre would be needed on the quest. Nevertheless, Roél denied him permission to come along.

Henriette stood sniveling, not only because Céleste was leaving, but also because Marlon would be riding away. Marlon was a young man of the warband, whom Henriette had within the week taken as a lover—spurred on, as she was, by the heat of listening to the sounds coming from Céleste's and Roél's quarters.

Vidal was at hand, along with Amélie. Theon and the houseguard were there as well. Marielle, Theon's wife, comforted sobbing Darci, for her husband, Captain Anton, was leaving. So, too, were others weeping, wives and lovers and loyal staff.

Altogether some two candlemarks passed before all was ready—horses and men and supplies and gear—and Céleste gave the signal to mount. Now the weeping intensified, and Henriette swooned, caught by Roche, who happened to be at her side.

And even as Céleste raised a hand to start the trek, "My lady," cried Leroux, the hawk master, "a falcon comes winging." Céleste commanded the warband to stand by, and Leroux ran for the mews.

Down spiraled the falcon, descending toward the cote, finally to land on the platform and stalk inside. Moments later, Leroux came running, the falcon now hooded. "'Tis a bird from the Autumnwood," he said, and he handed the small message canister up to his mistress.

Céleste opened the tube and fetched out the tissue within.

She unrolled it and read the words thereon. A smile broke across her face and she announced, "It is from Steward Zacharie of Autumnwood Manor. Sprites have come flying bearing the news that Princess Liaze and her betrothed, Luc, along with an armed escort, have entered the Autumnwood. She is safe and should be home in a threeday."

A cheer rose up from the Springwood Manor staff. Céleste read on, a frown on her features. Then she said, "Zacharie also reports that the witch Iniquí has been slain by Liaze, and warns us to be wary, for two of Orbane's unholy acolytes yet remain—Hradian and Nefasí."

A hushed murmur rippled through the gathering, but Céleste smiled and said, "Iniquí has joined her sister Rhensibé in death, and Liaze and Luc are safe; I think that calls for a celebration. Vidal, hold a feast this eve, for though we will be gone, this news deserves a fete."

"As you wish, my lady," said the steward.

Another cheer rose up from the staff.

Céleste called Theon to her, and leaned down and said in a low voice, "Keep the houseguard alert, Captain, for the remaining two witches, living foe that they are, might choose to attack Springwood Manor."

"Fear not, my lady, for we will keep the mansion secure."

Céleste motioned Vidal to her and said, "Four days from now, when Liaze is safely home, send falcons to my siblings and my parents with word as to what has happened here and the quest we now follow. Tell them of my betrothal, and say that when this quest is done, we will notify a king—my sire—and post the banns and plan the wedding. Give each of them my love as well."

"As you will, my lady," said the steward.

Theon and Vidal stepped back, and Céleste straightened in the saddle and gave the order to ride. New sobs erupted as forward the cavalcade moved; once again Henriette swooned, once again caught by Roche. Theon and the houseguard managed a respectable, thrice-shouted *Hip-hip-hooray!*

And with Céleste and Roél in the lead, warband and pack-horses trailing, across the lawn they fared and into the forest beyond.

8

Riddles and Redes

They passed into the woodland through a grove of flowering dogwoods there at the edge of the lawn, did Céleste and Roél and the warband. Scattered cheers from some members of the staff followed them within, but soon faded to silence in the quietness of the ever-awakening trees. And the only sounds were those of shod hooves on soft soil and the creak of leather and the quiet conversation among the riders.

But then Anton called, "Vérill, ride point. Garron, Déverel, one to each flank. Merlion, assume rear."

As those riders swung away from the cavalcade to take up their assigned positions, Céleste said, "Are you expecting more brigands, Anton?"

"My lady, with the news of another of the witches being slain, this one by your sister, we need ward against revenge. Hradian or Nefasí most likely were responsible for those brigands who attacked you, and who knows what they might do next?"

Roél nodded. "My love, Anton is most likely correct, for did you not say the leader spoke of his mistress wanting to see you dead or alive? And did not the crow itself cry out for revenge? And if not these witches, who else comes to mind as someone who might wish you ill?"

Céleste shrugged. "No one else I know of."

"How powerful are these witches?"

Again Céleste shrugged. "That I cannot say, though if indeed the crow was bewitched or— Oh, my, I wonder if the crow was actually one of the remaining sisters."

"Changed her shape? Transformed herself into a bird?" asked Roél.

"Oui."

"Is that even possible?"

"We are in Faery, my love," said Céleste, as if that explained all.

Roél's hand went to the hilt of his sword and he said, "Strange are the ways herein, and I can only hope Coeur d'Acier will ward us against any ills that might beset us."

Anton shook his head and said, "I'm afraid, Sieur Roél, sharp edges are no guarantee against sorcery."

"Anton is correct," said Céleste. "Many are the tales of witches and mages and sorcerers and the like overwhelming knights and warriors and paladins and others who solely rely upon weaponry."

"Oui," said Anton, "but there are just as many tales of warriors and their weapons overcoming such foe."

Céleste laughed and said, "My sire, King Valeray, says no matter the foe, stealth and guile are better weapons than force of arms. Of course, he started out in life as a thief."

Roél's eyes flew wide in astonishment. "Your father was a thief and is now a king?"

Céleste smiled and nodded.

"There is a tale here for the telling," said Roél, "and I would hear it one day."

"I will tell it one day," said Céleste.

Roél grinned. "From thief to king is quite a leap, my love. —Regardless, as to stealth and guile, my father says the same thing. Yet he also cautions there are instances when there is no time to bring them into play, and one must fall back on force of arms . . . either that or a rapid retreat."

"You mean run away?" asked Anton, cocking an eyebrow.

"Perhaps," said Roél. "It all depends on the situation. Let me give you an example. . . ."

They continued to ride throughout the morning, Roél and Anton and Céleste discussing strategy and tactics and the choices one might make, given the foe, his numbers, the terrain, and the numbers of allies one might have at hand to go up against the enemy. They discussed when it might be better to fall back to a new position, when it is better to create diversions, flanking attacks, ambushes, and when it is better to charge head-on, and other such choices of combat.

During these discussions it became clear to both Céleste and Anton that Roél was a master of strategy and tactics as well as being a knight of surpassing skills. They marveled at his grasp of battle, whether it involved armies or a handful of warriors or single combat, though he seemed unaware of the admiration in their eyes, so focused was he on the exchange of ideas, though in truth he did most of the talking.

When they stopped to feed and water the horses and to take a meal of their own, Céleste said, "Roél, I have often heard my sire and brothers speak of war and combat, but never so clearly have I understood all that is entailed."

"Oh, my lady, we have not covered even a small fraction of everything involved," said Roél. For a moment he paused, his gaze unfocused, as if he was lost in memory. But then he took a deep breath and said, "A grim business is war and combat and not to be undertaken lightly, but when it is unavoidable, one should fight to win, and that means turning every weakness of the foe into an advantage, while preventing him from doing the same."

They sat in silence for a while, eating bread and cheese and drinking hot tea that one of the warband had brewed. Finally Roél said, "Your brothers: are they knights as well as being princes?"

"Non," replied Céleste. "Although there are many knights in Faery, seldom do we fight great wars. I think the Keltoi never told long sagas of such."

Roél frowned. "The Keltoi?"

"Legendary bards," said Céleste.

"What would their stories have to do with there not being wars in Faery?"

"Ah. Well, this is the way of it, or so Camille thinks—and I happen to agree. You see, it is said that before there ever was a Faery, the Keltoi told such marvelous tales that they entranced the gods themselves. And the gods in turn made Faery manifest and populated it with all the many kinds of folk the Keltoi told of, be they human or Elves, Dwarves or Fairies, Trolls or Goblins, Sprites or Pixies, or whatever other kind you wish to name. And now we ourselves must be entertaining the gods, for the Keltoi seem to have gone to a green island somewhere beyond the rim of the world."

Roél frowned and said, "And these Keltoi never spoke of war?"

"For the most part, only in passing, my love. They told tales of knights going off to war, or returning from war, or of the folk left behind, but seldom of the war itself. Instead they spoke of the heroism of those who were on their way home from war, or of the hardships of those left at home, or of the terrible deeds done in the absence of the warriors.

"Oh, not to say that the Keltoi never told of battle, for some of their tales did speak of the great deeds done by heroes in combat or by heroic armies. Usually though, most of their tales of war spoke of a king and his army riding off to meet the army of a neighboring kingdom, or of war occurring in a realm far away. Where this so-called 'neighboring kingdom' might exist, I haven't any idea, nor do I know where the faraway realm lies.

"But for the most part these gifted bards told of heroic deeds done in pursuit of villains, or in the rescuing of maidens, or the doing in of Dragons, or of the slaying of Giants, and such: great deeds all, but by single men or single women, or by a mere handful of doughty people, and not by vast armies clashing.

"And so, you see, if it is true that the Keltoi did cause the gods to make Faery manifest, that's why war is seldom fought in Faery, or if it is, then it happens someplace away." Céleste fell silent and took another sip of tea.

"Hmm . . . ," mused Roél, "would that were true in the mortal world as well."

Again a quietness descended between them, but Céleste finally said, "It occurs to me that you and I and the warband are caught up in a heroic tale much like those told by the Keltoi, for you seek your sister to rescue her from the Lord of the Changelings, and we ride at your side to deal with whatever the Fates decree. If that doesn't become a saga to be told, well . . ."

Roél sighed and said, "It is not a tale much to my liking, though within it I have found my truelove, and *that* I would not trade for ought."

Céleste smiled, her eyes bright, and she squeezed Roél's hand, and in that moment Anton came to the two and said, "My lady, the horses are full watered and fed, the men as well."

"Then let us be on our way," said Céleste.

Roél leapt to his feet and handed her up, and in a trice all mounted and fared onward.

And as they rode they passed through a forest ever caught in the moment of spring, and in places snow yet lay on the ground and the air was chill and trees were barely abud, while elsewhere warm breezes wafted and forest and flowers and grass were full leafed and full bloomed and full green. Throughout the entire swing of the season did they ride, coming upon early here and late there and intermediate elsewhere. And limb-runners chattered and scolded; birds sang melodies with words unknown; deer bounded away with tails like flags held high in warning; a black bear waddled downslope toward a raging creek to move out of the line of the ride; and just within the edge of a briar thicket, a heavy boar bristled and snorted and turned and lumbered deeper in among the thorns. Partridges burst away in a thunder of flight, and hummingbirds darted among the flowers, though Roél now and again thought he espied among them tiny beings with iridescent wings flitting thither and yon. And he was certain that he had seen a wee man sitting in the knothole of a tree and smoking a pipe and watching the cavalcade ride past, even as small brown things—were they people, too?—ducked away on two legs.

They rode through a flurry of snowfall, which turned to rain, and then to hail, and they took shelter under the trees, even as the wind whipped at them. But the hail turned to a light spring shower and within a league they rode in sunshine.

"Your demesne is full of marvel, Céleste," said Roél, "caught as it is at the edge of winter on the one hand and at the verge of summer on the other; you have both the best and the worst of the season. I think it is fitting that a woman rules herein, for it is stormy and mild and cold and warm, pleasant and cruel."

Céleste cocked an eyebrow. "Are you saying it is fickle like a woman?"

"Non, my love," said Roél, grinning. "Challenging instead."

Céleste laughed. "Ah, Silvertongue, are you certain that you have no Keltoi ancestry?"

Roél shook his head. "If I have such blood, I know it not. Instead all I am saying is that I love this place, with its rushing streams, wildflowers, spring berries, its plentitude of game . . . as well as its wondrous tiny people."

"Not all are tiny, Roél, for some are great lumbering things, such as the Woodwose all covered in hair, or the *Hommes Verts* all covered in leaves. For the most part, they are shy, and rarely come to the manor, and then simply to show respect."

"When do they do this? —Come to the manor, I mean."

"In the Springwood, usually it is on the vernal equinox, though sometimes not. In Liaze's realm they mostly come at the autumnal equinox. In Alain's demesne it is at the summer solstice, whereas at Borel's it is at the winter solstice, though his *Hommes Verts* are covered in evergreen needles."

"Ah, I see," said Roél, "each in its own season."

Céleste nodded and said, "Indeed, most of their visits are governed by the sun. Often, though, some come at other times, usually to settle a dispute, but not always. Some simply come at their own hest to visit their liege and swear fealty."

"I would be at your side next equinox," said Roél, "for I am struck by the wonder of it all."

Céleste smiled and said, "And I would have you at my side on that day of balance."

They made camp that eve nigh a stream swollen with chill melt, and men began unlading gear. Horses were gathered in a simple rope pen, and Anton assigned several members of the warband to see to their care. A full day they had ridden, some twelve leagues in all. "At this rate," said the princess, "we'll be at the border shortly after the noontide two days hence."

Nearby, small tents were being pegged to the ground, for the erratic weather of the Springwood could just as easily send a great lot of wet snow as send a balmy night. Two men of the warband came bearing a somewhat larger tent for the princess. Roél said, "Here, I'll pitch it." But the warriors protested, and when Roél glanced at Céleste, with a faint shake of her head she indicated to him that he should let the men do the task. Swiftly 'twas done, and Céleste thanked them with a smile, and, beaming, the warriors moved on to other duties.

When they were out of earshot, "My love," said Céleste, "they vie among themselves to be the ones to serve me. Take not that away from them."

Roél grinned and said, "As I would vie were I among their company."

They walked down to the chill-running water and stood holding hands in the twilight, neither speaking. Behind them, men set campfires, and some began brewing tea. As Roél and Céleste dwelled in the comfort of one another, a polite cough caught their attention, and Roél turned to see Gérard standing nearby, his eyes fixed steadily on a point somewhere in the gallery of woods beyond the stream. Roél frowned. "Gérard, did I not instruct you to remain at the manor?"

"Indeed you did, my lord," replied Gérard, not shifting his gaze away from that distant point among the shadowed trees, "yet who would pitch your tent were I not about?"

"I'm of a mind to send you back even as we speak, Gérard."

Still standing at formal attention, chin held high, eyes peering off yon, Gérard said, "My lord, would you send me through these deep and dark and perilous woods alone? I think you cannot spare a warrior to escort me."

Céleste giggled.

Roél sighed in exasperation. "I did not see you among the company. How came you in the first place?"

"Why, on a horse, my lord. I knew you would need your valet de chambre, though it seems you yourself did not. A candlemark or so after you rode away, I realized where my duty lay, and so I saddled a mount, and took another one in tow, one laden with needed supplies, and I followed. I just now reached the camp, or, let me say, I reached the camp a short while ago."

Roél smiled and said, "You rode all the way completely alone through the deep and dark and perilous forest?"

"Indeed, my lord, though I believe it will be even deeper and darker and certainly much more perilous were I to have to ride back to the manor."

Roél burst into laughter; Céleste's own giggles turned to laughter as well. Gérard didn't blink an eye or shift his stance one hair as he let the mirth run its course. Finally, he made a slight gesture toward a newly pitched tent and said, "My lord, your shelter is ready. And would you and Princess Céleste like a good red wine to go with your evening meal?"

Once more Roél and Céleste fell into helpless laughter.

"I'll take that as a 'oui,' my lord." And with that, Gérard turned on his heel and strode away.

In the silver light of dawn, Céleste rose and walked past the sentry toward a wooded area designated as a place of privacy for her.

After she relieved herself, Céleste strode through the strip of woodland and toward the swift-running stream. As she neared, she heard someone weeping, and at the edge of the flow she came upon a small lad, no more than four summers old. In tattered clothes he was, and sitting on a rock and holding a trimmed branch in one hand—more of a long switch than a pole—and a length of fishing line in the other. Céleste looked 'round, but no adult did she see.

"Child, what are you doing here so early in the morning and all alone?"

Sobbing in *snucks* and *snubs*, the small boy looked up with tear-filled eyes. "I came to catch a fish for breakfast."

"Where are your père and mère?"

"Elsewhere, my lady. Very far elsewhere."

"They left you alone in the world?"

The child managed a whispered, "I have two sisters, and

they will have nothing to eat," and then he broke into wrenching sobs.

"Two sisters? No one else?"

"Non."

"Then come with me, my lad," said Céleste. "I will gather some food for you and your sisters."

"Non, non," cried the child, "I must catch a fish for them. But the string came loose from the pole, and a knot is needed."

Céleste sighed. "Here, let me." He held both out to her. She took them and quickly she tied the twine to the end of the switch, and then cast the hook into the stream. She handed the branch back to the lad, and he looked up at her and said, "Merci, Princess." And in that moment a shimmer came over the boy, and of a sudden before Céleste stood a slender maiden with silver hair and argent eyes, and from somewhere, nowhere, everywhere, there came the sound of battens and shuttles, as of looms weaving.

Céleste glanced at the dawn light growing in the sky and curtseyed and said, "Lady Skuld. Lady Wyrd. She Who Sees the Future."

Skuld smiled and said, "We meet again."

Céleste nodded, for on the day before the wedding of Camille and Alain, Skuld and her sisters—Verdandi and Urd—suddenly appeared before her family—her père and mère, her brothers and sister, and Camille and Michelle. Too, Hierophant Marceau had been there as well, though he had fainted dead away from shock when the three Fates abruptly materialized.

"My lady," said Céleste, "when last I saw you, you warned that the acolytes would seek revenge. Is that who—?"

Skuld held up a hand palm out, stopping the flow of Céleste's words. "Child, you know I cannot answer questions directly. I cannot e'en give you advice unless you first perform a service for me, and then answer a riddle. Because you tied my line to my pole when I was in the form of a small child, you have met the first requirement."

Céleste sighed. "I take it that you have something to tell me, and to hear it a riddle I must answer. Yet I have never been particularly good at riddles. May I at least fetch someone to help me? Roél perhaps?"

Skuld laughed and shook her head. "They are all yet asleep and will not waken—not even your truelove—until our business here is done."

Céleste groaned and glanced back at the camp. In the growing light, no one stirred, not even the sentry, who seemed locked in his stance. She looked again at Skuld and said, "In all fairness I must confess that I know the riddle of the Sphinx and the riddles you posed to Camille and Borel."

Skuld smiled. "I shall not ask you any of those, nor the one I posed to your sister."

Céleste's eyes flew wide in startlement. "You aided Liaze in her search for Luc?"

"Is that a question you would have me answer?"

Céleste threw out a hand of negation. "Non. Non. If you posed a riddle to her, one she correctly answered, then you aided her."

Again Skuld smiled.

Céleste took a deep breath and said, "As for a riddle you would have me answer, say away," and then she braced herself as if for a blow.

Of a sudden the sound of looms weaving swelled, and Skuld said:

"Trees on my back, dwelling below,
I fare when a wind does flow.
    Name me. . . ."

Even as the clack of shuttle and thud of batten diminished, Céleste's heart sank and tears sprang into her eyes. *I will never get the answer, never.*

"Wipe away your tears," said Skuld, "and think."

With the heels of her hands, Céleste dried her cheeks, and she looked at Skuld and then away. In that moment a small piece of wood caught in the flow went racing downstream. Watching it, Céleste recalled a happier time long past in her childhood, when she and her brothers stood by a brook and—

"A ship!" she cried. "Lady Wyrd, 'tis a ship, for the trees on its back are the masts, the dwelling below houses the crew, and a ship does fare when a wind flows." With hope in her eyes, she looked at Skuld.

Skuld now smiled and said, "Correct. And now I have something to tell you, and a gift for you as well."

"This something you are going to tell me, is it in the form of a rede?"

Skuld nodded, and again Céleste groaned. "Lady Wyrd, I am not good with puzzles and redes, can you not say it straight out?"

"No, Princess, I cannot, for my sisters and I must follow the rules."

"Rules," mused Céleste. "I wonder just whose they are."

"That I will not say," replied Skuld. "Instead, this is what I've come to tell you." And again as the thud and clack of weaving intensified, Skuld said:

"Seek the map, it is the key,
For Changelings dwell beyond the sea,
Yet beware, for there are those
Who bar the way: dreadful foes.

"A moon and a day, there is no more
For the lost sister you would restore.
Seven years all told have nearly passed;
A moment beyond and the die is cast.

"What might seem fair is sometimes foul
And holds not a beautiful soul.

Hesitate not or all is lost;
Do what seems a terrible cost.

Skuld fell silent, and Céleste said, "I understand some of it but not all. Lady Wyrd, would you please—?"

Again, with an upraised hand, Skuld stopped the flow of Céleste's words. "I cannot, Céleste. But this I can tell you: along the way you will face terrible trials, but you will also find aid as well."

Skuld glanced at the sky, the dawn bright, the sun yet below the horizon, but barely. "I must now go, Princess, yet remember all I have said. —Oh, and here, you will need this." Between thumb and forefinger, Skuld held out the gift she had promised. As Céleste took it, the sound of batten and shuttle swelled and then vanished altogether, as did Lady Wyrd.

In the distance, of a sudden the camp came awake. Men began stirring even as the limb of the sun rose above the rim of the world. Yet Céleste paid them no heed and instead peered at what Skuld had given her: 'twas nought but a small silver needle.

Dangerous Crossing

9

"And this is what she gave me." Céleste held out her hand; the silver needle rested in her palm.

Both Roél and Anton looked, and Roél said, "I don't see how that is going to help us."

"Well," said Anton, "needles are made for sewing. Perhaps it's to patch up something."

"Such as . . . ?" asked Roél.

Anton frowned. "The map?"

"The map needs patching?"

"Perhaps it's cloth, rather than vellum," said Anton, shrugging. "I mean, if it's a magic needle, and if the way to the Changeling realm is somehow obscured by a rip or a tear or a hole, then maybe if this needle is used to stitch the fabric, well, then the way will come clear."

Both Roél and Anton looked to Céleste for the answer. She merely shrugged and said, "Who knows the way of the Fates? Not I." They stood a moment in silence, but then Céleste added, "It seems neither my brothers nor my sister nor I can be involved in any kind of a quest without the Fates intervening."

Roél frowned. "Your family is somehow caught up in the entanglements of the Three Sisters?"

Céleste sighed and said, "Oui. First it was Camille in her search for Alain. Then it was Borel and his quest for Michelle. And just moments ago I discovered from Skuld that Liaze dealt with the Fates when she sought Luc. And now, it seems, it is my turn."

"At least there is one good, my lady," said Anton, "and that is, from what we know, the Ladies Wyrd and Lot and Doom aid rather than hinder. Even so, I do not care for the fact that Lady Skuld cast some sort of a spell over this camp of ours. Why, Goblins or Trolls could have attacked, or even the acolyte witches, and we would have been helpless."

Céleste shook her head. "Anton, I think Lady Wyrd would not allow that to happen. As you say, she came to help rather than hinder."

Roél shrugged and said, "I still don't see how a needle can aid."

"Neither do I," said Céleste. She turned her back and opened her leathers from collar to breastbone, and high on the bodice of her silk undershirt she stitched the needle into the fabric for safekeeping. Refastening her leathers, once again she turned to Roél and Anton.

Nearby, Gérard cleared his throat and said, "My lady, my lord, and Captain Anton, breakfast awaits."

"Well," said Anton, "needle or no, parts of the rede she gave to you seem clear enough, the first quatrain, in particular."

"How does it go again?" asked Roél.

Céleste frowned and said:

Seek the map, it is the key,
For Changelings dwell beyond the sea,

Yet beware, for there are those
Who bar the way: dreadful foes."

Anton said, "From that, it seems the map will show that we will have to voyage beyond the sea, and since the map is in Port Mizon, most likely that's where we'll set sail from."

Céleste nodded and said, "I am glad the warband is with us, for the last two lines of that quatrain speak of dreadful foes."

"Foes we can handle," said Roél, touching the hilt of Coeur d'Acier. "It is the second quatrain that has me most worried." He took another bite of bread.

Céleste set aside her cup of tea and said:

"A moon and a day, there is no more
For the lost sister you would restore.
Seven years all told have nearly passed;
A moment beyond and the die is cast."

"Oui," said Anton. "I agree it is worrisome, for if we do not reach your sister a moon and a day from now, it seems she will somehow be lost forever."

Gérard, who had been standing at hand, refreshed Roél's cup of tea and said, "I believe that will be at the dark of the moon, my lord."

Céleste frowned and glanced at the moon, now but a thin crescent racing barely ahead of the just-risen sun. "You are right, Gérard, for morrow night will be the dark of the moon, and we have but another moon beyond in which to find Avélaine."

"What of your brothers, Roél?" asked Anton.

Roél washed his bite down with tea and said, "Laurent started out a day after Avélaine was taken. We know he was well when he reached Sage Geron. Beyond Geron's cottage, he fared to the city of Rulon, or so his steel dagger would indicate, the one he traded for bronze. The ride from my sire's manor to

Rulon takes at least a moon and a fortnight. And so, even if he somehow immediately fell into the clutches of the Lord of the Changelings, perhaps we will have that much time after finding Avélaine to locate Laurent. As for Blaise, he set out nearly four years later."

Céleste said, "I know not how long it will take us to get to the Changeling realm, but the sooner started, the sooner arrived. And for me, the rede seems to tell us we have perilously little time to do so."

Agreed, said Roél and Anton together, and Roél stood and said, "Then I suggest we ride."

"'Tis the third quatrain most puzzling," said Roél. Céleste, riding alongside, nodded and intoned:

> *What might seem fair is sometimes foul*
> *And holds not a beautiful soul.*
> *Hesitate not or all is lost;*
> *Do what seems a terrible cost."*

"Beyond the obvious," said Roél, "I have no understanding of what that might mean."

"The obvious?" said Céleste.

"Well, clearly it refers to someone or something that will seem fair to us, but instead is foul."

"Mayhap it is the Lord of the Changelings," said Céleste. "Did he seem fair?"

"I did not think so at the time," said Roél. "I thought him dark and sinister . . . certainly not fair. But then I was a youth, a boy, and what might have seemed vile to me might seem fair to a demoiselle."

"Whatever it is," said Céleste, "we shall have to be on our guard and hesitate not, though what we must do at that time is not certain at all, nor why it would seem a terrible cost."

"Perhaps we need to slay it," said Roél.

"Or perhaps capture it," countered Céleste.

"Or perhaps let it go altogether," replied Roél.

"What if it isn't a person or a being, but an object, a thing?" said Céleste.

"Such as . . . ?"

"A gem, a crown, a weapon, a flower, a painting: something, anything, we might think beautiful, but could be wicked instead."

Roél sighed. "There are so many things in the world and in Faery that are beautiful, my love, at the pinnacle of which are you."

Céleste smiled and said, "I can be quite wicked, you know."

"Indeed," said Roél, grinning, and on they rode.

It rained all that darktide, but the next morning dawned clear and bright. Leaves were adrip and the air freshly washed, and Roél looked on in amazement as a troop of tiny beings—each person no more than an inch tall—came marching out from among the roots of a nearby grove and paid homage to Princess Céleste. They did so at the edge of the coppice, some bowing, others curtseying, and they presented her with a bouquet of tiny lavender flowers. One hung back to keep a wary eye on the men and the horses, for a single misplaced boot or hoof could easily destroy at least half of their wee band.

Céleste set the tiny bouquet behind her right ear, the soft violet hue in contrast to her pale blond hair. The princess in turn presented the tiny folk with a thimbleful of pepper poured upon a leaf. They bowed and curtseyed, and then several of them lifted the leaf up above their heads, and they all marched back among the roots whence they had first appeared.

"What were they, my love?" asked Roél.

"They have their own name for themselves," said Céleste. "Twyllyth Twyg, it is, but most folk call them Twig Men. They prize pepper above all."

Roél looked toward the place where they had gone and shook his head. "Why, they could ride mice or voles as their steeds, could they tame them."

"They sometimes do, Roél" said Céleste.

"Twig Men . . . ," mused Roél, and again he shook his head with the wonder of it all.

The cavalcade rode onward, the band pausing at the noontide to feed and water the horses and take a meal of their own. It was in midafternoon when they came upon the twilight border looming upward among the trees of the Springwood.

Anton sent scouts left- and rightward, and then the remainder of the cavalcade rode nigh the marge and dismounted.

"Now we must find the proper crossing point, my love," said Céleste, "for, if you'll recall Vidal's words, this bound is particularly complex."

"I believe he said it was 'tricky,'" replied Roél.

"Tricky indeed," said Céleste. "To reach Port Mizon, we must find the lightning-struck remains of a large black oak; 'tis there we need cross. We will wait here while the scouts fare along the bound. A bugle will sound when one finds the tree."

"Why not simply ride through and then, if it is the wrong place, ride back?"

"Oh, chéri, one of the crossings leads to a land of flowing molten stone; another leads to a great fall; still others lead to realms just as perilous. We need cross at the place that will not put us in jeopardy, and—"

Céleste's voice was lost under ululating howls, and a flood of Goblins and Bogles and monstrous Trolls came charging from the shadowlight. Above the onrush flew a crow crying, "Revenge, revenge." Céleste sounded her silver horn, even as men leapt to the backs of their steeds. Roél on his black drew Coeur d'Acier and took his shield in hand. Céleste drew her bow from its saddle scabbard, and nocked an arrow and let fly. It pierced the breast of one of the eight-foot-tall Goblinlike Bogles. Even as the creature crashed to the ground, a monstrous Troll leapt over the corpse and rushed at Céleste.

Roél charged forward, Coeur d'Acier cutting a bloody swath through the Goblins. He intercepted the Troll and gutted the twelve-foot-high monster.

Men of the warband lanced and hacked and flew arrows, only to be met in turn by cudgel and warbar and spear and arrows in return.

"Revenge, revenge," skreighed the crow, now circling above Céleste, and here the Goblins and Bogles and Trolls charged, surrounding the men protecting the princess, and clawed their way toward her.

With men all about her in mêlée, Céleste did not chance loosing an arrow, and she slipped the bow across her shoulders and drew her long-knife.

"Céleste! Céleste!" cried Roél, and he turned and drove his black toward her grey, taking down a Troll in his way, Coeur d'Acier keen and bloody.

Now a Bogle crashed its way through the men, and with a massive smash of his great club he slew Céleste's horse. She leapt free even as the grey tumbled to the ground. The Bogle loomed above her; he swung his bludgeon up to strike, but the blow never fell, for Coeur d'Acier took off his head.

"Céleste," cried Roél. He reached down and she grabbed on to his sword arm and swung up behind him.

Now with sword hewing and shield bashing and Céleste's long-knife slashing, Roél spurred his black forward through the mêlée and up a slope toward the shadowlight border, seeking higher ground.

Above them, "Revenge! Revenge!" cried the crow, yet marking the princess's whereabouts.

Roél's black screamed, and fell to its knees, a Goblin arrow jutting from one eye. Roél and Céleste sprang free, and they fought their way through Goblins and on up the slope, but Trolls and Bogles lumbered after, their great strides overtaking.

"Revenge!" cried the crow above, but of a sudden it scrawked and tumbled from the air, a crossbow quarrel through its breast.

Still Roél and Céleste fled onward, a horde in pursuit.

"Know you where this goes?" cried Roél.

"Nay, I do not," cried Céleste in return.

"Céleste, we must chance it," called Roél, bashing a Goblin aside and running onward, with the princess slightly arear and on his flank, her long-knife slathered with dark grume.

Up the slope they ran and into the twilight, Goblins and Bogles and Trolls in chase.

Dim it came and then darker, and Roél hissed, "Angle leftward—we'll lose them in the gloom."

On they ran, deeper into the border, the shadowlight becoming ebon as they blindly fled.

Headlong they ran, recklessly, shouting pursuit behind them. Now rightward they angled and raced straight on and past the pitch-dark midpoint, to hurtle out into empty space and plummet downward, plunging into blackness below.

10

Gone

"*Princess!*" cried the searchers. "*Princess Céleste!*"

"Did no one see where she went?" called Anton.

Men looked at one another in concern, yet none had followed her flight, for they had been caught up in the battle.

"Here is her horse," shouted Déverel, scrambling upslope toward the downed mare. Quickly he reached it and called, "Its skull is crushed."

Anton made his way among slain Goblins and Bogles and past a massive and gutted Troll. As he reached the dead horse, nearby a weak voice called out, "C-Captain."

Some yards away young Marlon lay wounded, and Anton stepped to him and shouted for Gilles.

"Captain," whispered Marlon, "she leapt free of her grey, and Sieur Roël fought his way to her, and she swung up behind. They went on toward the bound." The youth pointed.

Bearing his kit, Gilles arrived, his hands bloodied from treating others. He knelt beside Marlon. "Déverel, help Gilles," snapped Anton.

86

As Déverel moved to aid the healer, Anton strode in the direction Marlon had pointed. Within yards he came upon Roél's caparisoned steed lying dead. He swept his gaze wide, but he saw nought immediate to indicate where Céleste and Roél had gone. Then Anton knelt and closely examined the ground. *Ah, tracks, and many.* "Vérill, to me," he cried.

When Vérill arrived, Anton pointed and said, "Spoor."

"Goblins, Bogles, Trolls," said Vérill after but a glance, "and they are running. Mayhap to escape; mayhap in pursuit."

"See you any sign of the princess among them? Or Sieur Roél?"

Now Vérill studied the tracks closely, and he followed them upslope, moving slowly. "Ah! Here's a man's step. Possibly Sieur Roél's." After a moment he said, "And here the princess's. Captain Anton, they are running, and I ween the Goblins and Bogles and Trolls are in pursuit."

"*Merde!*"

On went Vérill, Anton following, and into the twilight bound they went. "Lantern. I'll need a lantern," said Vérill.

Anton stepped out from the boundary and called to Merlion, and quickly he brought a lantern to the two. But, as with all light, its glow dimmed in the mystical dusk of the marge. Even so, Vérill managed to follow the wide swath of the pursuers within the shadowy bound. Long did he track, covering a considerable distance. He found where Roél and Céleste had jinked to throw off the pursuit, and yet those chasing had eventually followed. And then through the ebon central part they all had sped—princess, chevalier, and pursuers.

"Get me a rope," said Vérill, and I'll see what is on the far side."

"I'll call a Sprite," said Anton.

"That might take a while," said Vérill, "and I can cross now." Merlion ran back to the battleground, now nearly a half mile away, eventually to return with a line and two more men. They tied the rope about Vérill and all took hold, and he stepped through the ebon wall.

The line snapped taut.

"'Tis a drop, but I think I hear waves," reported Vérill. "We will need a Sprite."

"Haul back!" cried Anton, and, straining, they pulled Vérill back through.

Out from the bound strode Anton, and he took his clarion in hand and sounded a call. Then again he called, and eyed the forest surround, and waited.

After a long while, a tiny diaphanous-winged being came flying among the trees. No more than two inches tall and naked she was, and she made straight for Anton, who held his horn on high. She landed on the bell of Anton's clarion; he lowered the trump and she looked up at him.

"Mademoiselle Sprite," said Anton, "we need your aid."

"I am Tika," she replied, brushing back a wisp of her brown hair. "And you are . . . ?"

"Anton, armsmaster and warband leader of Springwood Manor."

In that moment, more Sprites came winging, all in answer to the horn call. And some were greatly disturbed, for they had flown above the slaughter ground.

Anton waited until all the newcomer Sprites had settled on nearby branches. Then he said, "Tika, Princess Céleste is missing"—the wee Sprites gasped in alarm—"and we need you, all of you, to see what lies beyond the marge, so that we might go to her aid."

"Where did she cross?" asked Tika, the Sprite familiar with aiding humans at the boundaries.

"We think 'tis there where stands my man Vérill," said Anton, pointing.

Vérill raised his hand.

Tika turned to the waiting Sprites and spoke rapidly, and

she and they darted in a widespread line toward the twilight wall.

"Nought but ocean where the tracks cross?" cried Anton in dismay.

"Oui," replied Tika, her voice choking in pent grief, the gathered Sprites nodding in agreement, even as tears glittered against their tiny cheeks.

"Empty," said another of the Sprites, a russet-haired male.

"We found no one at all," said a third, a dark-haired female, tears flowing. "Just waves rolling o'er the deeps."

"There was a floating cudgel," said Tika, her voice breaking.

"Cudgel?"

"Like those borne by Redcaps," said Tika, gesturing in the direction of the slaughter ground.

"No one swimming? No one calling for help?" asked Vérill.

"Non," said Tika, bursting into sobs, her folk all weeping.

"I'm afraid . . . the princess . . . and her knight have drowned."

"Captain," said Vérill, choking on his own tears, "mayhap they were swept through the bound elsewhere and are safe."

"Non," said Tika, gaining control. "From the place of the tracks, we flew through the bound repeatedly both dextral and sinister, and always we came back into the Springwood; and we searched, and they are not herein. And back nigh that horrid battleground whence you said the Trolls and Bogles and Redcaps had first come, beyond the bound there is nought but wide, empty desert, and farther along the marge lies the realm of King Avélar, and the princess is not in either."

Tika burst into tears again, yet after a moment she managed to say, "Captain Anton, the princess and the chevalier, they most assuredly drowned."

Anton turned away, and peered at the shadowlight, and then he sighed and said, "Tika, I need you and the Sprites to bear word to Steward Vidal at Springwood Manor."

Her voice choking, Tika managed to ask, "And your message, Armsmaster?"

Anton sighed and said, "Tell him that during an attack by Redcaps and Bogles and Trolls at the sunwise twilight bound, Céleste and Roél crossed over and fell into an ocean and were drowned."

Yet sobbing, Tika nodded, and then she and the Sprites darted away.

His own cheeks wet with tears, Anton gathered the men and told them what the Sprites had found. And then, with men weeping, and with the most severely wounded riding on travois, back toward Springwood Manor they all turned. And they bore with them the trappings from Céleste's grey and from Roél's black, as well as a slain crow pierced through by a crossbow quarrel.

11

Pursuit

In but a heartbeat and before she could scream, Céleste crashed down onto a canted surface that rang like hardwood, and—"*Uff!*"—she fell forward to her hands and knees. Her long-knife was lost to her grip and went skittering away in the blackness. Floundering to her feet, "Roél, Roél," she called, but then she was grabbed from behind, and a rough hand was clapped over her mouth.

Céleste wrenched to and fro, and tried to stomp her heel onto the foot of whoever or whatever had her in its grasp, but she could not break free.

"Quiet, or I'll snap your neck," came a hissed command, and whoever had her twisted her head to one side.

Céleste stopped her struggle.

"My Lord Captain," the being said, keeping his voice low, "I have one here. A female, by the feel of her."

"There's another over here, my lord," someone else said, also in a hushed voice. "I think he's dead."

Roél dead?

Céleste moaned, but then fell silent as the grip on her mouth tightened in threat.

"Oi, now, wait a moment. He's breathing. I think he's just unconscious."

Thank Mithras, Roël's alive.

Footsteps neared on wood, but stopped, and the surface Céleste stood on slowly rose and fell. She smelled a salt tang in the air, and she heard the rush of water. A *ship. I'm on a ship.*

Her eyes now beginning to adjust to the darkness, Céleste could make out a dim shape standing before her.

"Madam, if my lieutenant takes his hand from your mouth, will you keep your voice down?"

Céleste managed a restricted nod.

"She agrees, My Lord Captain," said the one who held her.

"Then do so, Lieutenant."

The person took his hand from her mouth, yet held her tight, and in that very same moment and in the near distance there sounded terrified screams and roars and splashes.

"What th—?" breathed the one who held her.

"Goblins and Ogres and Trolls, Captain," said Céleste. "They were in pursuit of us. Now release me so that I might tend my consort."

"Consort? Who are you?"

Momentarily, Céleste hesitated, for she did not wish to be held for ransom. But then from nearby there came a groan. *Roël.* She took a deep breath and said, "Céleste, Princesse de la Forêt de Printemps."

"Princess of the Springwood?"

"Oui. Now again I say, release me so that I might tend my consort."

"Tell me something few know of your père," said the captain. *Does this man know my sire?* "Thief," said Céleste.

"Release her, Lieutenant."

Set free, Céleste turned in the direction of the groan, and in the darkness she could just make out the shape of something or someone—presumably Roél—lying on the deck, with someone kneeling at hand.

As she made her way toward the supine figure, the lieutenant said, "My Lord Captain, with those screams, surely we move not in secret any longer."

"Mayhap not," replied the captain. "Nevertheless we will hew to our course."

"But, Captain, the men grow ever more fearful, for should we cross over the bound—"

"I know, Lieutenant. We could crash the ship into a mountainside, or burn in a fiery flow, or plummet over an escarpment, or any number of other terrible disasters. Yet heed, if we are to overtake the corsairs, spring upon them unawares, then this is the best course. 'Tis a trick I learned from my freebooter days. Helmsman, just make certain the very ebon wall remains immediately on our port beam. That blackness is the midpoint we dare not cross."

"Aye, aye, my lord," replied another voice, the helmsman, no doubt.

Even as Céleste dropped to her knees beside Roél, for surely it was him, he groaned awake. "Wha— Oh, my jaw."

"Keep your voice low, beloved," said Céleste.

"Céleste?"

"Oui." She removed Coeur d'Acier from his grip and took his hand in hers and squeezed.

"I think my chin slammed into the edge of my very own shield," said Roél. "Where are we?"

Céleste looked about, her eyes now fully adjusted to the dimness. She could just make out the dark-on-dark silhouettes of railings and the helm and men and masts and sails and rigging. To the immediate port side there loomed a pitch-black wall.

"On the stern of a ship, chéri."

"A ship?" Roél struggled to a sitting position. He freed his shield arm. "What ship?"

The man—or was he a lad?—kneeling at Roél's side said, "The *Sea Eagle*, my lord, my lady. Three-masted and full rigged, she's the fastest in the king's fleet."

From the tenor of his voice, Céleste decided he was a youth. "What are we doing on a king's ship?" asked Roél.

"At the moment, chasing corsairs," said Céleste.

"Corsairs?"

"Pirates."

"I know what corsairs are, my love," said Roél. "Rather, I was wondering how we got here. Have I missed an episode in my life?"

Céleste smiled. "Non, Roél. When we ran through the border, we fell onto this ship."

"Oi, now, I'd say Lady Fortune must have been smiling on you two," said the lad. "I mean, what are the chances that we'd even be here, faring through this perilous dark, and the chances that you'd come running through the black bound just as we sailed underneath? Aye, Lady Fortune indeed."

"More likely 'twas the Fates instead," said Céleste. "Otherwise we would have been swimming, as are the Goblins and Ogres and Trolls who were after us, assuming they can swim."

"What of the warband?" asked Roél. "Did they plunge into the sea as well?"

Shock slammed into the pit of Céleste's stomach, tears following. "Oh, Roél, you don't suppose—?"

Roél embraced her. "We can only hope they did not."

And as he held her, the ship sped on through darkness, with a stygian wall immediately abeam, and the only sounds were that of the hull racing through water, the wind in canvas, and rigging creaking under the strain.

But then from somewhere in the distance to the forequarter starboard, there came the call of someone shouting orders.

A shadowy figure stepped nigh and knelt and said, "My lady, I ween you should go to the safety below, for we are about to o'erhaul the corsairs, and battle will soon be upon us."

"Captain," said Céleste, recognizing his voice, "have you any spare arrows? I am quite good with a bow." She stood and slipped the weapon from her back, then added, "And where is my long-knife? I will need it should battle become hand-to-hand."

Roél clambered to his feet and took up his sword and shield from the deck. "I can help."

The captain rose and said, "Well, now, I am not certain I should allow Valeray's daughter to be put in jeopardy."

Céleste started to protest, but Roél said, "Captain, you cannot win this argument. Believe me, I have tried. Besides, she is indeed quite good with the bow."

"All right, but this I say, Princess: we will board the corsair, but you need stay on my ship, for from here your arrows will reach the foe, but their swords will not reach you."

"Agreed," said Céleste.

Within moments, Céleste had resheathed her long-knife and had buckled over her shoulder a baldric holding a sheaf of arrows. The shafts were a bit lengthy for her draw, but there wasn't time to trim them. "Better long than short," she said, upon testing one in her bow.

As they sailed on through the shadow, Céleste said, "Captain, might I have your name?"

"Oui, my lady. I am Vicomte Chevell of Mizon."

"Mizon? Why, that's where we were bound when we were beset by the Goblins and Ogres and Trolls."

"Ah, I see," said Chevell. "You had business there?"

"Oui," said Céleste. "We wanted to look at the map that purports to show the way to the Changeling realm."

"Sacré Mithras!" blurted Chevell. "It is that very map we pursue."

"What? The map is on the corsairs' ship?"

"Perhaps; perhaps not. In the mid of night, the crews of three corsairs raided Port Mizon. Of the things they took, the chart was among them. We have already captured one of the ships, and our sister craft, the *Swift Mallard*, now bears the treasure from that vessel and escorts it and the raiders back to port to face the king's justice. Me, I would just have soon hanged them all and been done with it. Regardless, we did not find the map on that craft; if it is there, it is well hidden. There are yet two of the raiders' ships to overtake, one of which we believe has the chart."

"Oh, no," groaned Céleste. "We need that map to get to the Changeling realm."

"My lady, you cannot be seriously thinking of going to—"

Beyond the shadow and directly starboard, someone shouted another command.

"Lieutenant Armond," said Chevell, "ready the men. As before, you will lead the boarding party."

"Aye, my lord," replied the lieutenant, and he moved toward the bow.

"Chérie," said Roél, "I will go with them. As for you, ply your bow well, and stay safe aboard the *Eagle*."

Céleste's own heart was racing in fear for Roél, but she said nought as she fiercely embraced him and kissed him deeply.

They stepped apart, and Roél followed Armond.

Chevell said, "Bosun, 'tis into battle we go; pipe the sails two points to the starboard. Helmsman, follow suit."

Aye, aye, they both said, and as the bosun blew the command, the helmsman turned the wheel, and the ship began swinging rightward even as the crew haled the halyards about, yardarms swinging, sails turning to catch the best of the wind.

And out from the shadowlight came the *Sea Eagle* running in full, and less than a furlong to the starboard sailed a three-masted dhow, shock and alarm on the faces of the corsair crew.

"Ready grapnels," cried Lieutenant Armond, a tall, black-haired man.

The corsairs scrambled: some to take up weapons, others to swing booms and tiller to head their ship away, and still others to jitter about to no purpose whatsoever in spite of their captain's shouts.

Yet the *Sea Eagle* swooped down upon its prey, for it had the advantage of speed and surprise, as well as a ready crew.

Arrows flew from corsair to king's ship, and arrows flew in return. But Céleste waited, for she would be certain of her casts. She glanced at Roél; he stood at the starboard wale, now and again catching an arrow upon his shield.

Even as shafts flew back and forth, "Ship ahoy," came a cry from the crow's nest.

Céleste frowned. *Of course there's a ship.* But then the lookout cried, "A point to the port, Captain," and Céleste looked where Captain Chevell gazed. On the horizon the lateen sails of another vessel were just then passing out of sight o'er the rim of the world.

"'Tis the other corsair," said Chevell, a stocky redheaded man, some five foot nine or so. "Let us hope the map is aboard this one and not the other."

"I pray to Mithras you are right," said Céleste.

Now the *Sea Eagle* drew nigh, and at last Céleste began loosing shafts, each one aimed at a corsair archer; and one by one she took them out of the fight, her own aim deadly. Soon the pirates, especially the bowmen, were crouching down below the rails, for someone aboard the king's ship was lethal.

"My lady," said Chevell, "try not to slay the captain of the corsair, for I would have him lead us to the map, should he have it."

"Aye, aye," said Céleste, grinning, even as she loosed another arrow. "By the bye, Captain Chevell, which is the pirate captain?"

"I believe that's him cowering by the tiller," said Chevell.

"Ah, him," said Céleste, drawing another arrow from the quiver and nocking it. "Well, I wouldn't have shot him anyway, unless, that is, he threatens Roél, in which case I'll stick him like the cowardly pig he is."

Chevell barked a laugh and said, "Agreed. But the helmsman, now, he is fair game."

Céleste's next shaft slew that man, and the pirate craft fell off the wind and slowed.

Now the *Sea Eagle* began to overlap the corsair, and moments later they were beam to beam, starboard to larboard. Grapnels flew and bit into the boards, and pirates hacked at the lines, but more grapnels bit into wood, and the men of the *Eagle* haled ropes and drew the ships hull to hull.

Shouting, "King Avélar!" Lieutenant Armond led his men over the wales and onto the other ship, Roél among them, Coeur d'Acier slaying left and right, the blade cleaving straight through the corsairs' weapons of bronze to strike deadly blows. Some of the pirates leapt aboard the *Sea Eagle*, desperate to escape this purveyor of death, and there they fought gamely, for bronze met bronze and not steel.

One of the corsairs rushed at Céleste, but Chevell stepped in front of her and skewered the man. As Chevell jerked his sword free, Céleste said, "Merci, Captain, but I would have felled him myself."

Chevell turned to Céleste to see that she had an arrow nocked, and he grinned and said, "Oui, but sometimes a woman must let a man perform a chivalrous act."

Céleste whipped up her bow and aimed at Chevell's throat and then shifted a bit to the right and let fly. *Thock!* The shaft took an onrushing corsair in the eye, and he fell dead, his cutlass clanging to the deck at Chevell's feet.

"Tit for tat," said Céleste, grinning at the captain's surprised gape even as she nocked another arrow.

98 / DENNIS L. MCKIERNAN

The battle raged but moments longer; then aboard both ships, corsairs threw down their weapons and surrendered.

As the prisoners were rounded up, Armond dragged the corsair captain out from a hold, and marched him before Vicomte Chevell.

Céleste, an arrow yet nocked in her bow, stood at hand.

Chevell ignored the pirate for a moment and called out to the corsair vessel, "Ensign Laval, see that our wounded and dead are removed from that ship. And have some of the rovers come over and take their own wounded and dead back."

"Aye, aye, My Lord Captain," replied the young man.

"Lieutenant Florien," called Chevell. "Organize a search for that which was taken from the king."

"Aye, aye, my lord," replied the second officer.

Then Chevell canted his head toward the pirate and said, "Your name, Captain."

The small, swarthy man drew himself up to his full height and said, "I am Captain Zdnek, and just who are you to attack an innocent—"

"I would have the map you stole," said Chevell, his words harsh, his gaze icy.

"Map, map? What map? I have no—"

"From Port Mizon, pirate!"

"I have not in my life been to Port Mizon, and—"

"My Lord Captain Chevell," called Florien from the raiders' dhow.

Chevell turned toward the man.

"In the captain's cabin, we found the King's Bell and many of the other treasures taken, but the map was not among them."

"Keep searching, Florien."

"Aye, aye, my lord."

Grim-eyed, Chevell turned toward the pirate captain and said, "Hang him."

Even as Lieutenant Armond reached for the corsair, Zdnek

fell to his knees. "No, no, My Lord Captain," he wailed. "Barlou has it! Barlou!" Zdnek pointed in the direction along the horizon where the other ship had disappeared.

"I think you're lying," snapped Chevell.

"I swear by Holy Sybil, I do not have it," cried Zdnek, sobbing.

"Sybil is the goddess of many tongues," said Chevell.

"Then I swear by Holy Shaitan."

"God of liars."

Céleste said, "Swear by the Three Sisters: Skuld, Verdandi, and Urd. But hear me, the Fates will hold you to your word, and if it is false, then you will suffer torments beyond compare." Zdnek paled and trembled. "I swear on the names of Skuld and Verdandi and Urd, I do not have the map. Barlou took it. It was the main prize, and he has the fastest ship."

"The main prize?"

Zdnek clamped his lips shut.

"So you came after the map; I suppose the treasure you took was merely an afterthought."

Still Zdnek did not speak.

"Hang him," said Chevell.

"No, no!" blurted Zdnek. "Oui, it was the main prize."

"Who sent you for it?"

"I don't know. We were merely to get the map and deliver it to Caralos."

Chevell groaned, and Céleste raised an eyebrow, but said nothing.

As men began transferring treasure from the corsair to the king's ship, Chevell said, "Is he still on Brados?"

"Oui," said Zdnek.

Chevell sighed. Then he glanced at Céleste and turned to Armond and said, "Pledge the pirates in the name of Skuld and Verdandi and Urd. Warn them as did the princess that to break any pledge made in the name of the Three Sisters is to court disaster beyond belief. Then set them free to sail on their own back to Port Mizon to face the king's justice."

"What of Captain Zdnek, my lord?" asked Armond.

Chevell looked down at the cowering man. "Hang him from the corsair's main boom as an example to those who would break the king's peace."

Snarling, Zdnek snatched a kris from one of his voluminous sleeves and lunged up and toward Chevell, but he did not live to strike a blow, for Céleste's arrow took the pirate through the throat.

No matter that Zdnek was dead, they hanged his corpse regardless.

Uncertainties

12

Long did they search, but no map did they find, and so they transferred treasure and stolen goods from the pirate ship to the *Sea Eagle*. And after the swearing of the rovers in the names of Skuld, Verdandi, and Urd to sail to Port Mizon and give themselves over to the king's justice, "Cast off grapnels," Chevell ordered. Aboard the dhow the pirates loosened the hooks and tossed them onto the king's ship. A few members of the crew of the *Sea Eagle* began coiling the lines to stow the grapnels away, while other members stood by the halyards awaiting the captain's command. Chevell looked at Princess Céleste and said, "We've another corsair to catch."

"What be our course, My Lord Captain?" asked the helmsman.

"A point sunwise of sunup, Gervaise. That's where we last saw the third corsair."

"Aye, aye, My Lord Captain," replied the helmsman, taking a sight on the sun.

Chevell turned to the bosun. "Pipe the sails about to get us free of this raider, and then catch the best of the wind."

"Aye, aye, My Lord Captain," said the bosun, and he set whistle to lips and signaled the crew; the men swung the yards about, and the *Sea Eagle* began moving away from the corsair, and as soon as she was free, again the bosun piped orders, and once more the crew haled the yards 'round . . . and the ship slowly got under way.

Eyeing the wind pennants and the set of the sails, Chevell nodded his approval, and soon the vessel was running full.

Now Chevell turned to Lieutenant Armond. "The chirurgeon is tending the wounded, but I would have you see to the dead. Canvas and ballast: we'll bury them at sea."

As Armond moved forward to fetch the sailmaker, Chevell now stepped to where Roél and Céleste stood at the taffrail and gazed aft at the corsair ship just then getting under way.

"I wonder," said Céleste, "if the pirates will merely flee or sail back to Port Mizon to face the king's justice."

"Were it knights instead of corsairs," said Roél, "they would be honor bound to do so."

Chevell said, "They pledged in the names of the Three Sisters, and if they value their lives, they will keep their word, for the Fates have ways of punishing those who break their vows."

"Oh, look," said Ensign Laval, a blond-headed youth of twenty summers or so, "they've cut away the corpse of their captain."

In the distance the body fell and plunged into the waters, even as the dhow turned sunwise and picked up speed.

"Oi, now, wait a moment," said the helmsman, shading his eyes against the low-hanging sun, "that's not the course to take them to Port Mizon."

"Maybe they're tacking," said Céleste.

"Nay, m'lady," said Ensign Laval. "The wind's in our forelarboard quarter, and if they were going to Mizon, the breeze would be off their starboard aft, and they'd just ride it all the way to port. Nay, they're heading elsewise."

"Ah, me," said Céleste, shaking her head, "this in spite of their oath to the Three Sisters."

"There are those who know not the power of pledges and hold no belief in oaths, Princess," said Chevell, "and these rovers seem to be among them."

They watched moments more, and it appeared the pirates were jettisoning cargo. "What are they doing now?" asked Céleste.

Chevell sighed. "Throwing their dead overboard."

"Captain," asked the ensign, "won't that put blood in the waters, attract things up from the deep?"

"Aye, lad. That's why we sew our own in canvas, along with a ballast stone. It would not do to have sharks and things worse following the ship and waiting for a meal."

"Oh, Mithras!" cried the lookout from the crow's nest. "My Lord Captain, dead ahead, something dreadful comes."

Chevell stepped to the starboard side rail and leaned outward and peered ahead. He frowned and moved forward and again leaned outward. Then he ran to the bow and but an instant later cried, "All hands, ready weapons!"

Céleste whipped her bow from her back and set an arrow to string. Roél took up his shield and drew Coeur d'Acier. They both moved forward and leaned out over the side rail to see what—

"Oh, my!" exclaimed Céleste. "What is it?"

A great heave in the water raced toward the Sea Eagle.

"I know not," said Roél.

But then, even as men took up bows and arrows, cutlasses and cudgels, the lookout cried, "A serpent, Captain. I can see it now. 'Tis a terrible serpent of the sea."

Onward hurtled the great billow, the monster driving the wave before it in its rush through the water.

Ensign Laval stepped to Céleste and in a voice tight with stress said, "We're in for the fight of our lives, m'lady. Best you go below, for I think arrows will only anger it."

Her heart hammering in dread, Céleste replied, "Nay, Ensign, I'll not cower while others fight."

Roél turned to her. "If we do not survive, Céleste, know this: I love you."

Before she could reply the ship rose up as the leading edge of the billow reached them. "Hold fast!" shouted Chevell.

With her bow and its nocked arrow in her left hand, Céleste grabbed on to the side rail with her right, as up rode the ship and up, heeling over to the larboard side, rigging creaking under the strain. And the boiling wave passed alongside, part of it flowing under the *Sea Eagle*, and Céleste espied in the waters aflank an enormous creature hurtling past, its eyes like two huge round lamps, its body massive and long and dark emerald with spots of pale jade down its length, and running the full of its back stood a raised translucent, yellow-green fin held up by sharp spines. On sped the immense sea serpent, fully twice or thrice the length of the ship; on it hurtled and on, driving the water before it. And then it was beyond the *Sea Eagle,* the vessel left bobbing in its wake.

Her heart yet pounding with residual fright, Céleste resheathed her arrow and slung her bow across her back. Then she turned to Roél and slipped past his shield and sword and embraced him and in a delayed reply said, "I know, Roél, I know. Just as I do love you." And she took his face in her hands and kissed him, even as tears of relief slid down her cheeks.

Laval wiped a shaky hand across his sweating brow and said, "I thought we were deaders for certain."

"Nevertheless you stood fast and ready, Ensign," said Roél. He looked past Céleste and in the direction of the racing heave, and said, "Hmm . . ."

Céleste disengaged herself and turned to see what had caught Roél's attention. The wake of the serpent boiled toward the corsair.

Aboard that ship, pirates pointed and shouted, and then some began haling the sails about to catch the wind abeam and add haste to the vessel.

But then, without losing speed, the serpent lunged up and hurtled across the deck of the corsair, the creature's massive weight plunging the ship down. Across the craft and down and under and then back up and 'round the serpent coiled, the vessel now in its grasp. Wood splintered, the hull burst, masts shattered, and sails and rigging fell to ruin. Pirates leapt into the sea, and the water about them roiled and turned red, and fins sped to and fro as men screamed and screamed, their cries cut short in a froth of scarlet.

And then the ship was gone, masts and sails and rigging and hull dragged down into the depths below, the sea serpent vanishing as well. And all that was left behind was a frenzy of shark fins racing through a crimson swirl of water, and then that was gone, too.

"Well," said Chevell, taking a sip of wine, "if the map was somehow hidden beyond our search of that vessel, it's now lost."

Lieutenant Florien—a tall, long-faced man—shrugged and said, "My Lord Captain, well did we search, and no map was found."

Armond nodded his agreement. "Sir, the men did a thorough job. I truly believe the map was not there."

Céleste broke off a piece of fresh-baked biscuit and dipped it in among the beans on her plate. She peered at it a moment and sighed and looked across the table at Roél. "We can only hope it is on the last of the corsairs."

Roél nodded and cut another bite from his slice of smoke-cured ham and said, "Yet if it is hidden on the first ship captured, then we are sailing in the wrong direction."

"And if on the second ship, it's gone," said Officer Burcet, ship's chirurgeon—short and rather foxlike of feature, with reddish hair and pale brown eyes.

They sat 'round a table in the captain's quarters: Chevell, Armond, Laval, Roél, and Céleste, along with Florien and Burcet.

"Me," said Armond, "I believe the rover captain was telling the truth, and the map is on the last of the three raiders."

"Who can trust the word of a corsair?" said Chevell.

Céleste looked at the captain and smiled. "Did I not hear you mention you were once a freebooter?"

Chevell laughed. "That was long past, Princess. I've since become a king's man, and now my word is my bond. Your sire, Valeray, helped me to understand that."

"My sire?"

"Oui."

"When was this?"

Chevell glanced 'round the table and raised his left eyebrow and said, "This goes no further."

All the men nodded, including Roél, and Princess Céleste canted her head in assent.

Chevell lifted his glass of wine and held it up and looked at the ruby liquid, glowing with lantern light shining through. Then he took a deep breath and said, "Many, many summers now long gone, Valeray and I were partners. We were on a, um, a bit of a task, one requiring lock-picking skills. We had just managed to liberate what we had come for, when we were discovered. It was as we were escaping over the rooftops that I fell and broke my leg. The watch was hard on our heels, and I could not go on. Valeray, who had the . . . hmm . . . the items, dragged me into hiding and said if they found me, he would make certain to set me free. Then he fled on.

"Well, they found me, and threw me in gaol. A chirurgeon came to set my leg so that I would be fit when hanged. To my surprise, the 'chirurgeon' was Valeray. He did set my leg, and then, with a cosh, he stunned the jailor and managed to get me free. He had a horse-drawn wagon waiting, grunting pigs in the stake-sided wain. He slipped me under the floorboards, where I lay in a slurry of pig sewage, and drove right through the warded gate." Chevell burst into laughter. "The guards, you see, only glanced at the wain and backed away holding their noses and waved the pig farmer on. And even though I was retching as we went out the portal, my heaves were lost among the grunts of the swine."

Céleste broke into giggles, and the men at the table roared in laughter.

When it subsided, Chevell said, "We got quit of that city, and I asked Valeray why he had risked all to come back for nought but me. 'My word is my bond,' he replied." Chevell took a sip of his wine. "Later, we parted our ways, and soon I became a freebooter—rose to captain my own vessel. But always Valeray's words echoed in my mind: 'My word is my bond.'

"Up until then I had not had much experience with honorable men. Yet that set me on my course. I gave up freebooting and took my ship and a good-hearted crew—one I had been culling from among the corsairs—and joined the king's fleet. It was only long afterward I discovered Valeray himself had been a king's thief, working for a distant realm.

"Some time after that, there was that dreadful business with Orbane, and I hear that Valeray was key to that wizard's defeat." Chevell looked at Céleste. "Sometime, Princess, you will have to tell me how 'twas done."

There came a tap on the door. "Come!" called Chevell.

The door opened and a skinny, towheaded cabin boy said, "Beggin' your pardon, My Lord Captain, but the sailmaker says all is ready."

"Thank you, Hewitt. Tell the watch commander I'll be out at the mark of eight bells. Have the crew assemble then."

Roél looked at Chevell. "The funerals of those lost in the battle?"

"Aye," replied Chevell.

They ate in silence a moment, and then Officer Burcet said,

"Damn the corsairs. I spent a goodly time sewing up gashes and bandaging heads. Two died under my care. Would that I could have done something to keep them alive."

"The duties of a chirurgeon must be dreadful," said Céleste, "dealing with the aftermath of violence as you do."

"Oui. Even so, there are rewards as well."

"That's what Gilles says, too."

"Gilles?"

"One of the healers at Springwood Manor." Suddenly Céleste's face fell. "Oh, I hope he is all right."

When the officers at the table looked at Céleste, questions in their eyes, Roél said, "Gilles was one of those with us when the Goblins and Ogres and Trolls attacked."

"Ah, I see," said Chevell. "We can only hope if the men in your band did cross the twilight border, they did so at a place other than where you crossed."

A pall fell upon the table, and from the deck a bell rang six times, the sound muted by the cabin walls.

Finally, Roél said, "How does one cross an unknown border?"

"Very carefully," said Chevell.

Céleste looked up from her plate. "In the Springwood, in fact in all of the Forests of the Seasons—even the Winterwood—we ask the Sprites to help us. They fly across and back, and report what is on the other side."

"Why did you single out the Winterwood, chérie?" asked Roél.

Céleste smiled and said, "Sprites do not like cold weather, for they wear no clothing. And in Borel's realm it is always winter. Even so, we don special garments, with places within where the Sprites can stay warm. Then we bear Sprites 'round the bound and they help us note what is on the far sides. In the other three realms, no special garb is needed."

"Ah, I see," said Roél. "But doesn't that take a long while to map out a bound?"

Céleste nodded and said, "It is a long and tedious process, and we place markers signifying the safe routes, or note natural landmarks to do so."

Roél nodded. "I see, and there was no marker where we crossed."

Céleste frowned a moment and then brightened. "Ah, Roél, that works to the good. If men of the warband survived the attack—and they are most likely to have done so, since the Goblins and such followed us—they will be cautious when crossing over. Can they find one, they will fetch a Sprite to help, or rope a scout to cross over. And if we left tracks, they will most likely think we have drowned, for the Sea Eagle has borne us away." She grinned ruefully. "And here I was fearful for them, when instead they are almost certainly mourning us."

Ensign Laval said, "But won't that mean your brothers and sister and your parents will be in mourning, too?"

"Oh," said Céleste, her voice falling.

"Fear not, my lady," said Chevell. "As soon as we return to Mizon, we will send word of your survival."

"Ah," said Céleste, her voice rising.

With her spirits lifted, Céleste set to her meal with gusto. Roél grinned and said to Chevell, "You can report that, thanks to the Three Sisters, the Sea Eagle was at the right place at the right time, and the word of our demise premature."

"Hear, hear," said Second Officer Florien, his long face breaking into a smile. He raised his glass in salute.

"Aye," said Chevell. "I ween we can also thank the Three Sisters for sending the second corsair to the bottom, yet if the map was hidden thereon—"

Céleste shook her head. "Non, Captain. Although I do believe the Fates sent that serpent—for those corsairs broke an oath taken in the Sisters' names—I do not believe the Fates would have done so if the map were aboard."

Chevell cocked an eyebrow. "Why is that, Princess?"

"Because, Captain, somehow the Fates are tied up in this quest of ours, and Lady Skuld has given me a rede."

"Lady Skuld!" blurted Ensign Laval. "You spoke to Lady Skuld?"

"Oui."

Wide-eyed, Chevell looked at Céleste and said, "Princess, you will have to tell us of this quest you and Chevalier Roél follow."

Céleste looked at Roél and said, "Tis your tale to begin, chéri."

Roél nodded and said, "Some summers back my parents arranged a marriage for my sister, Avélaine, one she did not welcome. . . ."

". . . and that was when the Goblins and such attacked, the crow flying above and calling for revenge," concluded Céleste.

"Where is this crow now?" asked the ensign.

"Skewered," said Roél. "I believe Captain Anton slew it with a crossbow bolt."

"Then if it was the witch shapeshifted, she's dead. Right?"

Roél looked at Céleste, revelation in his eyes, and said, "Perhaps, Laval. Perhaps. We can only hope it is true."

Again the bell sounded, this time ringing eight. Another tap came on the door, and Cabin Boy Hewitt said, "The men are assembled adeck, My Lord Captain, and the slain await."

"Very well, Hewitt." Chevell stood, the other officers following suit, as did Princess Céleste and Chevalier Roél.

"Captain," said Céleste as they moved through the door, "if you will allow, I will sing their souls into the sky."

"Nothing would please me more, my lady," replied Chevell.

Céleste and Roél were quartered in the first officer's cabin, and Lieutenant Armond displaced Second Officer Florien, and he in turn displaced Ensign Laval, who then moved to share quarters with the chirurgeon, Burcet.

As Céleste and Roél lay in the narrow bunk, Roél, his voice heavy with fatigue, said, "Thank you for the sweet song, my love. It was well received."

"The men wept," said Céleste.

"As did I," murmured Roél. "It is difficult to see brave men go to their grave."

"Oui," said Céleste, but Roél did not hear even that single word, for, exhausted, he had fallen asleep.

Moments later, Céleste followed him into slumber.

Even so, in the wee hours after mid of night, Céleste awakened to find Roél propped on one elbow and looking at her by the starlight seeping in through the porthole.

Céleste reached up and pulled him to her and whispered, "Forever, my darling, forever," and they made love by the dark of the moon.

Yet for stolen Avélaine, but one dark of the moon remained.

13

Hazard

In the early-morning light, Captain Chevell stood on the bow of the *Sea Eagle* and stared at the horizon and brooded. He glanced down at the map in his hands and then called up to the lookout, "Anything, Thomé?"

"Non, My Lord Captain," called down the man in the crow's nest. "But for Low Island, the sea is empty to the rim."

Chevell again glanced at the chart, and then strode to the stern and said, "Gervaise, bring her to a course three points sunwise of sunup. Destin, set the sails two points counter."

As the helmsman spun the wheel rightward, the bosun piped calls to the crew, and men haled the yardarms about. The *Sea Eagle* heeled over in response to the brisk breeze. As soon as she came 'round, Gervaise straightened the wheel, and the ship now cut a new course through the waves.

Lieutenant Armond stepped up from the main deck and said, "My Lord Captain, what have you in mind?"

Chevell sighed. "The pirate Barlou has a long lead on us, and his ship is swift, and even though we are swifter, still he will make port ere we can o'erhaul him. Yet he sails a course to take his ship 'round the *Îles de Chanson.*" Chevell tapped the map. "We have just passed *Île Basse,* and so the Îles de Chanson lie along the course we now sail. If we fare through them, then we might intercept the corsair before it sails into Brados."

"But, my lord, isn't that a perilous course to take?"

"Oui, but it seems the only chance to seize the corsair before it reaches safe haven."

"But, my lord, what of the legends?"

"Legends?" asked Céleste, as she and Roél stepped onto the fantail.

"Good morning, my lady," said Chevell. He acknowledged Roél with a nod.

Roél nodded in return, and Céleste said, "Good morning, Captain, Lieutenant. And what's this about legends?"

"Princess," said Chevell, "in hopes of intercepting the raider, I have changed our course, and it will take us through the Islands of Song."

"Ah," said Céleste. "I see."

"I don't," said Roél. "What are these Islands of Song?"

Céleste said, "Lore has it that *Sirènes* at times dwell therein."

"Mermaids?" asked Roél.

"Oui."

Roél turned up a hand in puzzlement.

"It's their singing, Chevalier; they enchant men with their songs," said Chevell.

Roél looked at Céleste, and she nodded in agreement and said, "So the stories go."

Armond said, "It is told that the Sirènes sit on rocks and comb their long golden hair and sing, and men go mad with desire. Sailors leap overboard to be with them; ships founder; entire crews are lost to the sea, drowned in their own desire, drowned in the brine as well."

"Why not simply plug up the ears?" asked Roél.

Armond shook his head. "Contrary to an old legend, that does no good whatsoever. It seems the spell of the singing depends not on hearing at all, for even deaf men are enchanted."

Roél frowned and turned to Chevell. "Then, Captain, is this a wise course to take: sailing among these islands?"

Chevell smiled. "Some of what Armond has said is true: the Sirènes do sing, and men, deaf or no, are entranced by their songs. Yet heed: when I was a freebooter, I spoke to a raider whose craft sailed those perilous waters to evade one of the king's ships. He said the crew was indeed spellbound, but they did not leap overboard. Before they entered the isles, they lashed their tiller, and the course they had set carried them on through much of the perilous waters. When they could no longer hear the songs, they came to their senses just in time to avoid disaster and sailed on. The king's ship, though, did not think to do this, and so with her tiller unlashed and unmanned she foundered on the rocks and sank. The freebooter who told me this does not know what happened to the king's crew."

"Ah, and you plan on lashing our tiller?" asked Roél.

"Non, Roél. I plan on the princess guiding us through."

"Me?" asked Céleste, surprise in her eyes.

"Oui, my lady, for the songs of Sirènes do not affect the fairer sex."

"But Captain," protested Céleste, "I know nought of piloting a ship."

"Princess, 'tis likely that no Sirènes will be at the isles, but if they are, then we'll need you to steer. Helmsman Gervaise will teach you what you must know to maintain a course, for there is a rather straight run through the Îles de Chanson with but a single turn; it is shown on my charts and supports what the freebooter said."

"And you trust this man?"

"Oui, for he was my mentor as I worked my way up through the ranks."

"And who is this mentor?"

Chevell sighed and said, "Caralos."

"The same man the pirate captain said is the one who seeks the map?" asked Roél.

"Oui. He is now leader of the corsairs."

"And he is a friend of yours?"

Chevell shook his head and said, "Not any longer. We had a falling-out when I and my crew all became king's men. Before we left, I told him what we planned. He became furious and attacked me. I defeated but did not slay him. Instead I bound and gagged him and left him alive, but always have I known that we would meet again, for even in defeat he swore he would kill me one day." Chevell shrugged. "Perhaps that day draws nigh."

They stood for a moment, none saying ought, but finally Roél said, "Captain, I am well trained in strategy and tactics, and if we do not intercept the raider, then we will need a plan for recovering the chart, for without it the princess and I cannot carry on our own quest. I would have you speak to me of this safe haven where the raider goes. Mayhap I can help in laying out how we will go about retrieving that map should it reach Caralos."

Chevell nodded and said, "Come, we will go to my cabin, for there I have charts of the isle, as well as drafts of the corsairs' hold." He turned and said, "Princess, if you would, let Gervaise begin your lessons now, for though we might not need you at the helm, still 'tis better to be prepared."

The princess grinned and sketched a salute and said, "Aye, aye, My Lord Captain," and she turned to Gervaise.

As Chevell and Roél stepped from the fantail and turned for the captain's quarters, Céleste overheard Chevell saying, "Brados is an island with a sheltered bay with a raider town lying along its arc. Above the town sits a high-walled citadel, and in the center of that fortress sits a tower—Caralos's seat—and that's the most likely place where the map will be found, assuming the corsair reaches him . . ." They stepped through the door to the passageway below, and the princess heard no more.

"Ahem." Gervaise cleared his throat.

"Yes, Helmsman," replied Céleste.

"Steering, m'lady, now, this be the way of it. . . ."

That evening Céleste and Roél and Chevell sat at dinner in the captain's cabin.

"Today I handled the wheel," said Céleste.

"The training went well?" asked Chevell.

"Oui and non: there was a steady larboard wind, and so I had little practice at helming a ship. Even so, I learned much of the way of it. And Gervaise took relief from Helmsman Lucien and walked me the length of the ship, showing me the halyards and sheets and naming the sails and telling me what each one does, Bosun Destin accompanying us and adding a word now and then."

Chevell nodded and said, "My lady, Second Officer Florien tells me that the wind is shifting to the fore, and tomorrow we will be tacking. That should give you practice aplenty."

"Well and good, Captain. Well and good."

They ate without speaking for long moments, but finally Céleste ran her fingers through her pale tresses and sighed. "Ah, me, Roél, but the fact that we fled without any gear other than what we were carrying is dreadful. I mean, I need a bath and to wash my hair . . . and I believe I would kill for a comb. Too, I would clean my leathers, but I have nought to wear while they are airing."

Roél laughed and said, "For weeks on end during the war Blaise and I and all the men, we did not bathe nor change clothes whatsoever. Our leathers became stiff with sweat and grime and other matter. Rank we were, indeed."

"Nevertheless . . . ," replied Céleste.

Captain Chevell smiled. "My lady, I can provide you with salt water to bathe in, and then a small amount of fresh to wash the salt away. As for a comb and clothing, perhaps we can scare up some such."

"Oh, Captain, I would much appreciate that." Céleste hesitated a moment and then added, "I will also need a bit of clean cloth for . . . hmm . . . other needs. Perhaps I will see Chirurgeon Burcet for that."

Concern flooded Roél's face. "Beloved, are you wounded in some manner?"

Céleste smiled and said, "No more so than other women." Roél frowned, and then enlightenment filled his features. "Oh . . . ," and both he and Chevell became totally absorbed in cutting up their salted haddock.

Céleste shook her head and smiled to herself and cut at her fish as well.

The following day, dressed in cabin-boy garb, Céleste stood at the wheel, Helmsman Gervaise at her side, Bosun Destin standing nearby.

"The wind, she be blowing straight from the course we would like to follow," said Gervaise. "But we can't sail directly into the teeth of it. Instead, we tack on long reaches and run a zigzag toward the way we would go—in this case, the isles. We are about to alter course—to zig the other way—and head on a larboard tack; to make that change, well, it's called 'ready about.' "

Gervaise went on to explain to Céleste exactly how 'twas to be done. She listened intently and got the general gist of it, even though Gervaise used a plethora of terms—headsheets, jibs, spilling, luffing, aweather, let go and haul, mainsails, foresails, mizzen sails, halyards, helm alee, aback, and the like—most of which Céleste remembered from the lessons of the day before.

When he was finished, Céleste smiled and said, "Gervaise, if what they say about the Sirènes is true, there won't be men to hale the yards about, and I alone cannot handle the entire ship."

Gervaise scratched his whiskery jaw and said, "Well, if ye were runnin' on nought but jibs and staysails ye might, though ye'd have to tie the wheel while ye ran fo'ard and adjusted the sheets."

"Would I have the strength to do so?"

Gervaise looked at her slim form. "Well, m'lady, the *Eagle's* jibs and stays are quite large and usually require two men on each sheet, but one alone could handle them, though it'd be a strain. Now that ye call it to my attention, I think it'd be too much for a slip of a demoiselle such as you."

Céleste laughed. "Ah, then, Helmsman, we can forget about me dealing with the sails on my own, eh?"

Gervaise scratched his whiskery jaw and said, "Still, if we are to—how did you call it, ready about?—let us get on with the doing."

"Aye, aye, Princess," said Gervaise, and he glanced at Lieutenant Armond, who nodded to him and the bosun.

"Prepare ready about!" shouted Destin. He put his pipe to his lips and blew a call, and men adeck leapt to the halyards and sheets and waited. And Céleste caused the *Eagle* to fall off the wind a little to make all sails draw better to increase speed, and then the second part of the maneuver began.

As Céleste learned what she might need to know about helming a ship through the îles de Chanson, a knight and a former thief studied drawings in the captain's cabin in the event the *Sea Eagle* did not intercept the raider.

Chevell shook his head and said, "This outer fortress wall is sheer; my men are good at climbing ratlines, but not vertical stone."

Roél looked at the sketch. "Yet the walls are scalable, oui?"

"Oui, to one skilled at free-climbing."

Roél sighed and said, "As he taught his daughter."

"The princess can free-climb stone?"

"Oui," said Roél, harking back to the day he had asked Céleste if she would have him as a husband, when they had in fact free-climbed a sheer stone column named the Sentinel. Chevell made a swift gesture of negation. "Ah, we can't let her go on such a perilous venture."

"Captain, do you imagine you can stop her? I know I can't."

"No, Chevalier, I can't stop her either. After all, she outranks me. Do you suppose we can slip away unnoticed?"

Roél simply shook his head.

"She is quite a handful, eh?"

"I would not say she's a handful, Sieur, for that somehow implies I should be her master. Non, a handful she is not, yet headstrong she most certainly is. Even so, she has the skills we need, and I would not try to gainsay her. I love her, Captain, headstrong and all. We are betrothed, and plan to marry when we get back from our quest."

"If you get back," said Chevell.

Roél raised an eyebrow, a slight grin on his face. "If?"

"My boy, you are speaking of venturing into the realm of the Lord of the Changelings, a place from which few, if any, ever return."

The next morning the sky began to darken. "We've a storm approaching," said Lieutenant Florien. "I ween it'll be upon us by midafternoon."

"Good!" exclaimed Chevell.

"Good, My Lord Captain?"

"Oui, Lieutenant. It means we'll be running through the îles

de Chanson in foul weather. I think the Sirènes will not be singing this afternoon and eve."

They sailed onward, the skies ever darkening, and finally Chevell shouted, "Hewitt!"

Cabin Boy Hewitt came running aft. "My Lord Captain?"

"Hewitt, ask Princess Céleste and Sieur Roël to join me in my quarters."

"Aye, aye, My Lord Captain."

Hewitt dashed away toward the bow, where Céleste and Roël stood and watched dolphins racing the *Eagle* and leaping o'er the bow wave, then circling about to leap o'er the wave again. And every now and then, the two caught glimpses of swift swimmers among them—neither dolphins nor fish, but small finny folk instead, mayhap half human in size. Pale green they were, and some bore tridents, yet they used them not.

"What are they?" asked Roël.

"They are the *Couvée de la Mer*—the Sea Brood. 'Tis said they often use dolphins as men use dogs."

"Ah, but they are swift."

Hewitt came breathlessly to the bow. "Princess, Sieur Roël, My Lord Captain sends me to fetch you."

Shortly, both Céleste and Roël reached the captain's cabin. Chevell stood at the map table with a chart spread before him. He looked up. "Ah, Princess, Chevalier, good, you are here."

As Roël looked down at the map, Céleste said, "Yes, Captain?"

"My lady, the îles de Chanson lie dead ahead," said Chevell. "I will need you standing by the helm."

Céleste grinned and said, "Aye, aye, My Lord Captain."

"These islands," said Roël, "what are they like?"

"Ah, formidable: tall, rocky crags, little vegetation, no potable water, but for rain collecting in hollows. Not a place for man or beast."

"But fit for Sirènes," said Céleste.

"Oui, though only sometimes are they there."

"Then let us hope this is not one of the times," said Roél.

"Indeed," said Chevell. "Yet if any are nigh this day, I deem the oncoming storm will drive them into the depths."

"Is that likely to happen?" asked Céleste.

Chevell shrugged, and then tapped the chart. "I would show you our intended route."

Céleste glanced at Roél and then looked at the map.

"These are the islands: a long chain stretching some hundred sea leagues or so."

"Hmm . . . ," muttered Roél, "there must be a thousand here."

"More like twenty-three hundred," said Chevell. "A veritable warren with rocks to hole a hull and tricky winds channeled by the crags. Yet the Sirènes are the greatest danger."

"Are they that deadly?" asked Céleste.

"Perhaps not, though the tales say they lure men to a watery grave."

"I thought your onetime mentor said none of his crew leapt overboard."

"Aye, he did. Yet the king's ship foundered, and those men probably drowned . . . or died of exposure."

"I see."

Chevell pointed at the depicted islands. "Here the archipelago is narrowest; see how it necks down? It is the quickest way through, and a fairly straight run at that, though there is a larboard turn needed"—he jabbed a finger to the vellum—"right here, a total of three points to port."

Céleste nodded but said, "Oui. I see. But only if the wind is favorable—astern or abeam—yet if head-on . . . ?"

"Then we'll come through here," said Chevell, "and the turn will be a single point larboard." He traced the alternate route. "But at the moment, the wind is off our larboard stern, and not likely to shift greatly through the narrow part of the chain."

"Captain, did you not say the winds therein are tricky? Are they not likely to shift?"

"Oui. But we will run mainly on the topsails, for they are up where the air is less affected by the isles themselves."

"Ah. I see."

"And though I don't think we'll need you at the helm, Princess, before we enter the chain, we'll set all the sails for you to get us through in the event we do get entranced. With the sails fixed—no men to hale them about and take advantage of the shifts in the air—it won't be the swiftest run, but it will get us through."

Céleste nodded and said, "Captain, what if the wind comes about such that it's head-on out of the turn?"

"Then you'll need sail this way," said Chevell, tracing a third route. "Three points to starboard, and then bring her back on course right here. But heed: you'll need to make that decision before reaching the larboard turn; else we'll founder on these shoals."

"I see. The blue lines indicate shoals?"

"Oui."

"Oh, my, but there are so many through this . . . what did you call it? An archipelago?"

"Oui."

"Captain," said Roél, "who made this map?"

"Women sailors in small crafts, Roél."

"Ah."

Céleste frowned. "Then why not carry some females aboard every ship, Captain?"

"Ha!" barked Chevell. "My lady, having one woman aboard is somewhat of a strain on a crew. Can you imagine what having an entire bevy would do?"

"Pssh," said Céleste, but made no further comment.

There came a tap on the door, and Hewitt entered bearing a tray with three mugs of tea. "Beggin' your pardon, Captain, but Cookie said you would be needin' this."

"Ah, my thanks, Hewitt. Thank Master Chanler for me."

"I will, Sieur." Hewitt scurried away.

As she took up her tea, Céleste said, "Well, then, Captain, tell me the landmarks so that I'll know when to execute the turn, as well as those if the wind is unfavorable."

"Well, my lady, you'll need to be counting islands, first this one and then . . ."

In midafternoon, the wind running before the storm shifted to the larboard beam, the crew shifting the sails in response.

"Will we have to tack?" asked Céleste.

"Mayhap, m'lady," said Lieutenant Armond. "Though 'tis now on our beam, should it come 'round a bit more, aye, tacking we'll need do, and we'll approach the cluster by another route."

"So the captain said," replied Céleste.

The wind strengthened, the gusts now bearing spatters of rain forerunning the oncoming tempest. Hewitt came darting, bearing an armload of slickers. He peeled off the top one and, glancing at Chevell, he gave it over to Céleste. "My lady."

"Merci, Hewitt."

Then the cabin boy doled out the other slickers, Captain Chevell first, Lieutenant Armond second, Roël next, followed by Lieutenant Florien, then Bosun Destin, Helmsman Gervaise, and finally himself. The captain smiled at Hewitt's rankings, but said nought.

"My Lord Captain," said Armond, glancing at Céleste, "given the storm, the darkness, and the isles, is it wise to hazard the crossing during a blow?"

Chevell barked a laugh. "Wise? Is it wise? Mayhap not, yet it is the only chance we have of catching the raider ere he makes port. And as to the darkness, we should reach the far side of the archipelago just as full night falls."

Reluctantly, Armond nodded, and they all stood on the fantail and spoke not a word of the risk before them.

On drove the *Sea Eagle*, the day dim under the stygian overcast, and off to the larboard gray rain and whitecaps came sweeping o'er the deeps. And finally, dead ahead and dimly seen, a great scatter of tall, stony crags, stretching from horizon to horizon, rode up o'er the rim of the world.

"There they be," gritted Lieutenant Florien.

"They look dreadful," said Céleste.

"My lady," said Gervaise, "if need be ye at the helm, steer a clear channel 'tween each and we'll all be safe. The *Eagle*'ll take care o' the rest."

Now the full fury of the storm struck: icy rain came driving on a wailing wind, and lightning flared among the stone pinnacles, thunder following.

"Destin, the wind be off the larboard beam. Maintain the topsails full. Reef down half and goosewing all others on main, fore, and mizzen. Strike the stays and jibs. And set the sails for aft-to-larboard winds."

"But my lord," said Florien, "that means we'll be in the isles longer, and if the Sirènes are therein—"

"I know, Lieutenant, yet I'll not run in full in a storm in dismal light among islands of stone."

"Aye, Captain."

Now the bosun piped the orders, and as sails were struck and reefed and winged, and the yardarms were haled about, Gervaise said, "My lady, should ye have to take the helm, remember, keep the wind anywhere in the quarter from stern to larboard beam. Anythin' else and the sails'll either be luffin', or the wind'll be blowin' us hind'ards."

"I remember, Gervaise," said Céleste.

Roél reached out and took her hand, her fingers icy. He squeezed her grip, and she smiled at him with a bravery she did not feel.

And in shrieking wind and driving rain, the *Sea Eagle* clove through heaving seas and toward the massive blocks of stone, the great crags a blur in the storm, lightning stroking down among them, thunder riving the air.

"Stand by, Princess," said Chevell.

"Aye, aye, Captain," replied Céleste, her heart hammering against her ribs.

And in that moment the *Sea Eagle* drove in among the jagged monoliths.

14

Falcons

"Monsieur Vidal! Monsieur Vidal!"

The steward of the Springwood looked up from the parchment to see one of the gardeners hasten through the doorway. Vidal set his quill aside. "Oui, Morell?"

"Sieur, there is a Sprite in the arbor, and she says she has dreadful news for you."

"A Sprite?"

"Oui, and she is weeping."

Vidal stood. "Lead the way."

Moments later, it was Vidal who wept, and he called the staff together to announce the dire news carried by Sprites in swift relay: during a battle with Redcaps and Bogles and Trolls, Princess Céleste and Sieur Roél had drowned.

Battle? asked some; *Drowned?* asked others, while many burst into tears, though others choked back their grief.

But Vidal had little else to tell them, for the Sprite had known nought about those dire events except that Anton was leading the warband back to the manor, and there were wounded to tend.

127

Within a candlemark, falcons flew to the manors of the Winterwood and the Autumnwood and the Summerwood, bearing the terrible word.

The first to receive the falcon-borne news was Steward Arnot at Winterwood Manor, for it lay closest to the Springwood. He gathered the staff and made the announcement of Céleste's and Roél's deaths. Cries broke out and many wept, for the princess was well loved. The gala they had planned for the return of Prince Borel and Lady Michelle would now be set aside. "These will be sad times, and we must bear up," said Arnot. "A memorial will be held in Springwood Manor, and not only will Prince Borel and Lady Michelle pass through on their way there, but also passing through will be Princess Liaze and her contingent and Prince Alain and his, and so we will host all." He turned to the housekeepers. "Hang the door with black crepe and tie the candelabras with black ribbon." And then he said to the seamstresses, "We will need black armbands for all staff and visitors."

"Steward?" asked a skinny lad.

"Redieu," acknowledged Arnot.

"Are Prince Borel and his lady still at the Summerwood?"

"Oui, I believe they are yet there. Along with Jules and that part of the warband Lord Borel took with him, they are stopping over on their return from Roulan Vale."

"And the falcons have flown to each of the forests bearing this dreadful news?"

"Oui, Steward Vidal has sent falcons to all, including one to King Valeray and Queen Saissa."

"And so they will be here as well?"

"It depends on their route, but we will plan for them passing through."

On a croquet court at Autumnwood Manor, Liaze handed Luc her mallet and smiled as she took the message vial from Jean.

" "Twas another Springwood bird, m'lady," said the falconer.

"Two birds in less than a sevenday? What, I wonder, is my little sister up to now?" Liaze opened the container and unrolled the tissue.

She read the missive and fell to her knees wailing.

Luc knelt beside her and took her in his arms.

In the Summerwood, Alain, grim-faced and gripping a falcon-borne message, walked into the chamber where sat Camille and Borel and Michelle.

Alain's voice choked as he said, "I have some dreadful news."

Falcons winged back unto Springwood Manor bearing messages, and Steward Vidal announced to the Springwood staff that all kindred and their retinues were on their way.

15

Chanson

To larboard and starboard great crags reared up from the sea, sheer stone rising out of the depths and reaching toward the dark sky. Waves crashed against rock and pitched up and fell and rebounded, the water heaving and roiling, the pattern unpredictable as billows crossed and crisscrossed among the monoliths, reinforcing here, canceling there, the sea a boiling fury. And amid this chaos plunged the *Eagle*, the bow rising up and over a wave to hurtle down into the trough beyond. Rain hammered and lightning stroked and thunder shattered the shrieking air.

"Steady on, Gervaise, steady on," called the captain above the boom and howl.

"Aye, aye, My Lord Captain," cried the helmsman.

Céleste turned to Chevell and asked, "Captain, what if one of those bolts from above strikes a mast?"

"Most likely it'll splinter it," replied Chevell.

"Then I will pray that the lightning stays far away, or if not, that it altogether avoids the *Sea Eagle*."

130

The wind down upon the deck buffeted the crew, and it swirled this way and that, but aloft at the topsails it blew more or less steadily across the larboard stern and toward the starboard bow, the wind pennants atop the masts flowing that way.

"Princess, remember, keep your eye on the streamers," called Gervaise, pointing above, "for that shows the air what be driving the *Eagle* and not this muddle down adeck."

"Oui, Gervaise," Céleste called back, "I remember."

On they plowed through the raging waters, the ship rolling leftward here and rightward there and at times running eerily calm. And the rain descended in furious sheets, the churning wind driving it into face and back and flank. In spite of her slicker, Céleste became thoroughly soaked, chill water blowing into her hood and running down neck and shoulders and arms and breasts and stomach and onward.

Hewitt came running with capped mugs of hot tea, and all adeck savored the warmth.

And still the *Sea Eagle* plunged on. A candlemark and then another went by, and the day grew even dimmer, and still the storm raged, lightning cracking and thunder crashing and hammering rain pelting down.

Roél leaned over to Céleste and said, "Rather like a ride on a wild horse, eh?"

Céleste barked a laugh. "Given a choice between the two, I'd take the horse."

"Aw, this is nothin'," called Gervaise. "Why, once we were—"

"The wind is shifting deasil, Captain," said Céleste, her eye on the pennants above, the streamers now swinging out toward the starboard. "It's coming abeam."

"Oui, I see it," answered Chevell. "It means we'll have to change course."

"Go out the starboard way?"

"Oui."

And still the day dimmed as evening approached. The *Sea Eagle* plunged toward the turn, and Chevell called, "Ready, Gervaise?"

"Ready, My Lord Captain."

"Just past this isle, Helmsman."

"Oui, Captain."

And as the *Eagle* slid beyond the crag, there came drifting on the air the sound of singing—women's voices—and Chevell managed to say, "The Sirènes." But nought else passed his lips, as on halting steps he jerked toward the port wale.

Roël turned toward Céleste, an agonized look on his face, but then he, too, stumbled toward the larboard rail, as did Gervaise, and Anton, and Florien, and even Hewitt, the boy last of all.

Céleste leapt forward and took the helm and spun the wheel to starboard—"Come, my lady, it's just you and me now"—and slowly the *Eagle* swung rightward, toward the outbound leg of the passage through the Îles de Chanson. As the ship came onto the planned course, Céleste straightened the wheel, and onward the *Eagle* plunged, bearing her cargo of the entranced as well as a lone woman.

And still rain hammered down, and still lightning stroked and thunder roared, yet somehow the singing penetrated the din. How it could do so, Céleste did not know, yet do so it did. There did not seem to be any words to the song, just marvelous voices soaring. To Céleste's ear it was beautiful, but nothing more than that; yet to the men it was spellbinding.

Céleste looked in the direction toward which the men peered, but in the dimness and sheets of rain she saw nought of the singers. She turned her attention back to the ship and said, "Well, my lady, a candlemark more and we'll be free of these isles. Mayhap ere then, we will run beyond the reach of the Sirènes and the men will come to their senses. And so, fair maiden, sail on."

Another quarter candlemark passed, and if anything the

singing grew louder. Céleste sighed, and kept the ship running on course.

But then the wind began to shift deasil once more, the pennants above swinging 'round. Gervaise's words came back to her: "*My lady, should ye have to take the helm, remember, keep the wind anywhere in the quarter from stern to larboard beam. Anythin' else and the sails'll either be luffin', or the wind'll be blowin' us hind'ards.*"

"Oh, Mithras, Gervaise," Céleste said to herself. "If I turn rightward once more, that means—"

Céleste spun the wheel to the starboard, and the ship departed from the planned course. And still the day darkened as the fringe of night came on. Céleste frowned in concentration, trying to recall details of the map Chevell had used when they had planned their passage. But it was useless, for though she could remember the course they had laid out, they rest of the archipelago was a veritable maze. Céleste groaned. "Oh, why didn't I think to bring the map to deck?"

Ahead in the dimness a great dark mass loomed, and again Céleste turned the ship starboard, and deeper in among the monoliths plowed the *Sea Eagle*. And still the songs of the Sirènes followed, the men oblivious to all but the singing.

Night fell, darkness absolute, but for lightning flaring. And where before Céleste had prayed for the strokes to stay far away, now she prayed they would split the sky at hand.

Another quarter candlemark fled into the past, and onward through the storm and the dark drove the *Eagle*, now sailing for the wrong side of the archipelago. Another bolt hammered down, and Céleste gasped in fear and spun the wheel rightward, for looming up on the larboard bow stood a monstrous crag.

Slowly the *Eagle* heeled over. "Come on, my lady, come on," cried Céleste. And as the Sirènes sang an incredibly beautiful wordless aria, a terrible scraping shuddered along the hull, the ship juddering in response. Céleste called out to Mithras for aid, and then unto the Three Sisters. And of a sudden the *Eagle* came free, and once more she sailed in clear water.

Another lightning bolt flared out from the ebon sky, and Céleste glanced at the pennants above. Now the wind swung back widdershins, and Céleste haled the ship 'round to larboard.

On plunged the *Eagle*, plowing through black night in a raging sea, a storm hammering her sails. And among a labyrinth of deadly crags dodged Céleste, jinking the ship left and right, steering by lightning flares alone, and praying for the Fates to guide her through.

Starboard and larboard and to the fore loomed stone, all of it perilously close, and she heeled the ship this way and that, sometimes certain that she would crash and founder the *Eagle* and kill all aboard. Yet somehow she managed to evade disaster, though at times the hull scraped against stone walls.

Again and again lightning stroked, and once more the wind began to shift widdershins, Céleste turning the ship larboard in response.

Another quarter candlemark elapsed, and another quarter mark after, and still the *Eagle* veered and slued and cut among monoliths, and at times seemed to slide altogether sideways, riding on thwartwise waves.

And then of a sudden the wind adeck stopped whirling, and a strong flow blew against the larboard beam. The goosewinged sails took up the air, and the *Sea Eagle* leapt forward in response.

The storm began to fade, as did the songs of the Sirènes, and soon there was nought but a gentle rain falling, and the singing was gone altogether. And the men began to come to their senses, Cabin Boy Hewitt first of all, and he scrambled about lighting lanterns on the stern. And as the entrancement vanished, Roël turned and stepped to Céleste and put an arm about her, but he said nought as she kept a tight grip on the wheel.

"Merci, Princess," said Captain Chevell, "for getting us through a tight place; else we'd have all been drowned."

Gervaise beamed, his chest swelling with pride, for, after all, he was the one who had taught the princess how to handle the helm. "Any trouble, my lady?"

Céleste looked at him and then burst out laughing in giddy relief, and she managed at last to let go of the wheel. She reached for Roél and embraced him, and her laughter suddenly turned to tears.

16

Brados

"I could not help myself, chérie," said Roël. "I had no will of my own."

Céleste smiled and said, "They say the music of the Fauns does the same to women."

"Music of the Fauns?"

"Oui. A type of Fey. They have the legs, tail, and ears of a deer, but the faces of handsome youths. They play white willow-root pipes, and somehow women, or, rather, females—be they human, Elven, Nymphs, or ought else—become completely entranced. So, my love, to fall prey to something over which you have no control whatsoever, 'twas and 'tis no dishonor, for I know you love me still."

"How did you know I was feeling dishonor?"

"Your look told all, Roël."

"My look?"

"Oui. When the singing first came riding on the wind, you looked at me in distress, as if you were somehow betraying me, yet I knew that you were helpless before the lure of the Sirènes."

A fleeting smile crossed Roél's features. "It was an ordeal, though not an unpleasant one."

"Careful, my love, for my clemency only goes so far. Absolution, I give you, but I'd rather not hear the details."

"Oh, but I didn't, I mean, I—"

Céleste broke into laughter. "I'm teasing you, chéri."

They lay together in the narrow bunk, with Roél propped on an elbow gazing down at Céleste. And still a gentle rain in the night fell across the *Eagle* and the sea, the ship now running toward the pirate stronghold on the isle of Brados. All the crew had hailed the princess for bearing them to safety, and though she acknowledged their praise, all she really wanted to do was rest, for she was completely wrung out. And so, after a hasty meal, she and Roél had retired.

Of a sudden Céleste grew sober and a frisson shuddered up her spine. "Your ordeal might have been a pleasant one, but mine was anything but."

Roél kissed her on the forehead and said, "Yet you managed to get us free."

Céleste put her hand over her mouth and yawned, then said, "'Tis a miracle I didn't founder the ship, scraping against the stone as I did." Again she yawned.

"Miracle? Mayhap. Yet I ween the Fates are yet watching o'er you."

"O'er us," murmured Céleste, and then she fell asleep.

Dawn came upon a fair ocean, the sky clear, a goodly breeze blowing from just starwise of sunup. Standing nigh the helm, Chevell called to the mainmast lookout, "Any sails, Thomé? Lateen? Sunup or sunwise."

"Non, My Lord Captain. The sea, her bosom be empty," came the reply from the crow's nest.

"Keep a sharp eye, then, for the corsair; she's bound for Brados as are we."

"Aye, aye, my lord."

Chevell turned to Florien. "As soon as anything is sighted at all, let me know."

"Aye, aye, my lord."

"Pass the word on to Armond when he relieves you," added Chevell.

"Oui, my lord, I will."

Chevell retired to his cabin to break fast. In the passageway he met Céleste and Roél, just then emerging from their own quarters. "Join me, Princess, Chevalier. And, my lady, there's something I would discuss with you o'er the morning meal."

"As you will, Captain," replied Céleste.

Hewitt brought gruel and fresh-made bread and a pot of tea, along with a daily ration of limes. As Chevell ladled porridge into the bowls, he said, "Princess, if we don't see the raider by midmorn, I'll have to break off the pursuit." He held up a hand palm out to forestall her objections. "It merely means we cannot o'ertake the corsair before it reaches safe port in Brados. Yet even though we break off, I still plan on going after the map, but I would not have the lookout on Brados espy our ship, for that would put them on alert." Chevell looked at Roél and smiled, and then turned back to Céleste. "Instead, we'll need use stealth and misdirection to get the map: Sieur Roél and I will free-climb the citadel walls in the night and retrieve the chart, while Armond and the crew provide a suitable diversion."

Céleste nodded and said, "And my role would be . . . ?"

"I would have you remain on the *Eagle* and be safe," said Chevell.

Céleste looked at Roél, and he smiled. But she frowned and said, "Did you not tell him I can free-climb as well, chéri?"

Roél sighed. "Oui, I did."

Céleste turned to Chevell and cocked an eyebrow.

"My lady, with but two of us, just Roél and me, we will likely go unnoticed, especially with the proper diversion."

"Three is a small party as well, Captain," said Céleste, "and just as likely to go unnoticed, with the proper diversion, that is."

Now Chevell sighed and looked at Roél. "You said this is the way it would be."

Roél nodded.

Céleste now turned an eye on Roél. "Plotting behind my back, love?"

"Céleste, I knew you would come, but the good captain insisted he make an attempt to dissuade you."

"Blame it on me, would you?" said Chevell. Then he burst out laughing.

Soon all three were laughing, but finally Chevell retrieved the drawings and sketches he and Roél had pondered over. As he laid them before Céleste, he said, "Very well, Princess, should the corsair escape us this morn, here be the plan so cleverly contrived by Roél; hence this be the way we three will go about retrieving the map."

Midmorning came, and still the lookout had seen no corsair or ought else for that matter, but for a distant gam of whales blowing. And so Chevell, now adeck, altered course, setting the sails to come by circuitous route to the far side of the isle of Brados, where they would most likely not be seen. "Besides," said the captain, "'tis there where lies beached a single-masted sloop we can pull free at high tide." He turned to his first officer. "Armond, put Geoff to work on making sails for that craft. Her mast stands at some thirty-five or forty feet, her boom at twenty or so. A main and a jib ought to be enough."

"Aye, aye, My Lord Captain."

As Armond strode away, Céleste at the helm said, "Will a small sloop be enough, Captain?"

"I should think so," said Chevell. "It, along with part of the crew in the dinghies, should provide the distraction we need."

Céleste nodded and onward they sailed, the far side of Brados their immediate goal.

In midafternoon they dropped anchor in a small, narrow inlet, the isle itself a large and rocky upjut of land roughly circular and some five miles across, its craggy interior filled with scrub and twisted trees, though here and there groves of tall pines stood. The shoreline was nought more than a rocky shingle, sand absent for the most part, but for the root of the cove, there where a hull of a sloop lay on its side. Massive blocks of stone reared up along this part of the perimeter, and off to the right the brim of the cove was a long cliff of sheer rock rising up from the sea and curving away beyond sight.

Men lowered dinghies, and, leaving Armond and a small crew behind, the rest put to shore, Céleste and Roél among them. As they beached the boats, Chevell said, "Ensign Laval, take your part of the men and begin cutting brush and making the preparations we discussed. Lieutenant Florien, you and the rest will deal with the sloop. Princess, Chevalier, we've a long stroll ahead, but I know a path that will somewhat ease the way."

Chevell and Céleste and Roél marked their faces and wrists—all exposed flesh—with streaks of burnt cork, and Céleste bound her pale golden hair and slipped on a dark hat to cover all, and then they donned cloaks as well. Finally, armed and armored, the trio shouldered rope and grapnels and climbing gear and set forth, the captain in the lead. And up into the craggy land they fared, the day warm and humid, the way rough in stretches, while at other places they passed through with surprising ease. Céleste found it strange to now be walking on a surface that did not pitch and roll, and it took her a while to lose her sea legs. Birds with bright plumage fluttered among the occasional grove, and lizards skittered across the way. Now and again a snake would slither off into the rocks, and once a boar stood as if to challenge them, but then fled through the crags. "Pigs gone wild from those escaped from Brados Town," said Chevell.

Perspiring, they stopped in the shade of a grove, the air redolent with the scent of the surrounding pines. As they sat on a log and took water, "How long were you a freebooter, Captain?" asked Céleste.

"In mortal terms, twelve years, Princess. About the same length of time I was a thief."

"Did you capture many a ship?"

A frown of regret crossed Chevell's features. "Princess, I'd rather not think on those times, but yes, a goodly number fell to my crew."

"I'm sorry, Captain. I did not mean to dredge up old memories."

Chevell shrugged and turned up a hand. "There are things I'd rather forget."

"As would I," said Roél. "Deeds done in time of war."

A somber silence fell among them, and finally Chevell said, "Let's go."

Once again they took up the trek, passing among the tall trees to come to a rocky way, and there they aided one another across the difficult stretch, clambering up and across and down, only to clamber up and across and down again.

Finally, as the sun touched the rim of the world, they reached an upland on the far side of the isle, the highland nought but a jumbled plateau of scrub and rock and trees. In the long shadows Chevell led them to a low ridge, and just ere reaching the crest, onto his belly he flopped, and then eased his way to the crown. Following his example, Céleste and Roél did the same.

No more than a furlong downslope loomed a fortress of gray stone blocks, sitting atop a low rise jutting out from the fall of the land. On beyond and farther down, another half mile or so, stood a town, curving about a modest bay. Rover ships were moored in the dark waters, the cove enshadowed from the setting sun by the arc of the island shouldering up all 'round. As eve drew on in the dimness below, the trio could make out folk hurrying through the streets, and lights winked into being, and the music of a squeeze-box drifted on the air. It seemed to be quite a normal town and not a rover den.

As to the bastion itself, roughly square it was, an outer wall running 'round o'er the rough ground, some ten feet high and three hundred feet to a side and five feet thick at the top, wider at the base. "That wall is merely to slow invaders; it's not a primary defense," said Chevell, reminding them. "And though you can't see it from here, there's a gate along the starwise side. A road runs through and down a series of switchbacks to the town below."

Between the outer bulwark ringing 'round and the main fortress itself, lay nought but open space, the land completely barren of growth. "A killing ground for any who win their way up the hill and breach the outer wall," said Roél.

Centered within this outer wall and killing ground, the dark bastion itself stood: some fifty feet high to the banquette it was and also built in a square, two hundred feet to a side, with a great courtyard in the center, towers and turrets and a massive wall hemming the quadrangle in. "The main gate lies on the starwise side," said Chevell, "but you can see a postern here on the sunwise bound. We, of course, will use neither."

And in the very center of the courtyard stood a tall slender structure, mayhap some seventy feet high, window slits up its length, arrow slits up its length as well. "There it is," said Chevell, "Caralos's aerie. From there he surveys his kingdom. 'Tis at the top where he keeps his charts and plots his raids."

"Then that's where we are bound," said Céleste.

"Oui," said Roél. "But first we need get over the outer wall and then the inner one and into the courtyard."

"'Tis a good plan you have laid out, Chevalier," said Chevell.

"Let us hope it all goes well," replied Roél, "but like any plan of combat, it all falls apart the instant it begins."

They lay for long moments, watching the town come alive in the oncoming dusk, lantern glow or mayhap candlelight shining in nearly every house and building, songs drifting upslope. Finally, Roél slid a bit backwards and said, "One of the first rules of combat: take rest when you may."

"I'll keep first watch," said Chevell. "I'll wake you in four candlemarks."

"What of me?" asked Céleste. "Which watch is mine?"

"Third," grunted Roél.

Four days past new and on its way to setting, a crescent moon hung low above the sundown horizon when Chevell awakened Roél, and by the time he awakened Céleste the moon had long disappeared, and all was dark but for the stars, though a few windows in town as well as the bastion yet glowed yellow, including a lantern-lit window at the top of Caralos's tower.

Céleste yawned and asked, "What is the count?"

"Two candlemarks after mid of night," said Roél, now stepping back to the ridge and peering starwise.

Céleste slowly shook her head. "Ah, you trickster, you've cheated me out of my watch, for Armond and the crew are to—"

"My love, waken Chevell," said Roél. "I see the shadow of Armond's arrival."

And even as Chevell and Céleste came to the ridge, 'round the shoulder of the cove in the glimmering starlight came the dark shape of the sloop under full sail, dark blots in tow—dinghies, the trio knew.

"Quick," snapped Roél, "our gear."

Down the back of the ridge they darted, to snatch up rope and grapnels and weaponry and other such. And by the time they reached the crest again, the sloop was blazing in flames as amid the pirate fleet it sailed.

From somewhere below there came the clanging of an alarm gong, and on the fortress walls, horns blew. "Fire ship! Fire ship!" came the repeated cry. And in the light of the burning sloop, dinghies rowed for the outlying craft, and men from the *Eagle* threw torches aboard other dhows, with wads of oil-soaked brush following. The entire bay now came alight with blazing flame, the center of the fleet afire as the raging un-manned sloop crashed in among the corsairs.

Pirates ran down to the docks, cursing, raving, weapons in hand. They were met by volleys of arrows from the archers aboard the dinghies.

And as alarms rang and horns sounded—*chnk!*—the tines of a padded grapnel hooked onto the ten-foot-high outer wall at the rear of the fortress.

Up onto this beringing bulwark clambered a trio of dark shad-ows, their faces smudged with black streaks. Down the other side they scrambled, leaving a rope in place in case of need, for none patrolled this wall, and discovery of the line unlikely. Across the killing ground they slipped, nought but wraiths in the dark. They sped to one corner of the fortress, for there free-climbing would be easiest. And up they clambered, Roél in the lead, Céleste coming last.

Up the rough stonework they scaled, passing by arrow slits in the wall, darkness and silence within. Up they clambered and up, now and again slowed by a bit of smooth work. Finally, they neared the top, where Roél in the lead motioned the others to stillness, and they all clung to the stone without moving, for running footsteps clattered nigh. Cursing voices grew louder, along with the thud of boot. Lantern light shone brighter and brighter, and with their hearts hammering in their throats, the trio pressed themselves against the stone, as all 'round the dark-ness faded. Directly above on the wall the glow passed, and then sped beyond, voices and light fading as the pirates loped onward. Céleste exhaled, noting for the first time that she had been holding her breath. When the patrol was but a distant scuffle, upward Roél climbed, to slip over the parapet and onto the walkway above. Looking left and right as he slid Coeur d'Acier from its sheath across his back, he turned about to motion the others up, to find Chevell hoisting Céleste onto the banquette. They cast their cloak hoods far over their heads, for they would not have any see just who they were, strangers within the hold. Chevell drew a cutlass, and Céleste whipped the bow from her back and nocked an arrow.

Chevell took the lead, and down a spiral stair within the fortress wall he led them: one storey, two storeys, three storeys, and more. Five in all he descended, and out into the courtyard they passed, the place a turmoil of men and horses, some shouting commands as massive gates were opened.

Ignoring the pirates, across the courtyard they dashed, merely three more rovers amid others running. To the central tower they sped, and Chevell led them in through doors flung wide.

Now up a spiral stair they scrambled, the flight turning deasil, ever rightward, the stair giving advantage to right-handed defenders against right-handed foe. Past doors and chambers and arrow slits they wound, seven flights in all, passing through trapdoors flung back as to each storey they came.

Finally they reached the top, and Chevell led them into the chamber therein. A large, swarthy man stood at an open casement, peering out at the flaming chaos in his harbor below. Behind him a cloth map lay open on a table.

To one side in the shadows of the chamber stood someone else, dark and nearly invisible.

The large, swarthy man turned when the trio entered the room. Momentarily he frowned, his pitted face twisted in puzzlement.

"Caralos," said Chevell, casting back his hood.

The man's dark eyes widened in recognition and then he spat, "Chevell."

"The day has come," said Chevell, raising his cutlass. As Caralos sprang to take a like cutlass from the wall, Céleste drew her arrow to the full.

"Nay," barked Chevell. "He is mine."

Even as Caralos took the weapon in hand, the person in the shadows started toward the table, where lay the map.

"Non," gritted Roél, raising Coeur d'Acier and moving between the chart and the shadowed being. And then Roél gasped,

"You!" And as Roél sprang forward, the man in the black cloak whirled 'round and 'round, red limning flashing in his gyres.

"Yah!" shouted Roél, Coeur d'Acier slicing through the air, to meet nothing whatsoever, for the being had vanished, even as Céleste's arrow shattered against the stone chamber wall beyond where the man had been but an instant before.

Cursing, Roél slashed at the shadows, but his blade clove only darkness.

Chang! Bronze clanging on bronze, back and forth lunged Chevell and Caralos, swords stroking and counterstroking, parrying and riposting and drawing apart. They closed and hammered at one another, and Chevell jumped inward and smashed Caralos with the bronze basket hilt of his cutlass. Caralos staggered back, but then lunged forward again. And in that moment, Chevell spitted him through. Caralos stood an instant, his eyes wide in wonder as he gaped down at the blade. And then he fell dead, even as Chevell jerked his weapon free.

"You're bleeding," said Céleste.

"He got me across the forehead," said Chevell, blood running down.

Céleste quickly examined the cut. "A slight flesh wound; it looks worse than it is."

Chevell nodded and turned to Roél. "Who were you fighting?"

"'Twas the Lord of the Changelings," raged Roél. "He was here and then not, and once again I failed."

"The Changeling Lord? Are you certain?"

"I know my enemy," gritted Roél.

"And now so does he," said Chevell.

"Mayhap he knows me as well," said Céleste, "for I loosed an arrow at him, but he vanished e'en as the shaft flashed through the place where he had been."

Chevell sighed and shook his head. "Oh, Princess."

Stricken with the realization that both he and Céleste were now known to the Changeling Lord, Roél stepped to the princess and put an arm about her. Céleste looked at him and then at Chevell and said, "Roél is right, it was the Lord of the Changelings. I saw the red limning on his cloak. And who else can vanish simply by whirling about?"

"'Tis an ill thing he was here," said Chevell.

Roél gestured at the table. "He was after that map."

Chevell moved to the board and peered at the chart. "Voilà!" he cried. "It is what we came after."

"Then let us take it and flee," said Céleste.

They rolled up the map and then sped down the stairs, meeting no one. When they reached the courtyard, it was nearly empty, but the fortress gates yet yawned wide.

"As I surmised," said Chevell, and out and through the beringing wall and down the switchbacked road they fled.

"This way," cried Chevell, and he led them through the streets of the town and 'round the arc of the bay as ships burned, and men doused flames with water, and crowds milled about along the piers in the radiant heat. Dark smoke rose into the air and blotted out stars, acrid tendrils drifting onshore, the smell of it rank. Finally, the trio reached the end of the town, and at a small wharf sat a dinghy, a five-man crew waiting, three with swords in hand, two with arrow-nocked bows.

"Florien!" cried Chevell as he and Céleste and Roél came running. Swords were sheathed and bows slung and oars taken up even as the trio leapt aboard, and Florien barked, "Away!"

and the rowers put their backs to the flight, all unnoticed in the pandemonium centered in the bay.

'Round the larboard shoulder of the cove the dinghy hauled, to come to the waiting *Sea Eagle*. In but moments the free-luffing sails were haled about, and away she flew on the wind, a victorious bird of prey.

17

Parting

"It will make a nice scar, my lord," said Chirurgeon Burcet, standing behind the captain and tying off the bandage. "One that'll mark you as a warrior for all to see."

"I think instead it'll mark me as a fool for having made a mistake in a duel," replied the captain, a lock of his red hair spilling over the binding and down his forehead.

Roél smiled. "With that cloth band about your head, I think it makes you look more the freebooter than a king's man, my lord. What think you, Céleste?"

"What?" Céleste looked up from the vellum on which she copied the map. "What did you ask?"

"Given the bandage, does the captain more resemble a king's man or a freebooter?"

Céleste studied Chevell for a moment. "I believe it marks him as the duelist he is."

"Merci, Princess," said Chevell, bowing from the waist, though seated.

Céleste turned her attention back to the chart.

149

Burcet put away his needle and gut and said, "We'll make certain to put a clean bandage on it each day. I think tomorrow a red one will do; it'll give the men heart."

"I believe 'twould be better to give the men a double ration of rum, for a splendid task they did this night."

"Indeed, my lord," said Florien.

They were gathered in the captain's cabin, the rescued map on the table, Céleste and Lieutenant Florien at the board, Céleste making a copy under Florien's direction, the lieutenant a seasoned navigator.

"Ah," said Céleste, "here is the realm of the Changelings."

"Oui," agreed Florien, stabbing a finger down as Roél stepped to the table to see.

"And where are we?" asked Roél.

"Somewhere over here," said Florien, pointing to a place out in midair beyond the table's edge.

"Does it show a port?" asked Chevell.

"Oui, my lord," replied Florien, "Port Cíent."

"Ah, bon! That means we can drop anchor there in three days or so."

Céleste looked up from her drawing. "Merci, Captain."

"We are not going to Mizon, my lord?"

"Non, Lieutenant, not directly. First we will lay over in Cíent for the men to have shore leave for two or three days, and to set the princess and chevalier on the road to their destination, for Roél would rescue his sister and brothers and perhaps have another crack at the Changeling Lord."

"Oui," said Roél. "I would indeed like another try at that vile being." Then Roél frowned and said, "I wonder why he was at the pirate stronghold."

Céleste shrugged and dipped her pen in ink and traced another line. But Chevell said, "Clearly, Caralos sent the corsairs to fetch the map for the Lord of the Changelings."

Roél looked up. "Why would the Lord of the Changelings want this map?"

"Because, ever since King Avélar came into possession of it, we have had no maidens stolen from our domain, nor from any other part of Faery, as far as I know. Avélar, you see, promised the Changeling Lord that should he ever take anyone, our armies of ruin would march into the Changeling realm and destroy all. In return for leaving our women be, Avélar promised him he would make no copies."

"Ah," said Céleste in revelation. "Then *that* is why this map is considered a treasure."

"Oui," replied Chevell. "And the map was kept in a magically warded vault to guard against the Changeling Lord and his magery. Yet that was no proof against pirates, for they entered the old-fashioned way: brute force. I imagine Caralos was well rewarded for doing so."

"Then, the Changeling Lord was there to collect his prize," said Roél. "'Tis good we came when we did; else we would not have the map to copy."

"My lord," said Florien, "does making a copy not go against the pledge of the king?"

Chevell held his hand out level and wobbled it as of a ship rolling starboard to larboard and back. "Methinks the Changeling Lord violated the king's trust by trying to steal it; hence mayhap this be tit for tat."

Florien smiled and said, "Just so."

"And speaking of rewards," said Chevell, "Sieur Roél and the princess will need funds to continue their quest."

"Oui," said Roél, "yet we brought nothing with us but the clothes on our backs and a sword, shield, and a bow."

"Pah! You brought your skill and knowledge, and aided in the return of the map. And it just so happens you helped us capture a corsair with treasure in its hold—now in ours—some of which is King Avélar's, but much of which is not. As an officer of the realm, it is from that loot I will reward you. How much might you need?"

Roél glanced at Céleste, but she smiled without looking up and continued to draw.

Roél glanced at the map and said, "It seems a long journey, and we'll need horses—two for riding and two packhorses—and tack, food, bedding, and other gear for living in the wild." Roél frowned. "Hmm . . . in a port city, it's not likely they will have war-trained horses." He paused in thought, but finally said, "I would think—"

"Florien," said Chevell, "have we a hundred gold we can reward the chevalier and princess?"

Roél's mouth dropped open. "A hundred—?"

"Oui, my lord," said Florien. "Easily."

"But that is entirely too much, Captain," said Roél. He glanced at Céleste, and again she smiled to herself but kept drawing.

"Non, my boy," said Chevell. "One hundred is not nearly payment enough for the recovery of this map. When you and the princess return from your quest, come to Port Mizon. I am certain King Avélar will want, not only to meet you two, but also to properly reward you as well."

Roél took a deep breath and canted his head in acceptance. "As you will, My Lord Captain."

A silence fell among them, broken only by the creak of timber and rope from above and the *shssh* of the hull through water from below, and the scraping of Céleste's pen on the vellum. But then Céleste frowned and asked, "Hmm . . . what do you think this might be?"

Both Roél and Florien leaned closer in the lamplight to see.

"*EF*, it looks like to me," said Roél.

"I agree," said Florien. "But what that might mean, I have no idea."

"And here it is marked *WdBr*," said Céleste, "and over here *Spx* and *El Fd*, and *Ct Dd*."

Lieutenant Florien touched several more spots. "There are similar markings all across the map."

Again, none had any explanation, and Chevell shrugged and said, "Mayhap it's like Lieutenant Burcet's notations on his medicks: initials to tell only him what a vial or a packet contains. In this case, though, it's the mapmaker leaving arcane markings."

Burcet stepped to the map table and looked, but he was as puzzled as all the rest. "You'll just have to find out as you go nigh," he said at last.

"'Tis not only nigh we'll be going," said Céleste, "but we'll be at these points exactly, for that's where the crossings through the twilight bounds exist."

"Then mark them well," said Roél, "for I do not wish to fall into an ocean or a fiery pit or ought else." He paused a moment and, grinning, added, "Well, mayhap on the stern of a ship would be acceptable."

Chevell roared in laughter.

They sailed all that day and the next, and at dusk of the following day, they hove into the harbor in Port Cíent and moored in the sheltered bay.

But for a few key crewmen, the rest drew lots to see who would have first shore leave and who would have second and who third, for Chevell would not leave the map unwarded aboard the *Eagle* for three days.

As the first third of the crew prepared to go ashore, Céleste and Roél among them, "My lord," said Burcet, "are we not going to ask for volunteers from among the crew—ourselves included— to aid the princess and chevalier on their quest?"

Chevell shook his head. "Non, Burcet. I offered, but Roél says that two alone can go where a full warband cannot. Too, he reminded me that our duty lies in another direction: not in a venture into the Changeling realm to recover his sister and brothers, but instead to return the map to King Avélar. Besides, he reminded me of my very own words: that few if any ever return from the Lord of the Changelings' demesne."

"Ah, I see," said Burcet.

Chevell patted his breast pocket. "The princess has given me a letter to be delivered to Springwood Manor, and I shall arrange to do so as soon as we arrive in Port Mizon. The staff and family will no doubt be pleased to know she and Sieur Roél are in good health, but I suspect they will not be pleased to read that they plan on going into the Changeling realm alone."

Burcet nodded and said, "I shall miss them."

"I believe we'll see them over the next three eves," said Chevell, "for they have much to do ere setting forth."

"When we do," said Burcet, "I shall drink to their health." He leaned over the rail and waved to Céleste and Roél in the dinghy now pulling away from the *Sea Eagle*.

In their rooms at the *Tasse d'Or*, Céleste, wrapped in a towel but still damp, and briskly toweling off her wet hair, padded into the bedchamber. "Ah, Mithras, how splendid it is to once again have a hot bath."

"And in freshwater," said Roél, "not salt."

Céleste paused. "Do I smell witch hazel?"

"Oui," said Roél, leaning close. "A dash the barber patted on."

Céleste grinned and ran a hand across his clean-shaven cheek. "Ah, then, you are trying to bewitch me?"

Roél took the towel from her hands, as well as the one from 'round her slim form. "The question, my lady, is who is bewitching whom?"

He wrapped his arms about her and kissed her deeply, and when they broke at last, Céleste whispered, "I ween 'tis you wielding magic, my love, for my breath is completely taken away."

"Then let us see what we can do to restore it," said Roél, and he scooped her up in his arms and stepped to the waiting bed.

Over the next three days, Roél and Céleste purchased rations and utensils and cooking gear for the trail, and Céleste visited a fletcher and ordered two sheaves of arrows fitted to her draw and quivers to bear them in, while Roél purchased a light crossbow and a sheaf of quarrels and a quiver. They spent much time at various stables talking to the hostlers and examining steeds. It was as Roél had said: there were no horses trained for war. Regardless, they finally selected two feisty mares for riding and two placid geldings for bearing their goods, saddles and harnesses included, as well as a kit for dealing with thrown horseshoes and another for repairing tack. Roél engaged a smith to have a spear-lance made, as well as sought out a leatherworker for a slinglike saddle scabbard to bear the spear. Céleste, too, had a saddle scabbard made for her bow and quivers, but she also asked the worker to make an over-the-shoulder sling for the bow as well. At a clothier's, they purchased pants and shirts and undergarments to avoid having to constantly wear their leathers. And since they knew not what they might face in the realm of the Changeling Lord, at still other stores they purchased rope and grapnels and climbing gear. Rucksacks they bought, and lanterns and oil and candles, as well as flint and steel and tinderboxes and medicks and gut and needle and bandages, and other such paraphernalia as they might need.

Not all of their time was spent in acquiring goods for the journey, for in the evenings they sang and ate and drank and joshed with the crew of the *Sea Eagle*, and Céleste showed the sailors how to dance the reel, and they showed her how to clog. Sea chanteys the crew sang and Céleste sang ballades, and Roél added war songs to the mix, and with a shrug of an apology to the princess he also sang tales of willing women and randy men, and Céleste laughed right along with the crew and clapped her hands in appreciation.

And their nighttimes were spent speaking of many things as well as making sweet love.

Just after dawn on the fourth morning since dropping anchor, Captain Chevell bade, "Au revoir!" and the *Sea Eagle* sailed away on the ebb of the morning tide. Most of the crew stood adeck and shouted their farewells, not only to Céleste and Roél, but also to a goodly number of ladies of leisure who had come to the dock to bid their own adieu. And when the ship was gone from sight 'round the shoulder of the headland, Céleste and Roél returned to the Golden Cup to break their fast.

That eve the fletcher and smith and leather worker delivered the last of the ordered goods.

The very next dawn, Céleste and Roél saddled their horses and laded their pack animals with gear and, map in hand, rode out from the town of Port Cient and toward the Changeling realm.

There remained but eighteen days ere the dark of the moon would fall, just eighteen days until Roél's sister would be bound forever to the Changeling Lord.

18

Missive

Across the deeps sped the *Sea Eagle*, bearing a cargo of recovered wealth along with a treasured map, bearing as well a letter written by Princess Céleste to be dispatched to Springwood Manor telling everyone that she and Roél had survived and were even then on the way to the Changeling realm.

On the deck paced Vicomte Chevell, captain of this three-masted, full-rigged craft, and he eyed the sails and asked Destin if they were making the best of the wind.

"Oui," replied the bosun. "We're flying all canvas and the wind is on our beam, and nought better can she do."

And so the craft sliced through the waves with all due haste, the *Eagle* bound for Port Mizon.

On the third day after setting out from Port Cíent, "Land ho!" cried Thomé, lookout on the foremast above. "Mizon dead ahead."

"Steady as she goes," said Chevell.

"Aye, aye, My Lord Captain," replied Gervaise, the helmsman.

* * *

A candlemark later, Chevell debarked from a swift gig and sprang into the saddle of a waiting horse. In haste he rode to the palace, but e'en ere seeing King Avélar, he stepped to the stable where the king's messengers stood by. "Quint!" he called, and a lithe lad sprang down from the loft, his pants unbuttoned and his shirttail out, and there came a giggle from above.

"My lord?" he said, grinning, while stuffing in his shirt and buttoning his breeks and buckling his belt.

Chevell handed the lad a letter. "Quint, grab a remount and take your fleetest steed. Be as swift in delivering this as you are with the ladies."

"Where be I going, my lord?"

"To Springwood Manor. Know you the way?"

"Oui, my lord. 'Tis where Giselle lives."

"Ha! My boy, have you a doxy in every port?"

"Well, my lord, I would not call them doxies, but, oui, I know many a *femme*." Quint grinned. "Such is the life of a king's messenger that he spends much time in households away."

"Then be on your way, lad." Chevell handed the youth a golden coin. "Take care, and see this gets into the hands of the steward himself, or if not him, then give it over to the arms-master."

Moments later, away galloped the lad, Chevell watching him go.

"Someone in charge, my lord," said Quint, leading a saddled and provisioned horse out from its stall, and then another to tether to that mount.

Then the vicomte turned, and he made his way across the yard toward the palace, for there was much to tell the king.

19

Forest

Beyond Port Cíent the land rose up from the sea to become rolling hills, with scatters of thickets and groves amid ground cleared and filled with vineyards and fields of grain and cultivated rows of vegetables, as well as orchards and nut groves. Farmhouses dotted the land, some attached to byres, others not, and an occasional manor graced a hillside. Pastures with herds of grazing cattle and flocks of sheep gathered 'round these dwellings, and gaggles of geese hissed at the pair of sunwise-faring riders, but only if they ventured too near. The air smelled of turned earth and new-mown hay and the tang of fruit ripening, and of the dung of cow and sheep and horse, and of barnyard and henhouse and sty, and of sawed and chopped timber and woodsmoke from hearth fires. Traces and pathways and lanes and farm roads crisscrossed the region, and Céleste and Roél followed a well-travelled way as it wended among the hills and passed nigh many a dwelling. Field workers or drovers or farmwives and children would pause in their daily chores to watch these two strangers riding by.

"Where be ye bound?" some would call, and Roél would point ahead and answer, "Yon."

"Well, don't go too far—the forest be that way," said a straw-hatted man ambling along the lane in the same direction Céleste and Roél fared, the man leading yoked oxen pulling a wain filled with large, pale yellow root vegetables—parsnips, most likely, their sweet fragrance redolent on the air.

"The forest?" asked Roél.

"Oui. It be a terrible place."

"Terrible in what way?"

"Strange goings-on and mystifications, that's what."

"How far?" asked Céleste.

"Two days by horse, or mayhap three, all told," he replied, raising his voice to be heard above the grind of bronze-rimmed wheels now running over a rough patch of road. "They say it lies beyond the pass through the mountains, and that's just a day away."

"They say?" asked Céleste.

"Oui, them what should know, for I wouldn't be fool enough to go there myself."

Céleste glanced at Roél, and as he began to grin, she gave a faint shake of her head, and so he put on a sober mien and said, "Merci, mon ami."

"Eh," said the man, with a gesture of dismissal, as he continued his unhurried walk and led his oxen onward, the wagon trundling in tow.

Céleste and Roél rode beyond, leaving the man in their wake. By midday the pair had ridden well past the farming region, and the land had continued to rise.

When the noontide came, they stopped in a willow grove nigh a stream for a meal and to feed and water the horses. As soon as the animals had been taken care of, Céleste sat down among the tall, waving grass along the bank, the seed-bearing heads nodding in the faint breeze. Roél handed her a torn-off hunk of bread and a wedge of cheese and plopped down beside her. Céleste took a bite of each and peered at her map. "Hmm . . ," she said, chewing and then swallowing. "Roél, look at this." She tapped a spot on the chart. "This place might be two or three days hence."

Roél leaned over and looked. "A twilight bound, eh? Ah, I see, this is the one marked *EF.*"

"Oui," said Céleste. "And if what that crofter said is true, then *EF* might mean 'enchanted forest.'"

"Are there such things?"

Céleste smiled. "This is Faery, my love." She took another bite of cheese.

"Ah, yes," replied Roél, then frowned. "But, say, aren't all things in Faery enchanted, be it a forest or field or stream or whatever else might be?"

Céleste nodded. "Oui, yet some things are more charmed than others. And when something is particularly Faery-struck, then it is said to be truly magical. Hence, the *EF* on this map might indicate just such a place."

Around a mouthful of bread Roél asked, "And what might be in an enchanted forest?"

Céleste shrugged. "Wonderful folk. Terrible beasts. Magical pools. Dreadful pits. Who knows?"

Roél swallowed his bread and said, "Who knows?" He took a sip of water and then added, "Well, I suppose we will, once we reach it. —And by the bye, using your definition, I would call the Springwood an enchanted forest. It has wondrous folk, and it is ever springtime therein. Besides, it has a beautiful princess who rules that demesne."

Céleste laughed and leaned over and kissed Roél.

"Mmm . . . cheese," said Roél, licking his lips. "I love cheese."

Céleste giggled and pushed a crust of bread toward his mouth. "Here. Make your meal complete."

"I'd rather have another taste of cheese, if you don't mind." And he embraced her and they kissed again, and two hearts began to race.

"Love," said Roél, his voice husky with desire, "this grass is as soft as a bed."

"Yes, it is," she replied, her own voice laden with want.

Unclothed, they made reckless love amid the tall blades and stems and heads, flattening all in a wide and nearly circular swath. Breathless at last, lay they on their backs side by side. A sheen of sweat drenched Roél, beads running down in streamlets. A glow of perspiration covered Céleste, runnels pooling between her breasts and within the hollow of her navel. For long moments the lovers looked up through the limbs of swaying willows at swatches of blue sky above, and listened to the shush of the soft breeze whispering among the leaves and the murmur of the stream as it wended its way toward a distant sea. Finally, Céleste sprang to her feet and pulled Roél to his, and laughing, she jumped into the clear-running flow, and waist-deep, she splashed water upon her knight. "Oho!" cried Roél, and he leapt in after the princess.

Dressed once more and riding onward, Roél said, "Speaking of enchanted forests, I believe that willow grove arear now qualifies, for certainly you enspelled me. 'Tis a wondrous glamour you have."

Céleste said nought in return, though the contented smile on her face perhaps conveyed more than words.

On they rode, the land continuing to rise, and in the distance to the fore a range of snowcapped peaks came into view.

"Ah," said Roél, "the mountains the crofter mentioned. Are they on the map?"

Céleste unfolded the chart, saying, "I don't remember any thereon." She glanced at the vellum. "Non. They are not on the map, but it is rather incomplete, or so Florien said. It gives mostly directions in which to fare and landmarks to find at the twilight crossings. Little else does it convey, other than the obscure letters at each bound. I'm not even certain that the chart is to scale, for no scale was given."

"But didn't you say the marge was three days away?"

"I was merely relying on the crofter's words," replied Céleste. "Ah."

That night they camped in the foothills at the base of the range, and cool mountain air flowed down from above.

In the dawn, Roél and Céleste fed and watered the horses, and then took a meal of their own. As the sun broached the horizon, they saddled their mounts and laded the pack animals and got under way. As they rode to the crest of a hill, "There," said Roél, pointing ahead, "that must be the pass."

To the fore a rocky slot carved its way up and through the range, heading for a col high above.

"Oui. It lies directly along the course we bear," said Céleste.

"Mayhap a good place for an ambuscade," said Roél, peering ahead while lifting his shield from its saddle hook. "I suggest you prepare your bow, chérie."

Céleste smiled unto herself, for even as he said it she was stringing the weapon.

Roél pulled his spear from the sling and couched it in the cup on his right stirrup. Then he looked at Céleste. "Ready?"

"Oui. Ready . . ."

. . . And toward the pass they rode, Roél in the lead, trailing a packhorse, Céleste coming next, her own pack animal in tow.

Inward they went and upward, and sheer stone walls rose on both sides, and the slot twisted this way and that. The pass narrowed and deepened, and soon but a distant slash of sky jagged above, the depths below enshadowed and dim. And now and then stone arched out overhead, and here the way grew ebon. In these places the chill air turned frigid, and to left and right lay unmelted snow and ice, the sun unable to reach into the depths. But still the way continued to rise, as up toward an unseen crest the pair rode. Echoing hoofbeats clattered upslope and down, and Roél wondered if he shouldn't have enwrapped the animals' feet to muffle their sound. Black pools of darkness clustered in splits and crevices and slots along the walls, and little did the light from above penetrate these stygian coverts. The air smelled of granite and water and snow and ice, and whatever breeze might have been had vanished altogether.

In places the way grew even steeper, and Roél and Céleste dismounted and led the animals. Often they paused, allowing the steeds to rest, but ever they pushed onward, unwilling to spend any more time than absolutely necessary in this cold and shadowy place, with its stone walls rearing up hundreds of feet overhead and seeming to press ever closer, for at times it was no more than two arm spans wide, and mayhap as much as a thousand feet high.

They came into snow lying in the pass, for the most part quite shallow, though in places deep drifts stood across the way, and there it was Roél broke trail for the steeds, his breath coming harsh with the effort. They reached the crest nigh midday, where a cascade of melt ran down from above, and there they stopped to rest and feed and water the horses and to eat some hardtack and jerky. But shortly they were on their way downward, Roél saying, "I'd rather not stay at these heights in the night, where the cold will plunge beyond withstanding."

Down they went and down, now on the sunwise side of the pass, and water ran freely along the way, dashing down the slopes, and at times they splashed across shallows or waded through the swift-running flow. And still the way wrenched this way and that, and the walls yet soared upward on each side, and at one point they had to unlade the packhorses and hand carry the goods through, the cleft too narrow for the animals to traverse with the supplies upon their backs, and the chill water was deep, hindered by the slot as it was.

At last the walls began to recede, and late in the day they came out from the pass and into wide rolling plains.

Roél glanced back at the twisting slot. "If that were a main thoroughfare, then someone long ago would have placed a high, gated wall somewhere within and charged heavy tolls to pass through."

"At least there was no ambush waiting," said Céleste, now unstringing her bow.

"Non, chérie, there wasn't. It is a splendid place to defend, the way narrow such that a small force could hold off a much greater one. But as a place for an assault, I think it lacks the means for the assailants to spring an ambush upon the unwary traveller; after all, the way is strait and the walls very high, hence giving little chance for waylayers to lunge out from concealment in a surprise onslaught. And, just as a few could hold off many, so, too, could travellers hold off an attack."

"I take it you have been caught in ambushes?"

"Non, but in the war my comrades and I sprang many."

"How is it done?"

"Generally with a surprise attack on the flank," said Roél. "A place is chosen to give the ambushers concealment on high ground, and, if you have archers, divide them into two squads and set them at an angle to one another, and then . . ."

They made camp nigh a stream in a grassy swale in the foothills, and after unlading and currying the horses and feeding and watering them, and eating a meal, Roél and Céleste fell into an exhausted sleep, trusting to the Fates to keep watch o'er them.

The next morning they rested awhile ere making ready to ride, and as they broke fast, Roél said, "I wish we had thought to bring a dog along from Port Cíent, for I think we need a sentry in the night, and none is better than a dog."

"What kind would you have, Roél? A mastiff, a hound, a terrier, what?"

"My love, I think I would take the most nervous animal I could find, no matter the breed."

"Nervous?"

Roél smiled. "What better dog to keep watch than one on edge?"

Céleste broke into laughter. She suddenly sobered and asked, "Is that something you learned in war?"

"In a manner of speaking."

Céleste cocked an eyebrow at Roél, and he said, "When we would send a scout to seek sign of the foe, we always chose the most edgy man among the scouts at hand. For, you see, he would be the most alert to any sound or movement or odor. It seemed a good tactic, for we never lost a single scout, and yet many an enemy group we found. Hence, if it ever comes to a dog to keep watch, I will choose in a like manner."

Céleste grinned and turned up her hands and said, "Ah, 'twould be splendid to have such a noble dog cower at our side, one who trembles and whines at the snap of a twig or twitch of a leaf or the waft of an unexpected scent."

Roél laughed and said, "Better that than one who snores through the night though a dreadful thing be creeping 'pon us." Then he stood and added, "Come, chérie, it is time we were on our way."

They rode out across the rolling plains, where tall grass grew, the air filled with the sweet fragrance of the tiny blue blossoms nodding at the tips of green stems. And as they fared through the lush verdancy, in the angled light of the morning, high in the sky they espied a ruddy flash. 'Twas a raptor sweeping back and forth in the distance.

"A red hawk, do you think?" asked Roél, shading his eyes.

The princess nodded. "Most likely."

They watched the hunter for a while as across the land they rode. And then Céleste took in a quick breath. "Ah, he's sighted quarry."

Even as she said it, the raptor stooped, plummeting down and down, and just above the tops of the tall grass, its wings flared, and it disappeared down within.

Long moments passed, and then up the hawk flew, something small and brown within its taloned grasp.

"Hmm . . . ," said Roél. "We shall have to be careful, love, for I deem that was a marmot it took."

They swung wide of the place where the hawk had made the kill, but even so they came to ground riddled with holes and smelling of a rat warren. Céleste and Roél dismounted, and taking care, they slowly led the horses across the treacherous way, for they would not have one of the steeds step in a hole or break through a tunnel and fracture a leg . . . or go lame. Finally, they passed beyond the marmot burrows and once more mounted and rode.

In the noontide they paused by a river flowing down from the mountains arear, and they watered the animals and fed them a ration of grain. For their own meal they took waybread and jerky. As they ate and watched the river flow by, of a sudden Roél stood and shaded his eyes and peered sunwise.

"What is it, love?" asked Céleste.

"I think I see the twilight boundary," said Roél.

Céleste got to her feet and put a hand to her own brow and looked. In the distance afar, a wall of dimness faded up into the sky. "Oui. It is the shadowlight marge."

"Bon! I was beginning to think we would never reach it. You are familiar with these dusky walls; how far away is it, do you think?"

Céleste shrugged. "That I cannot say. Mayhap we'll reach it this eve. Mayhap on the morrow. We need to be closer to judge."

*   *   *

They forded the river, the water chill, made up of snowmelt as it was, and continued riding half a point sunup of sunwise, for somewhere along that way lay the crossing they sought.

In midafternoon and low on the horizon, they espied a wall of green. "The forest?" asked Roél. "The one the crofter said to avoid?"

"So I deem," said Céleste.

"But it is so broad," said Roél, spreading his arms wide as if to encompass the whole of it. "It runs for league upon league. Does the map say where to enter?"

"Non, chéri, it does not. What we are to look for along the shadowlight wall is an arc of oaks curving out from the bound and 'round and then back in, or so the chart says."

Roél sighed and said, "Then the best we can do is continue riding a half point to the sunup of sunwise, and hope we find it quickly."

They reached the edge of the forest at sunset, and there they made camp, Roél yet wishing he had thought to have brought along a plucky but nervous dog.

That night Roél was awakened by Céleste placing a finger to his lips, and he sat up to see a procession of lights low to the ground and wending among the trees, silver bells atinkle on the air.

"What is it?" he whispered.

"Who is it? is more the question," murmured Céleste. "Most likely the wee folk heading for a fairy ring. 'Tis nigh springtime in this realm, and they would dance the chill away and welcome warmth among the trees."

"But the woods are fully leafed," said Roél. "Is not springtime already come?"

"'Tis Faery, love, where the seasons of the mortal world do not always fully apply. There are realms with green trees and blossoms abloom though winter lies across the land, just as there are domains in winter dress though summertime reigns."

"Only in Faery," muttered Roél.

Slowly the march wended onward, and when it could no longer be seen or heard, Roél glanced at the stars above and said, "I ween 'tis mid of night and my watch is upon us. Sleep, Céleste, and I will stand ward."

"I would rather sit at your side."

"Non, chérie, as much as I love your companionship, you must rest, for dawn will come soon enough."

And so Céleste lay down and soon fell aslumber. Roél listened to her breath deepen, and then he threw another stick on the low-burning fire. He stepped to the horses, standing adoze, and checked the tethers and the animals. Satisfied, he returned to camp and sat down, his back to a tree, and faced into the forest.

How long he sat thus he did not know, but he suddenly realized something was afoot among the boles directly ahead, for he heard faint turning of ground litter, and something low and dark moved stealthily.

Roél took up his sword and waited.

In the blackness of the forest and nigh to the ground a pair of red eyes glowed, and then another pair shone in the dark, creeping nearer. Roél, his heart hammering, reached across to Céleste and gently put a finger to her lips. Silently she came awake, and by the light of ruddy coals, she looked to Roél. "Shh . . .," he murmured. "Something this way comes."

Céleste drew her long-knife, and lay alert, and still the red eyes crept closer, now five pairs altogether.

"Hai!" cried Roél, and leapt to his feet and kicked up the fire.

Startled and shying in the sudden light, a mother fox and her four kits turned tail and fled.

Roél laughed and said, "Ah, me, but the crofter's words of warning of a terrible forest filled with strange goings-on and mystifications have put me on edge."

"Foxes," said Céleste, giggling, her own heart yet arace. "You should have trapped one, love; 'twould make a fine nervous dog."

"Céleste, there is but one edgy dog here, and it be named Roél."

Dawn came at last, and Roél awakened Céleste. Neither had slept well, and both were somewhat glum and untalkative as they fed rations of oats to the steeds. But a meal and a hot cup of tea quickly returned them to good spirits, and they laughed at their reaction to the visit of the foxes in the predawn marks.

Shortly they were on their way again, and Roél asked, "How far to the twilight bound?"

"We should reach it just after the noontide, but then we must find the arc of trees, and I know not how long that will take."

And so on they pressed into the forest, *EF* on their chart.

Through long enshadowed galleries they rode, leafy boughs arching overhead, with dapples of sunlight breaking through in stretches, the radiance adance with the shifting of branches in the breeze. And across bright meadows they fared, butterflies scattering away from legs and hooves. Nigh a cascade falling from a high stone bluff they passed, the water thundering into a pool below, and therein swam something they could not quite see, though the size of a woman or man it was. "Mayhap an Undine," said Céleste, and then went on to explain just what that was.

Roél frowned. "A female water spirit who can earn a soul by marrying a mortal and bearing his child?"

"Oui," said Céleste. "At least that is the myth. In my opinion, though, 'tis but wishful thinking on the part of hierophants and acolytes who would have mankind be the only beings with souls, hence favored by the gods above all other creatures. Yet I believe souls are a part of all living things."

"All?"

"Oui. And some nonliving things as well."

"Such as . . . ?"

"Mountains, rivers, the ocean."

"The ocean?"

"Oui. Vast and deep is its soul."

"Céleste, are you speaking of spirits and not souls?"

Céleste frowned. "Is there a difference?"

"Mayhap; mayhap not. Perhaps they are two sides of the same coin."

"Souls, spirits—whether the same or different, I believe all things possess them."

Roél smiled. "Even Undines?"

"Especially Undines," said Céleste, grinning, "hence I'll not have you volunteer to marry one so that she can obtain a soul."

Roél laughed and then suddenly sobered. "Oh, Céleste, what of those whose shadows have been taken? What of their souls?"

"My love, I believe your sister yet has a soul, though most of it is separate from her."

Roél nodded and said, "And for those children born of a person whose shadow has been taken, Sage Geron says they are soulless."

"Perhaps so; perhaps not. Perhaps each one has a soul that is but a fragment of what it should rightly be. And unless the gods intervene, I know not what can be done for them."

Roél's eyes turned to flint. "Céleste, we simply *must* rescue my sister ere she can bear a child, for I would not have any get of hers to be so stricken."

Céleste nodded and they rode onward in silence, their moods somber.

They fared across a mossy field, and a myriad of white birds flew up and away, flinging apart and then coalescing and swirling away on the wind, each no larger than a lark.

Tree runners scampered on branches above and scolded the passage of these intruders in their domain.

And down among the roots and underbrush, small beings fled unseen.

And as the noontide drew on, Roél said, "Hsst! Ahead, Céleste. Listen."

And they heard someone cursing and muttering, and among the trees, and in a small clearing they espied a stick-thin hag dressed in rags and standing amid a great scatter of dead branches strewn upon the ground. In her knobby fingers she held two pieces of cord close to her faded yellow eyes, and she cursed as she tried to knot the twine together. Beyond the crone stood a small stone cottage with a roof of sod and grass growing thereon. A tendril of smoke rose from a bent chimney.

"Take care," whispered Céleste, loosening the keeper on her long-knife.

"Fear not," replied Roél.

They rode a bit closer, wending among the trees, and when they came to the edge of the clearing, "Ho, madam!" called Roél.

"Oh!" shrieked the hag, and she fell to her knees and held her hands out in a plea. "Don't murder me! Don't rob me! I have nothing of worth. I'm just a poor and widowed old goody." She sniveled and sobbed, mucus dripping from her hooked nose.

"We offer you no harm," said Roél.

"But you have that big sword at your side," said the crone as she glanced at the sun and wiped her nose on her sleeve.

"It will remain sheathed unless danger presents," assured Roél.

"You seem to be in some distress," said Céleste, riding forward.

"My string, my wood," wailed the hag, holding up the cord and gesturing at the scatter of sticks. "How can I cook my meals if I cannot gather wood? And how can I gather wood if I have no string to bind it?"

"Madam, let me help," said Céleste, springing down from her steed.

"Chérie," said Roél, an edge of warning in his voice.

But Céleste took the twine from the hands of the crone and quickly tied it, and then gathered the branches and woody twigs in a pile and swiftly bundled them. "Roél, would you please bear this into yon cote for the widowed goodwife?"

With the frail hag yet on her knees, Roél looked at Céleste and noted the keeper on her long-knife was loose, the weapon ready should there be a need. Sighing, he dismounted, and took up the sheaf and bore it into the cottage. Even as he passed through the door, the goody again glanced at the sun.

"By the mark of the day, I name you Verdandi, I name you Lady Lot, She Who Sees the Everlasting Now," said Céleste.

A shimmer of light came over the hag, and of a sudden there stood a matronly woman with golden eyes and yellow hair, and there came to Céleste's ears the sound of looms weaving.

"Clever, Céleste," said Verdandi. "How did you know? I could just as well have been a witch."

"When we first espied you the sun was just then entering the noontide, neither morning nor afternoon, but in the place between, the time of the Middle of the Three Sisters. And the moment you first glanced at the sun, I became suspicious, for my family somehow seems bound to you Three, and I knew I had to act."

"Ah, no mystery, then?"

"I was not certain until you glanced at the sun a second time. And of course I now see you as you are and I hear the looms."

Verdandi smiled and said, "Perhaps you see me as I truly am, but then again perhaps not. Regardless, I have come to aid you."

"Say on, Lady Lot."

"You must first answer a riddle, for that is a rule we Three live by."

Céleste nodded and said, "Might we wait for Roél?"

"He will not be coming," said Verdandi. "'Tis yours alone to answer, and to you alone will I give my rede."

Céleste sighed. "Ask the riddle, then."

The sound of looms increased, and Verdandi said:

> *"Without being fetched they come at night,*
> *Without being stolen they are lost by day,*
> *Without having wheels, yet they wheel,*
> *It is their name you must say."*

Céleste's heart sank, and she despaired. Oh, no, I'll never *get*— But then, without a moment of pondering, she blurted, "Stars, Lady Lot. Stars. They come at night without being fetched, and are lost by day, and they do wheel through the sky, and so 'stars' is the name I say."

Verdandi laughed. "Princess, did you realize you just now made a rhyme of your own?"

Céleste frowned. "I did? Oh, I see: 'lost by day' and 'the name I say.' I did make a rhyme. —Oh, wait: I merely repeated the rhyming words in the riddle."

Verdandi glanced at the sun riding across the zenith and said, "Child, we must hurry, for I have a rede to speak and some advice to give you as well as a gift."

Unconsciously, Céleste's hand strayed to her chest just above her left breast where a silver needle was threaded through her silk undershirt.

Verdandi nodded and said, "Yes, another gift, one to go with that given you by my elder sister, Skuld."

"Elder? But she is youthful and—"

"Hush, child. Ask Camille; she will explain it."

Verdandi again glanced at the sun and once more the sound of looms swelled, and she said:

> *"Difficult tests will challenge you*
> *At places along the way;*
> *You and your love must win them all,*
> *Else you will not save the day.*

"Ask directions unto his tower
In the Changeling Lord's domain;
The answers given will be true,
Yet the givers must be slain.

"Until the sister is set free,
With runed blade wielded by hand
Kill all those who therein do speak;
Question not; you'll understand."

Céleste's eyes widened. "Kill all who speak?"

Verdandi's face fell grim. "You know I cannot answer, Céleste. Yet this I will tell you for nought: blunt half of your arrows, for you will need them . . . both to kill and to not kill."

"But Lady Lot, I do not understand," said Céleste.

"Heed me, you will," said Verdandi. Again she glanced at the sun, and the thud of batten and the clack of shuttle swelled, and Verdandi said, "Here, you will need these," and she stretched out her hand, something gleaming held in her fingers.

Céleste reached forth, and Verdandi dropped the gift into her palm, and in that moment the trailing limb of the sun left the zenith, and the sound of weaving looms vanished, as did Lady Lot and the sod-roofed cottage as well.

"What th—?" Roél stood in the middle of the grassy clearing, his arms curled as if holding a bundle of branches, but he embraced only empty air.

Céleste frowned down at the gift she held: a pair of golden tweezers, their tips so rounded they would be hard-pressed to grasp anything.

20

Qualms

"Lady Lot? The crone was Lady Lot?"

"Oui, though she changed from a crone to a matron." Roél looked back at the place where the sod-roofed cottage had stood, where now was nought but the glade. Sighing, he said, "First Lady Wyrd and now Lady Lot. I suppose next it will be Lady Doom." He shook his head. "My love, it is as you say: you and your family are somehow involved in the intrigues of the Three Sisters."

"All mankind is caught up their weavings, though in my case—hence, yours as well, Roél—it seems they take a more direct hand."

"And this was Verdandi," said Roél, his words not a question.

"Oui," said Céleste, "and she gave me these." The princess handed over the golden tweezers.

Roél took the Fate-given gift and clicked together the smooth, rounded ends. Perplexity filled his eyes. "Skuld gave you a silver needle, and now Verdandi, golden pincers; whatever for? I wonder." He handed them back to the princess.

"She gave me a rede as well, along with some advice."

"Advice?"

"Oui. She told me to blunt half my arrows so as to kill and to not kill."

"To kill and to not kill? What kind of advice is that?"

Céleste shrugged. "I know not, chéri, yet I will follow it. Surely it will come clear."

"And the rede . . . ?"

"Ah, that. It seems quite straightforward in places and totally horrifying in others."

"Say it, love, and we will puzzle it out together."

Céleste smiled. "Just as we puzzled out the first rede, eh?"

Roél laughed. "Perhaps we can do better with this one."

Céleste nodded and said, "Oh, unlike the first rede, I believe there is not much mystery as to just what we must do. Yet it is, as I say, quite horrifying."

"Horrifying?"

"Oui. List:

"Difficult tests will challenge you
At places along the way;
You and your love must win them all,
Else you will not save the day.

"Ask directions unto his tower
In the Changeling Lord's domain;
The answers given will be true,
Yet the givers must be slain.

"Until the sister is set free,
With runed blade wielded by hand
Kill all those who therein do speak;
Question not; you'll understand."

Roél's eyes widened in shock. "Kill all who speak?"

"Oui. That's what Lady Lot said."

"And slay those who give us guidance?"

"Oui."

Roél shook his head. "In war I left slaughter in my wake. I do not relish doing so again."

"Nevertheless, it seems we must," said Céleste.

"Nay, love, 'tis not we who must do so, but only I instead, for Lady Lot's words say it must be done with a runed blade, and that means Coeur d'Acier."

Céleste turned up her hands and asked, "Then why did she tell me that I should blunt my arrows?"

"Did she not say 'half your arrows'?"

"Half, all, still the question is why."

Roél shrugged.

They stood without speaking for a moment, and then Roél said, "At least the first stanza seems clear. We will face many tests along the way, and those we must overcome."

"Roél, she said that we must win them all. We cannot lose even one. Else we will not save the day, and by that I think she means we will not save your sister and brothers."

Roél touched the hilt of his sword and said, "With my blade and shield and spear and horse, I have bested many a challenger."

"Oui, Roél, you have. Yet what if the test is not one of combat, but a test of another kind: riddles, games, puzzles, foot races, feats of strength, of skill, and the like?"

"Oh," said Roél, illumination filling his face. "I see." He shook his head in rue. "Ah, me. Ever the knight. Ready with arms and armor, ready to enter the lists; yet these might be lists of another sort."

Céleste smiled. "Indeed, yet recall, in the rede Verdandi said 'You and your love must win them all,' which means the two of us together will have a chance to prevail."

"Or each of us separately," said Roél.

"There is that," said Céleste, nodding.

"The second stanza in the rede seems clear as well," said Roél. "We must ask directions to the Changeling Lord's tower, and then slay those who respond."

"But only in the Changeling Lord's domain," cautioned Céleste.

Roél frowned, "Why say you that?"

"Because, Roél, I think if we get guidance from someone outside his domain, then we do not have to slay that person. Hear me: does not the third stanza of the rede say 'Kill all therein who speak'? And I deem that means all within the Changeling Lord's domain, as is stated in the second stanza. I do not believe the rede intends for us to kill all who give guidance if they are not in that realm. I mean, if that were so, then we should have killed Florien, and I would have refused to do so."

Roél frowned and said, "It is not clear, Céleste, for the second stanza tells us to 'Ask directions unto his tower in the Changeling Lord's domain,' and that *might* mean we need ask directions whether or not we are in his domain, and to slay those who answer. But on the other hand, it *might* also tell us to ask directions *when* we are in his domain, and only then to kill those who answer."

Céleste nodded and said, "As usual, the redes of the Three Sisters are ambiguous."

Roél pondered for long moments and finally said, "I ween you are right, Céleste, for to interpret it as I did at first meant we would have had to slay Florien, for he certainly aided us."

Céleste sighed and said, "Yet, Roél, we did not ask Florien for directions to the Changeling Lord's *tower,* but only to the lord's domain."

Roél slammed a fist into a palm. "Ah, Mithras! Why cannot the Fates speak plainly?"

Céleste turned up a hand and grinned. "But then what would be the challenge in that?"

Agape, Roél looked at her, and then he broke into laughter, his frustration evaporating. He stepped forward, took her in his embrace, and kissed her forehead—"I love you"—and eyes—"I love you"—and nose and finally her lips. "Oh, yes, my chérie, I do love you dearly."

They stood for a time holding one another and savoring the moment, but at last Céleste said, "Come, my handsome, let us find the arc of oaks."

As they mounted up, Roél said, "Mayhap one day I will get to meet one of the Three Sisters, and then I will ask why they do not speak clearly so that there is no question as to just what they mean."

Céleste laughed and said, "I think any answer you get will be a riddle itself."

Smiling, a half point sunup of sunwise, they rode onward toward the twilight bound.

"Well, here is the marge," said Roél, "but no arc of oaks."

Céleste shrugged and said, "We've come a long way; hence it is no surprise to me that we might have veered a bit off course. In fact, I would have been shocked had we ridden straightaway to the very point of crossing."

Roél nodded and said, "As would I."

Céleste raised her trump and said, "I have my horn; you have yours. I'll ride this way; you that. Three sharp calls upon finding the arc. Oui?"

"Oui," replied Roél. "Yet should you find foe instead and cannot slip away unseen, then sound repeated calls as you flee."

"Ah, oui," said Céleste, stringing her bow and nocking an arrow. "I assume you will do the same should you meet foe instead of charging in. Remember, chéri, I am rather good with this thing."

Roél laughed and cocked his crossbow and set a quarrel in the groove, and then he turned his horse rightward and rode away along the twilight wall.

Turning to the left, Céleste rode sunupward, her tethered pack animal following.

She wended among trees of oak and evergreen, of maple and elm, and of other varieties, and the fragrance of cedar and yew and pine wafted on the breeze. She splashed across streams flowing into the twilight, and as usual she wondered where they went when they crossed the border, for it seemed they never continued past the bound, or if they did, it was at some other bound they emerged. It was as if Faery was once a whole world, with no twilight boundaries at all, and streams and oceans and lands were the same as in the mortal realm. But then the gods interfered and placed the shadowlight walls where they would, and when folk stepped across, they did not go unto the very next place, but were whisked somewhere else altogether, or so Céleste and her brothers and sister had always speculated. Borel as a child had once suggested that they put red dye in a stream flowing into a bound and see where it came out, but that would call for knowing where the stream would emerge, and if they knew that, then the mystery would have already been resolved. So, the question remained: without being aware of it, did one get instantly borne to another place when crossing a marge, or instead was there a wholly different realm lying directly beyond? Céleste did not know. *Ah, me, but these twilight bounds are truly Faery struck.*

She was musing thus when from a distance there came three sharp clarion calls. *Ah, my handsome knight has found the arc.*

Céleste turned her steed about, the packhorse following, and sundownward she rode. A league or so in this direction she found Roél waiting within an arc of oak trees, and she wondered if the circle completed itself in some distant domain.

As Céleste rode to his side, "Should we tie a rope to me and let me cross over and see if the way is safe?" asked Roél.

"'Twould be best if I went," said Céleste, "for I am lighter and you are stronger. Even so, I think the map would not show this as a crossing if it were unsafe."

"Nevertheless . . . ?" said Roél.

In moments they had a line cinched about Céleste's waist, a good length in Roél's hand. Céleste then kissed Roél and said, "Let us give it a try," and into the twilight they strode, Céleste with her bow strung, an arrow nocked, and a quiver at her hip.

Dimmer it got the farther they went until finally they could see nought, so utter was the dark. Céleste paused and said, "Wait here and pay out the line."

Roél found her face in the blackness and kissed her again, and then he stepped back and arranged the line and finally said, "Ready?"

"Ready," she replied.

"Then go, chérie, but be careful."

Now Céleste stepped cautiously forward, and Roél, from the coil lying on the ground behind and with the rope over one shoulder and 'round the opposite leg as if he were rappelling, slipped the line and gave her slack and then added slack as she moved away. More he fed and more, as into the ebon wall she stepped. And of a sudden, the rope jerked taut, yanking Roél from his feet and dragging him after.

21

Memorial

Benumbed with grief, Borel and Michelle, Alain and Camille, Liaze and Luc, and King Valeray and Queen Saissa all sat in a drawing room in Springwood Manor, waiting for the mark when the service would begin. Hierophant Georges would preside, a tall and somber man. But for the nonce they sat alone, shielded from the sorrow of all others who had come—the retinues of the Winterwood, Autumnwood, and Summerwood, and that of the king—as well as from the heartache of the Springwood staff.

They sat for long moments without speaking, each wrapped in thoughts unshared.

Finally Camille said, "Alain and I think I might be with child."

Even this news brought nought more than a slight glimmer of gladness to the gathering.

"When will you know?" asked the queen.

"By the next full moon, I should think," replied Camille. But then silence fell and the glumness had returned.

The king sat with his foot propped up and in a tight wrap from toes to knee. "Damned horse," he said, peering at it.

"How?" asked Liaze.

"Eh?"

"How did you hurt your ankle?"

"He broke it, dear," said Saissa.

"Not I," said Valeray. "'Twas the horse that fell on me, not I on him."

"Still, how?" asked Liaze, seeking anything to take her mind from the matter at hand.

"He was trying to jump a rock wall," said Saissa.

"Well, that's where the stag went," said Valeray, huffing.

"Ah," said Liaze.

There came a light tap on the door, and tall, spare, silver-haired Vidal stepped in. "They are ready," he said quietly.

Alain sighed and stood, offering an arm to Camille. And so they all stood, Valeray using crutches to aid him along the way.

Out to the lawn they went, out to an arbor. And gathered in the garden before the vine-laden latticework were all retinues and staff.

When the kindred were seated, and after a short opening prayer to Mithras by Hierophant Georges, Prince Borel, eldest of the siblings, took stance behind a small lectern. And even before he began to speak, a soft weeping filled the air.

Tears ran down Borel's face, and nearby his Wolves whined in uncertainty; they cast about, seeking the cause of the woe besetting their master but finding none.

"Friends, family, loved ones," began Borel, "even though she was the youngest of us, my sister Céleste was the most headstrong. Always did she seek a challenge, and for that we loved her. Perhaps it was to show us that she could hold her own against Alain and Liaze and me, and hold her own she did, yet I think it was in her nature to—"

A distant horn cry interrupted Borel's words.

He frowned and looked toward the far woods.

Again sounded the horn, and bursting out from among the trees came a rider, a remount in tow. Across the sward galloped the stranger, and he wore the tabard of a king, but just which king it was—

"'Tis Avélar's man," said Valeray.

Once more sounded the horn, and up galloped the youth. He leapt from his steed and called, "A message from Vicomte Chevell."

The lad strode forward, and his gaze swept over the gathering, for all their faces were turned toward him. He then saw Giselle, her own face puffed and her eyes and nose red with weeping, and the youth frowned in puzzlement.

Now he saw Steward Vidal, as well as Armsmaster Anton, yet in spite of his instructions, he gave over the message to Prince Borel, whom he also recognized.

"We're having a memorial here, son," said Vidal quietly.

"Oh, my, I did not mean to interrupt," replied Quint.

Just then there came a whoop from Borel. "She's alive!" he cried, holding the letter aloft. "She and Roél did not drown after all, but landed on a ship instead!"

What? cried some, *Alive?* cried others, but most shouted in glee.

"I'm going to wring her neck," muttered Liaze, embracing Luc, tears of relief and joy running down her face.

22

Captive

Of a sudden the rope went slack, as if it had been snapped in two. Roél scrambled to his feet and drew in the line, only to find a frayed end. With his heart hammering in dread for Céleste, he disentangled himself and unsheathed Coeur d'Acier, and drawing the rope behind in case of need, he stepped through the ebon wall, wanting to run in haste, wanting to yell out her name, but moving carefully and silently instead.

Lighter grew the twilight, and then he was free of the bound. At his feet lay Céleste's bow as well as a scatter of arrows.

And in the distance he saw . . .

. . . he saw . . .

. . . the back of a retreating, fur-draped Ogre, a being fully twenty-five or thirty feet tall and bearing Céleste over one shoulder.

"Céleste!" cried Roél, but she did not respond, and at the sound of the shout the Ogre sped up, now loping toward stony crags beyond.

"Céleste!" Roél cried again, but the princess lay limp, as if unconscious.

Knowing afoot he would never catch the Ogre, Roél slammed his sword into its scabbard and snatched up the bow and arrows and turned and sped back through the twilight. Quickly he ran to the horses and slipped the bow into Céleste's saddle scabbard and the arrows into the saddle quiver, and using the retrieved line, he tethered her mount to his own pack animal. Then he leapt astride his horse and spurred forward, drawing the other steeds behind, and into the twilight he rode.

Darker it got and he passed through ebon, and then lighter it became, and he emerged from the twilight and into day. Ahead he looked, and left, and right, but the fur-clad Ogre and his prize had vanished.

Roél cantered forward, now scanning the ground for tracks, and he rode in a line toward where last he saw the monstrous being. Almost immediately he came upon great swaths of flattened grasses some eight or ten feet apart, there where the Ogre had stepped.

Following these dents, Roél spurred to a gallop, and soon the impressions came some fifteen or twenty feet apart, for Roél now rode along the track where the Ogre had been loping.

As he came in among the crags, Roél cocked and loaded his crossbow, and on into the rock-laden land fared the knight. Yet the ground was stony, and he had to slow to a walk, for he would not have any of the horses lamed.

And the easy tracks vanished, and now Roél had to follow traces where the Ogre's feet had turned up rocks, leaving fresh hollows behind, or the dark of stones where they had long lain with one side unseen by the sun but now were flipped over and exposed.

In places he had to dismount and cast about for spoor. He found an impression here, and an overturned slab there, and a slip of sand yet faintly trickling down. He was nigh in tears, and he cursed at the slowness of his progress, and his heart hammered in dread for his beloved, for the tales told that Ogres were man-eaters.

With his mind racing 'round all of the terrible things that might be visited upon her, Roël walked forward, his crossbow in hand, the horses plodding after.

And then he lost the track altogether.

Céleste came groggily awake as the Ogre reached into a stony crevice and pushed a great boulder in and aside to expose a cavern beyond. As she began regaining her full senses, she tried to get up from the ground and flee, but the moment she lurched to her feet, the monstrous being took her up, and on one hand and his knees, he crawled into a vast chamber beyond. He set her down and rolled the huge stone back into place. Light leaked in 'round the edges of the boulder, but Céleste saw that the crevices were too small for her to squeeze through. The cavern itself was lit with a reddish glimmer from embers somewhere within. In the dull scarlet gloom, Céleste heard a striker scrape, and then the glow from a large lantern filled the place. A huge chair and table loomed up in the shadows nigh the center of the lit chamber. Against one stone wall stood an enormous bed, and thereon a monstrous straw mattress and a jumble of blankets lay awry. A massive chest rested at the foot of the bed. Some thirty or so feet out from the opposite wall of the cavern sat an open-pit fireplace, ruddy embers within, and in the stone ceiling high above a jagged crevice acted as a smoke hole. Nearby lay shattered tree limbs and broken logs of oak, birch, maple, cherry, walnut, and the like with which to feed the fire. Beyond, lay a clutter of splintered bones from meals long past. Great copper pots and pans sat on an immense sideboard, along with huge utensils—knives, spoons, cleavers, and such. In midchamber a stone ring marked a wide well; a large bucket and a long rope testified to water below.

Céleste shook her head to dispel the dregs of her muzziness. The last thing she remembered was being snatched up by the heels just as she emerged from the twilight boundary, and there was a painful lump on the back of her skull, where it had hit the ground. She was sore 'round her waist, and there the rope was yet cinched. She discovered the line had been broken off short, with no more than ten feet remaining. *The Ogre must have snapped the rope in two when he found I was tied to someone or something. Ah, when I was grabbed, Roél was yet— Roél! Is he—? Did the Ogre—?*

The Ogre hung the lantern on a wall hook and then turned and leered down at her and rumbled, "Give up all hope, for your companion will not find you here."

My companion. That must mean Roél is yet safe.

Quickly, Céleste took stock. *No bow, empty quiver, but wait, I yet have my long-knife; even so, what can such a small pick do against this monstrous foe . . . ?*

She looked up at the huge creature. He was hairy and un-kempt, and he had a beard that reached down to his belt. Some of his teeth were missing, and those that were left were stained a scummy green. His breath smelled rancid, and it was clear he hadn't had a bath in months, if ever. "Why have you taken me hostage?" demanded Céleste.

"Hostage?" he boomed. "Ha! I want no hostage."

"Has a witch anything to do with this?"

"Witch?" The Ogre's eyes widened, and Céleste thought she caught a glimpse of fear within. "What have you to do with a witch?"

Céleste frowned. *If he is a friend of Hradian, or Nefasí, then he might turn me over to one of them. But if he is a foe, then he might aid me. On the other hand, he might slay me outright just for knowing their names. Mayhap I should remain silent as to the acolyte sisters.*

"I wondered if you were the thrall of a witch," said Céleste.

"Thrall? Me?" sneered the Ogre. "I, Lokar, am no one's thrall."

"Then why have you taken me prisoner?" Céleste demanded.

"If it is for ransom, then—"

The Ogre roared in laughter. "Ransom? Pah! I want no ransom."

"Then why?"

"To be my servant, my slave." But then Lokar's eyes filled with puzzlement. "Wait. Your voice is high-pitched." He leaned down for a clearer look. "Ah, in spite of your clothes, you are no man, but a woman instead." Again he roared in laughter and said, "You will be my wife!"

"Your wife?"

The Ogre nodded. "To cook and sew and keep the cavern clean, and to sing to me . . . and pleasure me in other ways as well."

Disgust filled Céleste's face. "Pleasure you in other ways?" Lokar reached under his hides and grabbed at his crotch and joggled his hand. "Here."

Céleste turned away in revulsion. But then her eyes widened in horror. *Mithras! His manhood will split me in twain. I've got to find a way to escape.*

"Cook for me while I rest," Lokar harshly commanded.

"After I eat, you can then pleasure me."

I must find a way out. And to do that I need to delay.—Wait! The fire. Smoke. Perhaps Roël will see. Then she looked at the wood and despaired. Oh, no. Hardwoods. Clean-burning hardwoods.

In spite of her desolation, "I will need pots and pans and the makings for whatever you wish to eat," said Céleste, bidding for time.

"Bah, there is already stew in the cauldron. All you need to do is stir it."

"Then set it on the fire and give me the ladle," said Céleste.

* * *

Among the crags Roél wound in an ever-widening spiral, or as close to a spiral as he could manage, for ridges and bluffs barred the way. 'Twas midafternoon and still he had found no sign of tracks, but for those he and his horses made. Roél looked up and about. *The Ogre could have stepped straight over some of these ridges and gone another way. Think, Roél, think! Which way would he have gone? Which way?—Wait! Go back to the last known trace of him and cross over yourself.*

Roél returned to a place where a slope of sand had been disturbed, the trickle of its slide now long spent. He looked up at the ridges on each side of the rocky slot and decided that one of them was low enough for the monstrous being to step across. Leaving the horses, Roél climbed up the fold and down the other side.

Sweeping back and forth across the stony floor beyond, at last he came to a recently overturned rock. Quickly he climbed back over the slope and down, and he took his mount by the reins, and he led the animals back to a low dip in the fold.

"The last wife I had knew how to give me joy. She would cover herself and my stiff pole with oil, and she would embrace it and . . ."

Céleste tried to shut out Lokar's voice as he sickeningly regaled her with how she was to "pleasure" him. Her thoughts were desperate: *I've got to find a way to escape. But how? Oh, Roél, where are you?*

She dragged two logs from the pile and cast them on the coals. As the fire blazed up she took the ladle in hand and began stirring the stew within the cauldron.

Lokar watched for a moment and then moved to the table and sat idling with dark tiles of some sort, and he continued to tell her just what she was to do: "And then you can use your tongue and . . ."

Céleste refused to listen, and even as she stirred, the ladle struck something hard, and then it surfaced. *What's this? A row of teeth glinted in the lantern light, and then rolled in the stew, and bone was revealed. Is that someone's jaw? Oh, Mithras, it is! It is a jaw!* Céleste cast a glance at the litter of splintered bones beyond the woodpile. *Human! They are all human bones. Or if not human, then humanlike.*

" . . . but in my pleasure I made the mistake of grabbing her, and . . ."

Céleste looked at the Ogre and gritted her teeth. *I've got to find a way to stop this monster.*

As Lokar continued to idle with the tiles, he went on talking of being pleasured.

"Are those pips?" asked Céleste.

Lokar looked up from the tiles. "Do you know the game?"

"My brothers and I play at times."

"As I eat," said Lokar, "you will be my opponent and learn that I am a master at pips. Then afterward you will delight me."

As Céleste stirred the cauldron, using the ladle much the same as if she were plying an oar, her mind raced: *Mithras, but how will I avoid "pleasuring" him?*

Then she remembered an ancient fable, and she struck on a plan. "Have you any wine?" she asked in all innocence. "I would flavor the stew."

Once again Roél climbed a ridge, up the near side and down the far. And in the stony vale beyond he moved along the slot, first one way and then the other, and he swept back and forth; this time he found nought. He crossed back over the ridge and climbed the fold opposite. And there an impression of a gigantic toe in a low swale pointed the way. He followed as soon as he had retrieved the horses, for he and Céleste might have to flee upon the mounts, once he had rescued her . . . or so was his intention.

*   *

*   *

"Aha!" roared Lokar. "Again I win."

"You are a master indeed," said Céleste, "but I think I will win the next one."

"Pah, woman! Do . . . do you . . . do you not by now understand I am far and away your s-superior?"

Céleste pointed at the great, foot-long tiles and said, "We shall see, Lokar. We shall see. Shuffle the tiles, while I pour more wine and refresh your bowl."

Lokar had eaten nearly the entire cauldron of stew, including crunching through long bones for the marrow, and through spines for the matter within, and he had drunk almost an entire cowhide full of wine. Groggily, he pushed the face-down tiles around on the table, while Céleste used one of the huge cups rather like a bucket to fill Lokar's wine goblet to the brim and then hefted more meat-and-bone stew into his great bowl.

Roél despaired, for the sun had set, and in spite of the light of the nearly full moon and that of the lantern he bore, he could not find the subtle signs of spoor. He sighed and finally made camp at the last trace of track that he had found. He unladed the steeds and curried and watered and fed them and took a meal of his own, though he had no appetite. Even so, he knew he needed to eat, for that was one of the lessons of war: eat when you can, and rest when you can, for you never know when the opportunity will come again.

Lokar pushed back his chair and wobbled to his bed. "Now you will pleasure me," he slurred as he shed the animal hides clothing him and stood naked and filthy and blearily looked down at Céleste. And then he fell backwards onto the mattress and immediately began to snore, his feet yet on the rough cavern floor.

Though his manhood hung limp, Céleste gasped at the monstrous thing. *Mithras, had he tried to bed me, I would be lying dead.*

She stepped to the woodpile and took up a sturdy billet, and then walked back to the bed and set it down. Then back to the fire pit she went, and drew her long-knife and shoved the blade into the red coals. Then she dragged one of the empty cauldrons over to the bed and upended it to use as a step to reach the mattress. Next, she upended a cook pot to use as a stool to climb onto the cauldron. With her stair built, she picked up the billet of wood and clambered up onto the cauldron. Across a blanket crawling with vermin she went, and she laid the wood down near Lokar's head.

Back off the mattress she climbed and went to the fire, and there she withdrew her long-knife from the coals, the two-foot-long blade radiant with heat.

Swiftly she ran across the floor and scrambled up onto the cook pot and then the cauldron and finally the bed; across the blanket she trod, where she took up the wooden billet and moved to stand at Lokar's cheek.

The Ogre yet snored.

Céleste positioned the point of the long-knife just in front of his right eye, and angled the blade, and raised the billet . . . and hesitated. Of a sudden, the Ogre ceased snoring, and he opened his eyes, and gasped.

With sharp blow of the wooden billet Céleste drove the red-hot blade through Lokar's eye and into his brain, the blade sizzling as it was quenched in his head.

The Ogre cried out and lurched up and fell back, and then his air left him in one long sigh, and he breathed no more. And his bladder and bowels loosed, and liquid and slurry splashed to the floor, and a great stench filled the chamber.

Gagging in the stink of urine and feces and burning flesh, Céleste reeled hindward, and turned and fled and scrambled down from the bed. Even as her feet touched the floor, she retched again and again . . . but no vomit came, only a thin, yellowish bile.

And she wept, for she had never before slain someone in his sleep or even in near sleep and perhaps would never do so again, no matter how vile.

Still sobbing, she strode to the great boulder blocking the exit. And there she confirmed that she could not squeeze past it to the outside. Nor could she roll it aside.

Along with his massive corpse, she was trapped in the Ogre's cave.

23

Escape

Céleste stepped to the woodpile and took up a length of sturdy limb to use as a lever, and she bore it back to the boulder blocking the door. She set one end in between the edge of the massive stone and the cavern wall and pried with all of her might . . . to no avail.

Next she sat with her back to the wall and placed her feet against the limb, and braced as she was, she tried to use her leg strength to roll the boulder. The limb flexed, but the boulder moved not.

Perhaps if I had a fulcrum . . .

She fetched a thick billet from the woodpile, and as close to the boulder as she could lodge it, she jammed the log upright between limb and wall. She moved to the far end of her improvised lever and pushed with all of her strength, trying to nudge the weight away . . . again to no avail.

With tears of frustration blurring her vision, she walked back into the cavern, and wiping her eyes, she examined the walls for a crevice or rift that would lead to freedom, but she found nought.

196

locket by its broken chain and held it up and said, "I have here the proof. Now go, Sauville, go!"

The small man rushed from the office, and for moments quietness reigned, though shouts from the street began breaking the silence. Finally, after one more look at the portraits, the mayor slipped the keepsake into his pocket. "Princess, my captain said you wish to see our armorer. Was your long-knife damaged when you slew Lokar? If so, we will gladly replace it."

"Non. My long-knife is quite satisfactory. Instead, I would have Monsieur Galdon blunt half my arrows."

Breton glanced at Roél and then back to Céleste. "Blunt half your arrows? Whatever for?"

Céleste shrugged. "Whatever for? That, Monsieur Breton, I do not know."

*

The news of Lokar's death hurtled throughout Le Bastion. Impromptu celebrations erupted. An innkeeper offered Roél and Céleste his very best rooms, but the mayor would have none of that, and instead put them up in his own modest residence. Armorer Galdon was fetched, and shaking his head, he took away half of Céleste's arrows to refit them with blunt ends.

Céleste retrieved the silver needle and golden tweezers, and then she and Roél gave over their leathers and undergarments to the mayor's staff to be cleaned. And the princess and her knight luxuriated in hot baths, and drank fine wine, and stuffed themselves with hot beef and steaming goose and savory gravy and onions and bread and artichokes and mushrooms and other such delicacies.

That evening, crowds gathered before the mayor's residence, and they called for Céleste and Roél to make speeches, and to repeat the story of the slaying of Lokar.

Long into the night did the revels last. As for the two heroes, they climbed into a soft bed, and the moment their heads

Taking a burning brand from the fire, she peered into the well . . . and water glimmered some forty or fifty feet below. Yet it stood still. *It does not flow; hence perhaps is not a stream leading out from this prison.*

Up at the smoke hole above she looked, and then examined the walls and the ceiling leading that way, but she saw no cracks or protrusions by which she could reach that cleft without climbing aids.

All I have is ten feet of rope— No, wait, there is also the rope on the well bucket. Even so, I have no pitons or jams, hence no way up unless I can improvise.

Céleste moved to the trunk at the foot of the Ogre's cot. She studied it a moment, and then stepped back to her improvised stair and climbed up. Holding her breath, for here the stench was strongest, she climbed up and onto the bed and strode past the corpse and to the chest. Using her length of rope tied to the hasp, after a struggle she managed to haul the lid back, where she tied it to the foot of the bed, and scrambled down into the trunk.

Inside she found clothing of a size for ordinary people, along with goods suitable for travel—rucksacks, flint and steel, tinderboxes, knives, a bow, arrows, some feminine supplies, a cutthroat razor, a jar of salve of some sort, and other such paraphernalia.

Oh, my, these are the possessions of Lokar's victims.

A glint caught her eye, and she took up an argent heart-shaped locket on a broken silver chain. She opened the leaves and inside and facing one another were small painted portraits in profile of a handsome, dark-haired man and a beautiful, red-headed woman. She snapped the locket shut and started to lay it aside, but on impulse she slipped it into her pocket.

She continued to search through the goods, finding combs and mirrors and various herbs and simples and boots and undergarments and scarves and other such fare, but she found no climbing gear.

Clambering out of the chest and crossing the chamber, Céleste scaled up to the top of the sideboard and examined the utensils there—huge spoons, knives, cleavers—none of which offered a way to reach the smoke hole high above the open-pit fire. Weary with defeat and needing sleep, Céleste sighed and sat down.

Oh, Roél, my Roél, where are you?

By lamplight and firelight, she surveyed the cavern for something she might have overlooked. Beyond the fire, beyond the well, a massive corpse lay on a bed.

And then she knew what she would do, and she lay down to sleep.

Roél was up before dawn, and he fed the horses and watered them and then took a meal of his own as he watched the sky slowly gain light.

Céleste, my love, are you even yet ali— Roél, stop that! She has to be alive. Oh, Mithras, please, Mithras, let it be so.

He saddled the steeds and laded the packhorses even as the sun broached the horizon, and he examined the stony floor where yester he had lost the track.

Nothing!

Sighing, he climbed the ridge on the left and down into the slot below. Once more he swept back and forth, seeking spoor— an overturned rock, an imprint of some sort, anything that would show him the way. Along the floor he went, sunwise and then starwise, but nought did he find.

Back up the ridge he clambered, and at the top he slowly turned about.

Céleste, oh, Céleste, where are—; Wait! What's that? Oh, Mithras, it must be her!

Quickly Roél scrambled down from the ridge and ran to the horses, and he leapt astride his mount and spurred away, the other animals in tow.

* * *

Hacking, coughing in spite of the wet cloth covering her mouth and nose, Céleste poured water upon the great armload of straw she had ripped from the mattress. She then cast it onto the fire where other wetted straw now burned, releasing dark smoke up toward the hole above, though it also filled the cavern.

At least it somewhat covers the reek of the dead Ogre.

Back to the straw-filled mattress she trod, where she tore out more of the bedding, and she carried it to the well.

Once again she tossed Lokar's rope-tied goblet into the shaft, for the drinking vessel served as her pail, the Ogre's wooden bucket too massive for her to use. She drew up the goblet and dipped her improvised mask into the water and then retied it around her nose and mouth. Then she wetted the straw.

She took it to the fire and set it aside.

Wood. I need more wood. Can't let the straw smother the burn.

To the woodpile she went, and took up an armful and headed back to the fire pit.

Even as she knelt to jam branches into the coals, a rope came snaking down from above.

Céleste leapt to her feet. *Oh, Mithras, please let it be.*

She grabbed the end of the line to keep it out of the fire.

She pulled away her wetted mask and cried, "Roél! Roél!"

There was no answer.

She stood, her heart in her throat, and moments later a figure came sliding down through the dark smoke.

It was Roél.

Even as his feet touched the floor, he reached for Coeur d'Acier, but he could not draw it, so fierce was Céleste's embrace.

And she wept, as did he.

"I thought I had lost you," whispered Roél.

And she hugged him all the harder.

And he kissed her and kissed her again—her eyes, her cheeks, her throat, her lips—and she mastered her sobbing long enough to take his face in her hands and fervently kiss him on the mouth, and then she laid her head against his chest and quietly wept again.

And Roél looked through the smoke and 'round the chamber.

"The Ogre, by the smell of it, is he—?"

"Dead," said Céleste, her voice small. "I slew him."

"You slew him?" Roél's eyes widened in astonishment.

"Oui." She looked up at him. "Oh, Roél, let us flee, for I do not wish to spend another moment in this dreadful place."

"Oui, chérie," said Roél. "Indeed, let us leave." He looked about.

"We need to climb," said Céleste, disengaging, "for a great boulder blocks the way."

"Up through the smoke, then," said Roél, grinning, and he pulled the wet, smoldering straw from the fire to diminish the column somewhat, and then he gestured for her to begin.

Céleste grabbed the rope, and even as she looked above, "Wait," she said, and she turned and ran back to the bed. Up she clambered and onto the cot, and strode to the cheek of the Ogre. And there she grasped the hilt of her long-knife and pulled it free. "This will teach you, Lokar, to leave princesses be."

She wiped the blade clean against his beard and sheathed and secured the weapon. Down from the bed she scrambled and back to Roél, and, together, Céleste first, Roél coming after, up the rope they went.

24

Warband

Back in the drawing room, Borel passed the letter 'round, and all read Céleste's words:

My dears:

I hope this finds all in good health and spirits, and I pray to Mithras that Anton and the warband came through the battle unscathed, though I fear some took wounds. If so, please keep them safe, and give them the best of care.

As for Roél and me, when we fled from the attack of the Redcaps and Bogles and Trolls, we escaped through the twilight border on the sunwise bound of my demesne. As you know, that bound is perilous, and perhaps we gave you a scare. You might have thought we drowned, since there is nought but ocean where we crossed. Yet when Roél and I eluded pursuit through that dusky marge, we fell (no doubt thanks to the Fates) upon a passing ship, the Sea Eagle, captained by Vicomte Chevell, a former colleague of Papa's (as the Fates would have it). Strangely enough, he happened to be after the very same chart Roël and I and Anton and the warband had gone to see (here again, I deem the Fates were involved). The map had been stolen by rovers who raided Port Mizon (as it turned out, it was the Changeling Lord himself who had arranged for the pirates to steal the chart).

To shorten this letter let me merely say we managed to recover the map, and I made a copy of a key part of it, the section that shows the way to the Changeling realm (and I deem this is why the Changeling Lord wanted the chart taken, for he would prevent those whose loved ones had been stolen from finding their way unto him).

Regardless, by the time you read this, know that Roël and I will be well on our way to rescue his sister, Avélaine, and his brothers, Laurent and Blaise. Pray to Mithras that we get there before mid of night on the night of the dark of the moon, else Avélaine is doomed.

Do not fret, for know we are hale and in good spirits, and we deem the Fates are with us. Know as well that you are in our thoughts.

With love, Tremain,
Céleste
Princesse de la Forêt de Printemps

"By Mithras, we must do something," declared Valeray. "We cannot just idly sit by and let them face the bloody Changeling Lord by themselves."

"I agree," said Borel.

"We have elements of our warbands with us," said Alain, "as well as the full Springwood warband at our behest. That makes a formidable force."

"Oui," said Luc, "yet the dark of the moon is but a fortnight hence, which gives us little time. I say we gather remounts for all and ride to Port Mizon."

"Mizon?" asked Saissa. "Why th—? Oh, I see: Mizon is where lies the map, and you will need a copy to find your own way."

"Seek Chevell," said Valeray, "for he knows where Céleste and Roél debarked. He is a good man and will aid." Valeray glanced from Luc to Alain to Borel and said, "Let us fetch the warband leaders. There is much planning to be done ere we can be ready to leave."

"Sire, you are not going," said Borel.

"What?"

"I am sorry, Papa, but with your broken foot, you will only be a burden, and as Luc has pointed out, time is short, and we must hie."

"But, but—"

"He is right, love," said Saissa, stepping to a nearby bellpull, "and you know it."

Borel turned to Liaze and Michelle and Camille. "You will not go either. Camille, if you are indeed with child, we cannot risk it. But even if not, to you and Michelle and Liaze I say, we will be freer and faster if we do not have to worry about you, especially in the midst of battle."

Even as the three began to protest, Valeray growled, "Borel is right: we must stay." In that moment a servant knocked on the door in answer to the bellpull, and shortly thereafter Armsmasters Anton of the Springwood, Rémy of the Autumnwood, Jules of the Winterwood, and Bertran of the Summerwood entered the room.

The very next day, out rode the combined warband, Borel and his Wolves at the fore, Alain at Borel's side, Comte Luc just behind, along with Anton and Rémy and Jules and Bertran. Remounts trailed after, just one apiece, yet they hoped to get more in Port Mizon.

A horn sounded, and away they galloped, Quint on point and running sunwise.

With tears in their eyes, Liaze and Camille and Michelle watched them go, as did members of the various staffs of the four Forests of the Seasons.

And when the last man disappeared into the woodland, Michelle sighed and said, "May Mithras protect them all."

"Oui," said Liaze.

Camille turned to the two and said, "Let us find Hierophant Georges and see what he knows of familiars."

"Familiars?" asked Michelle.

"Oui, for I suspect the crow Anton spoke of is a familiar of some witch."

"One of the acolytes?" asked Liaze.

"Mayhap," replied Camille, "for with Rhensibé and Iniquí dead there are two acolytes left, and who better to want revenge upon the house of Valeray?"

"Hradian and Nefasí both," said Liaze.

"Oui," said Michelle. She looked up at the balcony where Valeray and Saissa stood to watch the warband go. "'Twas Valeray who fooled Nefasí into revealing where she kept the Seals of Orbane. Let us see what he knows of familiars, too."

And into the manor they strode.

The warband reached Port Mizon in the noontide on the fourth day after setting out. There they exchanged all horses for fresh ones, most coming from King Avélar's stables. Avélar called Vicomte Chevell unto him and arranged for the *Sea Eagle* to transport the warband and their animals to Port Cient, for that's where Céleste and Roél had debarked to ride to the Changeling realm.

Borel and Lieutenant Florien were given access to the treasured map, and they copied down all that Céleste had drawn, for Florien had aided her in that task, just as he now aided her brother.

* * *

Some two days after and in the wee hours, they laded the *Eagle*. And when they were done, the holds and even the decks were jammed with men and horses, and, of course, Borel's Wolves.

At dawn they weighed anchor, and halyards were haled, and the sails bellied full, and the ship got under way.

25

Memories

Hacking and wheezing, they came out through a smoke-filled cleft nigh the crest of a rocky tor, and Céleste filled her lungs with sweet, fresh air, and she wept to see open skies. Roél embraced her from behind, and Céleste clasped her hands to his and said, "I thought I might be trapped forever."

Roél kissed her on the nape of the neck. "And I thought I might never find you."

"But you did, and I wasn't," said Céleste, and she turned in his arms and kissed him deeply; then she looked into his eyes.

Roél smiled down at her. "Burning wet straw was quite clever, chérie; else it would have taken me longer to fetch you. —But tell me, how did you manage to slay the giant Ogre?"

Céleste leaned her head against his chest and murmured, "I remembered an old tale of men being trapped by a giant being, and they got him drunk and blinded him. Me, I did not want him blind, but dead instead." She raised her face. "Where are the horses? I'll tell you the full of it as we ride."

206

"Yon," said Roél, pointing to one of the twisting canyons below.

"Then come," said Céleste, kissing him once more and then freeing herself from his embrace, "let us away from this Ogre hole."

Roél nodded, and from its anchorage, he untied the rope they had climbed to get free, and coiled it. Then he took her by the hand and down the slope they went.

". . . and so you see, I slew him, though in hindsight mayhap 'twould have been better had I blinded him and tricked him into rolling the boulder aside, as did the men in the tale, though I only thought of that later."

"Non, chérie, what you did was right; else he might not have been fooled and would have slain you instead."

Céleste shrugged. "Mayhap so, but I wouldn't have risked starving to death, for alone I could not move the rock."

Roél laughed. "You could have eaten the Ogre. He would have lasted for many, many days."

Céleste shuddered. "Don't even think that, Roél."

They rode without speaking for a while, and then Céleste said, "He was a man-eater, and many a victim had he consumed. His stew was of people he had captured and thrown into his pot. Oh, Roél, though I did not take pleasure in slaying Lokar, Faery is a better place without him."

"Oui, my love." Roél reached across the space between them and touched her arm.

In that moment Céleste gasped and cried in dismay.

Roél jerked his hand back and clutched the hilt of his sword, and he stood in his stirrups and scanned about, yet he saw nought but the rolling hills they had come into. "What is it, Céleste?"

"I deliberately let Lokar win at pips," said Céleste, despair in her tone.

"Oui, and . . . ?"

"Don't you see, Roél, Lady Lot told us there would be many challenges along the way and we must win them all. But I let Lokar triumph at pips."

Roél frowned in thought and then intoned:

"Difficult tests will challenge you
At places along the way;
You and your love must win them all,
Else you will not save the day."

He looked at Céleste and shook his head. "I think the test was not in playing pips, but rather in defeating an Ogre. That, and finding a way to get free. And in both of those, you managed skillfully."

Céleste sighed. "Well, I did slay Lokar, and together you and I got me free. Oh, my love, I do hope you are right."

In midafternoon, the wind strengthened and clouds scudded across the sky above, presaging an oncoming storm, for on the far horizon, a dark heave of clouds roiled toward them. Left and right and ahead they looked, but nought of shelter did they see. They paused long enough to fetch their oiled, leather cloaks from their bedrolls, and to make certain the gear on the pack-horses was well covered. On they rode—a candlemark and then two—and even as in the distance ahead they caught sight of a broad forest, spatters of rain forerunning the storm came flying on the wind.

"We can make shelter in its eaves," said Roél, spurring his mount to a trot, Céleste doing likewise. But a deluge came pouring down ere they reached the woodland, yet at last, and with the horses thoroughly drenched and chilled, they rode in among the trees.

"I deem we can—"

"Roél, wait. I think I see a dwelling, or rather the wall of one."

On they rode, deeper into the forest, where they found a high stone wall running to left and right, and along this barrier they turned rightward.

And the rain thundered down.

They came to a gate ripped from its hinges and lying across the way, beyond which lay a courtyard covered with litter and leaves, and beyond that sat what was once a stately manor, for it had the look of long abandonment: vines grew wildly, and shutters hung awry; windows were broken, and the front door stood ajar.

"Hello!" cried Roél above the hammer of rain.

There was no answer.

"Hello!" he cried again, louder.

Still there was no answer.

He turned to Céleste. "I deem this place be a derelict. 'Round side or back should be a stable; let us get the horses into shelter."

Through driving rain, past weed-laden gardens and overgrown flower beds they splashed, and beyond a broken fountain and a staved-in gazebo. Behind and off to one side of the manor sat a neglected stable, and casting back their hoods the better to see, they dismounted and led the horses in, Roél with his sword in hand, Céleste bearing her long-knife.

Rain pelted down onto the roof, filling the shelter with its drumming.

But for shadows, the place was deserted.

As vapor rose from the animals, Céleste sheathed her long-knife and said, "Roél, until we see what's afoot, let us leave the horses be, in case we need take quick flight."

"Oui. My thoughts exactly," he replied, slipping Coeur d'Acier into its scabbard.

They loosely tied their mounts to a hitching post, while leaving the packhorses tethered to the saddles. Roél took up his crossbow and cocked and loaded it, and Céleste strapped on a quiver and readied her bow and nocked an arrow to string.

Roél glanced at Céleste and received a nod, and out into the storm they went.

Angling across the overgrown yard behind the house, they strode to a service entrance. The door flapped back and forth in the swirling wind. Into the manor they stepped, and a hallway stretched out before them, its dust-laden floor unmarked by track other than those of mice. Doors and archways stood to left and right, and no sound other than that of the rain disturbed the silence. Along this way they quietly walked, past storerooms and a kitchen, its hearths unfired, gray ashes lying within. The chamber across the hall held a large pantry, its shelves yet laden with goods, these dusty as well. Past a laundry room they went, its ironing boards standing unmanned, its tubs empty, and nought but a few tattered jerkins hanging from the strung lines. More doors they passed, and all chambers lay untended; all were unoccupied. They came to a door, and beyond they found a welcoming hall, its marble floor covered with trackless dust and leaf litter. Sweeping staircases led upward to the floor above. 'Round the welcoming hall itself, doorways led to a music room, a parlor, a chamber with a desk and bookshelves, a dining room, a ballroom, and other such places where people gathered.

But all was in disarray, chairs o'erturned, tables smashed, leaves stirring in the wafts from the storm, and all the windows seemed broken inward as if by a great force from without.

"What shambles," said Céleste, looking about and sighing.

"Oui," said Roél.

Up the stairs they went, where they found bedrooms awry, some large, others modest, and some small. For here were the household and guest quarters, and dust lay thickly, and again the windows were smashed inward, even in the bathing rooms and privies.

"Something dreadful happened here," said Céleste, and Roél only nodded.

Back downstairs they went, and they came across an entry into the cellars, wherein they discovered dust-covered kegs of ale and casks of brandy and bottles of wine. But in one corner they also found an upturned open cask and dried human feces within, as if it had been used as a chamber pot.

"Perhaps some group took shelter in this cellar to escape the disaster above," said Roél, surveying the scene. "It looks as if they lived here for a while in isolation. Yet there are no bones of any occupants, so they must have eventually fled."

Céleste looked about as well. "Roél, there are no windows to the outside, and so whatever befell this manor, this is the only protected place."

Roél nodded. "Love, although there are beds above, beds we could make habitable, I say we spend the night in the stables."

"I agree," said Céleste. "Let us go from this damaged place now."

They unladed and unsaddled the horses, and they brushed the animals thoroughly to take away as much moisture as they could, and then took a currycomb to them. Then, as the steeds munched on their rations of grain, Céleste and Roél dried themselves, for in spite of the cloaks and hoods, their heads and necks and hands and forearms were quite drenched.

Roél built a fire, and together they made a hot meal of tea and gruel honey-sweetened, along with hardtack and jerky.

And the rain yet drummed on the roof as they made ready to sleep. Céleste insisted on taking first watch, and Roél nodded and lay down, the knight yet ruing the fact that he hadn't thought to bring along a nervous but plucky dog.

Some candlemarks later Céleste wakened Roél and whispered, "Listen."

Above the now-gentle patter of rain there came the strains of music.

It was the quadrille.

Too, there was soft laughter.

"Come, let us see," said Roél, taking up Coeur d'Acier and his shield. Céleste grabbed up a hooded lantern and lit it, then took her long-knife in hand.

With the lantern all but shuttered, together they crossed the yard and entered the service door. The house was dark, but the music yet played and the voices sounded as down the hallway they went.

Through the door at the end of the hall they crept, and the sounds—harpsichord, flute, violin, along with gentle chatter and the rustle of gowns and the measured steps of dancers—came from the direction of the ballroom, whence an aetheric glow emanated.

Moving quietly through the litter, Roél and Céleste eased across the marble floor and to the archway. But the moment they peered within, the light and sounds vanished. Céleste threw the lantern hood wide, and the luminance filled the chamber, but no one whatsoever did they see. The room was yet litter filled, and the dust and leaves stirred not. No tracks could be seen, and when Céleste walked to the harpsichord and looked at the keys, they had not been disturbed.

Roél frowned. "Ghosts? Spirits?"

Céleste took a deep breath and shook her head. "I know not. But whatever it is let us leave it in peace."

Back to the stables they trod, and even as they left the house, again music and gentle voices came from within.

"I'll take the watch," said Roél, and he stirred up the fire and brewed tea, while Céleste fell into slumber.

Again some candlemarks passed, and this time Céleste was awakened by Roél. "Hsst!" he cautioned. "Something large comes."

Above the sound of music and voices, the ground thudded with heavy tread, more felt than heard, and Céleste quickly strung her bow and nocked an arrow.

Together they stepped to the doors of the stable. The storm was gone, and the drifting clouds were riven with great swaths of starry sky, and a full moon looked down through the rifts and shone upon the abandoned estate.

"Though the steps come closer, I see nought," said Roél.

"Neither do—"

Glass shattered and screams rent the air, and running footsteps clattered. Something or someone roared and shouted in triumph, and more glass crashed, and wood splintered, and shrieks ripped out from fear-filled throats and split the night.

But nothing and no one could be seen tearing at the manor, though the moon shone brightly.

Again came a triumphant roar, and a crunching.

"Lokar," spat Céleste. "I know the voice."

"But Lokar is dead. You slew him."

"Yes, and of that I am glad."

"Are you saying that his ghost, his spirit, has come calling upon the ghosts of those who dwelled here?"

Even as the crashing of glass and the screams yet sounded, Céleste gazed through the moonlight at the once-stately manor, and her eyes filled with tears. "Non, Roél, not spirits, not ghosts. It is the house, my love. It is the house itself remembering."

They spent the rest of the night holding one another, each taking turns dozing.

And the next morn they saddled and laded the horses and rode away from a place where both gentle and terrible memories yet clung.

26

Le Bastion

Through the forest they rode, the leaves adrip with rainwater from yester eve's storm. The air smelled fresh and clean, as if the world had been washed and now sparkled anew. The dome of a cloudless sky arched above, and birds sang and small creatures scampered, and a deer and fawn broke from cover and bounded away. In spite of the bright morn, both Roél and Céleste rode in glum silence, their thoughts dwelling upon the occurrences in the night.

Finally Céleste sighed and said, "That poor house—perhaps cursed forever to recall a terrible eve."

Roél nodded but said nought.

After a moment, Céleste added, "Yet if someone lived therein, the manor might store new memories to displace the old."

As if in deep thought, again Roél nodded without speaking.

They rode in silence awhile, and then Roél asked, "Do you think most so-called haunted houses are simply ones who remember a tragedy?"

"No ghosts, no spirits, you mean?"

"Oui. Just events recalled."

Céleste shook her head. "I think spirits do roam abroad, as well as remain attached to a place. Yet I also believe we witnessed memories long held by that troubled dwelling; hence some so-called hauntings are of that ilk."

"And you think with new occupants those memories would be displaced?"

"Oui. Or at least I believe there is a possibility that will happen. For I would not like to think someone moving in would have that terrible event visited upon them every night."

Roél nodded and said, "Perhaps as long as the scars remain, so will the memory."

Céleste looked at him. "Your meaning?"

"Well, once the doors are rehung and the windows replaced and the manor repainted and swept and cleaned and set aright, then the vestiges of that night will be gone from the dwelling. In my own case I have scars, and when I look upon them, I am put in mind of deeds done in battle. Too, my companions and I—as well as many others—have scars of the mind, and they recall dread deeds done as well. Were these scars to vanish, both those in mind and form, then mayhap I would not recall those dire events, or at least not as vividly."

"But, Roél, would not that require taking away some memories entirely?"

"Oui, it would, and that is my point, for perhaps if the scars visited upon that manor were wholly removed—repairs made, painting done, and a loving family settled in—then gone would be the residual leftovers of that terrible eve."

"I suppose, but I think we'll never know," said Céleste.

And onward they rode.

As they passed through the woodland, they came upon a wide swath of destruction: trees downed and cast aside, as if something huge had passed this way, leaving wrack in its wake. Starwise to sunwise through the forest it ran for as far as the eye could see. Roél dismounted and looked for sign, yet he found no track to tell him what had made this waste.

Roél gestured at the run. "It's as if someone had started a road through the woods, but then abandoned the effort. Yet I think it not neglected, for if that were true, then weeds would have sprung up and saplings would be agrowing."

Céleste glanced about. "The uprooted trees have long been lying to the side; hence I deem this was done some time in the past, yet the way is still being used by something or someone."

"I agree," said Roél as he remounted. "Nevertheless, let us follow this windrow to make our way through the forest, for it seems to be going in our direction and will ease the ride."

Céleste strung her bow, adding, "As long as whatever uses it does not dispute our passage."

On they rode, following the wide path, and the sun climbed up the sky and across and down, and nothing and no one challenged them. As sunset approached, Roél and Céleste moved well off the swath, where they made camp in a small glade.

The next morn, again they took to the path, and with the sun mounting the sky, they followed the way, pausing now and again to feed and water the horses.

As the noontide wheeled past, they emerged from the woodland, and came unto derelict fields where crofters had once cared for the land.

And they passed abandoned farmhouses, some in nought but ruins, and Céleste gritted her teeth and said, "Lokar. It was Lokar who made the windrow through the forest. He used it as a way to fetch his dreadful fare."

Roél looked back toward the woodland. "Oui. I think you are right, chérie."

On they went, and more abandoned farms they passed. But in midafternoon they came to a roadway, and it led them across the fallow land to finally come in among tended fields. Along this way they went, and after some while and in the distance ahead they saw crofters driving herds and wagons in through the gates of a modest town, the settlement walled all 'round with a high palisade.

"Protection against Lokar," said Roél. "Mayhap against other enemy as well."

On they rode, and as they drew closer, Roél said, "Look! Along the wall they have huge ballistas."

"Ballistas?"

"Great, heavy bows. And these are arrow casters, or perhaps instead I should say spear casters."

"More protection against Ogres," said Céleste.

Roél nodded and said, "Those and other foes. But come, Céleste, let us pick up the pace. If Lokar be the only one who raids these environs, we have good tidings for them. Besides, the *ville* looks prosperous, and I have a taste for a good hot meal and a frothy mug of ale."

Céleste laughed and said, "Ah, men, always thinking of their stomachs."

"Only our stomachs?"

Again Céleste laughed. "Ah, not always, for they would have other pleasures to sate their needs. For me I would have a hot bath as well as a good meal and a fine goblet of wine. —Oh, and a soft bed to sleep in, for last eve I swear I slept on a rock the size of a boulder—grinding into my back it was—yet this morn when I found the stony culprit, it was no larger than a pea."

Roél broke into guffaws and managed to say, "Ah, the true test of a princess, eh?" And then he spurred forward into a trot, Céleste following, the princess laughing as well.

Closer they drew, and closer, and now they could see the very tall logs of the high palisade were sharpened to wicked points. Roél also pointed out that some of the wagons among the train moving toward the town were equipped with ballistas to guard the crofters and their herds.

Céleste and Roél reached the gates just as the last of the herds were being driven through. And as they waited for sheep to flock in, followed by a gaggle of geese, a guardsman came and, raising his voice above the bleating of lambs and honking of fowl, asked Roél, "Your names and your business here in Le Bastion?"

"I am Chevalier Roél, and my companion is Céleste de la Forêt de Printemps. Our business is to seek lodging for the night."

"And have you a smith or an armorer?" asked Céleste. The ward of the gate canted his head in assent. "Oui, demoiselle, Monsieur Galdon; he is a fine smith as well as a gifted armorer."

"And where might we find Monsieur Galdon?"

"We would see your mayor, too," added Roél.

"You have a need to see our mayor?"

"Oui," replied Roél. "We might have some welcome news."

"Welcome news?"

Gesturing at the palisade and the ballistas above, Roél said, "I note you are well defended. Is it perchance to ward off a giant Ogre?"

The man nodded. "Oui."

"More than one?"

"Non, Chevalier Roél. Just one."

"Would his name be Lokar?"

Alarm filled the man's face, and he looked over the fields in the direction of the unseen woodland. "Oui, that is his name." He shouted it often when he came to our walls."

"Stay calm, Sieur," said Roél. "You have nought to fear." He gestured at Céleste and added, "For my companion slew Lokar three days past."

A look of disbelief filled the guard's features. "Non. That cannot be. A mere demoiselle slay such a monster? Non. You are making a mockery of me."

"I swear on my honor as a chevalier it is true," said Roél, "and that is why we would see your mayor."

Céleste growled, "And this 'mere demoiselle' would also see your armorer."

The guardsman called his captain, and Roél repeated to him that Lokar had been slain by Céleste. The captain shook his head in disbelief; nevertheless he escorted the two to the town hall. Mayor Breton of Le Bastion was a tall yet portly man, baldheaded but for a ruddy fringe of hair running 'round the back of his head from one ear to the other. He invited them into his humble chamber, and there Roél introduced Céleste as la Princesse de la Forêt de Printemps.

A gleam of skepticism shone in the mayor's eye; even so he bowed to Céleste and treated her with deference.

When they were seated, Céleste told of her capture by Lokar, and her subsequent slaying of him.

Making noncommittal comments throughout the telling, the mayor clearly did not believe her. And when she was finished, Breton said, "Your tale is very interesting, Princess, and you describe him well, but perhaps you slew someone else, for Lokar is a giant of an Ogre."

Céleste sighed in exasperation, and before Roél could reassure the mayor, Breton said, "Tell me, what brings you two to my ville?"

Stifling his own frustration, Roél said, "We are on our way to rescue my sister and my two brothers."

The mayor frowned as if searching for an elusive memory. "And where might they be?"

"In the Changeling realm," replied Roél.

"The Changeling realm? I warn you, Chevalier Roél, no one ever returns from— Wait! Wait! Now I remember. You are the third knight to come through my town seeking the land of the Changelings."

"Laurent nearly seven years past? Blaise nearly four years agone?"

"Oui, those were their names."

"Hai!" exclaimed Roél, clenching his fist in joy. "They are my brothers, and they went seeking my sister, Avélaine, stolen by the Lord of the Changelings himself."

Breton looked closely at Roél. "I see the resemblance now, for you do favor them. Ah, me, but they were brave, these brothers of yours, for each in turn helped repel Lokar from our very walls. And each promised to make an end to him upon returning from the Changeling realm. But, alas, they did not heed my warning, and I fear both are lost."

Now the mayor looked at Céleste and then back to Roél.

"And you say you slew Lokar?"

"Not I," said Roél, "but Céleste instead. Mayor Breton, what we tell you is true. As I said to your gate wards, I swear it on my honor as a chevalier."

With wonder in his gaze Breton turned to Céleste. "Princess, you must forgive me, but I found it altogether preposterous to believe that a mere slip of a *fille* had succeeded in slaying Lokar. Such is quite improbable."

"I thought so, too," said Céleste. "Nonetheless, I did so."

Tears suddenly welled in Breton's eyes. "With Lokar dead, I can lead my people back to our lands."

"Back to your lands? Is not this ville your home?"

"Non. We fled from Lokar. Starwise is where we belong. On the other side of the forest."

"Did you have a manor there?"

"Oui. But Lokar came on a night of celebration, and only a few of us escaped his dreadful grasp. Some days after, I alerted the countryside. We fled through the forest and settled here. But seasons later Lokar found us, and he raided our farms and slew many, and took the corpses back with him. To prevent such a calamity in the future, we built this fortress and called it Le Bastion."

"That must have been some years ago," said Roél.

"Seasons upon seasons past," said Breton. Then he looked at the chevalier. "You are from the mortal lands?"

"Oui," replied Roél. "But how did you know?"

"Your use of the term 'years.'"

"Ah, I see."

"Mayor," said Céleste, "your manor remembers that night still."

Again tears welled in Breton's eyes, and he said, "As do I, for my own daughter was slain by that monster. It was her betrothal we were celebrating."

Of a sudden Céleste gasped, and said, "Did she have hair the color of yours?"

Breton touched his fringe of red. "Oui."

Céleste reached into her pocket and withdrew the silver locket she had all but forgotten, and handed it across the desk to the mayor, saying, "Perhaps this is rightfully yours."

Breton's eyes widened in recognition, and he took it up and opened the leaves and burst into tears. After long moments he said, "My Mélisande and her Chanler." He clasped the locket to his breast. "Princess, where did you find this?"

"In Lokar's cavern. He had it in a chest along with other possessions of those he had slain."

Breton looked again at the portraits. "I gave this to her on the eve of her betrothal. Oh, Mélisande, Mélisande." Once more he clutched the keepsake to his breast.

Again long moments passed, as tears slid down Breton's face. Finally, he closed the leaves and placed the pendant on the desk and said, "Merci, Princess. Merci."

Céleste canted her head in silent acceptance.

Breton then pulled a kerchief from his sleeve and blew his nose. Then he called out, "Sauville!" and when the door opened and a small man appeared, Breton said, "Tell the town criers that Lokar is dead, slain by Princess Céleste de la Forêt de Printemps."

"M'sieur?" His eyes flew wide and he looked at Céleste.

"Oui, she is the one," snapped Breton, and he snatched up the

touched the pillows, they fell into deep sleep, though the next morn they made sweet love in the onset of dawn.

It was not until the noontide that Monsieur Galdon returned with the twenty blunt, bronze-tipped arrows. "I made a special mold," he said of the teardropped points, their rounded ends forward. "I do not know what good these will serve, but here they are. 'Tis the best I can do given your strange request."

Céleste thanked him, and within a candlemark, she and Roél rode out through the gate to the cheers of the citizenry.

A league or so later, Céleste snapped her fingers and said, "Ah, me, but we should have gotten a dog."

"I asked, chérie," said Roél, "but none would part with any, for all said it is certain death to go into the realm of the Changelings, and the townsfolk do not want a vile shapeshifter to come back disguised as one of their dogs."

Céleste sighed and shook her head, and down the road they fared, and there were but ten days and a nighttide left ere the fall of the dark of the moon.

27

Span

Céleste unfolded the map and, after some study, said, "It seems as soon as we cross the next twilight bound, we need bear due sunwise." She passed the vellum to Roél.

After he looked at it for a moment, he pointed to a symbol. "What think you this marking means?"

Céleste swallowed the bite of bread and leaned over to look.

"Hmm . . . *WdBr.* I have no idea, my love."

"Think you it represents another one of the tests of which Lady Lot spoke?"

"Perhaps," said Céleste, "for the first test—defeating Lokar—came right after we met her, and that was at the twilight bound."

Roél frowned. "I think that was not the first test. For when I met you, it was brigands we fought. Then there was the poison of the blade. Then the attack by the Goblins, Bogles, and Trolls fell next. After that there were the corsairs. —Oh, and the Sirènes. Then came the giant Ogre. So, mayhap he was—what?—the sixth test?"

224

Céleste nodded and took a bite of well-cooked beef; it and the bread and other foodstuffs as well as grain for the steeds had been provided by the grateful citizenry of Le Bastion.

Roél sipped a bit of red wine. "Tell me, chérie, are the Fates the ones causing these tests?"

Céleste shook her head and swallowed. "Non, Roél. The Fates merely see what lies before us. It is rare that they actually interfere with the course of men or with that of any given individual. —Oh, when someone breaks a solemn oath or even a serious wager, well, then, I hear that one or the other of the Sisters steps in to take a hand. —Pity the one who has transgressed, for soon or late, he will pay, and dearly."

"If their interference is so rare, then why do they seem to plague you and your kith?"

Céleste shook her head in rue and peered into her own cup of wine. "My love, I do not know. Camille, Alain's wife, thinks it has something to do with Wizard Orbane, though she knows not what that might be, for, in addition to the Fates, it seems we are also plagued by Orbane's acolytes: Hradian, Rhensibé, Iniquí, and Nefasí."

"Did you not say the witch Rhensibé is dead? Slain by Borel?"

Céleste nodded. "Not directly, but by his Wolves instead . . . and Iniquí was slain by Liaze."

"And this Orbane . . . ?"

"Ah, him. One or the other of the Fates—perhaps all three— told Camille that he would pollute the River of Time itself, if he ever got free."

"And this pollution would . . . ?"

"I know not the effect, yet if the Fates think it dreadful, then I cannot but believe it would be terrible indeed."

Roél frowned. "Why do not the acolytes simply set him free? I mean, you have told me he is imprisoned in a castle beyond the Wall of the World. Why not simply storm the gates and free the wizard? During the war, my comrades and I assailed many a fortress—castles, palaces, bastions—and with our siege engines we were quite successful. So, why not simply attack with the proper forces and equipment and set Orbane loose from his shackles?"

Céleste shrugged. "I think the Castle of Shadows isn't like an ordinary palace or fortress. And as to the Wall of the World itself, perhaps it cannot be breached. Besides, what the castle actually is, I do not know. Mayhap it is simply lost beyond the Black Wall of the World, and not easily found. Perhaps it is a moving castle, and when approached it simply vanishes . . . goes elsewhere. When we have freed your sister and found your brothers, we will ask my sire these questions. Perhaps he has some answers."

Roél smiled. "Moving castle, eh? That *would* make it difficult."

Céleste laughed. "'Tis Faery, love."

On they rode, and the way became hilly, then rocky, and in the distance ahead they could see the twilight boundary rearing up into the sky. They came into a land of cliffs and massifs and deep gorges. And that eve they spent on the left bank of a swift-running deep river, with high stone walls rearing up o'erhead.

Swirling mist cloaked the next dawn as Céleste and Roél got under way. And still the passage was rugged. The gorge they followed was narrow, and became even more strait. And the river roared, the sound trapped as it was between opposing sheer stone walls. And the horses became somewhat skittish, especially the mares, and only by patting the animals on the necks and speaking to them soothingly did Céleste and Roél move forward. Finally, just ahead the river filled the entire width, and on the left wall and barely seen through the hanging vapor a wide ledge rose up out from the water, and at its far end a narrow path led up and along the face of the stone bluff.

"'Tis good we are on this side of the flow," said Céleste, "for I think we must follow that upward way. Even so, we need turn or cross over somewhere; else we will stray too far from our course."

"If we are to climb that path, we must reach it first, and here the river is narrow, the water likely deep," said Roél. "Yet given the curve of the gorge, mayhap along the left wall it will be shallow enough to reach the trail upward. Let me go first."

Roél tried to urge his mount forward, but the mare snorted and balked and laid back her ears and refused to enter the water, refused to go any farther into the roaring gap.

Roél ground his teeth and said, "Ah, me, would that I had my stallion. A splendid horse, he would brave anything."

Roél dismounted and tried to lead the mare into the flow, but with white, rolling eyes, the horse jerked back.

Now Céleste rode forward, her mare likewise balking at the thundering run, though it seemed a bit less skittish than Roél's horse.

But Céleste leaned forward and laid a soothing hand alongside the neck of her mount and called out calming words. And hesitantly, and with the whites of her eyes showing, and snorting in dread, still the mare entered the rush, and Céleste's placid gelding packhorse, though nervous, followed.

Roél's mare stomped and whinnied and belled, calling out to the other mare, as if to tell her to come to her senses and return to the safety of this side. But Céleste urged her horse forward, and clinging to the wall, ahead they went, and the water roared and clutched at the animals' legs, rising over hoof and fetlock, pastern and hock, and unto their very bellies.

And still Roél's mare cried out, and Roél, knowing that the herd instinct was strong, mounted the horse and heeled her. And now the animal, though her sides heaved with fright and her eyes rolled white and she snorted in terror, entered the roaring water as well.

Ahead, Céleste finally reached the ledge, and up onto the broad shelf she rode, up into the mist, and Roél's mare with his gelding in tow soon followed.

Roél's mare calmed when she came up out of the water and onto the flat, for once again the herd was whole. Roél dismounted and looked straight up the sheer stone wall. How high it went—a hundred feet or a thousand or more—he could not tell, for the fog shrouded all. He turned to Céleste and said, "The path looks steep, the way narrow. Best we lead the horses."

She nodded.

Roél took the reins of his mare in hand and said, "Ready?"

"Ready," replied Céleste.

And with Roél in the fore, afoot they began leading the horses higher into the swirling mist.

Whiter it got and thicker, and the roar of the river diminished, for sounds seemed muffled in the vapor's grasp. Wetness clung to everything: animal, man, gear, path, and sheer-rising stone. The way narrowed, and in places Céleste feared for all of their safety, and she wondered how she and Roél would cope had they to unlade the packhorses, for there was not space to do such.

Up they went and up, along the slender and twisting path, and the higher they got, the more nervous became the horses, even the geldings.

"Roél, is your mare reluctant?"

"Oui, but I know not why. Surely they do not fear heights."

"Ever since we entered this gorge, the horses have been edgy," called Céleste. "I thought it the water and the noise, yet now I am not certain, for that is far below, and should by now be forgotten."

"Mayhap 'tis the narrowness," said Roél.

"Perhaps, though I doubt it."

In spite of her reservations, it seemed to be true, for the animals continued to grow more uneasy along the constricted path. But then the way widened, yet even so, still the horses snorted and huffed, as if sensing an unseen danger, and both Roél and Céleste had to murmur soothing words to somewhat calm the steeds. Finally they came to a broad flat, though the walls of the bluff yet rose on high.

"A bridge," called Roél, still in the lead, but stopping. "I can make out a bridge straddling the gorge."

And still the mist swirled, obscuring here, revealing there, and then shifting anew.

The flat was wide enough for Céleste to pull her unwilling mount forward until she stood next to Roél.

And through the swirling mist she could see glimpses of a lengthy stone span reaching from one side of the gorge to the other. "Ah, perhaps *that's* what the *Br* in *WdBr* means: bridge."

"Mayhap," said Roél. "But what does the *Wd* mean? Surely it can't be 'wide,' meaning 'wide bridge.' 'Tis a bit too strait for that."

"It matters not, love," said Céleste, "for, in spite of this fog, somewhere just ahead must lie the twilight bound."

"Well, then," said Roél, and he started forward, Céleste following.

And as they moved toward the near end of the span, Roél could see along the length of the bridge short poles jutting up from the stone railings to either side, round objects affixed thereon.

Within ten strides he reached the stone structure, and there his mare flattened her ears and refused to take another step and pulled back on the reins. The gelding as well drew hindward, and together they hauled Roél back to where Céleste and the other animals stood.

"They sense something, love," said Céleste.

"Let me go forward and see what I can find," said Roél, and he handed the reins to Céleste, and then took his crossbow from its saddle scabbard and cocked and loaded it.

"Take care," said Céleste, as he moved toward the bridge.

No sooner had Roél set foot on the pave than at the other end a giant of an armored knight—a great two-handed sword in his grip—stepped onto the far end of the span.

A crimson surcoat he wore, and the mist swirled, shrouding him and revealing him only to veil him again.

"Friend, we would pass," called Roél.

He received no answer from the fog.

"Then we will hold and you may pass," Roél cried.

Yet the armed and armored man, now vaguely discernible, did not respond but stood waiting.

Roél sighed and turned to Céleste. "WdBr means 'warded bridge.'"

"Why would someone stand athwart this span?" asked Céleste.

Roél shrugged. "For toll? Perhaps that's it." Then he called out, "What be the toll?"

The giant of a man, some nine feet tall, made no response.

"Perhaps the Changeling Lord set him here to keep interlopers from his lands," said Céleste.

Roél walked back to his horse, and unladed and uncocked his crossbow and slid it into its saddle scabbard and the quarrel to the quiver. Then he slipped his helm on his head and took down his shield and drew Coeur d'Acier from its sheath.

"Chéri?" said Céleste.

"I must accept his challenge," said Roél.

"I'll simply feather him," said Céleste, reaching for her bow.

"Were the air currents still and could you see him clear enough, perhaps," said Roél. "But, non, my love, 'tis something I must do, for a gauntlet has been flung."

Céleste shook her head. "Men."

"Nay, love. Knights."

He tenderly kissed her and stepped onto the span and strode into the churning vapor. The moment he moved forward, so, too, did the massive warrior.

Her heart hammering with fear for Roél, Céleste strung her bow and nocked an arrow, not one of the blunts but a keen point instead.

Roél then passed a pike jutting up from the wall of the bridge, and now he could see the round object affixed thereon: 'twas the spitted head of a knight, helmet in place, rotted flesh dangling from bone. To left and right Roél looked as he trod onward. More pikes came into view; more knights' helmeted skulls gaped at the passing warrior.

Oh, Laurent, Blaise, let none of these be you.

On he went through the clinging vapor, the huge knight coming toward him, mist eddying about.

"To first blood?" called Roél.

In response the Red Knight swung his huge sword up and 'round and brought it across in a crashing blow, only to meet Roél's shield; yet the shock of the strike benumbed Roél's left arm.

Again the giant swung his great sword up and 'round, but this time the massive blade met Roél's Coeur d'Acier.

Clang! Chang! Blade met blade and metal screamed. And Roél feinted and parried and struck, and the blades whistled through the air as back and forth knight and knight struggled, the fog churning about them. The giant of a knight hammered at Roél, his blows mighty, and of a sudden Roél reeled hindward and fell, for he had been struck upon the helm, the bronze and padding and a partial parry all that saved him from a crushing death. And the huge knight sprang forward, his great blade whistling down, only to strike stone, chips flying, for his target had rolled away. Roél gained his feet, and as the next strike whistled past, he stepped inside the reach of the knight of the bridge, only to be flung aside by the backhanded sweep of a mailed fist.

At the end of the span, horses danced and snorted and huffed in fear, yet Céleste paid them no heed. As the mist cleared she could see struggling figures, closing, leaping apart, whirling about one another, blades swinging, the sound of their strikes like that of hammers on anvils. And Céleste drew and aimed, yet she could not loose her shaft, for in the blowing white vapor she could not be certain of her target nor the flight of her arrow given the swirling air.

And then the mist cloaked all, and still the cry of tortured metal rang along the gorge.

Forward, I must move forward. Yet what if I distract Roél? What will I—!

Of a sudden silence reigned.

Oh, Mithras, is it—!

"Roél!" she called, her voice choked with fear.

Footsteps neared.

Céleste drew the shaft to the full and aimed into the white.

A fog-shrouded form appeared, yet she could not see just what or who it—

—and Roél stumbled out from the mist and fell to his knees, his dented shield clanging down beside him. His chest heaved and blood slid down his face.

Behind her the horses suddenly calmed.

Dropping her bow and arrow, with a cry of anguish Céleste sprang forward. "My love, are you—?"

As she fell to her knees before him, he raised his head and looked at her and smiled. "Ah, Mithras, but he was mighty. Never have I fought so hard."

"But you're bleeding."

"I am?"

"Oui. Your forehead."

Roél reached up and touched his face and looked at the blood in surprise. Then he removed his helmet. "He struck my head a glancing blow. It must have happened then."

Céleste examined the wound, more of a scuffing of skin than a cut. She embraced him and gave him a kiss and said, " 'Twas your own helm did it, chéri. A bit of salve and a bandage should be enough."

"If you don't mind, I'll wait here," said Roél, yet panting.

Céleste stepped to the horses and rummaged through the gear. Then she returned with clean cloth and a small tin. In moments she had Roél's scrape salved and swathed. He took some of the remaining cloth and started to clean Coeur d'Acier, but the blade gleamed like new—there was no blood whatsoever upon the silvered steel.

"What th—? But I struck him through."

"Something mystic is afoot," said Céleste. Then she gestured hindward and said, "The horses knew."

Roél frowned down at his blade and then looked at the princess. "Come, let us see."

Groaning to his feet, Roél stepped to the now-placid horses and took up the reins of his steed, Céleste following. Walking, they moved upon the span, the white vapor swirling with their passage, and the horses calmly let themselves be led, no longer skittish and balking.

As they crossed, Roél carefully examined each and every knight's head spitted on a pike, fearing the worst for Laurent and Blaise, but whether those of his brothers were among the skulls so mounted he could not say, for with flesh rotted or gone and dangling hair in disarray he could see no resemblance whatsoever. He spent no time examining the helms, for doing so would yield nought, for, like him, Laurent and Blaise had traded all armor for gear of bronze in the mortal city of Rulon ere ever entering Faery.

When they came to the mid of the bridge, Roél looked about and frowned and said, "Here should lie the corpse of my foe, yet nought do I see."

On they went, Roél yet looking at the spitted heads but recognizing nought, and when at last he and Céleste came to the end of the span, there on a pike was mounted the visored helm of the giant Red Knight of the bridge, yet it was empty.

Roél turned to Céleste. "This was on the head of the one I fought, the one I slew. How can it be?" But ere she could answer, Roél muttered, "I know: Faery. 'Tis Faery."

Before them gaped a tunnel into the stone of the opposite cliff, and into this they strode.

The sound of shod hooves rang and reverberated within the rocky way, yet ere long they emerged from the passage to come out upon a narrow plateau.

Directly before them and rearing up into the sky loomed the twilight wall.

They had come unto the next bound.

28

Crossroads

Roél stepped back to a packhorse and took from it a length of rope and began tying it about his waist. "This time I will go first."

"But you are weary from your battle with the bridge knight," said Céleste. "Besides, I am lighter and you are stronger; hence 'twill be easier for you to haul me back than for me to haul you, should such be called for."

Roél handed Céleste the line. "Then tie me to your horse and mount up, and if need be, pull me back." He took his shield from his saddle and then drew Coeur d'Acier. "Ready?"

Sighing, Céleste tied the line to the forebow of her saddle. Then she tethered Roél's animals to her packhorse. She mounted and said, "Ready."

Paying out the rope, she let Roél move ahead and then followed. Into the twilight they went, the other horses trailing after. Darker it got and darker, and Céleste stopped just short of the midmost wall of ebon.

Roél stepped through.

The line jerked taut.

"Roél!" cried Céleste, and she spun her mare about and rode swiftly away, the other horses in a confusion but following.

And she dragged Roél after . . .

. . . and he was shouting.

When she realized Roél was behind her, Céleste haled her mare to a halt.

Disentangling himself, Roél stood . . . and dripped.

He was covered in yellow-green slime.

Concern and wilderment on her face, Céleste leapt from her mount and ran to him. "Are you injured?"

"I thought an Ogre or some such had you. The rope snapped tight. What happened?"

And he looked at her and burst into laughter. "Were you going to drag me at a gallop through all of Faery?"

"Oh, love, I merely fell down. 'Tis a swamp on the other side." He began wiping the odiferous sludge from his face.

Céleste wrinkled her nose and drew away.

Roél glanced at her and said, "Come to think of it, mayhap I should have let you go first." And he burst into laughter again.

Céleste and Roél had to lead the animals afoot through the treacherous murky waters, where quags and quicksand and sinkholes might lie. The horses were slimed to the hocks, and Céleste, too, was covered in slime full to her waist and up her left side to her shoulder, for she had taken a fall, and only her grip on the reins had preserved the relative cleanliness of her right arm.

Slow was their progress as they passed through stands of saw grass and reeds and wove their way among hummocks. Dark willows wrenched up out of the muck, and grey tree moss dangled down from lichen-wattled limbs. Things unseen plopped and slithered and gurgled, and oft great bubbles rose to the surface and slowly burst, releasing horrendous odors. Now and again they had to double back to find a safer route through the slime-laden waterlogged mire. But occasionally they came to more solid ground, and the first time they did so, Céleste looked down at herself and cried, "Leeches! Roél, leeches! Ghaa! I hate leeches!" And she whipped out her long-knife and began raking them from her leathers even as they oozed up her legs and sought entry to her flesh.

Roél, however, ignored those on his garb and began scraping the parasites from the legs of the horses.

When all of the animals were cleared of the bloodsuckers, Céleste and Roél mounted up and made good time until the solid ground gave way to mire again.

And that was the way of their travel through the morass: wading and leading the horses, scraping off leeches and riding, and then wading and leading again.

And gnats whined and flies bit and midges crawled into ears and nostrils and across eyes, and batting and slapping and raking, Céleste thought she would go entirely insane, though Roél seemed inured to it all.

Sunwise they fared, ever sunwise, as the day grew and peaked and waned, and just at dusk, they finally emerged from the swamp and onto solid ground, where rolling hills stretched out before them.

Exhausted and itching and well bitten, and filthy beyond their wildest imaginings, they made camp and built a fire and heaped pungent greenery upon the blaze and let the smoke drive all but the worst of the flying pests away.

They unladed and fed and watered the animals and groomed and treated them for their wounds, spreading a salve o'er the places where the parasites had sucked.

Then they used some of their drinking water to wash themselves, and they changed their clothes. Fortunately, they both had been wearing leathers and boots, which protected them from the leeches. Even so, they suffered from the many bites they had taken from the flying pests, especially the gadflies, a number of which were yet whining about.

"Would that we had tails," said Roél as they ate. He occasionally flicked a fly from his fare, though for the most part he ignored them and consumed gnats, midges, and all, unlike Céleste, who seemed to believe that each insect that landed on her food polluted it nearly beyond redemption, and she spent much time plucking away tiny pieces of her fare, where gnats and flies had walked, and flipping the infinitesimal pinches away, and taking bites in between landings.

As Céleste plucked and flipped another speck, she frowned.

"Tails? Whatever for?"

Roél merely pointed at the horses. Munching oats from their feed bags, head to tail they stood, each swishing flies away from the face of another.

Céleste laughed and said, "Ah, oui, tails would be a treat right now."

She flipped away another tiny piece of bread and quickly took a bite before another fly could land, and as she chewed she said, "I don't know about you, love, but I am going to sleep entirely under cover."

In spite of her matted hair and the odor yet clinging, and regardless of his own filthy state, Roél embraced her and kissed her tenderly and said, "Then do so, chérie. I'll take first watch and keep the fire going."

The moon was on high when Roél, sword in hand, quietly awakened Céleste. "Shh . . . ready your bow, for someone moves through the swamp."

Céleste looked, and a light bobbed among the trees. "Ah, love, 'tis the Will o' the Wisp you see. Follow it not, or it will lead you to a watery death."

"A watery death, eh?"

"Oui. Some think it a tricksy Boggart, out for a mere prank, while there are those who believe it's a ghost of someone who has drowned and wishes the same fate for others, and it bears a candle to lure the naïve; hence it is also called a Corpse-candle. It has many other names, yet regardless as to whether it is Boggart or ghost or something else altogether, it is not wise to stalk after one."

Roél frowned. "I know of ghosts, but what is a Boggart?"

"Generally a Brownie who's been soured by mistreatment."

"Well, ghost or Boggart, will it threaten us?"

"Non. It will remain in the swamp and bob about and try to entice you to follow."

"Then go back to sleep, chérie. I will remain on watch."

Céleste glanced at the moon directly overhead, the silvery orb some four days past full and said, "Roél, Roél, what am I to do with you? It is well beyond mid of night. It will do ill for you to be weary on the morrow and in the days to come. Non, love, you must sleep. I will set ward now."

Céleste was adamant, and so Roél took to his bedroll, and immediately fell into slumber, leaving Céleste to watch the ghostly light of the Corpse-candle drifting o'er the murky waters of the mire.

The sun was well risen when they set off again, for Roél had slept late, yet Céleste was aware of the urgency to get on with the quest, and so, at last, she had awakened him. And now they were on their way once more.

Across the rolling hills they fared, travelling due sunwise still, and in late morn they came upon a clear-running stream burbling out from a woodland. They watered and gave rations of grain to the horses, and then shed their clothes and waded in calf-deep to wash away the last of the mire. As Céleste scrubbed her pale blond hair, Roél began to harden at the sight of her, but feeling the need to press on, he plopped down into the chill flow. In spite of the cold water, he remained thrilled by her beauty and by her shapely form and her undeniable charms, and only by thinking of other things did he suppress his risen desire.

Free of grime and dressed once more, notwithstanding the underlying sense of urgency, they took time to clean their leathers—wetting and scraping away the semisolid muck yet clinging to the garb until pants and jackets were habitable once more—for who knew what might lie ahead? Who knew what the Fates might have in store for them?

After a quick meal of their own, they mounted up and on they went, and the hills began to flatten until they rode across undulant plains, mostly grassland, though a few thickets were scattered here and there.

Sunwise they went and sunwise, and they came to a road curving out from two points starwise of sunup and bending 'round to bear directly sunwise as well.

Now following this route, on they forged, and the sun crossed above and arced in its invariant descent toward sundown.

"Whence fares this road? I wonder," said Roél.

Céleste retrieved her vellum chart and began unfolding it. "That I cannot say, yet let me see if there is any clue on our meager map." After a moment she shrugged and said, "This route is not on our sketch, but that is no surprise, for many things are missing. This I can say: it seems there are only two twilight borders left to cross, and if the drawn gaps between notations are anywhere close to accurate, we should be in the Changeling realm within three or four days."

"Well and good," said Roél, "for there are only eight days beyond this one ere the fall of the dark of the moon."

"I do hope that is time enough," said Céleste, refolding the vellum.

"It will have to be," gritted Roél. . . .

. . . And on they rode.

As the sun lipped the horizon, "What's that in the distance ahead?" asked Céleste.

Roél stared down the track and frowned and held his hand to

the right side of his head to shade his eyes against the sullen rays of the setting sun glancing across the 'scape. Finally he said, "It looks like a gibbet."

"A gallows out here in the middle of the plains?"

"Oui. It seems so."

"Then that object dangling is— Oh, Roél, is it a person?"

"Oui, chérie. Ah, but look, there is someone beyond."

"Where? Oh. Someone sitting. Come, let us see what is afoot." Céleste spurred her horse into a canter, as did Roél, and as the last of the sun fell below the horizon, they could see that the gibbet had been placed at a crossroads, for running sunrise to sunset another route ran athwart the one they followed. Closer they drew, and closer, and now they could see the corpse of a young man hanging from the crossbeam of the gallows, and nearby and among low mounds a young woman sat weeping at the edge of an open grave. As the two came riding up, the demoiselle sprang to her feet and cried out, "Oh, monsieur, will you please help me? My Joel has been wrongly put to death, and I am sentenced to bury him, but I have no way to cut him down."

Roél frowned. "Wrongly put to death? And you must bury him? Who did this thing to you?"

"My papa, for he caught us making love, and we are not wedded. He said that Joel must be a devil to have done such a thing to me. He clubbed my lover and brought him here and hanged him, where other criminals have been put to death." She gestured at the low mounds. "I must bury Joel here among the other graves at this crossroad so that his ghost will be baffled, hence will not find its way to me or to haunt my papa." The girl broke into tears.

Gritting her teeth, Céleste said, "'Tis your père who should be hanged. Roél, cut the lad down. We must help this fille."

Céleste leapt from her saddle and embraced the sobbing demoiselle, while Roél, standing in his stirrups, clutched the corpse and cut the rope. He eased the body to the ground, and then dismounted and took him up and bore him to the graveside. He clambered into the cavity, and gently drew the boy in and laid him down. As Roél climbed back out, the demoiselle looked at Céleste and quietly said, "It seems you two are at a crossroads as well."

Céleste peered into the eyes of the girl, and black as midnight and deep they were.

The girl disengaged herself from Céleste's embrace and glanced duskward at the darkening twilight heralding the onrush of night, and then she smiled and said to them both, "Thank you for the favor. It is one of the required things."

Céleste sighed and said, "Roél, I think it is as you once deemed when you said whom next we would meet; I believe this young demoiselle is none other than Lady Doom."

A darkness enveloped the fille and then vanished, leaving behind a bent and toothless and cackling crone dressed in ebon robes limned in satiny ebon as well.

And from somewhere, nowhere, everywhere, came the sound of weaving looms.

29

Conundrums

R oël bowed and Céleste curtseyed, and Urd cackled and said, "Had you fooled, didn't I?" She made a vague, one-handed gesture, and the graves and gibbet vanished.

"Oh, my," said Céleste, "with those things gone, we did not do a true service for you."

"Heh! Nonsense, child. It is what is in your heart that counts, whether or no the need is real or illusory, vital or trivial, large or small. In this instance, Céleste, your heart was filled with rage at an injustice done, and sorrow for the victims of it, and the need to do something."

Urd turned to Roël and added, "And in your heart, Chevalier, you felt a momentary twinge of guilt, for you and your own lover are not married either, but o'erwhelming all, you felt the same rage and sorrow, and the need to seek out the perpetrator and exact vengeance. Yet, my boy, you need to take care when dealing out retribution, for such passions unbridled will blacken a heart."

"You can truly read what is in our hearts?" asked Céleste, wonder in her gaze.

"Oh, Princess, that is but a simple thing. This I do know: you two are deeply in love . . . fortunately with one another." Urd hooted in laughter, her ebon eyes dancing in glee.

When she finally stifled her joy she turned to Roél and said, "You, my boy, are yet certain that you—a mere chevalier—are not worthy of a princess, yet I tell you this princess knows you are. Set aside your doubts, Roél, for it is not station that determines merit, but heart and soul and spirit and deeds: the very fiber of your being."

Céleste looked at Roél, her heart in her eyes, and she said, "Oh, my love, did I not say it was so?"

"You did, chérie, you did. Yet I . . ." Roél fell into silence, as if strong emotions blocked his words.

"Heh," chortled Urd, "my sisters said he was a catch." Roél looked at Urd, a frown on his face. "Lady Doom, I did not see or speak with your sisters, yet you appear before me. Why is that?"

Urd waggled a finger at Roél, saying, "Now, now, Chevalier, don't you recall railing that we Three Sisters never answer something straight out?"

Roél's eyes widened in startlement, and Urd smiled a gummy grin at Céleste. "Didn't know I was listening, did he?"

"My lady, why have you come?" asked Céleste.

"Begging for a straight answer yourself, are we? Well, you know the second rule: first you have to answer a riddle."

"Might Roél help this once?"

"Of course, of course. Why do you think I let him see me? Silly girl." And again she crowed a laugh.

Céleste reached out and took Roél's hand in hers, then said, "Ask away, Lady Doom."

Urd looked from Céleste to Roél and back, and as the sound of looms swelled, she said:

"It can run but never walks,
Has a mouth but never talks,

Has a head but never weeps,
Has a bed but never sleeps,
When it tumbles, always grumbles,
Never bumbles when it rumbles,
Ever shouts in heady falls,
But mostly murmurs soothing calls,
At times wanders o'er wide fields
Wholly ruining crofters' yields,
Sometimes savage, sometimes mild,
Sometimes placid, sometimes wild,
Now I end this riddle game.
Can you give me this thing's name?"

Céleste's heart sank, but Roél gently squeezed her hand and said, "Lady Doom, given the manner in which you couched the riddle, I could answer by simply saying, 'No.' "

Urd clapped her hands and cackled in glee and hopped about in a small jig step and said, "Exactly so, Chevalier! Exactly so."

Céleste frowned and said, "But I don't understand."

Roél smiled. "The last line of the riddle asks, 'Can you give me this thing's name?' That question can be answered with a yes or a no. The name itself is not the riddle, but the question at the end is." He turned to Urd and added, "But my true answer, Lady Doom, is, 'Yes, I can give you the name.' "

"But you don't have to," said Urd, still grinning.

Frustrated, Céleste said, "Oh, Roél, tell me. Please, I want to kn— Oh, it's a river, isn't it?"

Roél broke out in laughter. "Oui, chérie. River it is."

Urd squinted an eye and pointed a knobby finger at Céleste and said, "And you think you are not good with riddles? My dear, you have answered all three: mine, Verdandi's, and Skuld's."

"But I didn't say 'Yes' or 'No' to the question," said Céleste.

"Instead I spoke the name; hence did I or did I not answer the riddle?"

Urd smiled somewhat enigmatically and said, "Give it some thought, my dear." She glanced at the sky and said, "But now we have little time left, and I have come here to provide you aid."

Roél sighed. "A puzzling rede, Lady Doom?"

"That, and a vision and a gift," answered Urd.

"A vision?"

"Oui. But first the rede."

And as the thud of batten and the clack of shuttle swelled, Urd glanced along the duskwise crossroad and intoned:

> "To triumph in the Changeling realm,
> Shift to a different trail.
> You must take the sinister path;
> Find the gray arrow or fail.
> Creatures and heroes and the dead
> Will test you along the way.
> Ever recall what we Three said,
> To fetch the arrow of gray."

"Shift to a different trail?" protested Roél. "But we are just two twilight borders from—"

"Hush!" snapped Urd, glancing at the diminishing dusk, growing darker with the onrush of night. "There is no time for this tomfoolery. Instead, step closer and . . . see."

With nought but a whispered word, a dark basin appeared in her hands, and it was filled with an ebon liquid. Céleste and Roél moved to stand before her.

"Peer into my farseeing mirror," said Urd.

The princess and her knight looked into the blackness, yet only glittering reflections of emergent stars above did they see.

"Lady Doom," said Roél, "there is nought to—"

Ripples disturbed the surface, the reflected stars dancing in the flux.

"I said hush, Chevalier. Now both of you, clear your minds."

Again Roél stared within the basin, and slowly an image began to form. It was . . . it was . . . two figures . . . two men. Gradually they came into focus. Roél gasped, then whispered, "Laurent. Blaise." The likenesses wavered and began to fade, and Roél clamped his lips shut and stilled his breathing.

With his silence the images strengthened, and Roél saw that they had grimaces on their faces and they were drawing their swords, as if readying for battle, yet to Céleste it seemed they were smiling and sheathing their swords, as of a battle finished.

Of a sudden the likenesses vanished, as did the basin, and Urd looked again at the darkening dusk, for night was nearly upon them.

"Here," she said, "you will need this," and she held forth her hand to Céleste, something gripped within.

The princess reached out, and Urd dropped the gift into Céleste's palm, and as the sound of looms swelled Urd said, "I will tell you one more thing, and it is this: left is right, but right a mistake; you will fail if the wrong path you take."

And now the rack of shuttle and the thump of batten surged in crescendo . . . and then vanished altogether, as did Lady Doom.

The dusk disappeared as well, for night had fully fallen.

Staring in bafflement, Céleste peered through the wan starlight at the gift Urd had given.

It was an obsidian spool of shadowy thread.

one carved to look like a man with the head of a falcon, the other a man with a jackal's head. An ebon darkness shimmered between.

"Mayhap it is a crossing," said Céleste.

"You mean like a twilight wall?"

"Oui."

Roél sighed and said, "Then I think we need go directly through, for it seems there is no other way out."

"You propose we use no rope?"

"Oui."

Céleste grinned. "Then let us have at it."

Up the steps they trod, the horses clattering after, but the moment their feet touched the dais, a man with the head of an ibis emerged from the black wall, and he held his hand out as if to halt them.

Roél paused, his grip on the hilt of Coeur d'Acier. But then he released his hold and bowed and said, "My lord."

Céleste curtseyed.

"I am Thoth, Lord of Wisdom, and I am here to test your worthiness to enter the realm of Lord Osiris. Hence—" Of a sudden he started in surprise. "By the thrice-named gods, you are of the living! You cannot enter Duat."

"We do not wish to enter Duat, My Lord Thoth," said Roél, "but the domain of Lord Hades instead."

"Hades?"

"Oui."

"Who sent you this way to reach that netherworld?"

"Lord Abulhôl, My Lord Thoth."

"Ever the meddler," growled Thoth. The guardian god of the way to Duat sighed and said, "Even so, he must have had a good reason. What is it you hope to find there?"

"We seek the Hall of Heroes in the Elysian Fields, for within that hall is a black portal leading to the City of the Dead, and within that city is a gray arrow, and that is what we seek."

30

Choices

Roél slammed a fist into palm. "Shift to a different trail? But we are so close—just two borders to cross—and there are but eight days left before Avélaine will be lost forever. We simply must rescue her ere then."

Céleste reached out and took Roél's hand and unclenched his fist and smoothed his fingers. "Chéri, we must follow Lady Doom's counsel. If we do not, we will fail."

Roél sighed and nodded. "It's just that . . ." His words trailed off.

"I know, my love. I know. We've come to an unexpected crossroads. Yet the Sisters see what might be, what is passing, and what is nevermore, and so we need to heed their guidance."

Roél shook his head and then softly intoned:

"To triumph in the Changeling realm,
Shift to a different trail.
You must take the sinister path;
Find the gray arrow or fail."

248

After long moments of silence, Roél said, "I wonder what this gray arrow is?"

Céleste shrugged. "Whatever it is, and whatever it is to be used for, we will not succeed without it, and Urd did say that we needed to fetch it. Hence, we must find it."

Roél nodded. "I note that when she told us to shift to a different trail, Urd glanced along the road in the direction you name 'duskwise,' and 'sundownward'—a bearing I would call 'west'—and she did tell us to take the sinister path; and certainly toward sundown is the leftward way from where we stand—here on what I would name the south side of the road—and we stood here when she said it. What does the map say lies in that direction? And will it take us to the Changeling realm in time?"

"Let us make camp, and then we will look," said Céleste.

And so they unladed the geldings and unsaddled the mares and curried and watered and fed them, and they laid out their bedrolls and made a small fire from scrub and an armful of branches gathered from a nearby thicket.

As they ate, Céleste unfolded the map, and by lantern light and firelight she traced out a path duskward to reach a boundary crossing. "Hmm . . . here is what we are to look for at the crossing itself, yet somewhat after the crossing, on a duskward bearing, it is marked *Spx*, whatever that might mean."

She showed the chart to Roél, and he shrugged and said, "I haven't the slightest notion either. But look, if we keep going sinister, the next crossing after is very close."

Céleste stared at the map and blew out an exasperated breath and said, "And just beyond that crossing the chart is marked *El Fd* and nearly on top of that enigmatic note is *Ct Dd*. I wonder if *El Fd* means we are bound for an Elven realm."

"Elven realm?"

"Where live Elves," said Céleste.

"Under the hills, you mean?"

Céleste laughed. "Roél, in Faery some Elves do live under the hills, but others dwell as do we."

"I see," said Roél. "In the mortal realm, though, 'tis said Elves betimes are seen abroad, but for the most they remain under the hills."

"A strange notion," said Céleste. "Still, I wonder about the marking: *El Fd.*"

Roél peered at the map. "Perhaps it refers to an Elven realm as you have guessed, chérie, but what about the *Ct Dd* right next to it?"

Céleste sighed. "I have no idea what that might stand for. Ah, Mithras, why couldn't whoever made this chart have spelled out the meanings?"

Roél snorted and said, "Mayhap the cartographer was one of the Fates."

Céleste laughed but then sobered. "Take care, love, for they might be listening."

Roél turned up a hand and said, "Most likely." Then he raised his face to the sky and called, "Why couldn't you have made the map plain?"

Céleste slapped a hand over her mouth to conceal a smile.

"Ah, well," said Roél, "whatever those initials might indicate, we do have a clue:

> *Creatures and heroes and the dead*
> *Will test you along the way.*
> *Ever recall what we Three said,*
> *To fetch the arrow of gray.*

"It seems we are to be challenged along the sinister path," said Céleste. "My bow and long-knife will be ready if they are tests of arms."

"And if not?" asked Roél.

"Then my wits," said Céleste.

Roél nodded, and then looked at the map again. "Think you we can fetch the arrow and then reach my sister in the eight days remaining?"

"I cannot say, for there is no scale," said Céleste, tapping the map. "Still, if the Fates have sent us this way, surely there is a chance."

They sat without speaking for long moments, eating waybread and jerky and drinking brewed tea. Finally Céleste said, "Lady Doom gave us one last admonishment ere she vanished: 'Left is right, but right a mistake; you will fail if the wrong path you take.' I wonder if she was speaking of these crossroads. Was she warning us to take the left-hand way and not the right?"

"Another puzzle," said Roél, "another confusing instruction. Mayhap what she was saying is that we *should* take the right-hand way, for if left is 'right,' but 'right' is a mistake, then doesn't that make 'left'—that is, the left-hand way—the mistake?"

Céleste groaned. "I don't know."

"Agh!" spat Roél. "I just had another thought: we were travelling due south—due sunwise—when we came upon Lady Doom. What if the left-hand way, the sinister way, is based on the direction we were going, rather than where we were standing when she gave us the rede? That would make the sinister path be toward the east, dawnwise, sunupward."

Céleste's face fell. "Oh, Roél, do you think that could be so?"

"I know not, chérie. Regardless, let us see what lies along the road toward dawn," said Roél. As his finger traced a sunupward route, he mumbled, "Hmm . . . *PR* and *WT* and over here *GY*. — Argh! That's no help whatsoever."

Céleste shook her head and said, "It all depends on which way one faces as to which of these roads—dawnwise, sunwise, duskwise, or starwise—is sinister. Yet the road running dawn to dusk is a 'different trail' from the one we were on, hence the one to follow, though in which direction, sunupward or sundown-ward, there's the rub."

Once again they fell into silence, but finally Roél glanced up into the star-filled night, and said, "Let us sleep on it. I will take first watch."

Céleste pushed out a hand of negation. "Non, love, for if you take first watch, you will let me sleep beyond my due. Instead, I will take ward now."

"What's to say you won't do the same to me?" asked Roél, a smile flickering at the corners of his mouth.

Now Céleste peered at the spangled vault above and said, "The sun will rise ten candlemarks hence. I will guard the first five, you the last. —Done?"

Roél reluctantly nodded and said, "Done," and he held her close and kissed her tenderly, and then lay down.

Céleste listened to Roél's breath slowing as he fell into slumber, and when he was fast asleep she stood and paced to the horses. They, too, were adoze, and so she returned to the fire and cast a branch thereon. And she sat in the warmth and reviewed Lady Doom's rede as well as Urd's final message, seeking answers that did not seem to be forthcoming. And slowly her watch passed as she pondered which way to ride on the morrow. Candlemarks eked by, and when she awakened Roél for his turn at ward, she had come to a conclusion. She embraced and kissed him, and as she lay down, she said, "Roél, think on what should be our course from here, and by morn let us see if we agree."

"My thoughts exactly, chérie," said Roél as he saddled his mount. "We must take the sinister path, and I believe we measure sinister from where we stood when Lady Doom spoke her rede. And as to 'left is right, but right a mistake,' mayhap it applies here—or not—though I do believe its true meaning is 'leftward is correct, but rightward is wrong.' Regardless as to whether that is the proper interpretation, I say we ride toward the west, in the sundown direction."

"Oui," said Céleste, pulling tight the girth strap 'round her mare. "Duskwise. Let us find this *Spx*, whatever that might be. Mayhap 'tis where the gray arrow lies."

And so they mounted up, and trailing the packhorses, sundownward they rode.

"Oh, now I understand," said Céleste, breaking out of her rumination.

"Understand what, chérie?"

"What Lady Doom meant when she said I was to think on the riddle she posed and the answer I had given."

Roél frowned, then cocked an eyebrow.

"Remember, she told me that I had answered all three riddles: hers, Verdandi's, and Skuld's. But I replied that I had said 'river' in response to her poser, which was neither a yes nor a no to the question at the end of the riddle. Anyway, she told me to think on it, and I have."

Roél smiled. "And what did you conclude?"

"That I didn't really have to answer the question, for by merely saying the name, or not being able to, that is answer enough."

Roél laughed and said, "Exactly so, chérie. But heed: even a wrong answer resolves the riddle, or rather the question as stated, for if one gives a wrong answer, then that means one's answer to the question is no."

"*Hmph*," grunted Céleste. "It's not much of a riddle if no answer at all as well as *any* answer—right or wrong—resolves it."

"Mayhap that's the way she planned it," said Roél.

"How so?"

"Love, I think the Fates truly wish to give us guidance, and so they make it as easy as they can without breaking those 'rules' they follow." Roél then shook his head and added, "As to why they would do so, I haven't a clue, yet I wish they could speak plainly instead of in murky redes."

Céleste nodded in agreement, but said, "I believe one of their rules must be that those they help must cipher out the meanings for themselves."

Roël nodded and on they fared, heading ever duskward as the sun rode up the sky.

Nigh midday, Roël said, "To the fore and left, Céleste, a long train of dust."

"A caravan, do you think?"

"Oui. Or the like."

Céleste frowned and said, "It is moving starwise and will cross our course. Perhaps we'll intercept it."

Closer they drew and closer, and Roël said, "Camels. It is a long train of camels."

"Oh, I've heard of them but have never seen such," said Céleste. "I hope we do cross their path, for I would see a camel."

Roël grunted and said. "I saw my fill of them during the war. They are swift, but are not as nimble as horses. And the warriors astride were quite good, especially with the bow; we were hard-pressed to defeat them. You and I must take care, Céleste, for should this be a military train, such men are fierce."

"Roël, someday, you will have to tell me of this war."

"Ah, me, chérie, I do not like to think about it, for many good men died . . . on both sides, I am certain."

"When you are ready, my love."

They rode without speaking for a while, and then Roël said, "It's not like single combat, where two knights agree upon the rules ere the fighting begins. Instead it is a charge of steeds and knights and footmen and a horrendous collision of armies crashing against one another, and confusion and chaos and a wild uproar filled with the clangor of weapons and belling of steeds and shouts of rage and cries of fear and the screams of the dying. All one can do is lay about and lay about and lay about, with hammers smashing and swords riving and spears stabbing and arrows piercing, with severed heads flying and entrails spilling forth like hideous blossoms blooming; hands and arms are lopped off in a dreadful pruning, and bones snap and skulls crunch beneath crushing blows. And then, finally it is over, and it seems a silence reigns, but the silence is only relative to what has gone before, for the field is littered with the dead and the dying, and men weep and cry out in an agony born of horrendous wounds, and horses scream of broken legs and ripped-open bellies; and the gorcrows and looters come to pick over the carrion, and—" Of a sudden, Roél became aware that Céleste had stopped the horses and had dismounted and now held him by the hand, and tears spilled down her cheeks as she looked up at him.

Her voice choked, yet she managed to say, "You need never tell me of this war you fought."

He nodded once, sharply, and whispered, "Let us ride on."

She looked up at him for a moment more, and then kissed his fingers and released his hand and turned and mounted her mare.

The caravan continued to fare starwise across the grassy plains, and as Céleste and Roél drew closer, Céleste said, "It looks as if their road will join ours. See, it curves 'round and does not cross over; I think it becomes one with this way."

Roél nodded but said nothing, and on they went.

Ahead, the caravan followed the arc and soon it was plodding duskwise, ahead of Céleste and Roél. It moved at a more leisurely pace than they did, and slowly the horses atrot overtook the ambling camels.

"It is a merchant train," said Roél, his first words in a while. "Not a military convoy. They have an escort of guards, though, so be wary."

Céleste slipped the keeper from her long-knife, and she

strung her bow, though she slipped it back into its saddle scabbard.

As they neared the tail end of the train, three camel-mounted guards—dusky-skinned and dressed in turbans and jodhpurs and boots and long riding coats under torso-covering bronze-plated armor, and armed with curved scimitars and lances and bows—slowed and waited for Céleste and Roél to reach them. One of the warders held out a hand palm forward and called out, *"Wakkif!"*

His meaning clear, both Roél and Céleste reined to a halt, and their mounts snorted as if to blow their nostrils free of the somewhat rank odor of camels, and it took a firm hand to keep the horses from sidling away.

"Min inte? Mnain jāyi? Intū kasdîn 'ala fên?" demanded the guard.

"Do you speak the common tongue?" asked Céleste.

The warder frowned. *"Kult ê?"*

Céleste sighed and said, *"Parlez-vous la vieille langue?"*

"Kult ê?"

She turned to Roél. "It seems he speaks neither Common nor the Old Tongue."

"I have heard such language as his in my travels, though I do not speak it," said Roél. "It sounds as if he is from Arabia."

The man looked at Roél and said, *"Betî? ham 'arabi?"*

Roél shrugged and shook his head, saying, "I think he just asked if I speak Arabic."

Another warder came riding back, this one with gold braid 'round his turban. He spoke to the guards, and they treated him with deference.

"It seems he's the captain," said Roél.

The man looked at Céleste and dismissed her with a gesture, at which she bristled but remained silent, but Roél he eyed with some respect. Yet he, too, did not understand either the Old Tongue or Common.

Roél clapped a hand to his own chest and said, "Chevalier Roél." He gestured toward Céleste and said, "She is with me." Again Céleste bristled, but still she remained silent.

Once more Roél slapped his chest and then pointed duskward along the road and said, "We ride yon."

The captain slowly scanned the plain; the land was empty as far as the eye could see. He said something to the three other warders, and they reined their camels about, the animals turning at the tugs on their nose rings, and with the beasts groaning and *hronking*, and blue tassels swinging from saddle blankets, and the riders thumping the camels with switches and crying, "*Hut, hut, hut, haijin. Yallah, yallah!*" they rode to catch the caravan and resume their posts.

The captain once more scanned out to the horizon, and then said, "*Kammil*," and he gestured for them to continue riding duskwise.

Quietly Roél said, "chérie, if they are from Aegypt or *Arabie*, they do not consider women the equal of men. It would be best if you rode slightly back and to my left."

Céleste hissed, and then muttered, "As you will, my master. Yet be aware, love, you will someday pay for this." Then she grinned at Roél's gape.

Roél then laughed and heeled his mare and together they rode onward, did the knight and his lagging princess.

And slowly they passed alongside the camel train, the beasts laden with trade goods. Dark-skinned men walked alongside, while others rode, trailing the pack animals on tethers running to nose rings.

"That must be painful," said Céleste, "yet fear not, my love, I'll not leash you that way."

Roél burst into laughter, and on they fared.

For the rest of the day they rode, and that evening as dusk was falling, and even as they espied in the distance to the fore the twilight bound looming up into the sky, they heard water running somewhere to the starwise side of the road, and there they found a spring bubbling out from the ground and running through the grass and down a gentle slope.

"That's odd," said Roël, looking about. "There are no hills or mountains nearby, yet here we have a fountainhead."

"'Tis Faery, love," said Céleste. She glanced at the darkening sky and added, "Perhaps we should camp here."

"Oui," said Roël. "It is a good place. And on the morrow we can cross through the twilight and mayhap find the gray arrow."

The next dawn, as they were breaking camp, a turbaned rider came to the spring and stopped to let his camel drink its fill.

"A scout, I think," said Roël, "from the caravan."

As the beast sucked water, Céleste stepped to the man and offered him a cup of tea. The scout took it and smiled and nodded his thanks.

Roël saddled the mares while Céleste removed the nose bags and stowed them away. As she tied the bundles, the turbaned man rinsed out the tin cup and stepped to her side, and smiling and nodding, he handed the vessel to her. Then he helped Roël lade the gear onto the geldings. Finally, all was ready, and Céleste and Roël mounted up, and the scout strode to his now-grazing camel and commanded the beast to kneel; then he, too, mounted and got the animal to its feet.

They rode together in a comfortable quietness for a ways, still going duskwise. The horses snorted and were somewhat nervous in the presence of the camel, yet Roël and Céleste held them firmly, and after a while they settled.

But within a league they came to a juncture, where a trail continued on toward the twilight bound, but the road began a slow arc starwise. Roël reined to a halt, Céleste stopping as well. The scout stayed his camel alongside them, a puzzled look on his face.

"Which way, chérie?" asked Roél. "What says the map?"

Céleste unfolded the vellum and looked and sighed. "This road is not on the chart, nor the fork and the path beyond. We are to look for three boulders at the crossing, though."

Roél nodded and said, "Then let us choose."

As Céleste refolded the map she said, "Perhaps 'left is right, but right a mistake' applies here."

"Hmm . . . do you think? If so, then we should take the straight-ahead path."

"I agree," said Céleste, nodding.

"Betif' tikir bi~ê?" asked the scout.

"I believe he wants to know where we plan to go," said Roél, and he pointed to himself and Céleste and then down the trail toward the wall of twilight looming in the near distance.

Frantically the scout shook his head and waved his hand back and forth in a negative gesture, saying, "Lâ! Lâ! Abulhôl! Abul-hôl!"

Roél shrugged and turned his palms up, clearly showing that he didn't understand.

The man then patted up and down the length of his own body from shoulders to hips and then moved his hands as if he were turning his torso sideways. And then he stretched and stretched the envisioned form and held out his arms wide, indicating a gigantic body. He drew forth from the lower tip of his spine a make-believe tail and added it to the pretend body. Then he framed his face and lifted an imaginary head and placed it on the conjured creature. Lastly he clawed at the air and roared and then said, "Abulhôl."

"Some sort of huge, man-headed beast," said Céleste.

Roél nodded. "Still, chérie, beast or no, I deem we must take the sinister way, for if left is right, and right a mistake, then somewhere ahead we must cross."

Céleste nodded and said, "Even if this isn't the right way, we can follow the wall till we find the three boulders."

"Just so," said Roél, and he turned to the scout and shrugged. Then Roél touched his shield and lance and said, "Large or not, my spear and a swift charge should do."

The scout moaned and shook his head and said, "Lá, lá, Inte raltán."

"Whatever he is telling us," said Céleste, "he thinks we are making a mistake."

"Nevertheless . . . ," said Roél, and he turned up his hands and shrugged, and then heeled his mare and started down the path, Céleste following.

For long moments the scout watched them ride away. Then he shook his head and turned his camel, and starwise along the road he fared.

A candlemark passed and then another, and nearer to the bound rode Céleste and Roél. Finally, "There are the boulders," said Céleste, pointing ahead. "I deem we have chosen aright."

Roél nodded and said, "If indeed we were to continue dusk-wise, though Lady Doom did not say."

Finally they came to the crossing and stopped. Roél dismounted and tethered his mount to Céleste's gelding, then tied a rope 'round his waist. He handed the coil to Céleste, and she tied the end to her saddle cantle. As Roél took his shield in hand and drew Coeur d'Acier, he grinned and said, "Try not to drag me across all of Faery, my love."

Céleste tentatively smiled but said nought.

Roél strode into the twilight, Céleste following, horses in tow. As they reached the midmost ebon wall, she stopped and payed out the line as Roél stepped on beyond. More and more length he took, and finally all rope was let out. Then it went slack, and Céleste began drawing it in and coiling it. At last Roél came through the midpoint, and in the darkness as he untied the line from his waist he said, "'Tis good that we filled all skins with water, for 'tis sand, all sand beyond, great dunes for as far as the eye can see."

"What of the monstrous man-headed creature?" asked Céleste.

"No sign of such," said Roél. "I believe the scout was speaking of a mythical beast that only exists in fable or imagination."

Though Roél could not clearly see Céleste in the twilight, she shook her head, saying, "Forget not, love, 'tis Faery."

Roél groaned and said, "Ah, me, you would have to bring that up." He stepped to his mare and hung his shield on its saddle hook, and then untethered the horse and mounted and rode forward to Céleste and said, "Shall we?"

"Let's do," said she, and laughed, and smiling, together they rode into the desert sands.

31

Cíent

Over the sea raced the *Eagle* and into a raging storm, and the decks pitched and men were hard-pressed to keep control of the animals. Many members of the warband lost their breakfasts and lunches and other meals throughout the day, and yet they persevered as under foul weather they ran. Yet the winds were strong and in their favor, and three days later they arrived in Port Cíent just as night drew across the land, and they spent much of that eve off-loading the animals and equipment and men.

It was here that Vicomte Chevell and some of his crew declared they would go with the warband, and so they depleted the fund of horses in that port city.

And running at a fair pace, the combined force rode away from Cíent the very next dawn.

There were but six days left ere the night of the dark of the moon, and they had far to go.

32

Sand

Into a world of dunes the chevalier and princess rode, under a cloudless sky. The desert stretched out before them like a golden ocean of long, rolling waves frozen in place. They had entered in midmorn, and the day was mild, rather than scorching, as across the sands they fared, as if spring or autumn lay upon this part of Faery, rather than a time of torrid summer or that of frigid winter.

As they had entered this domain, Roél had looked about and said, "I see no markers to get us back. What does the chart say?"

Céleste had then unfolded the vellum and had looked at the notation. "It says there is an obelisk at hand." She looked up and 'round. "Yet I see none."

Roél sighed. "Covered by sand, I think. Is there any other means to find our way to this very place again?"

Once more Céleste peered at the chart. "The *Spx* lies due duskward from here. Hence if we ride due dawnwise from whatever it might be, we can come back. . . . Ah, yet wait, there is a way to the Changeling realm from the *Spx*; hence we do not need to return."

"Another way?"

"Oui. Across two borders. If we find the gray arrow at Spx or El Fd or Ct Dd or mayhap somewhere beyond, it will be the shortest way to the Lord of the Changelings' tower."

"Bon! Then let us ride."

And so they had ridden.

And the day had waxed and waned, and in midafternoon they had fared beyond the dunes and into an arid wasteland with nought but sparse patches of thorny scrub dotting the barren, rock-laden 'scape.

On they went across the desert, and as evening drew nigh Roél said, "Watch for birds."

"Why so, love?"

"We need water and a place to camp, and at dawn and dusk they will lead the way."

"And you know this because . . . ?"

"Some of the war took place in an arid waste; I learned it from those who had been there as we rode home."

Céleste asked no more, for she was yet shaken by Roél's revelations with regard to armies in war, and she knew that he was deeply troubled by his experiences in battle. Oh, my love, my dearest heart, do you see blood on your hands? What was it you said? That good men had died on both sides? Oui, that was it. Until that very moment I had never thought of the enemy, the foe, as having good men as well. Non, but mayhap I have an excuse for never thinking such, for all I have known as an enemy are Redcap Goblins and Trolls and Bogles and other such vile beings. . . . Yet I wonder: are Redcaps ever good? Trolls? Bogles and the like? I do know that some Goblins are pleasant and well-mannered and kind: House Goblins for one, Barn Goblins for another. And I have seen—

"There!" called Roél.

Céleste looked where Roél pointed. In the near distance directly ahead two swift doves flew toward what appeared to be a great jumble of boulders. They spiraled 'round and down and disappeared among the huge rocks.

"We should find water there," said Roél, and he urged his mare into a trot, with Céleste following after.

Downslope they went, into a broad basin, in the mid of which there rose up the enormous pile of massive stones. As they approached, they could see enshadowed openings here and there, dark slots where the gigantic boulders rested against one another. "We'll have to be wary," said Roél, "for we know not what might reside within: asps, vipers, scorpions, jackals, even desert lions. If it's a large beast or a den of snakes, I deem the horses will give warning."

"Would doves likely go into a nest of vipers?" asked Céleste as she strung her bow.

"Mayhap," said Roél, cocking his crossbow and laying a quarrel in the groove. "Who knows what birds and other creatures will do for a drink?"

Céleste smiled. "Well, my love, we are about to find out, n'est-ce pas?"

"Indeed we are," replied Roél.

They rode to the foot of the great mound of monstrous boulders, rising up out from the barren plain much like a rocky tor. Roél said, "chérie, I would have you wait with our horses while I go within, for who knows what might come running out? And I would not have the animals bolt."

Céleste sighed in exasperation, but then she smiled and said, "And just what should I do if it is you who comes running out?"

Roél grinned and said, "Flee!"

"If so, perhaps I'll leave you a horse, but then again, maybe not."

Roél laughed and dismounted and handed Céleste his reins. As Céleste looped the lead about the forebow of her saddle and nocked an arrow, Roél took a lantern from one of the packs and struck the striker and opened the hood wide, and with his crossbow in hand, in through one of the great crevices he cautiously stepped. Moments later, the horses flinched and snorted in startlement and Céleste jerked up her bow as, in a thunder of wings, birds fled the jumble, desert crows crying and doves whistling as they hammered away. Off to the right a jackal ran out from the rocks and through the scrub, yipping in its flight.

"Roél!" called Céleste. "Are you well?"

"Oui," came a faint cry. "There is water herein . . . and scorpions."

"Rain?"

Céleste took in a deep breath and muttered, "Oh, my love, take care."

Finally, Roél emerged. "A deep pool, not a spring. Likely from rain."

"Oui, Céleste. Mayhap monsoons bring it, or perhaps the winter. The rocks protect the mere from the sun." He gestured back the way they had come. "Out there the water is sucked up by the sand, but here in this basin I think there must be a good layer of stone below, forming a wide catchment." Roél smiled and said, "There are some boulders in the pool, and that is where the birds roost, protected as if by a moat from the scorpions."

"Can we safely water the horses?"

"I believe so. Those poisonous creatures scuttled away from my footfalls. We cannot camp here, though, for sleeping among scorpions would be most painful if not fatal."

Céleste glanced at the sun, now on the verge of setting. Dismounting, she said, "Then let us water the animals and go, for I would find a camp ere the light completely fails."

Leading the mares, the geldings following, into the crevice they went, the horses balking somewhat at the narrow confines, but eventually the smell of water overcame their fears.

That night Roél and Céleste camped on the rim of the basin, a safe distance from the scorpion den.

*　　　*

*　　　*

The next morning, once more they let the horses drink their fill, and they made certain that their waterskins were full to the stoppers, and then they set out, again riding due duskwise.

Across barren ground and past clusters of sere vegetation they fared, and now and then they crossed down and through rock-laden wadis, ancient tracks of fierce water flow, now dry under the desert sun. On they rode and on, and in early morn a warm breeze began to blow at their backs, growing hotter with every league, and they cast their cloak hoods over their heads against the glare of the day. And once again they came to long, rolling dunes, and into the sand they passed.

With a now-torrid wind from behind and as the sun reached halfway to the zenith, they topped a dune and a league or so distant down a long slope of sand and across a flat lay a walled city, with tall pylons standing beside a wide gateway, past which a long row of massive columns led into the metropolis beyond. The buildings within were made of stone, or so it seemed, and some bore flat roofs with massive cornices, though others seemed to have collapsed.

Roél shaded his eyes and above the lash of wind he called, "I see no movement."

Céleste frowned. "Perhaps it is abandoned," she said, raising her voice to be heard.

"Oui, so it seems."

"Mayhap this is where we'll find the gray arrow," said Céleste.

"We can only hope," replied Roél, "as well as hope we find water therein. Come, let us ride."

With their cloaks whipping about, they started down the long run of sand, and Céleste said, "Think you this is the place marked *Spx* on the chart?"

Roél grunted and shrugged, and on they fared.

They had covered perhaps half the distance when the day

about them darkened. "What th—?" Roél looked up toward the sun and then back. "Céleste, we must fly!"

The princess glanced 'round; behind and hurtling toward them came a great dark roiling wall looming miles up into the sky and blotting out the very sun.

"Ride, Céleste, ride!" cried Roél, spurring forward.

Céleste whipped her mare into a gallop, the gelding running after, and down the slope and toward the city she and Roél and the horses fled. And rushing after roared a boiling wall of sand that would flay them alive should it catch them.

"Yah! Yah!" cried Céleste, driving her mare to even greater speed, and over the barren ground they now flew. Yet the storm was even faster, and for every stride they took it gained three.

Céleste drew even with Roél, and he called out, "Shelter behind the stone ramparts." And on they careered, the horses now running flat out, and Céleste, with her lighter weight, slowly drew ahead of Roél.

Oh, Mithras, I can't leave him.

But Roél, as if he were reading her thoughts, cried, "Ride on, Céleste, ride on!"

And so on she rode, as the great black wall of the storm hurtled after, now but mere heartbeats arear, now but mere moments ere it would roar o'er all.

Before her lay the gateway, flanked by two tall stone statues, a king and a queen, perhaps, their feet buried in drift, sitting on stone thrones beside the massive pylons; and as she flashed past and through the opening, she thought she saw the figures turn their heads toward her, but in that moment the stygian wall slammed into the gateway even as she veered leftward out of the slot to take refuge behind the high rampart; and the blast of sand screamed past and above and shrieked in rage at missing her, or so it seemed.

Céleste sprang down from her mare, and pulling the horses after, she headed for the base of the wall for better shelter. Finally she reached the stone bulwark, and there she stopped.

In the darkness she looked about.

Of Roél there was no sign.

Céleste called out, but the black storm ripped her words to shreds and flung the remnants away.

Oh, Mithras, Mithras, please let him be safe.

But only the howl of the tearing wind came in answer to her prayer.

33

Abulhôl

The storm roared among the pillars and buildings and steles and pylons and statues and ruins, sand hammering against stone as if to obliterate this anomaly within the pristine desert. And behind the protection of the wall where Céleste had taken shelter, dust swirled and tried to choke these interlopers, woman and horses both. Céleste tied a cloth across her mouth and nose, and she put a ration of oats into two feed bags and, with difficulty, she slipped them onto her mare and gelding, for they were affrighted, agitated by the ceaseless howl. And she soothed them, and food seemed to help. And when they settled somewhat, she loosely draped cloth 'round the brims of the feed bags to fend dust from their breathing as well. She tethered them to one of the slender pillars bracing an overhanging walkway; she unladed the gelding and unsaddled the mare, and then she sat down, her back to the stone of the wall, and waited.

Oh, my Roël, are you safe? Out of the wind, out of the storm? Or are you trapped within its clutches? Please, Mithras, let him not be in harm's way.

And the furious storm raved, the shrieking wind clawing at anything and everything in its path, yet in spite of the thundering blow, Céleste fell into slumber.

And she dreamed. . . .

. . . At one and the same time she sat on a cushion and watched herself dance, and she was naked, but for a small strip of cloth about her loins and the garlands of blue lotuses gracing her form. Her skin was dusky, and her hair raven black, and her eyes a brown so deep as to seem ebon. A man sat beside her and watched her dance as well, his enormous erection jutting out from his loincloth. And she was jealous of herself and enraged, and she felt exhilaration that as she spun and gyred she provoked such desire in this powerful man. He would be hers, he would be hers, and as she whirled the lotus blossoms lifted up from her breasts and the gauzy strip twirled out from her loins, each revealing and then concealing, and she knew he would build a city for her, and it would be a funeral monument as soon as she crushed the lethal juice from the deadly flowers and contrived a way to poison this little scheming, spinning slut with her kohl-painted eyes and red-ochre lips and her lithe, myrrh-scented body, who thought to take her place, for she would have no one become First Wife over her. . . .

. . . A jackal-headed man presided over the three-moons-long preparations as her envenomed organs were removed from her body and treated with sea salt and linen-wrapped and preserved in canopic jars; and her corpse was also treated with salt and then scented oils and fragrant spices and bestowed with gold and gems and rings and bracelets and necklaces, and then linen-wrapped to be sent on her way. A portrait mask was put over her face so that the gods would recognize her, and, along with the canopic jars, she was laid in a rosewood coffin, and that in turn was placed in her lapis-lazuli-decorated, gilded sarcophagus. . . .

. . . And the funeral was delicious, and the great man wept, and he turned to her for solace, even as she watched as she was solemnly entombed with her jewelry and wine and servants and provisions and trinkets and couches and divans and clothing and gold and food and other such goods she would need in the after-life. And as she took the great man to bed, she looked out from her vault as the boatman came to ferry her and her servants across to Duat and—

—Céleste jerked awake.

What th—? What was that sound?

She peered 'round. The horses stood adoze, their feed bags yet in place, and all was still, and stars glittered overhead. *The storm. It's gone. It's blown itself out. —Roël!*

Céleste scrambled up and pulled the dusty cloth away from her equally dusty face and called out, "Roël!"

There was no answer.

Keeping next to the wall, to the gateway she stepped and out, and she peered through the starlight and the glow of the half-risen half-moon and into the desert beyond.

No one was there: all was emptiness.

Back in through the gateway she trod, and she looked to her right, and in the distant shadows she saw large forms—horses—and Roël sat with his back to the wall, his sword unsheathed and lying at hand, and he was sound asleep.

"Oh, my love, my love," she cried, and she ran to him and dropped to her knees.

He opened his eyes, and he reached out and took her in his arms and pulled her into his lap.

Fiercely she embraced him, as tears of relief and the release of tension ran down her dust-laden cheeks, leaving tracks of mud behind.

"Oh, Roël, I thought you lost."

"Non, love, I galloped right behind, but I deemed you had turned dextral, not sinister. I should have known: left is right, but right a mistake, and it seems I made that mistake."

Céleste laughed through her tears, but she did not loosen her clutch.

"Your horses?" asked Roél.

"They are well. I put feed bags over their noses to save them from the grit."

Roél laughed and said, "As did I."

He kissed her and said, "I had the strangest dream."

"You did?"

"Oui. I was a king of some sort, in love with a young maiden, but she—"

"—she died of poison," said Céleste. "And all of this, all of this city, it is her funeral monument."

"Why, yes," said Roél, his eyes wide in amaze. "But how did you—?"

"I had the same dream, my love, but I was that dancing girl as well as the king's first wife. I was insanely jealous of me, and so I, the wife, poisoned myself, the dancer."

"How can we have the same dream?" asked Roél.

"I think it is much like the mansion Lokar savaged, only in this case it is the stone itself recalling a terrible tragedy and somehow showing it to us as we slept. After all, this entire city is a shrine to she who danced, and what better place to hold those memories?"

Roél smiled down at Céleste and said, "Given your predilections as First Wife, remind me to never look at another woman."

Céleste laughed and said, "Oh, you need not worry, my love, for, First Wife or no, I will always be your dancing girl."

Again Roél kissed her, and then he said, "Speaking of the city, let us see what we have here. Mayhap we'll find the gray arrow."

Céleste disengaged and stood, Roél gaining his feet as well. He stepped to his horses and removed the cloth and feed bags, and then he saddled his mare and laded the gelding and led them after.

They retrieved Céleste's horses and made them ready for travel, and they watered the animals and took deep draughts of their own, and then they set out to explore the ruins.

"What language is this?" asked Céleste, examining the carvings on the part of the stele jutting up from the encroaching sand. "I see birds and fish, cattle, beetles, flowers, and shepherds' crooks all mixed in with these strange glyphs."

Roél held up the lantern and peered at the blend of pictograms and characters. "I know not the tongue, and though I had not seen such writing ere now, I had heard of it from those who fought in the desert during the war. They say no one knows how to read it." He stepped to an adjacent side of the obelisk to find more of the same.

Céleste frowned, and in the moonlight she touched a carving and said, "Look here, Roél. Several symbols are collected together and enclosed in this oblong oval, while most other glyphs are not. Perhaps it's somehow important enough to be encircled. What think you this encasement means?"

Roél stepped back 'round and looked at the carving. "I do not know," he replied, running his finger along the outline. "Perhaps this is what one of the knights called a cartouche. Here is an ibis—he spoke of them—carrion eaters, and here I think is a jackal, rather like a fox of the desert—or so the knight said—but these other symbols I do not know. Oui, mayhap a cartouche is important, but as to what it signifies, that I cannot say."

They looked at the markings on the stele a moment more, and then turned away, and leading their horses, among the plinths and obelisks and columns and pillars and buildings of the abandoned city they went. And sand ramped up against walls and monuments, and some ruins but barely showed. At every structure where they could, they stepped inside and searched, but no gray arrow did they find.

Nor did they find a well or other source of water.

From the mid of night onward they trod among the stones of the shrine, neither Roél nor Céleste needing slumber, for they had slept through the full of the storm. And it took the rest of the darktide for them to explore each of the buildings and ruins, all to no end.

Yet throughout their sweep, there was something of a puzzle, for in every part of the city they had found widely scattered human bones—skulls, leg and arm bones, ribs, pelvises, spines, and the bones of feet and hands—some broken, others not, some with shreds of cloth yet clinging, most half-buried, some out in the open, but all sunbaked, sun bleached, and long dead, and seldom was any bone properly attached to its rightful mate. "It's as if someone or something has ripped people asunder," had said Roél upon coming across yet another skull, and he had loosened Coeur d'Acier in its sheath and on they had gone, finding nought of what they wanted, though more bones did they see.

It was as the sky began to lighten with the onset of dawn that they came to the far gateway through the opposite wall.

Céleste gazed back at the memorial city and sighed and said, "Roél, we must go on, for—"

"chérie, look."

Céleste's gaze followed Roél's outstretched arm, and in the shadows of dawn loomed a great stone figure of some sort. Roél began leading his horses toward the monument, Céleste following.

As the sky lightened even more, they could see that the statue was some form of creature resting in the sand and facing dawnward, facing into the city. Enormous it was and lionlike it seemed, and they walked in between the outstretched forelegs and toward its uplifted head. "Mithras, but it's huge," said Roél, gazing upward as they came to a stop. And now they could see that although it had the body of a lion, it had the features of a man.

"Ha!" exclaimed Roél. "Here we have what the caravan scout called an 'Abulhôl,' yet I know it as a Sphinx."

And as the first rays of the sun shone through the far gateway and down the wide avenue and out the near gateway to illuminate the stone creature's face, Céleste frowned and said, "Sphinx, oui, but why was the scout so frightened?"

In that moment the Abulhôl bent its head downward and fixed them with its stone gaze and grated, "Tomb robbers deserve nought but my fury," and it unsheathed its great claws to deal death.

34

Sphinx

Roél stepped in front of Céleste and wrenched Coeur d'Acier from its sheath and flashed it on high, and the silvered steel blade blazed like argent fire in the rays of the morning sun. But ere Roél could bring the weapon to bear against the monstrous creature of stone, Céleste cried out, "My Lord Sphinx, we are not tomb robbers nor did we come to steal ought."

Even as the Abulhôl raised his massive paw to strike, he roared, "That is what they all say!"

The horses reared and belled in fright, and Céleste and Roél, yet holding their leads, were dragged hindward. And even as she fought for control of her mare, Céleste cried, "In our case, it is true, my lord. No tomb robbers are we, but instead are on a quest."

The Sphinx stayed his strike, and one of his stone eyebrows rose. "Quest?" He lowered his huge foreleg.

"Oui, my lord," said Céleste, yet struggling with her mare. "A mission of rescue."

Although Roél sheathed his sword, the Sphinx did not

sheathe its claws, but instead interlaced them to close the way back out so that Céleste and Roél and the horses were trapped in its encirclement. And as the two gained control of the horses, the monster glared down at them. "Hmm . . ." it rumbled, and then inhaled through its nose a great breath. As a creature of solid stone how it could do so, neither Céleste nor Roél could say, yet inhale it did. "I smell gold, yet it is not gold from the tomb, nor do you have gems or other treasures from there."

Céleste spread her arms wide, her hands open and empty, and she said, "We have none, Lord Abulhôl."

"Abulhôl, Abulhôl? Ah, yes, the nomads call me that, they who are descended from those created by Lord Atum known as Amun known as Ptah, and though the nomads no longer speak the true tongue of the pharaohs, still it is one of my many names."

"Many names, my lord?"

"I am the Sphinx, the Abulhôl, sometimes mistakenly called Kheperi and Re and Atum; I am the Guardian of the Horizon, the Protector of the Dawn; I am the Seeker of Knowledge, the Asker of Riddles, the Enigma; I am set here by Osiris, Lord of the Underworld; I ward this shrine, and any who would violate it feels my wrath."

"Ah, oui, the bones," said Céleste. "We have seen your handiwork, my lord."

The Abulhôl glanced at the city and nodded. "Desecrating tomb raiders all."

"A well-deserved fate, my lord."

The Sphinx nodded, then said, "Speak of this quest, and perhaps I will let you live, mayhap even aid you. But first I would have your names."

"My Lord Sphinx, I am Céleste, Princesse de la Forêt de Printemps, and my companion is my betrothed, Sieur Roél, Chevalier du Manoir d'Émile." Céleste deeply curtseyed and Roél made a sweeping bow.

Clearly flattered by their courtesy, the Abulhôl canted his head forward in acknowledgment and said, "Ah, royalty and chivalry. Well, then, since you have passed through the shrine to Meketaten without taking ought, and since you are a princess and a knight, no tomb raiders are you. Hence, I will let you live." The Sphinx then sheathed his great claws and said, "But before I give aid, I would have you speak of this quest."

Céleste said, "'Tis a tale better told by Sieur Roél." And she stepped back while Roél stepped forward.

"It begins many seasons past, Lord Sphinx, when I was but a lad. My sister, Avélaine, was troubled by her upcoming arranged marriage to someone she didn't love, and she and I had ridden out to the ruins of a temple, where . . ."

" . . And so you see, we are not after treasure, but a gray arrow instead."

"And you say the Fates sent you to find such?"

"Oui. Without it we will fail."

"Hmm . . ." rumbled the Sphinx. "What you seek is the arrow that slew Achilles, for not even the gods could turn that one aside."

"Know you where this arrow lies?" asked Roél. "I would go through Hell itself to save my sister and brothers."

The Abulhôl rumbled a laugh and said, "Just so, my boy, just so, for to reach it, you will have to go through the realm of Lord Hades."

"Erebus? We must go through Erebus?"

"You know of Erebus?" asked the Sphinx, somewhat surprised.

"I have read a few of the Greek legends of old," replied Roél.

"As have I," said Céleste, "yet I knew not that Erebus is of Faery."

"It is not," said the Abulhôl. He gestured about and added, "Just as these sands are not of Faery."

Céleste's eyes widened in amaze. "Not of Faery? If we are not in Faery, just where are we?"

The Sphinx smiled and said, "Ever since you crossed out from Faery and into these sands, you have been in a remote area of a realm called Aegypt."

Roél shrugged and said, "Regardless as to whether we are in Faery or no, where lies this gray arrow?"

"It is held in the hands of an idol in a temple on the central square of the City of the Dead."

"And where might we find this City of the Dead?"

"Beyond the black doorway in the Hall of Heroes in the Elysian Fields."

Céleste frowned as if trying to capture an elusive thought. Of a sudden her eyes widened in revelation. "*That's* what they mean. Roél, our map: *Spx*: Sphinx. *El Fd*: Elysian Fields. *Ct Dd*: City of the Dead." But then her face fell and she said, "Oh, my love, I thought all we needed to do was follow our chart duskwise, but if we are to go to the underworld of Erebus, I know not what to do."

The Sphinx smiled and, with a grating of stone, slowly shook its head. "Quite right, Princess; you will not reach the City of the Dead by riding duskwise."

Roél said, "My Lord Sphinx, you are the guardian of this shrine, one in which I witnessed in a dream a ship that came to bear a loved one away to the afterlife in the underworld. Can you help us find that ship? If not, then our mission will fail, for we need the gray arrow, and time grows perilously short."

Solemnly the Abulhôl nodded. "Indeed, for there is not but this day and four more ere the night of the dark of the moon. Yet it is a terrible thing you ask, for the living have seldom ridden the ferry to the underworld. Still, where you must go is not to Duat—the domain of Osiris—but to that of Hades instead, to his netherworld; hence you will not ride that ferry, but another one altogether."

"Nevertheless, Lord Sphinx, can you aid us?"

Slowly the Abulhôl nodded, stone grating on stone. "I can start you on your way, yet I am bound much as are the Three Sisters: you must answer a riddle of mine ere I can give aid. And if you fail, I must slay you."

Céleste groaned, but Roél said, "Speak your conundrum, then."

But Céleste held up a hand and said, "My Lord Sphinx, in all honor, I find it only fair to warn you, I know the answer to your most famous riddle."

"The one Oedipus solved?"

"Oui."

"Ah, that is not mine but the riddle of one of my sisters, she of the eagle's wings and lion's body and a beautiful woman's face. Nay, I will not ask her riddle, but another one instead."

Céleste sighed and signed for the Abulhôl to proceed.

And from the surrounding air there sounded the song of the plucked strings of a lyre, and the Sphinx intoned:

I go on no legs in the morning,
And my no legs are my last.
I go on two legs in the noontide,
I have just had a repast.
Four legs I dine in the dark nighttide,
Now you must name me at last."

Once again the great deadly claws of the Abulhôl came sliding forth.

Céleste glanced at Roél, and his face was filled with distress. He turned up his hands, and she despaired: *Roél has no answer, and neither do I. Think, Céleste, think! No legs? What has no legs? And how can no legs become two legs and then four legs? This Sphinx, this Abulhôl, this creature of the desert, has posed an unsolvab—*

She looked up and smiled and said, "My Lord Sphinx, a being of the desert you are, and so creatures of the desert are perhaps the answer."

The Abulhôl looked down at her and said, "And what would they be?"

Céleste took a deep breath and braced herself and said, "'Tis a dying asp in the morning whose corpse is eaten by an ibis at noon which in turn is eaten by a jackal at night; hence no legs in the morning is taken in by two legs at noon, and two legs with no legs inside is taken in by four legs in the dark night-tide."

The Sphinx nodded and said, "Very good, Princess," and it sheathed its claws.

Tears of relief sprang into Céleste's eyes.

Roél said, "Lady Doom was right: you are quite good at riddles. But how did you . . . ?"

"Oh, love, the answer is in the second line of the riddle."

Roél frowned. "'And my no legs are my last'? But how can that—? Ah, I see: when something is on its last legs, it is dying. And a no-legs thing on its so-called 'last legs' is a dying snake, an asp in this case, and it becomes carrion."

"Oui, and what eats carrion? An ibis. You said so yourself back at the stele. And I guessed the four legs was a jackal, for one of those was on the stele as well."

Roél embraced Céleste and kissed her. "Oh, my love, if we succeed in saving my sister and brothers, it will be because of you—your wit, your courage, your prowess with a bow. I could not ask for a better companion."

Céleste took Roél's face in her hands, and she kissed him deeply, only to be interrupted by a grinding "Harrumph!"

She turned and looked up at the Sphinx, and it was smiling.

"If you two are finished with this unseemly display of affection . . ."

"We are, Lord Sphinx," said Céleste.

". . . then I shall start you on your journey to the land of the dead. Yet heed, your path will be quite difficult, for, as Lady Doom said, creatures and heroes and the dead will test you along the way. Well, I am a creature, and I did put you to trial, but there are more ordeals to come. And recall, as Lady Lot said of the tests you will face along the way, you must win them all, just as you won the one with me."

"Yes, Lord Abulhôl, well do we understand," said Roél.

"Then I will lead you to the gateway to the land of the dead, but heed me, take nothing you see in the tomb of Meketaten; else I will hunt you down and slay you outright."

"You have my pledge as a knight," said Roél.

"And mine as the Princess of the Springwood," said Céleste.

The great Sphinx nodded his acceptance, and said, "Then follow me," and he stood, and sand cascaded from his flanks and came roaring down in a great pour. The horses snorted and reared, and it was all Céleste and Roél could do to maintain control.

Now looming above them, the massive creature strode forward, its ponderous steps thudding, seeming to judder the very world with each thundering footfall.

"His tail!" cried Céleste, and she sprang into her saddle as Roél leapt into his, and they turned the horses and galloped out from under the belly of the monstrous Sphinx just as his massive stone tail dragged through the place where they had been. And the Abulhôl laughed, his gaiety sounding as would an avalanche of tumbling boulders.

Toward the city he walked, and each step shivered the ground, and the sloping sand against the ramparts shuddered and ran down. Céleste and Roél trailed at a safe distance, and as the Sphinx came to the wall, he lifted his tail and delicately stepped within the bounds of the shrine.

And now like a great cat he padded, gently easing his feet down. Toward an enormous cube of stone in the city center he softly stepped, carefully passing by steles and pylons and buildings and columnar rows and ruins, and when he reached the huge block he stopped and looked 'round at Céleste and Roél following.

"I think you will need to dismount and lead your horses," said the Sphinx, "for the entrance is quite low. And light a lantern; you will need it to find the way."

And so the princess and her knight dismounted, and Céleste took his reins while Roél fetched a lantern from the packs and set it aglow.

When all was ready, "Keep in mind your pledge concerning Meketaten's tomb," rumbled the Abulhôl.

"We will, my lord," said Céleste.

"And remember, you must pass all tests; else you will not find the arrow of gray."

"We understand, Lord Sphinx," said Roél, "and we stand prepared."

The Abulhôl sounded a chuckle like sliding rocks and said, "I doubt that." And then the creature turned to the great slab and whispered an ancient word, and a dark opening appeared; then the Sphinx stepped aside. "Fare well, and I pray the light of Re shines down upon you both."

Céleste curtseyed and Roél bowed, and Céleste said, "And may Mithras find favor in you, Lord Abulhôl."

The Sphinx roared in laughter and said, "Do you not know, Princess, that Mithras and Re are one and the same? Now go; you are keeping me from my sleep."

"As you wish, my lord," said Céleste, and then she turned and followed Roél into the shadows beyond.

35

Thoth

Into the mausoleum they went, and when the last horse clattered onto the marble floor, from behind there came a thunderclap that reverberated throughout the looming shadows. Céleste turned 'round, and by the light of the lantern Roél carried, she could no longer see the opening they had entered; only solid stone met her gaze. . . .

. . . There was no way back out.

Tall columns loomed up into darkness above, and from left and right aureate glints came winging to the eye from gilded chests and rich fabrics and golden goblets and other such treasures. Sparks of sapphire and scarlet and emerald and sunshine glittered forth from gems and jewels and jades. Silver chalices there were, filled with crystals of quartz and amethyst and chrysoberyl.

"Oh, my, what wealth," breathed Céleste.

"But look beyond, my love," said Roél.

And deeper in the shadows there stood linen-wrapped forms, shields on their arms, spears in their hands.

"Guardians?" asked Céleste.

"Oui."

"Did they murder men simply to have an honor guard for Meketaten?"

"It would seem so," said Roël.

"Oh, how utterly cruel."

"Mayhap not cruel, chérie. Instead I deem it a useless waste. Still, I think they might have gone willingly, for I ween they believed it assured them a place of honor in the afterlife."

Céleste growled, but said nought.

Roël held his lantern on high, and it shone upon a sarcophagus, and on the lid a carved black jackal with golden eyes and golden ears and a golden collar reclined on its stomach, its head held up, as if alert, as if it, too, was a guardian.

"It is my *sarcophage*," said Céleste, "or so it was in my dream."

"I remember," said Roël.

"Oh, Roël, look."

Standing in ranks beyond the sarcophagus were the mummified remains of perhaps a hundred people.

"The servants," gritted Roël. "How sad their lives were taken for this."

Céleste looked away. "Perhaps they, too, are assured of a place in the afterlife."

"Afterlife or no, Céleste, still it was needless sacrifice."

They paced onward, their boots ringing on marble, the horses' hooves clattering with echoes resounding all 'round.

"What I am wondering," said Roël, "is how do we get to the underworld?"

"Surely the Sphinx did not betray us and sentence us to a lingering death."

Roël did not reply, and on they trod.

"Look, chérie, ahead, a dark wall of some sort."

Up three steps and on a broad dais stood two marble statues:

"And what do you hope to do with that arrow?"

"My lord, we do not know. Yet without it our quest will fail, or so said Lady Doom."

"Urd?"

"Oui."

"Then you *must* use this gate. Nevertheless, I cannot let you pass unless I find you worthy. And to do so and since you are yet living, I will examine but two of the seven parts of your souls: your *Akhu*—that part of your spirit containing your intellect and will and intentions. I will also examine your *Ab*—your heart—which holds the source of good and evil within a person, for moral awareness resides therein as well as the center of thought."

Roél cocked an eyebrow, and Thoth said, "I see you are skeptical."

"Lord Thoth, I believe my moral awareness and center of thought does not reside in my breast."

"Indeed it does not," said Thoth. "But the closest I can come to translating the word 'Ab' into your tongue is to name it your heart."

At Roél's side Céleste was nodding in agreement, and Thoth looked at her, and though his mouth was that of an inflexible ibis beak, somehow he conveyed a smile through his eyes.

"Then judge away, my lord," said Roél.

Thoth held out his hands wide with palms upraised and said, "I call upon the goddess Ma'at to aid me."

A golden glow suffused throughout Thoth's form, and then with his keen ibis eyes he stared at Céleste. Long moments he studied her, and then he turned to Roél. "Oh, my son, there are many dark deeds in your past, yet they are exemplary endeavors of honorable warriorkind, and your Akhu and Ab remain unstained."

Thoth turned and faced the dark gateway and called out, "By my wisdom and the judgment of Ma'at, I declare these beings worthy to pass through the gate to Erebus, for that is the realm of Lord Hades."

In that moment the golden glow vanished from Thoth's form. He turned to Céleste and Roél and said, "These things I do advise: each of you place a small coin in your mouth, for you will need it. Do not drink the waters of the rivers in Erebus, for one bestows the rancor of hate, another the oblivion of forgetfulness, still another the torment of sadness, and yet another the misery of lamentation, and one is a river of fire. Too, do not visit the Palace of Hades, for he will summarily eject you."

"Thank you, my Lord Thoth," said Roél.

Thoth waved a negligent hand and said, "Now go, for that netherworld awaits you," and then he vanished.

Céleste rummaged through a pouch at her belt, and she withdrew two small copper coins. She handed one to Roél and placed the other in her mouth. Roél followed suit, and then he nodded to her, and she nodded back, and together and leading their horses, they stepped through the wall of black.

36

Erebus

They found themselves under a leaden sky and among sobbing women and moaning men and weeping children all standing on a bare slope leading down to a dark river, where a long and broad, gray stone quay jutted out into the ebon water.

In spite of the coin tucked in her cheek, and though she did not speak the mother language of those who come to Erebus, still Céleste had some hope of being understood, for it is said that the dead speak all tongues. She stopped at the side of a woman and asked, "Why do you lament?"

With tears running down her face, the woman turned to Céleste and said, "Many here grieve for they are the shades of the unburied—those who died at sea or in remote fastnesses or in faraway lands, and no coins were placed in their mouths. Others of us grieve for, although we were buried, our kindred were too poor to yield up the least *obolus*, a mere sixth of a drachma. Hence all of us are lost souls who cannot pay Charon his fee to ferry us across the Acheron and through the Dismal Marsh and over the Styx beyond, and so we will never reach Erebus to mingle with our kindred, and none of us will ever drink of the Lethe in order to be reborn."

Ah, so that's what the coin is for: a ferryman's fee.

Céleste looked about, wondering how to help, yet there were so very many shades without even a sou.

"Come, Céleste," said Roél, "I see a boat approaching."

And so down to the jetty they went, leading the horses after, and when they reached the gray pier, although they could step onto the stone, their horses could not.

"What th—?" asked Roél, puzzled, for although the animals were willing, it seemed they could not place a single hoof on the quay.

"Ah," said Céleste, enlightened, and she took four small coins from her purse and tucked one each into the tack of the four animals, and onto the dock she led them.

In the distance across the torpid dark water they could see the ferry approaching, and Roél said, "It seems too small to hold us and the horses, too. Yet we must reach the other side, but I care not to leave the animals behind."

"Let us see what the ferryman says," suggested Céleste. "Perhaps he has another craft."

On came the small boat, ebon in color, with a high prow and stern. And now they could see Charon poling the vessel. He was dressed in black robes, and a hood covered his features. Closer he came, and now they could see his withered, almost skeletal hands, yet his hood held the darkness of a moonless night, and nought of his face did they see.

He stopped alongside the pier, the top wale of his ferry level with the capstones, and with a shriveled, taloned hand he silently gestured for Roél and Céleste to board.

"Ferryman," called Roél, "we would take our animals with us."

Charon pointed a skeletal finger at the horses and beckoned.

"chérie, though it will take several trips to get all across, I think the boat is large enough to accept one of our mounts. I will lead my mare aboard."

Untethering his packhorse, Roél stepped from the dock and into the boat.

Charon held out an atrophied hand, a hand rather like that of a long-dead corpse. Roél spat out the coin from his mouth and gave it over to the ferryman.

Roél pulled on the animal's reins, and the mount stepped from the dock into the boat, and—lo!—the craft lengthened.

Charon then gestured at Roél's mare and beckoned.

Again Charon held out a withered hand, and Roél took the coin from the mare's tack and gave it over.

The ferryman then gestured for the gelding to board, and Céleste tossed Roél the lead from his packhorse, and he pulled the animal into the ferry, and once again the boat grew, and once again Charon demanded his due.

And in a like manner did Céleste and her horses board the craft, each time the ferry lengthening to accommodate them.

Now Charon plunged his pole down into the waters of the River Acheron, and slowly did the boat turn to leave the dock, and as they pulled away, Céleste withdrew a handful of coins from her drawstring purse, and she flung them onto the bank, and the forlorn rushed forward in a mad scramble to snatch them up.

"I just wish I'd had enough for all," said Céleste as she watched the ruction ashore.

"Did you save six coins for our return?" asked Roél.

Céleste blanched. "Oh, love, I didn't think of that."

Roél smiled and shook his head. "I believe we have more coin in our baggage, but if not, we'll manage somehow."

Beyond the width of the Acheron, Charon entered a fogbound drear marsh, and across weed-laden waters he fared, and if the torpid current of the river flowed through this foetid swamp, neither Roél nor Céleste could discern it.

Behind them, the bank of the poor and the unburied disappeared in the gray fog, and onward Charon poled.

"How can he see his course?" whispered Céleste.

"I know not, love," Roél murmured in return, "yet it seems he does."

Finally they emerged from the stagnant waters of the Dismal Marsh, and once again it seemed a current flowed, though slowly, as did the River Acheron.

"This must be the Styx," said Céleste, as on Charon poled.

At last he came to another stone pier and glided to a stop alongside. And then with a gesture Charon bade them to disembark.

This time Céleste led, and onto the quay she and her horses stepped; Roél and his mare and gelding followed; and as each person or animal left the boat, the ferry shrank.

As Charon swung about and poled away, Roél said, "A marvelous craft that, for it changes size to accommodate its passengers."

Céleste nodded and said, "I think it must be because at times—as in war or during a plague—many souls come all at once for transport into Erebus."

They trod to the end of the pier, where before them they saw a gateway, and in the opening and tethered on a long and heavy bronze chain lay a monstrous three-headed dog with a serpentine tail much like that of a Dragon.

And as they approached, the dog lifted its heads and stood and snarled, its crimson eyes glaring, and its scarlet tongues lolling in three foam-slavering jaws filled with dark and terrible fangs.

The horses screamed in terror and shied back and would have bolted but for Céleste's and Roél's adamant grips.

Roél called out as he struggled with his animals, "I feared 'twould be so, for I deem this is Cerberus, the guardian to the gates of Hades' dominion, and he will not let the living pass."

"Then what will we do?" Céleste called back, now managing to get her mare under control.

"I will take up my shield and spear and—"

"Oh, Roél, you cannot slay this creature, for then Lord Hades himself will hunt us down."

"Then what do you suggest?" asked Roél, as he finally got his own mare under control.

Céleste thought furiously: *What do I suggest? What do I suggest? What do I suggest?*

"Killing! That's it, Roél. Killing!"

"That's what I suggested, love, and now—"

"Oh, Roél, don't you remember what Lady Doom said?"

"She said many things, Céleste."

"Oui, but a key thing she said was:

Creatures and heroes and the dead
Will test you along the way.
Ever recall what we Three said,
To fetch the arrow of gray.' "

"Oui," replied Roél, "I remember, but what does that have to do with—?"

" 'Ever recall what we Three said,' *that's* a key phrase of Lady Doom's rede, love. And so, I bring to mind what Lady Lot said: *'Yet this I will tell you for nought: blunt half of your arrows, for you will need them . . . both to kill and to not kill.'* Roél, we did not understand what she meant when she said it, yet I deem this is a time to 'not kill.' Hold my horses, and I will defeat this dreadful dog."

Roél took the reins of Céleste's mare, and she strung her bow and fetched her quiver of arrows and nocked a blunt-pointed shaft.

As she stepped forward, Roél said, "Ware, chérie, for 'tis said his bite is deadly poisonous."

Céleste paced toward the monstrous beast, and snarling, it charged, yet even as the princess flinched, Cerberus came to the end of its massive chain.

As it roared in frustration, Céleste drew the blunt arrow to the full and aimed and loosed, the shaft to hiss through the air and strike the middle head between the eyes, and that one fell unconscious. The remaining two howled and tore at the pave trying to get at her, yet the chain held, and Céleste nocked a second blunt arrow, and she let fly again, and once more the shaft struck between two of the creature's eyes, and this time the right-hand head fell stunned.

Yet baying, the dog drew hindward a step, and again Céleste loosed an arrow, but Cerberus dodged aside, and the missile glanced off his shoulder. But the next one struck between the third head's eyes, and the dog fell stunned, though like a deadly whip its tail yet struck out toward her in rage. Céleste moved 'round to the flank, though she remained beyond the reach of the long, Dragonlike lash. Another blunt arrow struck at the base of the tail, and it, too, fell limp.

Even as she dashed forward, she cried, "Now, Roél, before it regains its senses!"

Past the monster Roél ran with the animals, the horses snorting and shying in terror, but nevertheless following his lead. As for Roél, he cried out, his voice tight with fear, "Céleste, get away from that beast!"

But even as the dog was rousing, Céleste ran to Cerberus and she snatched up her five spent arrows, and then she darted onward. The snarling monster lurched to its feet and lunged after, its fangs bared and snapping. And it missed her by a mere hand's breadth as Céleste fled beyond the reach of its chain.

She ran to Roél, and he embraced her trembling form. And with his voice filled with distress, Roél said, "Oh, my love, why did you do that? An arrow is not worth your life."

"Because Lady Lot said we would need them 'to kill and to not kill,' and since I used them this time 'to not kill,' we might need all of them 'to kill' someone or something. I could not take the chance that we would run out of blunt arrows at a critical time."

Roél kissed her on the forehead and said, "Even so, chérie—" But he was silenced as she drew his face to hers and kissed him on the mouth.

Leaving Cerberus raging behind, they mounted up and rode on, and 'neath the dismal sky they fared in among broad plains. To the fore they saw more souls, these in aimless wandering, or so it seemed.

"We need find the Elysian Fields," said Céleste.

"And the Hall of Heroes," added Roél.

"Then let us ask one of these souls," suggested Céleste. The first one they asked looked up at them curiously. "You are yet alive," she said. "What are you doing here?"

"We are on a quest," said Céleste.

"Ah, like Aeneas," said the shade. "Well, I cannot help you, for I do not know where lie the Elysian Fields."

Neither did the second soul they asked, nor the third nor fourth, nor many others. But finally one, an old-seeming man, said, "Yon"—and he pointed—"where the everlasting day is bright, where the sun ever shines down through sweet air to fall upon green grass and bright flowers and the beautiful faces of the favored. But beware the rift, for 'tis said to lead to Tartarus itself."

"Tartarus?"

"Yes. It is the Abode of the Accursed, the pit where the very worst souls are sent after judgment. There it is where Sisyphus ever toils, and Tantalus reaches for the unattainable fig and tries to drink from the vanishing pool. There, too, are imprisoned Cronus and the rest of the Titans, and others. Deep is this chasm: it is said an anvil dropped into this abyss will take nine days and nine nights to reach bottom. And just as bottomless is the small rift nigh the Hall of Heroes, for I am advised it plummets to Tartarus as well."

"How know you this?" asked Roël.

"I was told by Achilles himself, for he roams at times and pauses here in the Fields of Asphodel and speaks with me now and then. During twelve years of travail in our former lives, on one dark night I made his acquaintance."

"And you are?"

"Priam, the last king of Troy."

"I have heard of Troy," said Roël. "Once mighty."

"But now gone," said Priam, and he wept shadowy tears.

Leaving the grieving shade behind, on they rode in the direction the former king had indicated. Awhile they fared under dismal skies, and off to the left they espied a great dark dwelling.

"The Palace of Hades, do you think?" asked Céleste.

"Perhaps. If it is, remember Thoth's warning to not go there."

"Ah, I do not plan to," said Céleste, smiling, and on they pressed.

Finally, in the far distance ahead, they saw a glimmer of brightness, and toward this they fared. The sky grew lighter the farther they went, and finally they rode into sunshine. And all about was green grass and bright flowers and the air was sweet, just as Priam had said.

And now they could see an enormous, rectangular, white-marble building, perhaps three hundred paces in length and half that in width and some sixteen fathoms high. Soaring columns lined a broad portico, beyond which huge bronze doors marked the entrance. And below the eaves of its peaked roof, carven figures graced a wide frieze, showing chariots racing and naked men grappling with one another and throwing javelins and discuses and loosing arrows and engaging in fisticuffs and other such sporting events. To the left of the building they could see an oval track for chariot racing, and a straight track for running sprints. There was a ring for hurling the discus, and a field for the javelin throw. Nearby was an area for the standing broad jump. Other venues for athletic events were scattered here and there.

"By the depictions above and the fields to the left, no doubt this is the Hall of Heroes," said Roél.

"The gymnasium is enormous," said Céleste.

"A mighty hall for mighty men," said Roél, grinning.

On they rode, coming closer, and just ere reaching the great portico, they came to an area fenced off by a chain. Within that enclosure yawned a rift in the ground, some six paces in length and perhaps two wide at the center. Céleste said, "Think you this is the crevice of which Priam spoke, the one plunging to Tartarus?"

They paused a moment by the chain and peered at the fissure. Céleste dismounted, and as Roél gritted his teeth to keep from telling her to take care, she leaned forward to look as the daylight shone down within.

"I see no bottom whatsoever," she said. She turned to Roél.

"It must be a way to the Abode of the Accursed."

"Perhaps," said Roél. "Yet let us not tarry, but enter the hall and find the black portal to the City of the Dead."

Céleste remounted, and they rode to the steps.

And even as they alighted, one of the great bronze doors opened, and draped in the pelt of a lion, a large muscular man stepped out and said, "Seeking death, are you? Perhaps I should slay you outright."

37

Challenges

"Who is it, Heracles?" called a voice from inside the hall.

"A pair of mortals, Chiron," replied the large man.

"Mortals?" There sounded the clip-clop of hooves, and a Centaur came trotting out and peered at them. "You two, what are you doing in Elysium? Do you not know that without special sanction mortals are forbidden to be in this place upon penalty of death?"

"My Lord Chiron," said Céleste, "I believe we are indeed here on special sanction, for we have been sent by the Fates themselves."

"Clotho, Lachesis, and Atropos?"

"Perhaps those are your names for them, but we know them as Skuld, Verdandi, and Urd, as well as the Ladies Wyrd, Lot, and Doom."

Chiron smiled. "All gods are thrice named, did you not know?"

"You call the Three Sisters gods?"

"I do, but perhaps they are above all pantheons, for the gods themselves seem ruled by the Fates," replied Chiron. "Regardless, why have you come?"

Céleste gestured at Roél and said, "We are on a mission to rescue my companion's sister and his two brothers."

Heracles growled and said, "How do we know these mortals are telling the truth?"

Chiron shrugged. "Let us first hear their story, and then we shall judge." He turned to Céleste and Roél and said, "Come. Enter the Hall of the Champions so that all might know your tale."

"But Chiron," objected Heracles, "for a married woman to witness our athletic contests means she must die. Virgins and young maidens are the only ones permitted to see." He turned to Céleste and asked, "Are you a virgin, or are you instead married?"

Before Céleste could answer, Chiron said, "Oh, my son, if these two are sent by the Fates, then such needless rules must give way." The half-man, half-horse turned to the pair and gestured for them to enter.

"As you wish, My Lord Chiron," said Céleste, and together with Roél, she walked up the steps and past the great bronze doors.

Heracles, a sour look on his face, followed, but Chiron was smiling instead.

The hall was a vast gymnasium equipped for indoor sports, with weights to lift and circles for wrestling and boxing and ropes for climbing and other such.

Inside one of the large circles a pair of naked men grappled, and a third man with a brief skirt wrapped 'round his loins and sandals on his feet seemed to be judging the match. Ringed 'round the contestants a gathering of men—some nude, others not—watched and shouted encouragement.

Chiron called out to them, and the match stopped, and men turned to see what the Centaur wanted.

As Céleste came in among them, the men looked at her in

amazement, and some unashamedly responded to her beauty and form, while others looked questioningly at Chiron and Heracles. Chiron smiled.

Heracles scowled and shook his head, as if to declare it was not his fault that a female had entered their sanctum.

Chiron said, "These two mortals declare that they have been sent by the Fates." He turned to Céleste. "I did not catch your names."

"I am Céleste, Princess of the Springwood, and my consort is Sir Roél, Knight of the Manor of Émile."

"Ah, a princess and a knight. How fitting that you are on a mission of rescue."

One of the men, his hair honey gold, said, "Mission of rescue? Ah, how heroic that sounds."

"Indeed it does, Achilles," said Chiron. "I suggest we all move to the amphitheater, for we have a tale to hear and judge."

A small amphitheater stood in one corner of the vast hall, and all the men were soon seated in the tiers all 'round. Chiron led Céleste and Roél onto the floor of the circular stage, and then stepped to one side and said, "Now, Princess, your tale, if you please."

"Much of it takes place ere I met my companion Roél, and so he is the one to tell our story in full."

Céleste stepped to Chiron's side, leaving Roél in the center of the floor. Slowly he turned about, eyeing the heroes and demigods above. And then he began: "When I was but a lad, my sister and I rode to the ruins of a temple, for she was distraught over being pledged to marry someone she did not love. And at these ruins . . ."

". . . and so you see, the Three Sisters sent us to find the gray arrow, for if we do not obtain it, then we are doomed to fail. Hence we must go through the black portal in the Hall of Heroes, for that is what both the Abulhôl and Lord Thoth said."

Achilles scowled and rubbed his left heel. "The gray arrow is the shaft that slew me. What will you use it for?"

"That we do not know," replied Roél.

"Ha, the Fates are ever ambiguous in their foretellings," said another of the heroes.

"True, Odysseus," said Chiron.

"Is there a dark doorway within this hall?" asked Céleste.

Reluctantly, it seemed, Chiron nodded. "The one you seek leads to the Waste City of Senaudon, also known as the City of the Dead, which lies in the underworld of a fabled land called Cymru."

"Cymru," said Roél, his word not a question. "I have heard of such from other knights. It lies somewhere on an island to the east, it is said."

"Yes," said Chiron. "In the world of the Cymry, Senaudon is the dreadful place where the souls of those who commit the most heinous deeds go when they die. It is somewhat like our Tartarus."

A youthful-seeming man stood and said, "But not as escape-proof."

"Aye, Philoctetes," said another.

"Say on, Jason," urged Chiron.

Black-haired Jason rose and said, "Now and again one of those dead ones manages to escape their dread city, and they come through their black portal to enter the Hall of Heroes. Ah, but then Heracles grasps them and"—Jason gestured in the direction of the fissure outside—"tosses them into the crevice yon that leads to the pit of Tartarus, a place from which they cannot get out."

As Jason sat down, a silence fell on the gathering, but then Heracles said, "A nice tale told, Sir Roél." Heracles turned to his comrades and said, "Even so, how do we know it is true? After all, these two mortals might be going to Senaudon to raise a dread army."

A burst of chatter broke out among the heroes, but Chiron raised his hands and said, "Whether true or false, we do not know for certain, yet I am inclined to believe them. How many of you do?"

A goodly number raised their hands.

"And how many are uncertain?"

A greater number raised their hands.

"Ah, it seems you lose," said Chiron.

"But we are telling the truth," protested Céleste.

"Perhaps so," said Chiron, "yet how do you propose to prove it? Has any a suggestion?"

Roél started to speak, but all eyes were turned to Odysseus, the clever one of the lot. He frowned and then said, "As we have done before, let us settle this by trial. Let them meet three challenges—two individual contests and one team challenge— and they must win all three."

Céleste gasped and said, "But you are demigods and heroes and are favored of the gods, and with such supremacy at your behest, how could we prevail?"

Heracles sneered and said, "Pah! We need no aid to defeat you, nor use of divine power."

Céleste turned to Roél for support, but he said, "Odysseus's suggestion is the same as my own: trial by combat, or through tests of strength and skill."

A murmur of approval muttered throughout the gathering.

Céleste stepped to Roél and whispered, "But as I say, they are demigods, and if we are to win, it must be through cunning, through guile."

Roél frowned, for it went against his grain. Even so, he understood the worth of it, and he said, "We shall first try guile, but if that fails, then combat or other tests it be."

Céleste nodded her acceptance, and she turned to Chiron and said, "We accept your challenge on the condition as Heracles has put it: your champions must neither accept divine aid nor use any divine powers against Roél and me, for we are but mortals."

Chiron turned to the gathering and said, "Do you so pledge to compete as would a mortal? If so, then the goddess Athena and her companion Nike, to whom this athletic temple is dedicated, will certainly hold you to such."

"I do so pledge," declared Heracles.

"As do I," said Achilles.

"And I," said Philoctetes.

"Enough," said Chiron. "Three champions for three tests, and if no one objects"— Chiron took from a pouch at his waist a scroll and a plume with which to keep tally—"I will be the judge."

A roar of approval rose from the heroes, for after all, Chiron was the famed tutor of Heracles, Achilles, and Asclepius, and others within the hall, and none could be fairer.

"Very well," said Chiron, and a quietness fell as he made a notation on the parchment.

During the silence, Céleste turned to Roél and whispered, "Remember, Roél, we must use guile."

Nearby, Chiron smiled, as did Odysseus, even though he sat in the stands.

Heracles stepped forward and gestured toward the enormous weights at one end of the hall and said to Roél, "I challenge you to a test of strength."

Roél glanced at Céleste and winked and then said, "Nay, My Lord Heracles, a test of strength would not be fair, for I did hear that you held the entire sky on your shoulders, while Atlas took golden apples from the garden of the Hesperides. Yet, my lord, I name a different challenge, and it is this—" Roél turned and took the plume from Chiron's hand and held it on high and turned about so that all could see. "Light as is this plume, I name that which e'en you cannot hold for six hundred of my heartbeats. If you loose it ere then, let it count as a victory for Céleste and me. If you succeed, then it is a victory for you."

Heracles snorted in derision and said, "I accept your challenge," and he reached for the feather.

But Roél said, "Oh, My Lord Heracles, did you think it was this plume you would hold? Non, instead it is your breath."

"My breath?"

Even as Heracles said it, the heroes burst out in laughter, Odysseus loudest of all.

When it abated, Roél gave the plume back to Chiron and said, "Oui, My Lord Heracles, your breath, for surely it is as light as a feather. Now take a deep one and I shall begin the count." Roél placed a finger on his wrist and found his pulse. "And remember your pledge, Lord Heracles: you must compete as would a mortal—no acts of divinity nor acceptance of divine aid."

Glowering in ire, Heracles deeply inhaled thrice, and on the third breath he clamped his lips tight and nodded.

Roél began the count: "One, two, three, four . . ."

And now Heracles smiled at Roél, for surely he could hold his breath that long. He had done so many times, though that was with divine aid. Nevertheless . . .

". . . one hundred eighty-one, one hundred eighty-two, one hundred eighty-three . . ."

Heracles was now red in the face, but he yet held his breath.

". . . two hundred thirty-nine . . . two hundred forty . . . two hundred forty-one . . ."

Still Heracles grinned at Roél, though his face was redder still.

". . . three hundred eighty-one . . . three hundred . . . eighty-two . . ."

Heracles' face was now nigh purple, and he squinted his eyes shut, and tears streamed down his cheeks. As for Roél, he frowned and glanced toward Céleste, but he yet kept the count.

Of a sudden, with a great whoosh followed by a frantic panting of air, Heracles blew and gasped and blew. And once again laughter broke out among the heroes, for mighty Heracles had been bested.

"That's one for the team of the princess and the knight," said Chiron, and he stroked the parchment once.

"It was not fair, Tutor," protested Heracles. "I demand a different trial."

But Céleste called out, "Who is the best at hurling the discus? I would challenge him."

All eyes turned to Heracles, and he grinned in triumph and said, "That would be me, Princess."

Céleste looked crestfallen and said, "Oh, my, it seems I have bitten off more than I can chew. How far can you cast it?"

Heracles sneered and said, "Ha! Surely farther than you."

"Well, then, my lord, let me set the terms: take up the discus and stand where you will and fling it. And wherever it stops, that shall be the measure of the throw. Then I will do the same. We will have one cast each. Do you agree to the terms?"

"Oh, yes, my lady, I accept your challenge, and I do agree to the terms."

"As you will, my lord," said Céleste, glancing at Roél, who frowned in worry.

Two of the heroes ran and gathered up two of the circular wooden objects rimmed about with bronze, and all marched outside and to the discus ring. Heracles took up both of the disks and judged their weight. Then he laid one down and said, "You can cast the lighter one; I will take the heavier of the two."

Heracles then stepped into the ring, and with a spinning toss he hurled the discus; up it sailed and up, as if borne on the very wind, and then down it arced and down, finally to land and skip along the ground, and when it came to a stop, it lay easily 150 paces away, and perhaps as much as 160.

"A mighty cast, my lord," said Céleste, "mayhap four hundred feet in all."

"Think you can best that?" asked Heracles.

"Oh, yes," she replied nonchalantly.

Heracles snorted in disbelief, and he bent down and took up the remaining disk and handed it to her.

"Hmm . . ." Céleste frowned. "'Tis much heavier than I imagined."

A smile of victory spread over Heracles' face, and he gestured at the ring.

But Céleste shook her head and walked toward the front of the gymnasium and beyond, all the men following, Odysseus laughing.

To the crevice she went and pitched the discus within. As down it fell beyond seeing, Céleste turned to Heracles and said, "I understand you should be able to measure the full distance of my cast after nine days and nine nights, but as you can see, it has gone well beyond the trivial toss of yours."

Hilarity erupted among the men, and the look upon Heracles' face was one caught somewhere between humiliation and rage. But of a sudden he burst out in laughter, and he bowed to Céleste and said, "Well played, my lady, well played." He glanced at Odysseus and added, "As clever as the very slyest of us."

Céleste smiled and stepped to the large man and she reached up and pulled his head down and stood on tiptoes and kissed him on the cheek. The men hooted and whistled, and one said, "Let not Deïaneira hear of this; she will claw Heracles' eyes out for accepting a kiss from another beautiful maiden."

Again there was more hooting and laughter, but finally Chiron said, "Now comes the team challenge; has anyone a suggestion?"

Achilles stepped forward and said, "My Lady Céleste, is that your bow I see upon one of the mares?"

"Oui."

Achilles nodded and turned to Chiron and said, "Since Philoctetes, the prime archer of the Argonauts, and I both took the pledge, then I suggest that we return to the gymnasium and he take up the bow and contest with the princess, while I take up the sword and contest against the knight."

"But my lord," protested Céleste, "this is really two challenges, and therefore the total is more than three tests in all."

All eyes turned to Chiron, for he was the judge. He pondered a moment and then said, "Nay, Princess, it is really just one, for in team play, oft are many different matches waged."

And so, Céleste retrieved her bow and arrows, and Roél took up Coeur d'Acier, and back into the Hall of Heroes all trooped, Céleste thinking furiously, for Philoctetes was a fabled archer, and Achilles a champion with a sword.

Finally, inside the hall, she said, "Let the archery contest be the first match, and then the sword duel commence."

Both Philoctetes and Achilles nodded, for no trickery within the suggestion did they see.

Several small targets—a chit of wood, a small flask, a coin on edge, a cup, a chalice—were set at one end of the hall, and the archers told to strike the target of their choice. At the other far end of the hall, one of the circles was chosen for the duel, and the men were to battle to first blood.

Chiron then said, "Heed me, for these are the additional rules: if Céleste and Roél are bested, then they lose, and the black portal is denied."

"What if there is a tie between teams?" asked Odysseus.

"If the teams tie, there is no victory for the princess and the knight; hence going through the black doorway is denied them in this case as well."

Roél groaned and looked at Céleste, and she said, "Agreed."

"Well, then, archers, take your positions."

Céleste marched away to the end most distant from the wee targets. Philoctetes' eyes widened in surprise, but he followed her.

Roél and Achilles also went to the far end of the hall, for that is where lay the circle they had chosen for their match.

Chiron gave the signal for the contests to begin, but Céleste turned to Roél and Achilles and said, "Let not your own match start until my arrow is loosed."

Achilles looked at Roél and shrugged, and they both agreed; the loosing of her arrow would be their signal to begin.

Céleste smiled and nocked an arrow but then said, "Philoctetes, after you."

Philoctetes looked at the faraway targets, and after a moment of deliberation he said, "I declare my target is the small coin standing on edge."

The gathered men gasped, for never had any shot ever been made at so small a target from a distance such as this.

Philoctetes nocked his arrow and drew it to the full and took long aim at the target nigh three hundred paces away. Finally he loosed and up flew the arrow, sissing in its flight. And all held their breaths as the shaft hurtled in its long arc and sailed down to—*ching!*—strike the coin. Pent breaths were released in wild cheers, for it was a shot worthy of the gods themselves.

Philoctetes turned to Céleste and smiled and said, "Your turn now, my lady. Choose your target and loose."

Céleste drew her own shaft to the full and said, "I choose"— she quickly turned and shot Achilles in the foot with a blunt arrow—"Achilles' left heel."

Crying out in pain, Achilles fell to the floor, and as Odysseus laughed, Chiron said, "The arrow is loosed; let the duel begin."

Roél stepped to writhing Achilles and with Coeur d'Acier simply pinked his left heel, and said, "First blood."

The hall erupted in argument, some men shouting, others laughing, and a few saying it was a gambit worthy of Odysseus himself. *What do you mean?* cried others. *Clearly they should forfeit the match.*

When quiet fell, Céleste said, "According to the rules, I was to select a target of my choice, and my choice was Achilles' left heel, for only there is he vulnerable."

Again argument erupted, and finally all eyes turned to Chiron. "Indeed it was clever, and certainly within the rules as stated. And since both archers struck their targets of choice, that match is declared a tie. Yet Roél drew first blood; hence he is clearly the winner, and so the contest of the teams goes to the princess and her knight."

Odysseus clapped, as did many others, yet a few grumbled at the outcome. But Achilles finally got to his feet and shook Roél's hand and bowed to the princess, and she kissed Achilles and Philoctetes each on the cheek.

Céleste turned to Chiron and said, "Then the black portal is ours to enter and go to the City of the Dead?"

Chiron nodded but said, "Yes, Princess, you and your knight have earned that right, yet there is one final test."

"A final test? But we have met your three challenges. Surely you cannot force another upon us."

Chiron held out a hand to stop her words. "Princess, it is not I, nor we, who force this test, but Lord Hades himself instead."

Céleste sighed. "Go on, Chiron. Tell us of this final deed."

Chiron gestured to the far end of the hall and said, "There are two dark exits: one leads to Tartarus, from which there is no return; the other leads to the Waste City of Senaudon. You must choose between them, for at no time whatsoever do we know which is which."

Céleste looked at Roél and said, "Love?"

"We must chance it, chérie; else my sister is lost forever. Yet I can go alone."

Céleste shook her head. "Never, Roél." Then she grinned and said, "Let us retrieve the horses and choose."

And so Céleste took up the blunt arrow she had used on Achilles. And then she and Roél fetched their mounts and led them into the hall, where they followed Chiron to the far exitent. There he bade the princess and the knight to stand in a modest circle inset in the floor. "Now you must put all else out of your minds except the desire to open the portals, and then, together, say the word *Phainesáton!*"

"*Wait*," said Roél, and he stepped to his mount and took up his shield from its saddle hook. Then he stepped back into the circle where Céleste yet stood, the princess with an arrow now nocked to her bow. He drew Coeur d'Acier and glanced at Céleste. At a nod from him, they spoke in unison—"*Phainesáton!*"

Before them appeared two black doorways, seeming much like the gate in Meketaten's tomb, or the ebon at the heart of Faery's twilight bounds.

Roél turned to Céleste and said, "Choose."

And Céleste said, "Left is right, and right a mistake." And leading their horses, into the leftmost portal they went.

38

Senaudon

Out onto a decrepit stone pave emerged Céleste and Roél, out between two ancient pillars, the fluted columns raddled with cracks, and a cold swirling wind groaned about the stone. The animals followed after, snorting and blowing in the sulfur-tinged sobbing air, and Céleste, pulling them and squinting against the acrid whorl, turned and looked behind to see not one but two black portals just then fading from view. Scribed in the riven stone at her feet was a faint outline of an ages-old circle, much like the one they had left.

"Is this Tartarus?" asked Roél, as left and right and fore and aft he scanned for foes, yet there were none.

"I know not, Roél, but if it is, then we will be trapped forever. Yet there is hope that it is not, for I did see two portals when we emerged, as well as what is perhaps an invoking circle scribed on the floor. I would think these things would not be in Tartarus."

Roél grunted but said nought.

Céleste added, "If we need come back this way, once more we will have to choose."

312

Roél nodded, and still cautious—sword in hand, shield on his arm—he started forward, Céleste at his side. Across the broken pave they trod, cracked pillars standing along its perimeter, to come to the last of its extent, and they found themselves on a dark hilltop. Outward they gazed across the world into which they had come. The land before them was sere and dark and of ash and cinder and sloped down toward widespread stone ruins lying just past the base of the hill. Far beyond those shambles and over the horizon crimson light stuttered across the dull gray sky and a deep rumbling rolled o'er the blackened 'scape.

"Oh, but what a dreadful place," said Céleste, her face twisted in revulsion against the reek of cinder and char and brimstone borne on the coiling wind. "Perhaps it is Tartarus after all."

"If not, then yon," said Roél, pointing down at the ruins, "must be the City of the Dead—Senaudon."

Céleste turned her gaze toward the remains.

The town itself had once been walled about, yet much of that barricade had fallen, and great gapes yawned through the stone. Crumbling houses and broken buildings made up the city proper, though here and there parts of such structures yet stood, some nearly whole. And but for rubble lying strewn, empty were the streets within.

Roél intoned: *"It is held in the hands of an idol in a temple on the central square of the City of the Dead."* He glanced at Céleste. "That's what the Abulhôl said. Hence, if it is Senaudon, the arrow must lie"—Roél turned and pointed downward—"there."

Céleste's gaze followed Roél's outstretched arm, and arranged about a square in the heart of the shambles a large group of imposing buildings remained, though holes gaped in their roofs.

Again the distant ruddy sky flashed bright, and the ground shuddered, and across the land a wave of thunder came rolling.

Roél glanced at Céleste. "Come, let us ride."

They mounted, and with packhorses in tow, down they rode, down through the twisting wind, down toward the vestige of what had once been a mighty city, now nought but a city of ruin.

And Roél yet gripped Coeur d'Acier, and his shield remained on his arm. Céleste held her bow, a keen arrow nocked to string.

The horses' hooves crunched through ash and cinder, and small puffs of dark dust rose with every step taken, only to be borne away on the chill wind. As Céleste and Roél neared the broken walls, they could hear a banging, a thumping—and in the coiling air at the main entry into the city a gaping char-blackened gate swung loose on its hinges and thudded against its support.

The horses shied, but at Roél's command and that of Céleste, forward through the opening they went and into the rubble-strewn cobblestone streets. To either side stood broken houses, doors agape, shutters banging in the groaning air.

Céleste's horse flinched leftward, and the princess looked rightward to see what had affrighted it, and there in deep shadows of an alley she saw— "Roél!" she hissed, and pointed. In the darkness a form lurked: manlike it was, but no living man this, for bones showed through gapes in its desiccated skin, its flesh stretched tight like wetted parchment strung on a ghastly frame and then dried taut in sunlight. And the being shambled toward them, and it snuffled, as if trying to catch an elusive scent, and the creature emitted a thin wail, but the sound was lost in the sob of the wind.

"Keep riding," said Roél, and they continued onward, head-ing for the city square.

They passed more alleys, more wrecked buildings, of which some had been dwellings, others once establishments of one sort or another. And the air wept among the dark ruins.

From the gloom came more of the beings, living corpses who once had been human. Some had shreds of clothes yet clinging, while most were completely exposed. Many were nought but fleshless beings, while others had tissue hanging on their frames and straggles of long hair stringing down from their pates. Some still had eyes in their skulls, the lids gone, the skin flaked off, leaving behind huge glaring orbs, somehow not shrunken away. Lips were stretched tight, drawn back from yellowed teeth in horrid, gaping, rictal grins. Most were wasted men—with long bony arms and legs and grasping taloned fingers, their ribs jutting out, their groins bare, their manhoods blackened and withered, some of which had rotted away or had dried and broken off—but many of the beings were gaunt women—flat dugs hanging down, tufts of hair at their groins, their womanhoods shriveled and flapping—and Céleste shuddered in horror at the sight of all.

"Liches," muttered Roél. "The walking dead."

"How can this be?" asked Céleste. "Some are nought but skeletons, and yet they move."

Roél shook his head. "I know not the ways of the departed, but surely these are cursed, for did not Chiron say that for the Cymry this is the dreadful place where the souls of those who commit the most heinous deeds go when they die?"

"All of these committed heinous deeds?" asked Céleste, looking 'round. "But there are so very many."

Roél nodded but said nought as on they rode, a crowd of corpses shambling after, and the farther they went, the more of the living dead joined them, all snuffling, as if to inhale the essence of life that this man and woman and these horses had brought into their world.

And in the distance the leaden sky bloomed red and the ground shook, followed long after by a grumbling roar.

Now they came unto the central square where the once-stately buildings stood.

"Which is the temple?" asked Céleste, gazing about.

A ghastly laugh greeted her query and echoed among the

ruins, the wind twisting it about so that its source could not be found.

As Céleste's and Roél's gazes searched the square, again the eldritch mirth resounded. Céleste said, "There," and pointed. High up on the wall of one of the buildings, in an array of dark niches stood torchbearers, yet none of their flambeaus were lit.

"We seek the temple of the gray arrow," called Roél.

The macabre beings looked down with glaring eyes and once more there came nought but a hollow jeer, and one called out in a ghoulish voice, "Death awaits. Death awaits."

Again the dull sky flared scarlet afar, and the ground shuddered, and a rumble rolled across the dark land.

Roél turned to Céleste and said, "Mayhap that is the temple, for it is the only place so warded." And they rode forward toward a set of wide steps leading up into the stately building where the torchbearers stood high above. Beyond the stairs and between columns and across a broad landing a doorway blackly gaped onto empty dark shadows within.

And behind Céleste and Roél the dead shuffled close.

And as the princess and her knight came to the foot of the steps and stopped, outstretched hands reached for the pair. And one of the living corpses laid a skeletal palm on a gelding, and the horse screamed. A dead being grasped at Céleste, and as its desiccated fingers clutched her leg a deathly chill swept through the princess. Shrilling, Céleste kicked at the creature, and its arm cracked off and fell to the ground, the brittle bones shattering on impact.

"Roél, ride!" Céleste shrieked, and she spurred her mount forward. But Roél had cried out a warning at the same time, for one of the living corpses had touched his mare, and at the squeal of the horse, Roél swung Coeur d'Acier and took off the undead thing's head.

Straight up the steps Céleste galloped, Roél coming after, and the torchbearers in the niches high above shrieked in rage, for living beings were defiling the empty hall below. And one of those corpses put a horn to its lips and sounded a thin call, more of a wail than the cry of a clarion, and the moaning wind carried it throughout the ruins of the city, and beings shuffled forth through the dark.

Across the landing galloped Céleste and through the gaping portal, and just inside she leapt from her mare and shouldered one of the doors to. At the other door, Roél did the same, and—*Boom! Doom!*—the massive panels slammed shut. On the back of Roél's door a beam rested in a pair of brackets; with a grunt Roél slid it across to mate with a like set of brackets opposite and bolted shut the entry.

Corpses outside mewled and hammered at the doors, and scratched the panels with their talons.

And even as Roél and Céleste looked at one another, from above dim light came streaming down as portals at the backs of the niches opened, and the skeletal torchbearers, now holding their unlit flambeaus as cudgels, stepped onto a walkway high above.

Roél's gaze swept the great chamber. Across a marble floor inlaid with arcane markings, to left and right and in the shadows at the far end stood open doorways to rooms beyond. To the back of the hall on either side stairwells rose up to the walkways above. Also in the darkness at the rear of the chamber a statue of a woman stood on a pedestal, but what she signified Roél knew not, nor at the moment did he care. "Céleste," he called, "the stairways afar, the liches must come down them to reach this hall. I will take my stand at the one on the right; take the left and use your bow to keep any from reaching the main floor."

Céleste nodded and ran toward the left-hand stairwell, and she reached it just as the first of the torchbearers started down. Céleste took aim and loosed, and the shaft flew true and struck the creature in the chest. And it looked at the arrow jutting out from its ribs and laughed, and continued on downward.

Céleste flew another shaft, and it shot completely through the dead being, leaving nought but gaping holes fore and aft in the taut, yellowed, parchmentlike skin. Again the creature jeered, even as a second one of the beings reached the landing above and started down.

My arrows are useless. Oh, why did not the Fates warn—¿

Of a sudden Céleste laughed, and she called out, "To kill and to not kill, that's what Lady Lot said. I thought it only applicable to Cerberus and Achilles, yet here it is more to my liking." And she nocked one of the blunt-tipped arrows, and taking careful aim, she let fly at the descending creature's exposed pelvis. *Whmp!* The arrow struck, and brittle bone shattered into fragments, and the creature toppled over to come tumbling down the stairs, and when it reached bottom, nought was left of it but the rags of its garments and the cudgel it had borne all lying in a scatter of shards, and clattering down after came her arrow as well. A thin wail sounded, and an ephemeral gray twist in the air rose up from the splinters of the sundered being, and Céleste wasn't certain whether it was a spirit rising or simply a whirl of motes lofted up from the fragments.

Céleste flew a second blunt shaft at the pelvis of the next torchbearer, and that creature, too, fell and tumbled down the stairs to become nought but shattered bone. Again and again Céleste loosed, each time slaying a torchbearer, and each time a faint keen and a wisp of gray mist arose from the strewn shards. Fifteen blunt arrows she loosed, and fifteen corpses died; no more were left on her stairwell. Quickly she turned to help Roël. But he stood amid a pile of fragmented bones and rags and cudgels, and no torchbearers were left on his stairs either, and he looked over to see that Céleste was hale, and he grimly smiled.

Céleste took up her spent arrows, most of which had rattled to the bottom of the steps, though she had to climb up after a few.

As she fetched the last of the shafts, "Aha!" crowed Roél. Céleste turned to see him standing on the pedestal of the statue, and in his right hand he held an arrow. And he called out: "Céleste, this is not Tartarus but Senaudon instead, for the gray arrow: I have it!"

Céleste darted down the stairs and to the plinth.

"Here," said Roél, and he handed her the arrow.

Céleste examined it. The shaft was dark gray as was the fletching, and the arrowhead was of a dull gray metal. "It looks like *plomb*," said Céleste. She tested it with her thumbnail, leaving behind a faint mark. "Oui, indeed it is lead."

"It was in her hands," said Roél, gesturing at the statue.

Céleste looked up at the depiction. A woman stood, a crown on her head, her arms outstretched, palms up, as if in supplication. "She seems to be a queen," said Céleste. "Mayhap the queen of Cymru."

"Or the queen of the Waste City of the Dead," said Roél. "I wonder why she had the arrow that slew Achilles?"

Céleste shrugged, and as she started to speak—

Thdd! Thdd!

The chamber doors rattled under massive blows.

Roél turned and peered at the juddering panels. "They must have fetched a ram, and those simple brackets will not withstand such battering."

Céleste slipped the gray arrow into her quiver. "What will we do, my love? There are entirely too many for my blunt shafts and your sword."

Thdd! Thdd! Bmm!

Roél frowned then looked 'round at the chambers. "Mayhap there is a back way out."

Quickly they searched, and the pounding went on, the doors quaking, the bolt rattling in its loosening clamps.

And the horses skittered and whuffed with each blow.

Dmm! Dmm!

Neither Céleste nor Roél found any other exit.

Bmm! Bmm! hammered the ram, and the doors began to give and thin wails and a mewling grew louder, as if the undead creatures anticipated victory.

Céleste shuddered, remembering the touch of one of the beings, and she looked down at her leg where the creature had clutched it, and she gasped, for her leathers held what appeared to be a scorched imprint of a hand, as if the grip was of fire. Yet no scald this, but rather one of intense cold, as she could well attest. "Freezing!" said Céleste. "I felt a deadly numbness, a bitter chill, when one of those corpse folk grabbed me, Roél. Yet we ward cold with fire; think you flames will deal with these creatures?"

Bmm! Dmm!

"Perhaps," said Roél. "In fact, it might be our only hope." With a few quick strides he went to the foot of the stairs he had defended and took up four of the unlit torches from the pile of splintered bones lying there. "I wonder if these flambeaus yet hold enough oil to burn?"

"If not," said Céleste, stepping to one of the geldings and fetching a lantern, "we have lamp oil here."

Clang! One of the brackets fell to the floor, and the door gave inward. Outside, the mewling of the undead mob pitched even higher.

As she poured oil on the torch rags, Roél said, "But where will we go once we are free of these corpse people?"

Bmm! Bmm! Dmm! Clang! Another bracket fell, and the doors gaped even more, and now the crowd yowled.

Céleste glanced over her shoulder at the yielding entrance. She struck the striker on the lantern, and it flared into flame. "The only way we know out of this place is back through the gate whence we came."

Dmm! Bmm!

Roél lit the torches, and as Céleste extinguished the lantern and shoved it into a pack, Roél said, "Oui, yet that way out only leads back to Erebus—either to the Hall of Heroes or to the pit of Tartarus, and neither place will set us free or get us any closer to my sister. And even should we get back across the Styx and the Acheron and find our way back through Thoth's portal, that will but leave us trapped in Meketaten's—"

"Oh, Roél, you have hit upon it!" called Céleste above the crash of the ram and the cries of the mob. "I think I know just how to get us out of here."

"You do?"

"Oui." Céleste laughed and said, "Thoth told us the way."

Roél frowned in puzzlement, and Céleste said, "Trust me, my love." And she grabbed two torches and leapt into her saddle, and cried, " 'Tis time to flee through the gauntlet and up the hill whence we came."

And in that moment with a crash the doors flew wide, and the horde of howling corpses pushed inward.

39

Bridge

Hard they rode, did the warband, long under the sun and stars. They took little rest, only that needed to spare the steeds. Even so, horses went lame, and gear was shifted, and men took to new mounts, abandoning those that could no longer run. And some four days after leaving Port Cíent, the riders entered yet another forest, but this one had a windrow through it, and so the woodland did not slow the force as had the previous forest they encountered. They emerged at a run under the stars and hammered across fertile fields, though the crofts were abandoned, as were the steads thereon. In starlight they came unto a palisaded town: 'twas Le Bastion.

Guards aimed great ballistas laded with spears at the milling band, for the citizenry was sore afraid to let such a force within; after all, they could be raiders. Mayor Breton was called, and when he appeared on the wall above, Borel explained that it was Céleste and Roél and Avélaine and Laurent and Blaise they were out to save, and Breton ordered the gates flung wide.

They exchanged as many horses as they could with those

322

from the town, and after but six hours respite, the warband galloped away.

"The Wolves are edgy," said Borel, as up the narrow pathway they went along the wall of the gorge. "Horses, too. Something dire lies ahead, I ween."

Mist swirled and twined, and as they came to a flat, a stone bridge stood before them. And a huge armored man bearing a great sword and wearing a red surcoat stepped on the far end of the span, the whorls of white alternately revealing and concealing the knight.

And neither the horses nor the Wolves would set hoof or paw upon the stone of the bridge.

"We would pass!" called Borel.

The monstrous knight did not reply.

Donning his helm, Luc dismounted and took up his shield and sword, saying, "I will go parley with him."

With a bit of blood running from his left arm and his shield cloven in twain, Luc returned through the swirling fog and said, "We can go onward now."

And across the bridge they all went, the horses no longer skittish and shy, the Wolves padding forward without delay.

At the far end, the Red Knight's empty helm sat on one of the pikes, but as to where his slain body had gone, none could say.

They came to the twilight border and passed on through to find themselves in a dank swamp, and slime floated on the water therein. And now no matter how hard they pressed, they could move no faster than a swift walk, and at times they moved much slower.

And there was but a single day remaining ere the dark of the moon.

40

Escape

Torches aflame and shrieking a war cry, toward the squalling mob drove Céleste, with Roél shouting and charging after, fire in his hands as well. And the mares and geldings smashed into the throng, and brittle bones shattered under the onslaught. Corpses fell and were trampled under, never to rise again. The horses screamed at the touch of the undead things, and yet they hammered ahead, trying to get free of the deadly and draining chill. The princess and her knight laid about with their torches and tattered clothing blazed up, and dangling flesh burst into flame, and burning creatures mewled thin wails and fled back into the horde, only to spread the fire as more of the undead caught flame and squealed and ran into others and those into others still. The corpses gave way before horse and flambeau in fear of hoof and blaze, and some took up rubble and threw it at these living things to try and bring them down. But Céleste and Roél and the horses crashed onward, and finally the princess was free of the mob . . . and Roél broke free right after.

Yet bearing their torches, up through the streets they galloped, a howling throng running after. Past broken-down houses and collapsed buildings and other wrack and ruin they fled, and beings emerged from the side streets and alleyways and reached out to grasp with their deadly cold hands. But the two and their horses ran onward, sometimes smashing over the corpses, bones snapping and popping like dried sticks under the pounding hooves.

Out through the gate flashed Céleste and Roél, and across the barren cinders and ashes and up the hill toward the ruins of fractured stone columns and broken pave high above.

And the horde of the undead corpses came yowling after.

And in the distance beyond the horizon where the leaden sky glowed red, the air flashed bright crimson, and the ground rumbled and thunder rolled o'er the land.

Céleste and Roél galloped up and up, guiding the horses by knees alone. Finally they reached the crest of the hill, the horses to clatter onto the fragmented stone. Céleste and Roél leapt down, and casting the flambeaus aside, they took the horses by the reins.

Behind them, skeletal beings, some seeming nought but fleshless bones, came swarming up the hill.

Céleste pointed ahead at the broken stone floor. "There, Roél, there lies the circle." Together they stepped into the ring, and as before, at a nod from Roél, in unison they said *Phainesáton!*

Nothing happened. . . .

No portals appeared. . . .

And the horde came howling up the hill.

Again Roél nodded . . .

. . . and again they said *"Phainesáton!"*

And again no portals appeared.

Roél looked over his shoulder, and he drew Coeur d'Acier.

And the undead things came on, their squalling growing louder.

"Why do not the doorways manifest?" asked Céleste, even as she took up a torch.

"I know not," said Roél. "Mayhap—"

"Oh, wait," said Céleste, "I think I might know why."

Roél looked at her.

"Remember what Chiron said: 'Now you must put all else out of your minds except the desire to open the portals, and then, together, say the word *Phainesáton!'* Roél, the word alone is not enough; we must have the intent. Hence, we need to calm our thoughts, no matter that a mob comes.'"

In the distance, a huge blast of scarlet flared the entire sky red, and the ground gave a violent jolt, and even as Céleste and Roél and the horses fought to keep their feet, one of the huge pillars on the left side of the ruins toppled and crashed down, stone bursting apart.

Under a now-ruddy sky above, as the aftershocks diminished and died, Roél said, "If the portals do not appear, we must flee from here, and return later when the liches are gone."

"Agreed," said Céleste.

WHOOOM. . . ! A vast wave of thunder from the distant explosion at last rolled across the hill.

The horses belled in fright and shied, but Roél and Céleste managed to keep control.

And the howls of the oncoming throng grew louder.

Céleste said, "Flee we will, if necessary, but now let us clear our minds of all but the need to open the way."

Roél nodded and Céleste looked down and took a deep breath and slowly exhaled, and she brought her gaze up to where she had last seen the gateways and then glanced at Roél and—

The mob topped the hill and rushed toward the living beings standing in the ruins.

—he nodded, and together they said *Phainesáton!*

Two black doorways appeared before them.

Squalling, living dead ran forward.

One of the geldings screamed as an undead thing laid a hand upon its flank.

"Left is right and right a mistake," shouted Céleste, and together she and Roél fled through the leftmost portal, corpse folk hurtling after.

41

Hades

Through the portal and into the Hall of Heroes dashed Céleste and Roél, the horses clattering after, and right behind them howling undead poured into the great chamber as well.

Across the gymnasium a circle of men turned at the sound of the din, and Chiron shouted, "Cymry!"

Achilles snatched up a bronze sword and Ajax a warbar and others took up weapons nearby, all but Heracles, who came running forward armed with nought but his bare hands.

Roél spun about and with shield and sword took on the first of the horde, and even as he struck and fragmented the enemy the portals began to fade. Céleste flew blunt arrows into the throng to bring down corpse after corpse.

Heracles waded in and smashed left and right, Achilles and Ajax charging after. And then the remainder of the heroes reached the mob, yet—lo!—Heracles' fists and the champions' weapons did not break the undead apart, though the squalling foe fell to the blows.

Only the weapons of Céleste and Roél seemed to deal death to the undead. Mayhap it was because, unlike the weapons of Erebus, the arrows were from Faery and the sword was from the mortal world; yet whatever the reason, wherever they struck, the wailing undead fell slain.

Yet it seemed the frigid grasps of the living corpses had no effect upon the heroes of the Elysian Fields, whereas in the midst of the mêlée whenever one touched Roél he felt the dreadful cold.

On went the battle and the portals closed and no more undead Cymry came through. And soon all the corpse foe lay stunned or shattered, depending on who or what had dealt the blow.

With the fight now over, laughing and slapping one another on the back, Heracles and the men began gathering up the defeated, and they bore them out to the crevice to Tartarus and without ceremony cast them in. Likewise, they took up the splintered remains of those slain by Roél and Céleste and cast those to Tartarus as well. Then they unstopped wineskins and passed them about, hailing one another as well as Céleste and Roél. And Philoctetes said to Céleste, "Those arrows of yours: quite deadly," and he helped her reclaim them from the floor.

"Thanks to the Fates," said Céleste.

"Ah, yes," said Philoctetes, "they do work well," and he glanced toward Achilles, who was sharing a wineskin with Ajax.

Chiron joined them, and Céleste said, "We did not intend to bring enemies into your domain."

Chiron smiled and said, "Princess, I believe the men enjoyed it."

Heracles laughed and said, "I haven't had that much fun since I performed the twelve labors." He handed his wineskin to Roél.

As Roél started to tip it up for a small swallow, Céleste said, "No, love. Mayhap 'tis like unto the Elf King's domain in Faery, and we should forgo food and drink."

"Ah, oui," replied Roél, and he passed the skin to Odysseus. After drinking, Odysseus said, "Did you find that which you went for?"

Céleste nodded and pulled the gray arrow from her quiver and held it up for all to see. From across the hall Achilles looked, and tears sprang into his eyes, and Ajax threw an arm about him in comfort. Céleste sighed and put the arrow away.

Roél turned to Chiron and said, "We cannot tarry and celebrate with you, for our mission is urgent, and it's to the mortal world and Faery we must go."

Chiron frowned. "Charon will not ferry you back across the Styx and the Acheron; his trip is one-way only. I'm afraid once in the underworlds you cannot return."

Odysseus shook his head. "Are you forgetting about me, about Aeneas, Theseus, and others?"

"Nay, Odysseus," replied Chiron. "Yet Lord Hades himself has closed those ways out of Erebus."

A debate broke out among the men, and Céleste called for quiet, and when it fell she said, "Lord Thoth himself told us how."

"Lord Thoth?" asked Chiron. "Oh, yes, I remember. You did tell us that he had helped you to come unto Erebus, yet not how you could return."

And so Céleste told the way it was to be done, and the men and Chiron clapped and laughed and saluted her cleverness, for it was worthy of Odysseus himself. Roél merely shook his head in admiration, for such means had not occurred to him.

Céleste and Roél took their leave of the heroes, and out from the hall they strode. Mounting up, across the plains they fared, out from sunlit Elysium to come once more under the leaden skies of the Asphodel Fields.

On they rode, and at last in the distance ahead they once again saw the great dark dwelling they had seen as they had ridden opposite less than eight candlemarks prior. Toward this massive palace they went.

Up out from the plains it towered, its ebon stone rising in tiers toward the somber vault o'erhead. Toward a wide entryway at ground level they fared, the opening yawning darkly wide.

"We must take our horses with us," said Céleste as they came upon black basalt pave.

"Oui," replied Roél.

Now they rode into the enshadowed gape, and Céleste turned to Roél and said, "Oh, my love, I do hope Lord Thoth is right."

Roél grimly nodded but said nought.

Dark stone pillars lined the way, and hooves rang and echoed from the gloom-laden surround.

Following the directions given by Chiron, they came to a broad stair climbing up into darkness; dismounting, they led the horses clattering upward.

Into a long ebon hall they emerged, torches in sconces lighting the corridor with eternal flame, or so Chiron had said.

Rightward along this hallway they trod, their horses trailing after, to come at last to a wide archway.

Across a polished black marble floor they went and toward the far wall, where before ebon curtains sat two thrones, a beautiful maiden upon one, a dark male on the other.

This pair was in deep converse and did not look up even as Céleste and Roél came to stand before them.

Céleste cleared her throat and said, "My Lord Hades, my Lady Persephone."

Now the pair looked toward the two, and rage crossed Hades' features, and he shouted, "Mortals! Again! Will this never end?"

And with a bellowing shout, he swept the back of his hand outward, and as if from a mighty blow, into roaring blackness Céleste and Roél hurtled.

42

Desperate Run

When the great rush of blackness subsided, Céleste and Roél found themselves and their horses standing in sand before the great stone Sphinx outside the City of Meketaten's Tomb. And in that moment the first rays of the rising sun struck the face of the Abulhôl, and it looked down at them and smiled, rock grinding on rock with the grin.

"Ah, summarily ejected by Hades, eh?" it asked.

"Oui," said Céleste. "Just as Lord Thoth said Hades would do."

"Did you find what you sought?"

"Oui," replied Céleste. "The gray arrow is ours, and for that I say merci, my lord, for your aid; without it we would have failed."

With a grating of stone upon stone, the Abulhôl inclined its head in acknowledgment.

Roél frowned and glanced over his shoulder at the morning sun. "I do not understand, Lord Sphinx. It was just after dawn when we went into Erebus. Have we come back the same dawn we entered?"

332

Slowly the Abulhôl shook its head. "Nay, Chevalier. Two days have elapsed since you first broached the realm of the dead."

"Two days?" exclaimed Roél. "We spent but ten candlemarks at most therein."

"Time marches at a different pace in the netherworlds," said the Sphinx.

Céleste gasped in dismay and said, "Oh, Roél, that means there are but three days left ere the dark of the moon, and we have far to go."

"Then I suggest you set out," said the Abulhôl.

After a quick glance at her map, Céleste pointed sunwise and said, "Yon."

"South it is," cried Roél, and he and Céleste sprang to their mounts and rode into the dunes, the Sphinx murmuring after, "May the smiling face of Atum be turned your way." Then it closed its eyes and went back to sleep.

Across the sands they fared, stopping now and again to feed and water the horses as well as themselves. It was at one of these pauses when Céleste remarked that during the time they were in Erebus, even though two days in the world had elapsed, they had not felt the need for food or water.

"Mayhap one never gets hungry or thirsty in Erebus," said Roél.

"In Tartarus they do," said Céleste. "Remember Tantalus, love."

"Ah, oui," said Roél. "Yet mayhap it is his eternal punishment for the deeds he did. Perhaps none else suffers such pangs."

Céleste nodded, and they mounted and rode onward, up and over and down tall golden dunes—great still waves of sand— and across long stretches of gritty flats, the surface baked hard, and through rocky wadis, some salt encrusted, which spoke of leaching streams of ages agone, and then back into dunes again.

They ran out of water in midafternoon, and only sand and grit did they see; there were no wells, no piles of rocks, no birds to follow across the waste where they might find an oasis or a pool.

Yet in the evening in the distance ahead they espied a looming wall of twilight, and within a candlemark they reached it. It took them another candlemark to find the fallen obelisk at the crossover point, and back into Faery they passed. They came into a world of green trees and lush grasses and cool air. The sky above was deep violet with dusk, and almost immediately they came upon a stream. They let the horses drink, and they drank as well and replenished their waterskins.

"We have to press on," said Roël as they brushed the animals clean in those places where grit would chafe, "for we cannot tarry."

"Yet we must not enfeeble the horses," said Céleste, examining the legs of her mare. "Else we will most certainly lose any chance we have."

"I know, my love," said Roël, shaking sand from the saddle blankets.

"What we need are remounts," said Céleste.

"Oui, remounts for getting to the tower ere midnight of the dark of the moon, horses which will become mounts for Avélaine and Laurent and Blaise on the way back. Is there a city or ville between here and the next boundary?"

As Roël resaddled the mares and laded the goods on the geldings, Céleste unfolded the vellum chart and studied it in the failing light. "Ah," she said at last. She stabbed her finger to the map. "I think this must be a town along the way. Perhaps there we can get horses."

Roël looked. On the chart were the initials *FdTn*. "A town?"

"Oui. That would be my guess. I mean, it doesn't seem to be by a twilight border, and though I don't have a notion as to what the *Fd* might mean, I think the *Tn* might stand for 'town.' It is slightly out of the way, but if it has horses, that will more than make up for the extra distance."

Roél sighed and said, "Once again, whoever made the original map seemed to want some of it to be in cipher. Yet if the scale of this chart is anywhere close, without remounts we haven't a chance. Let us go to whatever this *FdTn* might be."

With their own horses flagging, in the noontide of the next day Céleste and Roél topped a hill to see a goodly-sized town along the banks of a river meandering through a wide valley below. And as the waterway wended past the ville itself, it broadened to nearly three or four times its width elsewhere.

"Ford Town," said Roél. "The *Fd* stands for 'ford.'"

Down the slope they rode, and soon they came in among the buildings, and after inquiries, they reached a stable. Roél traded their mares and geldings for three fresh mounts. And spending some of the gold given them by Vicomte Chevell of the *Sea Eagle*, Roél purchased three more, bringing the total of their horses to six: two were to be ridden, while the other four would trail behind on long tethers as remounts to share the task of bearing the princess and the knight on a headlong run into danger. He also purchased additional tack so that when shifting from one horse to another they would not have to switch gear, saying, "It will save time. Besides, we need tack for Avélaine and Laurent and Blaise."

"Speaking of needs," said Céleste, "we need select enough supplies to feed us and the horses coming and going, and your siblings on the way back. How many days will we be in the Changeling Lord's realm?"

The hostler gasped upon hearing this. "Oh, Sieur, mademoiselle, you must not go unto the land of the Changeling Lord. Terrible things live therein, hideous things. They will kill you, Sieur, and take your demoiselle captive and do dreadful things to her—use her until she is worn beyond living."

"You mean breed me?" asked Céleste.

"If you are a virgin, mademoiselle, then oui, they will use you to strengthen their line. If you are not a virgin, then they will merely use you for pleasure, one after another after another. Yet virgin or no, into the land of the Changelings you must not go."

"We have no choice, Sieur," said Céleste. "Three lives hang in the balance—a sister and two brothers."

"Yours as well," said the hostler, shaking his head.

Roél looked at Céleste, anguish in his eyes. "chérie, I beg of you, stay here. I will go on alone."

"Non, my love," replied Céleste, "where you go, so go I."

"Ah, zut!" declared the hostler. "Sieur, mademoiselle, it is but madness to venture into that dreadful realm, no matter the reason."

Roél looked at Céleste, a plea in his eyes, but she shook her head in silent answer to his wordless appeal. He sighed and turned to the hostler and said, "Mayhap indeed we are insane, yet go there we must."

The man then looked at the sword at Roél's side and said, "If you are bound to take this unwise course, then this I will tell you: turn not your back upon any therein, for to do otherwise is perilous. This I tell you, too: the only sure way to kill a Changeling is to cut off its head, though an arrow through an eye will work as well."

"Merci, Hostler," said Roél. Then he turned to Céleste and said, "We have but the rest of this day and all of tomorrow up until midnight to reach the Changeling Lord's tower and save Avélaine. And then we need to find Laurent and Blaise, and surely it will take no more than three days for the five of us to get back from there."

Céleste nodded and she and Roél selected just enough supplies to last the journey to there and back and but a single day more, and they evenly distributed the goods among the six steeds to equal the loads. The remainder of their supplies they left with the stableman.

At last all was ready, and, with an au revoir to the hostler, out from the town they went. Behind them, the man watched them leave and smiled unto himself, and then stepped back in among the stalls, and the sound of looms weaving swelled and then vanished, and gone was the hostler as well.

Sunwise across the shallows splashed the horses, and upon emerging on the far bank Céleste and Roél broke into a run, two of the mounts bearing weight, four running but lightly burdened. Roél set their gait at a varied pace, and the leagues hammered away beneath their hooves. All day they ran thus: trotting, cantering, galloping, and walking unburdened, and then doing it all over again. Roél and Céleste changed mounts every two candlemarks or so, pausing now and then to stretch their legs and feed the horses some grain or to take water from the streams flowing down from nearby hills.

Long they rode into the late day, past sundown and well beyond, taking the risk of running at speed in spite of the darkness. When they stopped at last, it was nearly mid of night. They had covered some forty leagues or so, yet they had not come unto the twilight bound. But ere the two cast themselves to the ground to sleep, the horses were unladed and rubbed down and given grain and drink.

At dawn the next day, once more they set forth upon the sunwise track. Céleste was weary nearly beyond measure, and she wondered whether the horses could hold the pace; yet the steeds bore up well, for even though they had run swift and far, still half of the time they'd carried no burden. It was she and Roél who felt the brunt of the journey, for they had spent weeks on the quest, and little rest and but few hot meals had they had in those long days.

Yet on they strove, running sunwise—south, Roél would say—and among hills they fared, and they passed through vales and they splashed across streams. A woodland slowed them greatly, yet in the candlemarks of midafternoon, in the near distance ahead they espied the twilight wall rising up into the sky.

"What be the crossing?" called Roél.

Céleste opened the map and looked, and then called back, "A small waterfall on a bourne."

"A brook?"

"Oui."

And on they rode.

When they reached the twilight bound, no stream did they see.

"I'll take the left," said Céleste, raising her silver horn.

"Mayhap even here left is right and right a mistake."

"I'll take the right," said Roél, his face grim, for this was the day of the dark of the moon, and but nine or ten candlemarks remained ere the mid of night would come.

Away from each other they galloped, remounts trailing behind. And within a league Céleste topped a hill to see a stream in the vale below. Down she rode, and there a small waterfall tumbled o'er a rock linn and into a pool beneath, to run on into the boundary.

She raised her horn to her lips and blew a long call. And in but moments it was answered by Roél's clarion cry.

Céleste let her animals drink, and she fed them a ration of grain, and as Roél rode up, she moved her bow and arrows to the horse of hers whose turn had come.

Roél shifted his own gear likewise, and as soon as his steeds were fed and watered and he had changed mounts, with his shield on his arm and his sword in hand, and with an arrow nocked to Céleste's bow, across the stream they splashed and into the twilight beyond.

*   *   *

They came in among high tors, nearly mountains rather than hills, and a passage wound downslope before them and out into a land of woodlands and fields.

"I don't know what I was expecting," said Céleste as they carefully wended their way down the narrow slot, "but certainly not a land such as this." Then she grimly laughed. "Mayhap I thought it would be all ashes and cinders, much like Senaudon, with fire beyond the horizon and the smell of brimstone on the air. But this, the Changeling Lord's realm, is rather like much of Faery elsewhere."

"Me," said Roél, "I was expecting bare stone and a cold wailing wind, yet it seems to be rich farmland and bountiful forests."

Even as he spoke, Roél's gaze searched the horizon for as far as he could see, yet no Changeling Lord's tower did he spy nor a building of any sort. In the far distance ahead, dark mountains rose up, and a black storm raged among the peaks. Roél studied the crests and rises, and no tower or other structure on those stony heights did he see, yet they were far away and a tower could easily be lost to the eye against the rocky crags.

As they reached the foot of the passage and debouched into a grassy field, just ahead a child of a goosegirl, a willow switch in her hand, herded her flock toward a mere, the drove gabbling as they waddled forward.

Roél and Céleste reached the girl just as the geese reached the pond and splashed in.

"Ma'amselle Gooseherd," said Roél, "know you the way to the Changeling Lord's tower?"

"Oui, Sieur," replied the child, her voice piping as she looked up at the man on his horse. She pointed. "That way, I think."

"Roél," murmured Céleste, "no matter what Lady Lot said, this fille can be no more than eight summers old. Let us leave her and ride on."

Roél nodded, and as they turned to look toward the mountains—

the direction the child had indicated—a darkness came over the girl, and she bared her teeth.

"Merci, Ma'amselle Gooseherd," said Roél, turning back, even as the glaring child sprang, spitting and hissing, her leap carrying her shoulder high to mounted Roél, her hands like claws reaching for his throat.

Roél wrenched up his shield barely in time to fend her, and as she fell away, with a sweep of Coeur d'Acier, Roél took off the child's head. She struck the ground, her body dropping one way, her head tumbling another.

Céleste cried out at the sight of the decapitated girl, and Roél looked on in horror at what he had done, for he had slain nought but a poppet, a wee *fillette* but seven or eight summers old. Roél looked at Céleste, tears in his eyes, and he started to speak, yet no words came. But then Céleste gasped, for in that moment both body and head changed into a monstrous thing with fangs and glaring eyes and a hideous bulbous brow and a twisted face and a barrel chest and long hairy arms and legs and broad hands with lengthy, grasping fingers ending in sharp talons. And even as the horses danced aside, the hideous creature dissolved into dark mucus, and a putrid stench filled the air.

The horses snorted and blew and backed and sidled as the slime liquefied and seeped into the ground, leaving barren soil behind, the grass burnt away as if by virulent acid.

"Oh, Roél," said Céleste, "Lady Lot was right."

Still shaken, Roél merely nodded, and Céleste intoned:

"Kill all those who therein do speak;
Question not; you'll understand.

"Roél, the girl was a Changeling, a monstrous thing, even though she seemed nought but a beautiful and innocent child." Céleste looked away from the charred soil and toward the distant mountains and chanted:

"Ask directions unto his tower
In the Changeling Lord's domain;
The answers given will be true,
Yet the givers must be slain."

Roél nodded in agreement and said, "Oui, the Fates are right. Even so, it seemed a dreadful thing I had done."

"But necessary," replied Céleste, yet looking in the direction the Changeling had pointed.

Roél's gaze followed hers, and he said, "Somewhere yon lies the tower and my sister, perhaps my brothers as well. We must ride, for time grows perilously short."

And so, once again they took up the trek.

Often changing mounts, across the land they hammered, passing o'er hill and riding down through dale and across wide fields, as toward the mountains they raced. Occasionally they stopped at streams to water the horses and feed them rations of grain to keep their strength from flagging. And Céleste and Roél took food and drink themselves to keep their own vigor from falling any further, though fall it did. Even so, after but a brief respite, they would remount and fare onward, heading ever toward the mountains.

And along the course they asked a herdsman the way to the Changeling Lord's tower, followed a candlemark later by a tinker, and later still by an old lady. Each pointed toward the stormy mountains, and Roél beheaded them every one, and hideous and garish monsters they became and then a gelatinous mucus that dissolved into a dark, foul-smelling liquid that burned the soil as it seeped away.

As the sun set, the mountains seemed no closer, and on galloped Céleste and Roél. Twilight turned into darkness as night pulled its black cloak across the world, and stars emerged, yet there was no moon to light the way. Once more taking great risk by riding swift in the night, the pair hammered on, hooves strik-ing the ground at a trot, a canter, and a gallop.

And candlemarks burned away as on they raced, and it began to drizzle. They pulled up the hoods of their rain gear and sped on, hooves splatting against the wet ground.

They came to the foot of the mountains, and there a road led up into the massifs and crags, up into the raging storm, and a gate stood across the way. An elderly gatekeeper bear-ing a lantern hobbled out in the pour to ask them their busi-ness, and Roél said, "We seek the Lord of the Changelings' tower."

Lightning flashed and thunder boomed, both riving the air.

"Eh, eh?" The keeper put a hand behind an ear. "What's that?"

"The tower of the Changeling Lord, old man," cried Roél, louder.

"Oh. Up the road." Slowly shuffling in the wetness, the man opened the gate, and as Roél charged by, he swept the old man's head off even as the creature began to change into a monstrous Ogreish form.

Leaving a pool of slime in the road, up the way they splashed, and now they had to slow, for the road was steep and running with water, and the horses labored.

Lightning flared and thunder roared and rain fell down in sheets. . . .

. . . And time fled. . . .

Now and again at twists and turns in the road, high above sil-houetted by lightning against the raging sky, they could see a tall tower standing.

And another candlemark burned.

Yet at last they came to a flat, and before them stood a stone wall, an archway leading under and into a passage where torches in sconces shed a flickering, ruddy, sorcerous light, for though the flambeaus burned, they were not consumed. Beyond the wall as lightning glared they could see the roofs of buildings all attached to one another, and looming above all in the riven air stood a tall dark tower.

And with less than a candlemark remaining ere Avélaine's doom would fall, into the archway they rode.

43

Failure

The warband paused at a crossroads to feed and water the animals and to take food and drink themselves. Borel looked at the stars and sighed and said, "Tis the mid of night of the dark of the moon. We can no longer save Avélaine. In that, we have failed."

"Twas the bloody swamp," growled Chevell. "Had it not delayed us . . ."

"Avélaine is not the only sister needing aid," said Alain. "If Céleste is a captive, we can still rescue her, as well as Roél and his brothers."

"How far?" asked Luc.

Borel unfolded the vellum. "Two borders remain; at the second one we will enter the Changeling realm. As to where therein we need to go, I cannot say, other than we must reach wherever our sister might be. After that, we can deal with finding Roél and his brothers."

"If she is a prisoner," said Luc, "I would think the Changeling Lord's palace is the most likely place he would hold her."

"Or manor or tower or wherever it is that he lives," said Chevell.

"We have spoken of this all along the way," said Alain, "and I say we must ask those living therein as to where their lord dwells."

"What makes you think that by asking Changelings they will tell the truth?" asked Chevell.

"What else would you suggest, Vicomte?" coldly asked Alain.

"Mayhap holding a sword to their throat," shot back Chevell.

"Peace," growled Borel. "We are weary, and there is no need to squabble among ourselves."

Luc grunted his agreement. He glanced about and saw that the horses and men were done. "Let us ride."

And so, worn down and testy and somewhat dispirited, they all mounted up and galloped onward, midnight of the dark of the moon now gone.

44

Perils

Into the flickering-torchlight way they went, Roél in the lead, Céleste following, and behind them lightning flared and thunder crashed, and the corridor flashed bright in the strike. And revealed by the glare, at the far end stood a tall figure in black, his cloak limned in red.

"You!" cried Roél, and he spurred forward, but an axe came flying the length of the passage to bite deeply into Roél's shield. A second axe flew out from the wavering shadows, and a third, and they struck and slashed at Roél, wielded by no hands at all. And horses snorted and blew and recoiled and jerked this way and that in the clanging din as axes met shield and Roél fended with Coeur d'Acier. Yet a fourth axe joined the fray, and a fifth, and Roél was hard-pressed as the blades flew about and slashed at him.

Behind Roél, Céleste's mount flinched and stutter-stepped, yet in spite of its frantic dancing the princess drew her arrow to the full and aimed and loosed. Even as the shaft hurtled through the fluttering light, the figure at the far end whirled and van-

346

ished, and the arrow hissed through where he had been and shattered against stone.

And the axes fell to the pave of the corridor, no longer under sorcerous control.

His breath coming in gasps, Roél said, "'Twas the Changeling Lord."

Yet even as he said it, at the far end a huge knight in black armor and bearing a battle-axe with flames running along its blade rode out from a side archway on a horselike steed; but no horse was this mount, with its serpent scales and flaring yellow eyes and a forked tongue and cloven hooves.

And with a howl, the black knight charged down the corridor, his flaming axe raised for a killing blow.

Roél spurred his mount forward to meet the onslaught, Coeur d'Acier's edge gleaming argent in the flickering torchlight.

Even as they closed, an arrow hissed past Roél to—*thuck!*—pierce the serpent horse and plunge deep into its breast. A skreigh split the air, but still the creature thundered on.

Down swung the black knight's fire-edged battle-axe, and with a mighty crash, it shivered Roél's shield in twain, yet at the same time, Roél's silver-chased, rune-marked blade swept under the black knight's own shield and ripped open his gut. Roél spun his horse, and with a second blow, he sheared through the knight's neck to take off his head, even as another arrow flashed along the corridor, this one to pierce the serpent horse's left eye, and that creature shrilled and crashed to the stone. The black knight's body smashed down beside his monstrous horse, and his head yet encased in his helm clanged to the pave just behind, his axe blanging down nearby, its flames now extinguished.

Céleste quickly nocked another arrow, but the grotesque knight and his hideous beast began to pool into slime. And a horrific stench filled the passage.

With their horses snorting and blowing in the malodor and

trying to jerk back and away from the sickening smell, gagging in the reek, both Roél and Céleste prevailed and spurred past the now-runny sludge and on down the corridor.

To the right and through the archway whence the black knight had come, they found an extensive, torchlit stable.

"Mid of night is drawing upon us," said Roél as he and Céleste rode halfway down the row of stalls and dismounted. "We must find Avélaine ere then."

"*Hsst!*" cautioned Céleste. "Roél, at the far end, something or someone moves."

Down to the far extent they crept, to find several horses in stalls. "Céleste, there is Impérial, Laurent's horse, and Vaillant, Blaise's. They are here; my brothers are here. But, if that's true, then why haven't they—? Oh, are they prisoners?"

Mayhap dead, thought Céleste. *No, wait, Lady Doom showed us their images in her farseeing mirror. Surely they yet live; else why show us them?*

Quickly they tied their horses to stall posts, and then wrenched down two of the sorcerous flambeaus, and up a flight of stone stairs they went, to find themselves in a courtyard, the rain yet sheeting down.

As they crossed, lightning flared, and Roél gasped. "Céleste, it is Laurent and Blaise."

"Where?"

"Yon."

In that moment another flash brightened the courtyard, and near a gaping entryway stood two figures.

"Take care, Roél, for the Changelings are shapeshifters, and this could be a trap."

"Laurent, Blaise!" called Roél, and, sword in hand, he and Céleste ran through the rain to where they had seen the two, slowing as they neared.

Another flare.

The figures had not moved.

Stepping closer and raising their torches on high, they found two life-sized statues.

Céleste recognized both from the image in Lady Urd's dark basin. And just as they had seen at the crossroads some nine days past, both Laurent and Blaise stood with their hands on the hilts of their swords, the weapons partially drawn or mayhap partly sheathed. And their faces reflected either smiles or grimaces. Were they preparing to do battle, or instead were they putting their swords away? Neither Roél nor Céleste could tell.

"Oh, Mithras, my brothers, an enchantment, have they been turned to stone?"

"I do not know," said Céleste, "yet we cannot stand and ponder. 'Tis nigh mid of night, and we must find your sister."

In through the opening they went, and they found themselves in a long corridor. From somewhere ahead came the sound of soft weeping.

"Avélaine!" called Roél, and down the hallway they trotted.

From a doorway at the end of the passage there stepped a maiden. "Avélaine, we have found you," cried Roél in triumph. "We have found you in time."

"Is it you? Is it truly you?" asked Avélaine, sweeping forward, a beautiful smile transforming her face.

Céleste's heart plummeted even as Roél rushed forward and embraced Avélaine. Then he stepped back to look at his sister and said, "Where are Laurent and Blaise?"

Céleste came to stand beside Roél, and Avélaine glanced at her and smiled. "Roél, she spoke to us," said Céleste in a low voice.

Roél shook his head. "Céleste, she is my sister," even as Céleste held her torch up for a better look at this maiden, the light casting shadows against the walls. Céleste drew in a sharp breath between clenched teeth.

And as Roél started to sheathe his sword, "No!" cried Céleste, and she dropped her bow and torch and grabbed Coeur d'Acier away from Roél, and in spite of his shout, with a back-handed sweep she slashed the keen blade through Avélaine's neck, the head to go flying.

Down fell the body and the head.

"Céleste," cried Roél, horrified, "what have you done?"

But then the head began to transform into a visage of unbearable hideousness 'neath hair of hissing snakes. And as Céleste and Roél looked on, their own bodies began to stiffen, to harden, yet at that moment the corpse and its head collapsed into mucous slime and then to a malodorous liquid, and Céleste and Roél felt whole and hale again.

Céleste said, "She was not Avélaine."

"But how did you know?"

Céleste handed Coeur d'Acier back to Roél and retrieved her bow and torch and said, "She had a shadow, and Avélaine does not. And I remembered Skuld's words:

"What might seem fair is sometimes foul
And holds not a beautiful soul.
Hesitate not or all is lost;
Do what seems a terrible cost.

"When I held up the torch, her shadow showed her true soul, her true form—that of someone with writhing snakes for hair—a Gorgon. Besides, she spoke to us, and Lady Lot said that until Avélaine is fully restored to slay all those who do so."

"A Gorgon?" Roél glanced at the puddle that was her head and then looked over his shoulder toward the statues in the courtyard. "Laurent and Blaise, this is how they . . . ?"

Tears brimmed in Céleste's eyes. "I'm afraid so."

Gritting his teeth, Roél said, "The Changeling Lord will pay dearly for this. Come, we yet need to find Avélaine."

As they started down the hallway, again they heard the soft

weeping. They came to a cross-corridor, and Céleste murmured, "This way," and rightward she turned toward the sobbing.

To either side open doorways showed chambers furnished with tables and chairs and cabinets and lounges and other such. In some, fireplaces were lit; in others the rooms were dark, and some were lit by candles.

They arrived at the doorway whence the weeping came, and they stepped into a chamber where a maiden sat on the floor quietly crying. At hand stood a narrow golden rack o'er which a dark wispy garment draped.

Céleste raised her torch and approached the girl to find she cast no shadow, though there was a thin line of darkness at her feet that shifted slightly as the torch moved about. "Is it Avélaine?" asked Céleste.

Roél knelt before the maiden and whispered, "Avélaine?"

The demoiselle looked up, yet there was no recognition in her eyes, and she cast her face in her hands and wept on.

Céleste looked at Roél, a question in her eyes, and he nodded and glanced down at Coeur d'Acier and stepped well back and murmured, "Oh, Mithras, do not let her speak."

In that moment, Céleste gasped and pointed, where on the wall a huge celestial astrolabe slowly turned, the large disks of the golden sun and silver moon and the smaller disks of the five wandering stars—red, blue, yellow, green, and white—all creeping in great circular paths.

"Roél, look, the disk of the moon is nigh all black. 'Tis but a faint silver line remaining, and even it is disappearing."

"We must hurry, for mid of night is upon us," said Roél.

Frantically Céleste looked about, her eye lighting on the golden rack. "Can this be her shadow?" asked Céleste, reaching for the dark garment. But her hand passed through; she could not grasp it.

"It must be," said Roél. "It looks just like the one the Changeling Lord had draped over his arm."

Céleste frowned in puzzlement. "If we cannot even touch it, then how do we restore it to her form?"

Roél frowned and looked at the golden rack and then his face lit up in revelation. "Céleste, the Fate-given gifts!"

"Oui!" cried Céleste, and she set her bow aside and took the three gifts in hand: the golden tweezers and spool of dark thread from her pocket, and the silver needle from her silken under-shirt.

With the golden tweezers and their very rounded, blunt ends, she found she could take hold of the shadow on the rack.

But when she tried with her fingers to pluck the loose end of the wispy dark thread from the obsidian spool, she could not grasp it either. Once again she used the golden tweezers, and with some difficulty, she managed to thread the silver needle. Then she lifted the shadow from the rack and moved it to the thin line of darkness at Avélaine's feet, and after comparing one with the other, she turned the shadow over to mate with the line.

And on the wall the astrolabe showed a black moon with but a trace of silver remaining, and it began to disappear.

Taking a deep breath and praying that she had gotten things right, Céleste began to stitch, the seam sealing perfectly as she went.

Roél stepped to the door to stand ward, only to hear a distant rising and falling of an incantation echoing down the hallway.

"Céleste," he called quietly, and when she looked up, he glanced at the astrolabe where but a faint glimmer remained. "Someone is chanting . . . mayhap the Changeling Lord. If so, it might be to entrap Avélaine's soul forever, for mere moments are left of time. I must stop him ere it falls, but you must continue sewing."

Céleste paused in her stitching and glanced aside to make certain her bow was in reach, and then she nodded and whispered, "Go," and began sewing again.

With Coeur d'Acier in hand, Roél stepped quietly along the

corridor toward the canting. Past doorways he trod, and he turned at a cross-hall, the sound growing louder. Down the passage before him, an archway glowed with wavering light, and as he approached, a brief flare of brightness glared through the portal, followed by the boom of thunder. At last Roél came to the entry, and it led into a grand room bare of furniture, with a great, round skylight centered overhead. Again a stroke flashed through the sky and starkly lit the entire room, thunder crashing after. But the storm above was not what caught Roél's eye, for there in the flickering candlelight, with his back to the door, in the center of the chamber at the edge of a circle engraved in the floor with five black candles ringed 'round, each joined by five straight lines forming a pentagonal shape, the Changeling Lord stood with his arms upraised, and he chanted, invoking some great spell.

Running on silent footsteps, across the broad floor sped Roél, his sword raised for a strike. But ere he reached the Changeling Lord, in the circle appeared a tall, thin, black-haired woman, dressed in a dark flowing gown. And her imperious face twisted in rage, and she shrieked, *"You!"*

But it was not the Changeling Lord who evoked her venom, for, even as the lord turned to see Roél hurtling forward, the woman raised a black-nailed hand, and with a gesture she spat a word.

And Roél was frozen in his tracks, and try as he might, he could not move.

Sneering in triumph, the woman started forward, but the lines on the floor seemed to stop her. She looked down at them and with a negligent wave, as if flicking away a fly, she stepped out from the pentagon, out from the circle, and, with but barely a glance at the Changeling Lord, she strode past him and toward her impaled victim: Roél.

45

Reckonings

As the woman stopped before Roél and looked him up and down and smiled wickedly, "I did not expect you, Nefasí," said the Changeling Lord.

"Then why did you summon me, Morgrif?"

"I did not summon you by name, Nefasí, but rather I summoned this one's deadly enemy, for he is a most deadly foe."

Nefasí laughed. "Indeed, I am his deadly enemy, for he set back my revenge against Lord Valeray."

At the name Valeray, the Changeling Lord's eyebrows rose in surprise. "He, who is most responsible for the defeat of Lord Orbane?"

"Oui, Morgrif, the very same. And this fool twice kept me from seizing one of Valeray's get: Céleste."

Nefasí turned to Roél and put a hand behind her ear in a pretense of listening. "What's that you ask? How did you interfere? Pah! You fool, 'twas I who sent the brigands to capture Princess Céleste, Valeray's youngest spawn. And 'twas I who sent my minions to attack at the twilight bound. And it was you who in-

354

terfered both times, for I watched as you slew brigands and again as you slew Redcaps and Bogles and Trolls and fled with the princess."

"You watched?" asked Morgrif.

The woman ground her teeth. "I looked through the eyes of my familiar and called out for revenge, ere some fool put a crossbow quarrel through my bird, and oh, how that pained me, and for that this man shall also pay . . . and dearly."

Nefasí turned to the Changeling Lord and said, "You will be well rewarded for this, Morgrif. And when Orbane is set free, you will sit near the throne."

"I think I have another gift for you, Nefasí," said the Changeling Lord. "This knight has a woman with him."

"A woman?"

"Oui. Elegant and slender and of pale yellow hair and green eyes."

Nefasí crowed. "Ah, even sweeter than I thought. Surely it is Céleste. She has not escaped my revenge after all."

Sweat ran in rivulets down Roél's face as he strained to move, yet he could not. And Nefasí laughed to see him struggle, and, preening in her power, she strutted back and forth before him, her long black gown flowing behind. "Why, you ask, do I wish to harm your love, the princess? Idiot, I am one of four sisters, two of whom are now slain: Rhensibé, killed by Borel, and Iníquí, murdered by Liaze. Those two assassins are siblings of your Princess Céleste, all of them foul get of thief Valeray and his slut Saissa. And I and my sister Hradian plan to kill them all; we will have our revenge, we two who remain Lord Orbane's acolytes."

Hatred filled her eyes, and spittle flecked at the corner of her mouth, so rabid was her desire for vengeance. "There will come a day when we set him free, but you will not be around to witness it, nor will your whore Céleste." Nefasí raised her hand, her black talons gleaming ebon in the candlelight, and she reached for Roél's exposed throat.

"Whore, am I?" came a call from the enshadowed doorway. Nefasí turned to see Céleste standing in the opening, her bow in hand, an arrow nocked. Behind her stood someone else in the darkness.

The witch hissed, but then she laughed. "Have you come to save your love, Céleste? This is even better than I expected."

Céleste drew her bow to the full and aimed.

Again Nefasí laughed, and she raised her right hand toward Céleste, her index and little fingers hooked like horns and pointing at the arrow, and her middle fingers pointed down and her thumb pointed leftward. "You fool! Set aside your pinprick, for neither you nor it can harm me."

"Oh, no?" said Céleste, and she loosed, the shaft to hurtle through the air toward the witch.

"Avert!" cried Nefasí, and then her eyes widened in fear, and she shrieked as the arrow sped true and pierced her through the heart. Momentarily she looked down at the gray shaft, and then at Céleste.

"Not even the gods could turn that one aside," said Céleste coldly.

And Nefasí fell to the floor, dead before striking the stone.

Suddenly Roél could move, and he stepped toward the Changeling Lord.

But Morgrif leapt into the circle and spoke an arcane word. And he laughed and looked at Céleste even as Roél approached.

As the princess nocked another arrow, the Changeling Lord called out, "Though somehow you have managed to defeat your deadly enemy, I have now called out to my minions to come to my aid, and by their very numbers, they will o'erwhelm you both."

Céleste aimed and loosed her shaft, the arrow to hiss through the air, only to shatter as if against an invisible barrier at the perimeter of the circle.

Once more the Changeling Lord laughed and called out to

Céleste, "I am in a ring of protection, a place where your weapons of bronze cannot harm me." His gaze then fell upon Roél, and Morgrif stepped to the very brim of the design toward the knight and added, "Not even that silver-chased bronze sword of yours, fool."

Roél, now reaching the circle's edge himself, gritted and said, "Coeur d'Acier is no weapon of bronze." And with a back-handed sweep, he took off the Changeling Lord's head.

46

Flight

Lightning flared and thunder roared throughout the chamber as the Lord of the Changelings collapsed and became a great pool of dark slime, which then degenerated into viscous liquid. A gagging stench rose up, and Roél backed away and turned to find Céleste right behind. He took her in his arms and kissed her, and then said, "Avélaine, my sister, is she—?"

Céleste smiled and, disengaging, gestured toward the enshadowed doorway and beckoned. Out stepped a lovely, raven-haired young woman, her sapphire-blue eyes clear and sparkling. "Sieur Roél, may I present Dame Avélaine du Manoir d'Émile. My Lady Avélaine, this is your brother Roél."

Avélaine gaped and said, "Rollie, is it truly you?"

"Oui, Avi, it truly is."

She rushed forward, and with tears in his eyes, Roél embraced her and kissed her on the forehead and whispered, "Oh, Avi, we searched so very long: Laurent, Blaise, Céleste, and I."

Avélaine drew back and looked about. "Laurent and Blaise are here?"

Roél sighed. "I have some ill news, Avi. You see—"

"*Hsst . . . !*" silenced Céleste, and in the quietness following they heard distant oncoming yells and the drumming of running footsteps.

Roél looked about, but there seemed to be no other exits, or if there were, they were well hidden.

Céleste nocked an arrow, and Roél raised Coeur d'Acier. "Avi, get behind us."

"I can fight," said Avélaine.

Roél glanced at Céleste, and she looked at the door and then to Avélaine and said, "Do not leave her unarmed."

Roél loosed the keeper on his long-knife and handed it to his sister, and then he ran for the archway, shouting, "Kill any who get past me." He came to a halt beside the opening, his back to the inside wall.

A howl sounded, and Roél risked a quick glance down the passage and then ducked back. Some kind of great black doglike beast loped on all fours toward the chamber. Behind it came more creatures, some on two legs, others on four, some flapping on great awkward wings.

As the black dog hurtled through the doorway—*shkk!*—Coeur d'Acier took off its head. A gangling man ran through, and, shouting a war cry, Roél swung again, striking off another head. A flapping creature shot past above, and an arrow pierced it through a yellow eye, and scrawking, down it tumbled.

A vast roar echoed down the corridor, and Roél chanced another quick glance, and a great Troll lumbered toward the opening.

Roél took a deep breath and then stepped into the entry, and on came the monstrous being, other of the shapeshifters giving way before it.

"*Vive la Forêt de Printemps et le Manoir d'Émile!*" shouted Roél, raising his sword to the ready.

And from the far end of the hall, there came an echo—or was it a cry?—*Vive le Manoir d'Émile!*

But then the Troll was upon him, and even as it reached for the knight, Roél swung Coeur d'Acier in a wide swath and opened up the thing's gut.

The monster roared and entrails spilled forth as of a horrid flower coming abloom, and still the Troll reached out with its great hands and clutched at Roél and grasped an arm and lifted him on high.

Thakk!—an arrow pierced the thing's eye, and howling, it dropped Roél and crashed down, even as more of the shapechangers rushed into the chamber, and they slipped and slid in the putrid pools of reeking slime and dark liquid.

Roél gained his feet and began laying about, hacking, slashing, taking off heads. Yet there were too many, and soon he was mobbed.

But in that moment two sword-swinging knights crashed through the Changelings at the archway and joined Roél in the mêlée.

"Laurent! Blaise!" Roél shouted, but they did not respond, so fierce was the battle.

In a back-to-back triangle they stood, and the good bronze of two of the swords and the sharp rune-bound steel of Coeur d'Acier and the arrows from a bow soon prevailed over tooth and claw and fang, and the Changelings fled, those who had managed to survive, though many were maimed.

Panting, the brothers looked upon one another, and Blaise clasped Roél and said, "Roél, whence came you?"

Laurent looked at Roél and said, "This is Rollie?"

"Oui, Laurent. I have grown some since last you saw me."

But in that moment, Avélaine came running, and Laurent swung up his sword and shouted, "'Ware, Gorgon!"

But Roél stepped in front of his brothers and said, "Non! It is Avélaine. We rescued her."

"We?" asked Blaise.

"Céleste and I," said Roél, and even as he spoke, the princess came in among them, wiping dry the arrows she had used in the battle as well as the gray arrow she had retrieved from the corpse of Nefasi, though its shaft was now cracked and its soft plomb point now blunted.

As Laurent and Blaise embraced Avélaine and she them, Roél made quick introductions all 'round. Then he said, "We must leave, and swiftly, for the Lord of the Changelings has summoned his minions."

"We'll not go before we kill him," gritted Laurent.

"Already done," said Céleste, grinning and gesturing at the dark liquid in the pentagon within the circle. "Roél took off his head."

Laurent gazed at his little brother, now no longer a lad, and Blaise said, "There is a tale here for the telling, yet if the minions have been summoned, it can wait."

Out through the archway and down the hall they hurried, Roél and Laurent in the lead, then Avélaine and Céleste, and Blaise coming last.

As they made their way toward the stables, horns sounded from within the castle, as if in rallying cries.

Quickly they reached the horses, and as Laurent and Blaise saddled their mounts with their very own gear found nearby, Roél and Céleste tethered remounts after.

Out from the stables they rode, Avélaine upon a fresh horse, Roél and Céleste upon fresh animals as well, and all trailed strings of horses after. And in the passageway beyond the stables they had to fight their way through Changelings, these armed with weapons. Forward they charged, blades swinging, arrows flying, spears lancing, and out through the exit beyond.

Down the roadway they hammered, leaving much of the foot pursuit behind, though some winged creatures flew above, and four-footed beasts trailed after.

And still the storm thundered and raged, lightning limning the tower aft, a tower now lacking a lord.

* * *

One by one the Changelings killed the remounts, one by one by one. They would fly down to land in the darkness and shift shape and lie in wait. And when the humans rode past, the Changelings would loose arrows at the horses and kill at least one or two. Then they would shift shape and take to the air and fly ahead and land and wait in ambush and do it over again.

And those Changelings following afoot would pad through the darkness on the fringes and wait for an opportune moment, and then they would silently attack in a swift foray, and just as swiftly retreat.

Of Roél and Laurent and Blaise, all had been wounded, though lightly. And blood seeped as they rode on, for they could not afford to stop; else they would be o'erwhelmed.

Daylight came, and now they could see likely places where ambushers might lie in wait, and they veered this way and that to avoid such pitfalls. Even so, Changelings rose up from the grasses to loose arrows and take down more horses. And at last there were no remounts remaining.

Still the five rode on, fleeing on a different heading from the one taken inward by Roél and Céleste, for Laurent and Blaise both assured them that it was a shorter ride.

And loping Changelings sped onward, and others flew o'er-head, all of them outrunning the flagging steeds. And they bayed and skreighed loudly, summoning others to the hunt, or so Laurent surmised. And many of them ran on beyond without at-tacking, as if to cut off any escape.

As the five passed through a swale, Roél's mount was shot out from under him, and he crashed hard to the ground, and his left shoulder was wrenched out of joint. Up he sprang as beasts closed in, but Laurent and Blaise and Avélaine and Céleste cir-cled back and drove them away. With his right hand Roél grasped his left elbow and pulled it across his body and popped his shoulder back into place. Even so, it was weak and would bear no strain. Avélaine leapt from her horse and gave it over to Roél and cried out, "Céleste and I will ride double." And as she sprang up behind the princess, Roél swallowed his protest and mounted the steed.

And with but four horses and the women riding two-up—for they were lighter than the men—across the plains they sped.

Of a sudden Laurent's horse was felled, and he leapt free as it went down. But a bone snapped in one of his wrists, and an ankle twisted and popped in the tumbling fall.

They continued on three horses—Céleste and Avélaine riding double, as now were Roél and Laurent.

When there were but two horses remaining, Laurent had said, "Avélaine, Céleste, take them and run for the border. Blaise, Roél, and I will stay behind and delay the Changelings."

Céleste had shaken her head and had spoken of the hostler's warning. "If we are captured, the Changelings will do dreadful things to us. They will ride me until I am worn beyond living, and breed Avélaine time after time to strengthen their line. As for me, I would much rather die fighting at Roél's side than to be taken captive and used as a plaything by these monstrosities."

Avélaine had nodded in agreement and had said, "And I will not become a broodmare for them."

And so, Céleste and Avélaine had ridden at the men's side until the horses were gone, and then had travelled afoot with them toward the border.

When they came within sight of the twilight bound, a flying reptile of a *thing* swooped down upon Blaise, and though Blaise dodged away from its claws, the creature gashed a deep cut in his side with one of its deadly wing talons. As it flew up and circled 'round for another attack, Céleste slew the creature with a well-placed bow shot.

On they ran, blood seeping from Blaise, Roél with his left arm dangling, Laurent nursing a broken wrist and limping on a sprained ankle. But Céleste and Avélaine were relatively un-harmed, for the Changelings had other plans for them.

And now they came to a great pile of boulders, the marker for crossing out of the Changeling realm, the twilight bound no more than a furlong past. But a host of shapeshifters barred the way, and they swept forward in a wide arc, the ends to come to-gether to entrap their victims. And about Céleste and the others the ring slowly closed.

Roél said, "Let us make our last stand atop these rocks; there lies some shelter against arrows, and it will be difficult for creatures to come at us except from above. Céleste, with your remaining shafts, you can guard that way. The rest of us will watch the ramps. And now, my loved ones, let us give them a battle of which the bards would ever sing if they only knew."

All nodded in agreement with Roél's words, and up onto the great pile they clambered, Roél helping Laurent to the crest, Céleste and Avélaine aiding Blaise.

Now they took shelter from the Changeling arrows behind boulders ajumble, and they waited.

Quickly Avélaine tore a strip from her dress and bandaged Blaise's side, but the blood yet seeped through.

And cautiously the shapeshifters closed in.

Céleste looked at her arrows. Not counting the broken one of gray, she had but three remaining, and two of those were blunt tipped.

Horns sounded, signaling among the Changeling ranks, and some lines delayed while others moved forward, making ready for a final rush.

Roél gripped Coeur d'Acier and looked on. Laurent held his sword in his left hand, for his right wrist was the one broken. Blaise struggled to his feet and stood swaying but ready. Avélaine gripped Roél's long-knife and remained at Blaise's side.

At last the signal for the attack sounded.

And as they charged, Céleste raised her own horn to her lips and called out the war cry of Springwood Manor.

And—lo!—it was answered in kind. And she whirled to see Anton and the full warband of Springwood come charging on horses through the border, and elements of the warbands from Autumnwood and Winterwood and Summerwood manors along with Vicomte Chevell and crew members of the *Sea Eagle*. And horns blew and war cries sounded. Borel and his Wolves led the charge, Alain in the fore as well, and he leapt from his horse and a darkness came over him, and a huge grizzled Bear smashed into the Changeling ranks.

And Céleste fell to her knees and wept with joy as all around chaos reigned.

47

Return

Horses, men, Wolves, and a Bear: they crashed into and through and over the ranks of the Changelings. Swords rived, spears impaled, arrows and bolts pierced, hooves trampled, fangs rent, and claws savaged. Shapechangers screamed and fell slain in pools of slime and slurry, and surviving Changelings broke and fled, only to be hauled down from behind, though a handful outran the pursuers. Some rose up to flap away, and several of these were brought to earth by bolt or arrow—including one brought down by the last pointed shaft from Céleste's bow—and only a few escaped.

The warband formed a protective ring about the great jumble of boulders, and up clambered Borel and Alain, the latter no longer a Bear. And they embraced Céleste and held her close, and she wept in relief, as did they. And Borel said, "Oh, Céleste, we thought we had lost you, that you had drowned, but then your letter came, and we set out straightaway, warbands and horses, to help you rescue Roél's sister. But we were too late for that."

"But you did rescue Avélaine, for this is she," said Céleste, pointing to the maiden, "as well as rescue the rest of us."

Then up came Vicomte Chevell, and he roared in laughter and said that he and his men would not have missed this for all the world, and he eyed in admiration the twice-rescued beautiful demoiselle Avélaine, and she blushed most modestly.

Clambering up came Anton of the Springwood, and Rémy of the Autumnwood, and Jules of the Winterwood, and Bertran of the Summerwood: armsmasters all.

Accompanied by Gilles the Healer, a tall, slender, dark-haired man climbed up, one who had been exceptionally devastating in the fight; it was the chevalier Luc, betrothed of Princess Liaze of the Autumnwood, though Borel introduced him by his full title: *Comte Luc du Château Bleu dans le Lac de la Rose et Gardien de la Clé.*

There at the top of the mound, Gilles treated the wounds of Blaise, Laurent, and Roél, and the scrapes of Céleste and Avélaine, while down at the base of the boulders, Chirurgeon Burcet treated the ten or so warriors who had been injured in the battle with the Changelings.

Finally, aiding Blaise and Laurent, down they all clambered, and when they reached the ground Céleste said, "Come, let us leave this dreadful place and find an inn, for hot food and good wine I would have, and a bath and clean clothes, but mostly I would have sleep."

And so they set out and along the way, they stayed in inns and wayside manors and even in a bordello. And they ate hot meals and drank fine wines and took long baths and slept, and, of course, Céleste and Roél made sweet love.

When they came to the swamp, the men groaned, for they would have to pass through this distressing place again.

Late in the day they at last emerged from the mire and came to the Bridge of the Red Knight. Yet that fearsome warrior was not there, nor was his helm on a pike. Why he was absent, they knew not, though Céleste proposed that he stood ward against only someone passing the opposite way.

After they had crossed over and had made their way down to the river below, as all men bathed in their turn to remove the muck of the mire, Luc said, "The toughest battle I ever fought was against the knight of the bridge."

"He was indeed hard to kill," replied Roél

"I agree," said Laurent.

"Ah, oui," added Blaise.

And these four chevaliers all eyed one another in speculation and broke out in laughter, and they all agreed that sooner or later, lances and chargers ready, they would take to the lists against one another, and then unto the fields.

The great warband was welcomed in Le Bastion, and they stayed there for a sevenday, and fetes were held every eve as they told and retold their many tales. It was during this time that Céleste learned that Luc's steed Deadly Nightshade at the command of Liaze had been the one who actually killed Iniquí—". . . kicked the witch into the fire he did, well-trained knight's warhorse that he is." Too, Alain and Borel and all others had learned that Nefasí had been slain by the gray arrow loosed by Céleste.

"It means that there is but Hradian left of the four acolytes," said Borel.

"But there is yet Orbane," said Alain, "and even though he is entrapped in an inescapable prison, one day, I deem, he will have to be dealt with."

They paused at the ruins of the manor devastated by Lokar the Ogre, and Céleste laid a wreath of wildflowers at the door and prayed to Mithras to give the manor peace.

On they went, and finally, two full fortnights in all after the battle in the Changeling realm, they came to Port Cient.

* * *

Roél and Céleste stood on a candlelit veranda in the twilight and looked out over the harbor. There rode the *Sea Eagle* at anchor, her crew readying her for the voyage home. In the garden below the balcony, Vicomte Chevell and Avélaine sat in quiet conversation, and Chevell said, "Lady Avélaine, might I come courting?"

"Oh, my lord, I am most sorry, but I am betrothed to another."

"Betrothed?"

"Oui. He is someone I do not love, yet my parents arranged it so."

"Non, Avélaine," called down Roél.

When Avélaine turned and looked up at him, Roél said, "I did not mean to eavesdrop, Avi, but you are no longer betrothed. Maslin did not wait for you, but married another. You are free to choose for yourself."

Avélaine squealed in joy, and she blew a kiss to Roél. Then she turned to Chevell and cast down her eyes most modestly and said, "Oui, my lord, you may indeed woo me, though you have my heart even now."

Across the brine sped the *Sea Eagle*, and the lookout above called out, "Land ho!" And within a candlemark the *Eagle* rode at anchor in the harbor at Port Mizon.

Vicomte Chevell escorted Céleste and Roél, Borel and Alain and Luc, and Avélaine and Laurent and Blaise to stand before King Avélar. When he had heard the full of their tale, Avélar praised them highly for what they had done, especially Céleste and Roél for ridding Faery of the Changeling Lord.

There was great joy in Port Mizon that eve, and the next four nights as well, but on the fifth day, during a noontide meal at the palace, even as Céleste spoke of their plans to set out for the Springwood on the morrow, a page came in and whispered to the king. Avélar nodded and the page sped away, and moments later a man in robes strode in, a roll of cloth under his arm.

"What is it, Sage Gabon?"

"My king, the map, it is— Here. Let me show you." He un-rolled the cloth. It was blank on both sides.

Startled, Chevell said, "This is the treasured map?"

"Oui . . . or perhaps I should say it was," replied Gabon.

Céleste reached into the breast pocket of her leathers and pulled out the vellum chart she had borne so very many days. Spreading it out, she gasped, for it, too, was blank.

Now Borel did the same with his copy of the map, and it was blank as well.

Blaise and Laurent also drew forth their copies to find those vellums unmarked.

"What does this mean? I wonder," asked Avélar.

"Hsst!" said Demoiselle Avélaine. "Listen. What is that?"

In the subsequent quietness, all heard a faint sound of looms weaving, which faded into silence.

"Huah!" exclaimed Roél and shook his head. "I ween we now know just who the cartographers were. Cryptic, a cipher in places, a chart that only they could see would be needed, first by you, my lord, then by my brothers, then by Céleste and me, and finally by the warbands who rescued us. And it is—or rather was—on woven cloth."

Avélar looked at Roél in puzzlement, and Céleste said, "My lord, Roél deems, as do I, that the Ladies Wyrd, Lot, and Doom have reclaimed the patterns woven into that piece of fabric, as well as those we drew."

"But why?"

"Mayhap, my lord, so that Faery itself—or, that is, a great portion of it—will now remain a mystery."

Avélar held up his hands in a modest gesture of surrender and said, "Who are we to question the Three Sisters?"

Chevell laughed and said, " 'Tis better this way, for ever would I rather sail off into the unknown than to follow the tried and true."

Avélaine gazed at her vicomte, and there was nought but adoration in her eyes.

Just after dawn of the following day, siblings and siblings-to-be and the warbands and a pack of Wolves set out for the Springwood, Vicomte Chevell riding at Avélaine's side, Céleste and Roél together, with Luc and Blaise and Laurent laughing at some bon mot as out through the gates they rode.

Some four days later they crossed into the Springwood, and with her silver horn, Céleste summoned a Sprite and asked the wee winged being to relay the message to the manor that she and the others were on their way.

Three days after, they rode onto the grounds of Springwood Manor, and waiting for them was the full staff of the estate, and elements of those from the manors of the Winterwood and Autumnwood and Summerwood. And a great cheer rose up as the cavalcade emerged from the forest and fared onto the lush green lawn.

There, too, were waiting King Valeray and Queen Saissa, and their hearts swelled and tears came into their eyes at the sight of their offspring unharmed.

As well awaited two princesses and a princess-to-be: Liaze and Camille and Lady Michelle. And as the riders came to a stop, Luc leapt from his horse and swept Liaze up in his arms, and Alain sprang down and embraced his Camille, and Borel alighted and passionately kissed Michelle.

And in that moment, Alain gave a great whoop and lifted Camille up and whirled 'round, but then gently set her down. When the others looked at him in startlement he said, "My Camille is indeed with child."

During the ball that night, in between dances and among those who stood to the side and sipped wine, stories flew and tales were exchanged, their fragments overheard in passing:

". . . and when Laurent and I came to, we were standing in a courtyard dripping wet from the raging storm above. We had been fooled by a Gorgon, you see, and had been turned to stone, and—"

"Stone?"

"Oui, but apparently when Céleste slew the Gorgon, our enchantment ended and . . ."

". . . and, oh, my, you should have seen Luc battle the Red Knight, a huge man, if man he was, because when Luc defeated him, the Red Knight vanished, but his helm . . ."

". . . horses were jammed together in Vicomte Chevell's Sea Eagle, and we had to keep them calm and from biting one another, and when we reached Port Cient, they were frisky upon leaving the . . ."

". . . heard the sounds of conflict, and then a battle cry, and Blaise and I ran to aid whoever was in hard combat with the Changelings, only to find Roél in mêlée and . . ."

". . . the worst part? Oh, it was the swamp. Never have I been bitten by so many . . ."

". . . I think he broke it when an arrow took his horse out from under him . . ."

". . . oh, yes, but he is quite handsome, isn't he, now? I deem Lady Avélaine is quite fortunate to have . . ."

". . . and it seems we galloped all the way from Port Cient to the land of the Changelings, and when we passed through the bound, we heard the Springwood battle cry; it was the princess . . ."

". . . and so, Valeray, Avélar made me a vicomte, with lands starwise of Port Mizon, though much of my time is spent aboard the Sea Eagle, escorting merchants across perilous waters and . . ."

". . . ah, oui, there will be weddings, for kings have been notified—King Avélar in the case of Vicomte Chevell and Lady Avélaine, and King Valeray in the case of Princess Céleste and

Roél . . . oh, and of course for Liaze and Luc and Borel and Michelle—and there are banns to post and weddings to plan and a Hierophant to be acquired, and . . ."

Thus did the tales and gossip and conversations go.

And dances were danced, and food and drink consumed, and lovers slipped out into the cool spring eve and embraced in the silver light of the argent full moon and kissed . . . and more.

At the midnight mark, King Valeray called a halt to the music, and he took stance upon the ballroom dais, and as servants passed among the gathering and doled out goblets of wine, Valeray called for quiet, for he would make a toast to the successful quest and to those who rode thereon, and he would toast the brides- and grooms-to-be, and of course he would toast the child to be born to Alain and Camille.

But the moment that all had a goblet in hand, including the servants, of a sudden there came the sound of shuttles and looms, and before the gathering stood three women: Maiden, Mother, and Crone; the Ladies Skuld, Verdandi, and Urd; the Fates Wyrd, Lot, and Doom—one slender, her robe limned in silver; one matronly, her robe limned in gold; and one seemingly bent with age, her robe limned in black.

A gasp went up from the gathering, yet Valeray and Borel and Alain, and Luc and Roél and Chevell, all bowed, the other men in the gathering following suit; and Saissa and Liaze and Céleste and Camille and Michelle and Avélaine curtseyed, the other gathered women doing likewise.

"Mesdames," murmured King Valeray upon straightening.

"Valeray," said Verdandi.

"What would you have of us?" asked the king.

Verdandi looked at Urd, and she in turn peered at Céleste among the gathering and said, "The gray arrow?"

"It is in my quarters," said Céleste. "Shall I fetch it? It is broken."

Urd cackled and said, "Broken? Nay." And with a gesture, of

a sudden the arrow appeared in her hand, and even as she held it, the shaft became whole and its leaden point keen. Then she looked at it and murmured, "Even were I to let it stay broken, still it is too deadly to remain in mortal hands."

"Why else have you come?" asked Borel, stepping forward.

Slowly Urd turned her head toward him and canted it to one side. "Just as when once I met you by a stream, ever bold, I see. Questioning the Fates, are we?" And then she cackled in glee.

Borel pushed out a hand in negation, and Michelle looked at him quizzically.

"I believe what my son means," said Valeray, "is—"

"We know what he meant," snapped Urd, and she turned to Skuld.

"Yes, we came to give warning," said Lady Wyrd, "and it is this: for a while there will be peace, yet upon a dreadful time yet to come you will all be needed, as will others. Heed me, stand ready and relax not your guard, for there will be a— Ah, but I cannot directly reveal what I have seen, yet know that one among you will be the key."

"The key?" asked Camille.

Skuld looked at her and smiled and said, "The key."

"So peril yet comes," said Valeray, his words a statement, not a question.

"It does," said Skuld.

"Be ready," said Verdandi.

"And on guard," added Urd, and her gaze swept across the gathering to momentarily stop upon Luc, and then moved to Camille.

And the sound of looms swelled and then vanished, and the Sisters Three vanished as well.

The gathering stood stunned for a moment, but then Valeray lifted his glass and, with a rakish grin, said, "Here's to interesting times!"

"To *interesting times!*" cried they all.

Epilogue
Afterthoughts

And thus ends this part of the tale that began three moons and a day past, when, upon a spring morn, Princess Céleste of the Springwood sat in a tree pondering, and a gallant knight rode to her rescue.

Yet the whole of the tale is not quite over, for on the night when all celebrated the successful quest, the Fates themselves appeared and hinted of dire times to come.

Days passed, and the sense of unease slowly abated, though vigilance did not, and finally Laurent and Blaise and Avélaine and Chevell, along with Céleste and Roél, all rode to the mortal lands, where Sieur Émile and Lady Simone wept to see that their daughter had been rescued and that their three sons were hale. Chevell did ask for the hand of Avélaine and the blessing of their union, and it was freely given. And, of course, Roél had his parents meet the Princess of the Springwood, his own bride-to-be. Within a fortnight, a wedding was held, Avélaine so beautiful in her white gown, Céleste her maid of honor, with Roél the best man to Vicomte Chevell.

Afterward, Céleste mentioned that in her demesne there lay an abandoned estate, one not too far from Springwood Manor, and if Sieur Émile and Lady Simone were of a mind, they would be more than welcome to make it their home. Subsequently, when all returned unto Faery, Émile and Simone did find the estate to their liking . . .

. . . and more weddings were held and pledges given: in the Winterwood, Borel and Michelle exchanged vows out in a snow-laden 'scape, though afterward all moved indoors for warm drink and food and the gala that followed. A moon beyond, in the Autumnwood, Luc and Liaze plighted their troth beneath an arbor laden with grapes, and the celebration afterward lasted well into the wee hours. Another moon passed, and in the Springwood, Roél and Céleste were wedded beside a tumbling waterfall, and joy and song and a sumptuous banquet and dance followed.

A few moons afterward, in the Summerwood wee Prince Duran was born unto Camille and Alain. . . .

. . . And three years, seven moons, and a five-day passed.

It was then that the witch Hradian, the last surviving acolyte and consumed by hatred over the death of her sisters, conceived of her plan to set the wizard Orbane free. It was so simple, all she had to do was—

Ah, but that is another story altogether. . . .

'Tis better this way, for ever would I
rather sail off into the unknown than to
follow the tried and true.

Afterword

Although I have woven the main threads of two fairly well-known fairy tales together, as well as having injected facets from many others, to tell this single story, to my mind all of these elements truly belong in a single tale. Perhaps the original bard who might have told this saga stepped through a twilight bound, and after he was gone, various parts of the single story were split away to become individual tales. Thank heavens, they are now back together again.

The two story threads that I have woven together are "Le Bel Inconnu," an Arthurian tale I believe by Renaut de Beaujeu, where a knight who knows not who he is goes on a quest to rescue a maiden, and "Childe Rowland," author unknown, an English folktale, wherein a maiden's shadow is stolen by the King of Elfland, and her three brothers, knights all, one by one, go on a quest to rescue her, the last one being Rowland, who succeeds where his brothers do not. Of course, *Once Upon a Spring Morn* somewhat echoes elements of these two tales, for there are parallels. But my tale has witches and Fates and Trolls and Bogles and Goblins and Changelings and Sprites and other such throughout.

Additionally, I have included a princess in the quest, something that many ancient bards did not do (though many did) except as a victim of a nefarious being. But in my story the princess, in addition to being beautiful and clever, is quite handy with a bow, and without her aid, the male hero of this saga would have failed.

And since I have a knight and a princess as the central characters in the tale, I have cast the story with a French flavor, for, in addition to a magical adventure, this tale is a romance at heart, and French is to my mind perhaps the most romantic language of all.

One other note: throughout the telling, I have relied upon the phases of the moon. I used the earth's own moon cycles to do so, and I hope they correspond to those in that magical place. But perhaps I am quite mistaken in my assumptions. . . . Who knows? For, once you cross the twilight borders and enter Faery, strange and wonderful are the ways therein.

Lastly, I enjoyed "restoring" these two fairy tales to their proper length by putting them back together to make a much longer story, as well as adding back those things I think should have been there in the first place, but which may have been omitted bit by bit down through the ages.

I hope you enjoyed reading it.

Dennis L. McKiernan
Tucson, Arizona, 2006

About the Author

Born April 4, 1932, I have spent a great deal of my life looking through twilights and dawns seeking—what? Ah yes, I remember—seeking signs of wonder, searching for Pixies and Fairies and other such, looking in tree hollows and under snowladen bushes and behind waterfalls and across wooded, moonlit dells. I did not outgrow that curiosity, that search for the edge of Faery, when I outgrew childhood—not when I was in the U.S. Air Force during the Korean War, nor in college, nor in graduate school, nor in the thirty-one years I spent in research and development at Bell Telephone Laboratories as an engineer and manager on ballistic missile defense systems and then telephone systems and in think-tank activities. In fact I am still at it, still searching for glimmers and glimpses of wonder in the twilights and the dawns. I am abetted in this curious behavior by Martha Lee, my helpmate, lover, and, as of this writing (2006), my wife of over forty-nine years.